HARBINGER

OTHER FICTION BY A.J. CALVIN

THE RELICS OF WAR
The Moon's Eye
The Talisman of Delucha
War of the Nameless

The Ballad of Alchemy and Steel

Serpentus

THE CAEIN LEGACY
Exile
Guardian
Harbinger
Legend

HUNTED

WRAITH AND THE REVOLUTION

PRAISE FOR HARBINGER

"A heart racing penultimate novel which delivers the action and bloody battle scenes just hinted at in book one… Longtime fans of John Gwynne will love where the story is heading."

– *Under the Radar SFF Podcast*

"The world building in this series is exquisite. I love that with each book I not only learn more but that what I did know is expanded and given new context. It's a beautifully organic way to build the world and it works magnificently without making the reader feel overwhelmed."

– *Cat Bowser, author of The Second Star trilogy*

"Another fantastic entry in one of my favorite ongoing series."

– *Timothy Wolff, author of The Legacy of Boulom series*

"This series continues to deliver! Calvin writes gripping tales that are equally strong in plot and character. Her fantasy worlds are tangible and information is delivered steadily throughout, which kept me turning the pages."

– *C.B. Lansdell, author of Far Removed*

HARBINGER

THE CAEIN LEGACY
Book Three

A.J. CALVIN

HARBINGER

ISBN 979-8-9883193-9-9

Cover illustration and design by Jamie Noble
(www.thenobleartist.com)

Map illustration by Dewi Hargreaves (www.dewihargreaves.com)

For Joshua

You're the reason I never gave up on this series
even when I thought I should, when the prospects
of publication seemed out of reach and unattainable.
Thank you for helping me see this through.

You were right—and it *has* been worth it.

AUTHOR'S NOTE

The Caein Legacy was originally planned as a trilogy, but as I was midway through writing what eventually became Harbinger, I realized there was just too much story left to fit in a single volume. I made the decision to split the third book in two, which made the series a four-book adventure.

The trouble with cutting what was intended to be one book more or less in half was that it forced me to do something I don't like to do. I had to end it on a cliffhanger. And for that, dear readers, I am sorry.

But Legend, the fourth and final book in this series, is complete at the time of this writing (a few details, including release dates, can be found at the end of this book, or on my website, www.ajcalvin.net.) I promise you will not have long to wait before reading the conclusion.

Harbinger is the book where most of the major action really begins in earnest for this series; Exile and Guardian were merely the foundations, the building blocks leading up to the inevitable. So if you've made it this far in The Caein Legacy, you have my sincerest thanks for humoring Alexander's banter, enduring Andrew's grief and depression, and for reading a series of books that I poured my soul into.

I hope you enjoy Harbinger.

Thank you and happy reading,
A.J. Calvin

NOVANIA AND THE SOUTHLANDS

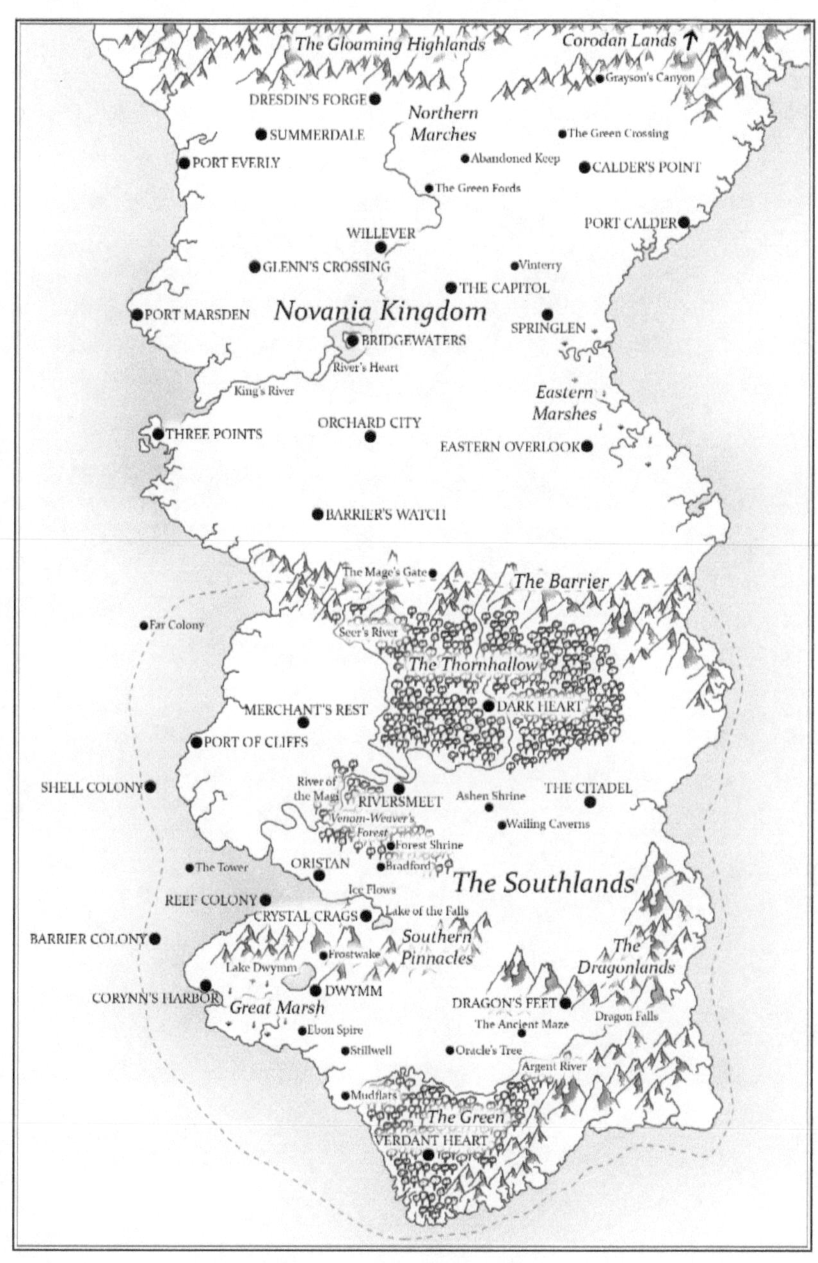

ONE

The spiral staircase felt endless as we ascended to the mosaic room near the top of the Oracle's tower. I was weary; we'd spent the past eight days traveling from the Dragonlands, and the only thing I wanted in this moment was time to rest. But it was not to be.

We pass countless landings along our torchlit path, but the tower is uncharacteristically silent. Our previous visits were met with numerous tower servants at each level, some on errands for the Oracle, others tasked to oversee the comfort of her guests. Conversation had filtered from each level, voices carried through tiled corridors to mingle and blend. Not so today.

It had been nearly four months since Alexander and I had last been here, though it seemed almost a lifetime ago. Much had happened in that time, not the least of which was the completion of his trials and his becoming a true mage.

I wasn't looking forward to our meeting with the Oracle, not after our final words before departing the tower. Alexander's wounds were still raw, though he'd never openly admit it.

And she'd been expecting our arrival. No matter how much I protested, we would not be allowed rest until after the Oracle had her say; the woman was as stubborn as she was powerful. I was resigned to follow her orders, despite my fatigue and the knowledge that our visit was purely for Alexander. I was merely his guardian, duty-bound to accompany him even though I had no place in the coming meeting.

Lileen said little beyond her initial greeting in the tower's foyer. She led us upwards, following the winding, white steps that spiraled toward the top of the tower in silence. As we emerged from the staircase and entered the circular room with a tile mosaic set into the floor, Lileen paused and turned to face our group. We'd *all* been summoned to speak with the Oracle.

"Please wait here for a moment. I'll inform the Oracle of your arrival. She'll be down soon." She hurried across the room to a shorter spiral stair that led up to the Oracle's personal chambers.

I turned and walked a short distance away from the others to peer out one of the curved arches facing the balcony ringing this level of the tower. Beyond the balcony, the city sprawled far below, lights twinkling in windows to ward off the coming darkness. The sky was overcast and I could see nothing of the moon or stars as the last rays of sunlight faded.

"Why do you suppose she wants to see all of us?" Rynn asked as she came to stand at my side. "It's…unusual."

I shrugged, pulling my gaze from the windows to study her. She stared through the arch, her vibrant blue eyes taking in the view of the city below. Her expression was pensive.

"I suspect it has something to do with our plans." I referred to the scheme Alexander and I had begun to lay out during our journey from the Dragonlands. "After all, she claims to have seen us in her visions. You've agreed to travel with me, Emmarie will remain with Alex, and Lydia…"

We were all connected with one another in some way, and it made sense that the Oracle wanted to speak with us together. In my former life as Novania's commander, I'd learned it was often simpler—and faster—to speak with a group rather than individuals. I suspected the Oracle felt the same.

Rynn turned away from the window and looked up to meet my gaze. "Perhaps. Still, she has broken many of her own rules with the two of you. It's concerning."

Footsteps sounded on the floor behind us. I turned to find Lileen descending the staircase once more, a tall woman with long white hair and the ageless countenance of a mage trailing in her wake. She wore a flowing garment that billowed around her form, obscuring much of her figure.

I frowned, uneasy. I suspected she was dressed as she was to disguise her growing pregnancy, a potential source of discord between herself and Lydia.

I flicked a glance at Alexander, who appeared thoroughly uncomfortable as the Oracle's eyes met his. Beside him, Lydia's face was an expressionless mask. Even though no one had spoken, I could sense the tension brewing in the air as though it were a living entity.

Emmarie stood just behind them. She was edgy and anxious, though for very different reasons. The young Merael partially blamed the Oracle for her uncle's decision to exile her. The Oracle certainly hadn't done anything to prevent it.

The Oracle stopped a few paces away from Alexander and studied him silently for several moments with her strange violet eyes, her face unreadable. Finally, she nodded and said, "I welcome your return, Alexander. You are the first mage-warrior in several centuries to have successfully completed the pilgrimage. I didn't doubt you would succeed." She extended her right hand, palm up. "Give me your hand."

Alexander stiffened, but at a nudge from Lydia, he accepted. She closed her eyes for several moments while a faint citrus aroma emanated from their location.

"I see." She opened her eyes and released him. "Your trials went well, but many difficulties plagued your journey. Many I did not foresee."

Alexander snorted derisively but made no further reply.

"The assassins I expected," she continued. "The loss of your guide, as well. The behavior of Elder Stanley at the Oracle's Tree I did not envision. I will select another for that post in the days to come."

I clenched my jaw at her mention of the elder, the man who had threatened harm to Lydia, the man who had attempted to deceive us, the man who now lay dead at Rynn's hands. He'd been a monster, a predator, and she seemed to dismiss his crimes as inconsequential. I was incensed.

"You should have removed him from his post years ago." The bitter words spilled from my lips unbidden. "That man was a damned menace."

Her gaze shifted to meet mine, but her expression remained inscrutable. "The matter has been dealt with. Andrew, please come forward."

I drew a breath and shoved my anger aside. Clearly, she had no intention of discussing the elder further, despite his crimes.

A sudden pang of uncertainty shot through my core as I crossed the distance between us. I may have been dragon-kind, but the Oracle unnerved me. It wasn't her magical ability, nor her unsettling eyes, but her perpetual scheming and long history of manipulation that set me on edge. She'd helped us when we'd last visited the tower, but she'd also hurt Alexander deeply—and continued to show little remorse for her actions.

I couldn't bring myself to forgive her yet, nor did I trust her.

"I have news that concerns you both. It's why I have asked you here." She studied each of us in turn, then said, "The troubling visions I suffered when you were here previously are beginning to hold more meaning. Events have transpired that are of great concern. The Barrier is faltering and an army has gathered in the north, threatening the Mage's Gate."

Lydia's sharp intake of breath was accompanied by a pointed question from Rynn. "What do you mean, the Barrier is faltering?"

"I mean exactly what I said," the Oracle replied placidly. "The magic that sustains the Barrier was never meant to last indefinitely. It has begun to unravel. This by itself would not be of concern, but the army's proximity to the Mage's Gate makes it a serious matter. The army was sent in pursuit of you, Andrew Caein."

"We heard Colin had moved some of his troops to the gate," I replied uneasily. "I didn't know their sole purpose was to pursue *me.* Can you do nothing about the Barrier?"

It would take months to gather the forces required to oppose Colin, but it seemed our time was rapidly running out. If the Barrier could be made to hold even a few months longer, it would provide us with the time to gather the necessary people and resources. We couldn't hope to face Colin without them.

The Oracle shook her head, sorrow in her eyes. "I have foreseen the Barrier's fall, but I am not certain when it will occur. It may be tomorrow, or it may hold another five years. I cannot say. But it is my belief the army must be dealt with—and swiftly."

"We have a plan," Alexander cut in, "but it's dependent on your aid. You owe me that much." He crossed his arms, his tone bitter.

She frowned, her eyes darkening. "I owe you nothing, and I do not typically acquiesce to such demands." Her eyes narrowed further as she regarded him critically. "I suppose you remain angry about what occurred between us. Given your upbringing, I admit it was my fault that you didn't understand my intentions. You could not have known the honor I bestowed on you." She tossed her head, pale hair flying behind her. "I will hear your demands, but I will make no promises until I have time to think them over."

Alexander's jaw was set stubbornly and his green eyes flashed in momentary anger. "It was my understanding that for each mage who completes the pilgrimage, you allow them to ask one favor of you. Do you not owe me that much?" His voice had dropped in both volume and pitch as he spoke, and I knew the Oracle had struck a nerve. I had rarely witnessed my younger half-brother so enraged.

The Oracle studied him for a moment, her expression steely. "Very well. I will uphold that portion of my duties. If you ask any more due to our *other* circumstance, I may choose to ignore you, as is my right. I have explained why you cannot interact with the child."

Alexander's eyes narrowed and his nostrils flared. Lydia placed one hand on his arm, and he turned his head toward her, startled. She shook her head, indicating this was not the time nor place for this discussion. He closed his eyes briefly, and when he turned to face the Oracle once more, much of his ire had faded.

I marveled at the effect Lydia had on him. I would not have been capable of diffusing his rage as effectively, if at all. If anything, I'd have stoked it further.

"I only ask that you send a summons—to *all* magi—asking them to join me. If we are to bring the fight to Colin and save the damned Barrier, we require allies. As many allies as we can muster." Alexander glowered at her, but I no longer believed he would lash out in his frustration.

She nodded once, her violet eyes unreadable within her ageless face. "Return here in the morning, and we will speak again. I will think over your proposal." She turned away from us, a clear indication the conversation was finished.

I sighed and ran one hand through my hair. She hadn't been forthcoming, and we hadn't been afforded the opportunity to explain our plans. I was beginning to believe we'd be forced to embark on the endeavor of raising an army alone, without the means to do so as swiftly as the Oracle believed was necessary. Having come from Novania ourselves, we understood the threat Colin's army posed, but we knew almost no one in the Southlands. Gaining the help of the magi would be difficult, if not impossible, without the Oracle's assistance.

As soon as the Oracle had ascended the stairs to her private quarters, Alexander spun around and swore in frustration. "I'd hoped now that I've become a mage, she'd be a bit more reasonable," he seethed. "She's only grown more inscrutable during our time away." His eyes sought mine, his unspoken desperation clear in his expression. "If she refuses to help us, I don't know if we'll muster the forces necessary to put an end to Colin's insanity."

I nodded my agreement. "Nevertheless, we did come up with a plan. If she chooses not to assist, it will simply take us longer, though I don't see why she should refuse… She began by stating we must deal with the northern army, after all."

Alexander crossed his arms. "You still intend to travel north."

"Yes. Tom needs my help, and by providing that, we can begin to build some sort of army on our own. *Without* her."

Alexander nodded, resigned. "At the very least, give me time enough to convince Bryson Feige to help us before you depart. Then we can communicate despite the distance." His gaze flicked to Rynn, who remained at my side. "Do you still plan to go with him?"

When she nodded, Alexander sighed and Lydia frowned. "I hope you know what you're doing, brother," he said with a shake of his head.

Ignoring his jibe, I turned to Emmarie. "Do you still wish to help us? Things have become more dangerous than we anticipated."

She nodded, her dark eyes fierce. "I have nowhere to call home. You and Alex have become like a family to me, and I won't abandon you now." She looked down at her delicate green hands for a moment, then straightened, her jaw set in determination. "I'm ready to put my skills to the test. Even if I can't return home when this is over, I still mean to defend it."

At that moment, Lileen returned from the chamber above. "The Oracle will send word to you when she is prepared to speak with you again." Her expression was troubled. "She has asked me to find rooms within the tower for your use."

As we descended the spiral stair, I found myself walking alongside Alexander. "I plan to stay here for a time," I informed him. "I know the news we just received makes our plans more urgent, but I won't leave before your wedding, brother."

He grinned then, his gaze drifting to Lydia's retreating form. "Thank you. It means much to me—to both of us—that you want to be a part of our ceremony, small as it may be."

"I hope to seek out my father tomorrow as well," I continued, "but I don't know if Lileen will be free to facilitate the conversation, given what the Oracle said."

I had many questions for my father after traveling to the Dragonlands, and I needed to speak with him before leaving to join Thomas. I craved answers.

Alexander nodded in understanding. "I hope you have time to speak with him. The more you learn about yourself, the more it will help our fight in the end." He looked down with a frown, his eyes filled with concern. "It seems everyone we meet comes up with an immediate agenda for you, brother. I know it's due in part to what you are, but...you still don't fully understand yourself."

I shrugged uncomfortably. Each time I'd revealed to someone that I wasn't completely human, there had been an immediate response. Some simply looked at me with wonder, but many sought my help. As a skin-changer, I was much stronger than the average human, capable of rapid healing, and my vision was unmatched—all that aside from my ability to transform.

But Alexander was right. I still didn't fully understand my own limitations. I had many questions that only my father could answer, but I couldn't simply approach him and have a conversation. Only with the assistance of a mage with the proper attunement could I hope to speak with him, and Lileen was one such mage. I had not yet asked for her help, but I would do so before I was forced to depart.

Lileen located rooms for the others first. It wasn't until we were nearly back to the ground floor that she stopped. She led me across the landing to a corridor, then to the first door, indicating it was my room. She lingered as I opened the door, an uncertain frown on her lips.

"The Oracle said I should take you to visit your father tomorrow," she said. "She has seen something of your future beyond the battles that will ensue, but she refused to elaborate. All she would say is that you must speak with Zayneldarion." She sighed with a shake of her head. "The child she carries is unlike the others that have come before… It has changed her, and not for the better, I fear."

I lifted my eyebrows. "She's colder than I remembered. More distant. I thought it was due to Alexander's presence and their…history."

Lileen shook her head again. "No, she has been this way for several weeks. While your brother's proximity doesn't help matters, she was 'cold' long before your arrival tonight. She believes the child will be her heir, and regarding this matter, the Oracles of the past have never been wrong. She hasn't said as much, but there is something different about this child. I don't know what it is, and she's afraid."

I frowned. "Does it have something to do with Alex being a mage-warrior?"

She shrugged. "I don't know, but it's a possibility. Your brother's power is unique, and what's more, he's incredibly strong. His Mark proved irresistible to the Oracle, even before he began to train, and now… We can *all* sense him." She looked away, seemingly at a loss for words.

"Is there anything I can do to help?"

She managed a smile. "No, Andrew, but thank you for the offer. What I meant is that all magi who come near your brother can sense his power. Even if the Oracle doesn't see fit to aid him, he will have little difficulty in recruiting others to your cause. I've decided I will lend what aid I can, even if it's in defiance of her orders."

"Do you truly believe she'll refuse his request?" I asked.

"I can't say, but she has been erratic of late and closed to the rest of us. She hasn't been herself, and I believe it's because of the child. Alexander's child… He doesn't know what it has done to her. I'm not certain he *should* know." She sighed heavily and began to turn away. "I'll seek you out tomorrow. We'll speak with your father then. I have kept you long enough."

We were summoned before the Oracle as noon approached the next day. For our second audience, she called only Alexander, Rynn, and myself. While Lydia's displeasure at being left behind was evident in her glare, she didn't openly protest. I knew—as did she—that Alexander would share the details with her afterwards.

Lileen led us to the mosaic room. Once there, she departed, leaving us alone with the Oracle.

"I have considered your proposition, Alexander," she said by way of greeting. Her tone held no warmth, and her expression was unreadable. "I will send a summons to the magi on your behalf, but beyond that, I must not interfere. Events shall unfold as they will."

Though I was immediately relieved to hear she would honor Alexander's request, I had a nagging suspicion this favor would not come without a steep price. I hoped, for my brother's sake, it wouldn't be too high. He'd suffered enough through her schemes.

"Tell me of your plans," she stated after a moment's silence. "You indicated last night that you have some, and before I send the summons, I must know what you intend." Her eyes met mine then, and I had the distinct impression she was prepared to impose some form of judgment—and I'd be held responsible.

"I will gather forces in the Southlands," Alexander replied. "Andrew has suggested staging them north of the Thornhallow, where we can monitor the enemy's movements more readily. I'd like to muster as many mages as are willing, along with anyone capable of wielding a sword."

"And what of you?" the Oracle asked me pointedly.

"I'll travel north to rendezvous with our brother, Thomas." I glanced at Rynn briefly, then said, "Rynn has expressed the desire to accompany me."

"Yes, it wise for you to remain together." The Oracle nodded as though satisfied. "I have seen something of your brother's movements in the north. He will not remain safe long. If you linger in the Citadel, your arrival may come too late." Her eyes slid to Alexander's. "Make your plans for the ceremony quickly, for your brothers need one another—and I can sense Andrew refuses to leave until he sees you wed." She sniffed imperiously and crossed her arms. The action served to cinch the billowing fabric of her dress, and the rounded outline of her belly became visible beneath the cloth.

Reddening, Alexander looked away. I frowned at the Oracle in response, convinced she was goading him.

"I hope you carry out your end of this bargain," I told her through clenched teeth. "I think we're finished."

"Alexander no longer needs a guardian, yet you continue to leap to his defense." The Oracle shook her head as though she found the situation amusing. "I will send the summons on your brother's behalf. I don't believe we will speak again for some time, Andrew Caein, but this is far from our last encounter. You may go."

I longed to say more, to further argue my point, but the dismissal was final. Any response I made would be ignored. I stalked toward the stairs and heard her order the others to remain despite my departure.

I fumed in silence until I reached Lileen's location on the first landing below. She gave me a curious look when I returned alone.

"I don't believe the Oracle can suffer my presence any longer," I growled. "I'll wait for Alex and Rynn. Then, if you're free, perhaps we can speak with my father? I sorely need a distraction after…that."

She nodded. "I am free. I was merely waiting for you to finish your business. I'm sorry she sent you away as she did."

I laughed bitterly. "You should not be forced to apologize on her behalf. I believe what you said last night. She has changed—and I fear what she plans for Alex."

Her eyes widened with surprise and fear. "Do you think she means to harm him? That would go against her code—"

I barked another laugh and shook my head. "I've been told she's broken her code when it comes to my brother on more than one occasion. I don't think we can trust her to follow her own damned rules."

It was several minutes before Alexander and Rynn descended the steps. Alexander was scowling, and Rynn appeared decidedly uncomfortable. One glance at my brother told me it was best to give him time to cool his temper before I pressed him for details.

"I'm going to visit my father," I said after a moment. "I've had enough of this tower for one day."

He nodded in acknowledgment and stomped wordlessly away. I glanced at Rynn, who shrugged helplessly.

"I'll tell you what happened on the way to the Stone Grove," she replied. "I hope you don't mind if I accompany you, but I'd like to speak with Caelmarion while we're there. I understand he can converse without the aid of another mage."

I nodded. "He can, and I don't mind." I frowned at the staircase below, troubled by the Oracle's words and Alexander's foul temper. "I'm worried about Alex."

TWO

We followed Lileen through the teeming streets of the Citadel, threading our way through the throngs of people drawn to the trade district and marketplace that surrounded the tower. It took a half hour to wind our way through the masses before we arrived in a quieter, residential area of the city. Not long after, we reached a path that led into the surrounding forest.

Once beneath the eaves of interlacing branches and away from the noise of the city, Rynn launched into her tale of what had transpired with the Oracle after I'd been summarily dismissed.

"She disapproves of Alex's attachment to Lydia," Rynn stated with a shake of her head. "I think she means to drive them apart, but knowing them both as I do, she'll only reinforce their love for one another. It took every ounce of restraint your brother possesses to hold his temper. I've never seen him so livid…"

I sighed and raked one hand through my hair. "Alex won't leave Lydia, not for all the promises in the world. What does she hope to accomplish with this meaningless ploy?"

"It's because of the child," Lileen said over her shoulder. "As I told you last night, something is different, and it troubles her."

Rynn snorted. "Yes, I hadn't got to that part of my story yet. She mentioned the child, and she claimed she may have been wrong in her initial assessment. Apparently, she told him he could not be a part of the child's life. It's an unwritten mandate all Oracles have followed for centuries. But as Lileen said, this time is different. She claims she may have need of Alex's proximity after all."

I groaned. "No doubt he felt she was trying to drive another wedge between him and Lydia. *Damn.*"

Rynn nodded. "Exactly. But I think there's more to it… What do you know of the child she carries, Lileen?"

Lileen shook her head. "Nothing beyond what I've said. *She* claims it's different, but who are we to second-guess her? She is the Oracle."

Rynn frowned. "In any case, Alexander wants nothing more to do with her. She promised to send the summons, but I'm not certain Alexander even heard her through his rage." Rynn paused to gather her thoughts. "His anger is justified. He and Lydia are a good pair, and she should not interfere in their lives like this. Especially not now, given the news of Novania and the Barrier."

We walked in silence for a time; the only sounds were the birds in the trees above and our boots crunching through drifts of fallen autumn leaves. I considered our options. Our plan could succeed even without the Oracle's assistance, though it would be more difficult—but we'd planned for that possibility. And neither Alexander nor I were strangers to trial and strife. We would move forward, with or without her aid.

"Knowing Alex, he'll hope to depart the Citadel as soon as he's able," I said after a time. "I don't blame him."

We rounded a bend in the path and the forest opened into a solemn glade. The trees ringing the perimeter were long dead, petrified decades ago when the dragons had opened the gateway and fled our world. The ground appeared to have been blasted by a tremendous force, and near the center of the glade were what remained of the three dragon-magi responsible for opening the gateway. Each was frozen in place, their bodies long since hardened and turned to stone. Even after so many years, the evidence of their final act remained clear, as though even the forest feared to encroach on the scene of their final sacrifice.

My eyes sought the figure of Zayneldarion Caein. His was the farthest from our location, but his form was the most familiar. When I shifted, I looked like him, after all.

The nearest of the stone dragons was larger than my father. A long scar ran down his flank, marking his unfortunate history with Novania's laws. I gestured to him in passing, indicating to Rynn that this was Caelmarion Zorai. At a point halfway between Caelmarion and Zayneldarion was a third dragon, forming the last segment of their triangle. She was half the size of Caelmarion, her features more refined and delicate than that of the two males who flanked her. She was Miranetha Fohn, the only member of the trio I'd never spoken with.

Rynn stared around the grove in silent wonder as I made my way toward my father with Lileen. Rynn had never entered the Stone Grove, and I knew from experience she would sense the magical power that remained trapped inside the grove. Alexander had reacted in a similar fashion.

Lileen placed one hand on Zayneldarion's foreleg, then swiftly took my hand with the other. Through her connection, I could hear my father's voice.

"It gladdens my heart to see you again, Andrew."

I smiled, pleased to hear his words after the previous events of the day. I had many questions, but I didn't know where to begin. He sensed my uncertainty and asked the first question instead.

"Did you locate the vault?"

"Yes, I found the armor. Thank you. It will be invaluable in the days to come." I paused for a moment, then said, "I also found the chamber of histories."

He was silent for a time, contemplative. "Did you speak with Davereth?" When I nodded, he released a sigh. "Then you know of our family's unfortunate stance when it came to the other peoples of this world."

I nodded again, chewing my lower lip. "He mentioned something of it, yes. It seems there were never any skin-changers in the Caein line until I came along." I looked up into his face, wishing I could see some indication of his emotions—but his face remained frozen in stone.

"Know that I never agreed with that line of thinking," he replied with emphasis. "I have *always* believed every race that inhabits this world has its place. It was we who were the anomalies. Did Davereth tell you of our origins?"

"Only that this was not the first gateway the dragons had opened," I replied. "He said he counseled against this one. He believed our people were better off here, but I don't know anything more."

Zayneldarion chuckled. "This world is the third we inhabited. Our people have always been reluctant to remain in one place, but this was the first world we found where we could sire children with its other races. The magic of this world is far stronger than the others, or so I was told." He was silent for a moment, and I had the distinct impression he studied me carefully. "Even if we had not opened the gateway, I would still claim you as my son. I don't give a damn if it would have caused a stir amongst the clan elders or that my father would have disowned me. I loved your mother, Andrew, even if she grew to resent me. I hope Davereth saw fit to place your name on the panel, linked with my own."

"He did, but my symbol was different. I think it's because I'm a skin-changer. I noticed there weren't many others…like mine." I looked down, uncomfortable with the admission. "I grew up hearing tales of dragons and the dragon-kind. There were so many stories about skin-changers that I expected we were more numerous, but there were only a handful."

"The skin-changers have always been few. The union between the dragon-mage and the other person must be attuned precisely… Only the most powerful of the dragon-magi had the ability to assume another form as I did, and our mate must also bear the Mark. But it was still not a certainty anything would result from the union."

I gaped at him for several seconds, digesting his words. "Does that mean mother was…a mage?"

He chuckled. "She was never trained as such, no, but she bore the Mark. Given that I encountered her in Novania, it was fortunate it branded her scalp and that she had such thick hair to hide its presence." He chuckled again at the memory. "Did she never tell you?"

I shook my head. "No, but now I understand why she was so protective of Alexander. We speculated, but we didn't know for certain."

"Her Mark was powerful, but it was nothing compared to what your brother bears."

The mention of Alexander drew my attention to the matters that lay ahead. "Alex and I must leave the Citadel soon," I said. "He'll gather an army, and I must return to the north. I don't know how much time I'll have to speak with you after today, and I still have many questions."

"Then ask me whatever you wish," he replied. "Until Lileen needs rest, that is."

During the course of the afternoon, I learned my father had been considered an outsider amongst his own clan, which supported Davereth's claims. He didn't share their view that pure-blooded dragons were superior to other races, much to his own father's chagrin. He'd befriended Caelmarion nearly two hundred years before they opened the gateway, during a rather heated and prolonged dispute he'd had with my grandfather. Zayneldarion had left the Dragonlands to distance himself from his clan, seeking solace and adventure elsewhere since he could assume the guise of a human to blend into their society. For a time, he wandered through the various human lands—Novania amongst them—using the name Zayne Blackwell. He'd met Caelmarion as he was returning from one of his forays into the northern lands while he waited for passage through the Mage's Gate.

Caelmarion Zorai was an elder amongst his clan and was pleased to see another mage of similar caliber. When he learned of my father's origins, he immediately understood why Zayneldarion wandered alone. The Caeins had no love for "sympathizers," as they referred to them, to which Caelmarion had scoffed and called them a long list of colorful names.

The two struck a lasting friendship, and it was at the behest of Caelmarion that my father was allowed to return home and assume the role of emissary between the dragon clans and the Oracle. Even with his newfound role, my father could never fully mend the rift with my grandfather. It seemed Zandorion Caein believed his son should pursue a more "noble" path and should not belittle himself by acting as an ambassador to "lesser" peoples.

Their tense relationship only became more strained when my father willingly donated his dragon scale to craft the armor I now possessed. He'd relayed the story of the armor before I left with Alexander on his pilgrimage, but now I understood why it had been left in the vault when the rest of our family moved on. Dragon scale was coveted by the other races and was rarely given so freely; my father's actions were admired by many, but condemned by the Caein clan.

When talk of opening the gateway began to take place, there were only a handful of dragon-magi left with the magical prowess to summon the power required. Foremost amongst them was

Caelmarion, and he willingly volunteered, hoping to provide a more tolerant world for his descendants. My father also volunteered, though for far different reasons; he'd grown tired of the prejudice rife within his family and wanted nothing more to do with it. For him, it was a means of permanently severing all ties—with his father in particular. Miranetha had volunteered simply to remain at Caelmarion's side. He'd been her mentor, and later, she became the mother of several of his children.

"By the time I met your mother, we were well on our way to opening the gateway. Even had I known of your existence, I would not have chosen a different fate for myself," he explained. "My place was here. If I'd known she was pregnant, I could have arranged for your mother to follow the others through the gateway if that had been her desire. The Caeins would have shunned her and would have made life miserable for you, but many of the others would have welcomed you. Perhaps it's for the best that you remained here. It's not the life I would have wanted for my son."

"If she had gone, I'd be without my brothers," I replied.

"Perhaps. If things had been different, I wouldn't know you as I do now. You're my only child, Andrew, and I'm grateful you're here. Perhaps it's a selfish sentiment, but it has made my time trapped here worthwhile, knowing that one day you'll return to visit again."

"I have one more question, if you don't mind," I said after a time. Lileen was growing weary and she would need to rest soon.

"Of course."

"I met a pair of…historians, I suppose you might call them," I said slowly. "We were at the Frostwake. One of them mentioned a story about another skin-changer who had lived for several hundred years. Is that longevity…*normal?*"

Zayneldarion laughed good-naturedly. "None of the dragon-kind age, Andrew. Some of the elders were more than a thousand years old, and Caelmarion is no exception. If injury doesn't claim your life, you will live many centuries."

I shook my head, bewildered and terrified by the confirmation. Perhaps it was because I'd always assumed I would live a *human's* lifespan that the notion of centuries made me uncomfortable, or perhaps it was the knowledge that with such longevity, I would be forced to watch everyone I'd ever cared for succumb to the ravages of time. I had not yet spoken of this to Alexander, though I suspected Lydia had informed him at some point during our journey.

"You appear troubled."

I merely nodded; there was nothing more I wanted to say on the matter.

"We will always be here, should you wish to speak. You will not be alone, even many years from now when the others are gone."

I knew he was attempting to comfort me with his words, but frozen in stone as he was, our relationship would always be markedly different. I could not interact with the dragons as I could with everyone else.

"I must ask you one more question before you leave today," he said. "The woman who has been speaking to Caelmarion—who is she?"

I smiled faintly. "Rynn Gwyllias. She's a mage, but she was…changed by her power. She assisted with Alexander's pilgrimage."

"Ah, I think I understand," he said, amusement in his tone. "I can see by the way she looks at you that she cares for you. If she was changed as you say, I can only assume she cannot safely interact with many of her own kind. Am I correct?"

"Yes…"

He chuckled. "I take it your feelings are not so concrete as hers appear to be. Given what you've told me of your past, I'm not surprised." He paused for a moment, then said, "If you return before you depart, I would very much like to speak with her."

My eyebrows lifted in surprise, and I wondered what my father hoped to say to Rynn. "I'll tell her."

"Good." I could hear a smile in his voice. "Lileen grows tired. I think it's best that we end our conversation here. I look forward to speaking with you again."

Dusk was falling as we made our way back to the Citadel. Rynn was in an unusually buoyant mood, having thoroughly enjoyed her conversation with Caelmarion. When I asked what they'd discussed, she smiled enigmatically and changed the subject.

"If we return, my father would like to speak with you," I said. "He wouldn't elaborate, so I don't know his reason for making the request."

"Will you be rested enough for us to return tomorrow?" Rynn asked Lileen.

Lileen nodded. "I believe so."

With a shrug, Rynn said, "Let's plan to return then. Of course, the timing may depend upon your brother and Lydia." She flashed a knowing grin.

By the time we arrived at the Oracle's tower, night had enveloped the city. Lileen took her leave, her face pale and drawn from exertion. The lengthy conversation she'd facilitated between us had consumed most of her energy, but as ever, she didn't complain. I thanked her as she departed, grateful for her selfless assistance.

I bade Rynn a good night soon after and retired to the room I'd been assigned. I had much to think over and little time in which to do it.

When I entered the small room, I found a tray of fruit and bread had been left within, most likely by one of the Oracle's many assistants. Taking an apple, I walked to the window. My room sported a view of the street not far below, but at this late hour, it was nearly deserted. A few people scurried by, their steps fueled by a desire to return home.

I remained near the window for some time, thinking over the events of the day. I'd learned much about my father's family, but the confirmation of Davereth's claims had been disheartening. So many of the notions I'd entertained since childhood lay in shambles, shattered by harsh reality. The Caein clan had not been the benevolent people I'd dreamed they'd been, and with the exception of my father, I was glad they were gone. I'd been an outsider amongst the humans and detested the notion I would have fared the same amongst the dragons.

I shook my head and tossed the apple core on the tray before selecting a firm pear, then reminded myself that not all clans felt as my father's had. Davereth had implied it, and Zayneldarion verified it. I would have been shunned only by my own family, but accepted by most others.

It softened the blow, but didn't eliminate it.

Early the next morning, I was awakened by insistent knocking.

I groaned. It had been weeks since I'd been afforded more than a single night's full sleep in a row, and to be roused as dawn had just broken was disappointing. I pulled on my trousers and a rumpled shirt, then went to answer the unwelcome summons.

Alexander stood outside, bouncing on his heels nervously. I was still adjusting to the change that had been wrought in his features with the completion of his mage trials. He appeared neither old nor young, just as all magi did, but I continued to be taken aback each time I studied him. He no longer looked ten years my junior. Now it was I who looked the part of the younger brother.

I blinked at him groggily. "Alex? Is something wrong?"

He shook his head. "No. It's just… Well, Lydia and I decided to have our wedding ceremony as soon as possible, and the magistrate is free this morning. I want you to be there." He looked down and fidgeted, something I'd seldom seen him do.

I laughed. "Relax! You're getting married to a woman who obviously loves you, and as I've said before, you make a fine pair. When is it?"

"Ah… As soon as we arrive at the magistrate's house." Alexander chuckled uneasily. "I meant to tell you last night, but you didn't return until after dark. And by then I was…otherwise occupied." He flushed crimson and stared at the floor.

I clapped him on the shoulder. "She's good for you, brother. Let's go before your bride tires of waiting. Just give me a moment to dress."

He flashed a grin and continued to bounce nervously while he waited in the doorway.

He led me to a large manor house with whitewashed walls and a well-tended garden a short distance from the tower. A series of broad steps led from the garden to the wide double doors that marked its entrance, and a collection of earthen pots filled with the last of the year's flowers decorated the space.

At the base of the steps, Rynn and Emmarie awaited our arrival. An elderly man who could have only been the magistrate stood alongside Lydia at the top. She wore a pale blue gown which complimented her eyes, and her long sandy hair was loose, falling to her knees.

Alexander paused at the base of the steps to straighten his jacket and smooth out unseen wrinkles in his trousers. He glanced at me with a nervous smile.

"Go, Alex. Don't keep her waiting."

He chuckled uneasily, then bounded up the steps to join Lydia. The magistrate smiled at the pair before he began the brief ceremony. Alexander took each of Lydia's hands in his own, his eyes locked on hers while the magistrate spoke. I didn't listen carefully to his words, but the love the two shared for one another was clearer than the sky overhead. Alexander beamed, Lydia blushed prettily, and the magistrate continued with a twinkle in his eye.

I smiled, both elated at their union and melancholy with the reminder of my own recent loss. They were good for one another. Vera would have approved of their match.

As the magister finished speaking and announced the newlyweds as Alexander and Lydia Marsden, the two turned to face us once more, beaming. They strode to the bottom of the steps, where we offered our congratulations.

As if on cue, a fluttering, like the sound of many hundreds of wings beating the air, erupted overhead, interrupting our celebration. I peered skyward and was startled to see countless messenger birds taking flight from the balcony encircling the Oracle's tower.

Alexander gazed upward, then broke into a relieved grin. "She kept her damned word! That was the summons." He turned to Lydia and gathered her into his arms, kissing her passionately. "This is the most wonderful day of my life. Married to a beautiful woman, and everything else seems to be falling into place as well."

Rynn handed a carefully folded sheet of parchment to Lydia, deftly avoiding any contact with the other woman as she did so. "It isn't much, but I felt it was the least we could do. Enjoy it."

Lydia unfolded the sheet, and her eyes widened in surprise. "Oh, Rynn, if only I could hug you, I would! This is wonderful! And Andrew, thank you."

She showed Alexander the sheet, and he glanced between Rynn and me with one eyebrow lifted in surprise. I didn't know what Rynn had done, but clearly my brother believed I had a hand in it.

"What is it?" Emmarie asked excitedly.

"They've paid for two nights at the finest inn the city has to offer," Alexander replied.

I shot a meaningful glance at Rynn. We would discuss this later, though I was glad she'd managed to cobble together a gift of sorts—even if she'd attached my name to it without my permission. The newlyweds deserved something more than the meager words I'd offered, and I certainly wasn't drowning in coin.

"You deserve some time together," Rynn replied with a ready smile. "It was the best we could do on short notice, but perhaps later, we'll purchase a proper gift." She glanced at me with a knowing smirk but said nothing more.

"Enjoy yourselves," I added with a laugh. "We'll speak with you again before we leave."

THREE

Rynn, Emmarie, and I made our way back to the Oracle's tower after a final round of congratulations were offered to the newlyweds. Alexander and Lydia planned to wander the Citadel for a time, then retire to the inn Rynn had paid for.

I was happy for my brother. I liked Lydia and believed she'd remain at his side no matter what lay in store for us in the future. And Alexander would do anything she asked of him. I hoped their time together would be joyous—and that he'd have Lydia in his life for many years. He deserved this chance at happiness, of making his future without fear of who and what he was. He would never have been granted this opportunity in Novania.

"I assume you signed my name to your gift," I said to Rynn after a time.

She blushed and offered me a sheepish smile. "I did. I hope you don't mind. I know you and Alex left your homes with almost nothing… I thought you'd like to give something to your brother."

I appreciated the sentiment. "Thank you. But now, it seems I'm in your debt."

"Is that such a bad thing?" she asked coyly before gesturing ahead.

We'd arrived at the Oracle's tower. Lileen stood outside the entrance awaiting us while she leaned against its smooth stone exterior. I seized the opportunity to change the course of the conversation by greeting Lileen.

While I was grateful to Rynn for what she'd done, her attraction to me was a poignant source of discomfort. I genuinely liked her, but I wasn't prepared for another relationship so soon after losing Vera.

We'd discussed it more than once, but she was undeterred, willing to wait years if that's what it took for me to change my mind.

I doubted I would. She was wasting her time, and I wished she'd focus her energy elsewhere. Others may have been flattered, but it left me feeling morose. The wounds Colin had inflicted when he'd attacked Vinterry remained raw, infecting my very soul.

Lileen appeared rested, but her expression was troubled. As she led us away from the tower toward the outskirts of the city, Rynn asked if she was feeling well.

"I'm fine," she replied carefully, "but I fear the Oracle is not. She summoned all of her assistants this morning to help with Alexander's summons. As soon as we were finished, she sent us all away and locked herself inside her chambers. Erek knocked and asked if she was ill, but she shouted and ordered him to leave. It isn't like her."

I frowned. I suspected the Oracle's strange behavior had something to do with Alexander's wedding, though I kept my thoughts to myself. The timing was too perfect to be a coincidence.

"Perhaps she is merely unwell?" Rynn suggested, ever the optimist. "I've heard most women experience illness during pregnancy."

"Perhaps." Lileen didn't sound convinced, but she said nothing more.

We walked in relative silence for the remainder of our journey. Emmarie paused a few times during our trek through the forest to speak with the birds we passed, and again with a red fox. None of the creatures appeared to have news relevant to the Barrier or Colin's movements, but they readily shared tales of the forest with the young Merael.

I smiled as I watched her, glad she had this time to be herself. If she stayed with Alexander after my departure, I feared she'd have little more. Training at arms and preparing for battle would occupy most of her time.

As we entered the Stone Grove, I stopped alongside Caelmarion. I planned to speak with him while Rynn spoke with my father. He'd given me sound advice in the past, and now that I understood his relationship with my father, I wanted to learn more about him.

Lileen paused as she neared Zayneldarion. "Andrew, I require your assistance."

I blinked in momentary confusion. "What?" As the word left my mouth, I realized my mistake. Rynn could not make direct contact with Lileen.

"Of course," I said, then strode across the glade. "I should have known you would need my help with this. I'm sorry."

Rynn appeared amused, and Lileen managed a small smile, the first I'd seen from her that morning. I glanced past them to note Emmarie had located a pair of squirrels near the petrified edge of the glade and was engaged in animated conversation with them.

"There has already been much for you to consider today," Lileen replied gently. "It's only natural you'd be distracted." She studied me for a moment, then said, "I must use you as a conduit of sorts. I don't know if you will sense anything, though given your nature, it's likely. Until your father wishes for you to be part of the conversation, I'll merely pass my power through you to Rynn. You won't hear any of what is said between them."

I nodded, though I was hesitant. I'd never been part of magic akin to this, and I didn't understand its mechanism. Lileen's ability had not caused any adverse reactions in me yet, despite my sensitivity to magic as a whole, but the notion of her power channeling directly *through* me would be a new experience. I didn't know what would happen, if anything.

But my father wanted to speak with Rynn, and this was the only way. I trusted Lileen wouldn't knowingly harm me.

Lileen took one of my hands in hers and indicated that I should take one of Rynn's with my other. "Are you ready?" she asked, her dark eyes piercing in their intensity.

When I nodded, she placed her free hand on Zayneldarion's foreleg. A moment later, I felt a surge of energy pass through my body, pulsing from Lileen to Rynn. I shuddered involuntarily; the sensation left me uneasy, and my stomach threatened to purge its meager contents. I was suddenly thankful I had skipped breakfast.

A moment later, another pulse of energy passed through me, traveling from Rynn to Lileen. It took every ounce of willpower I could muster to prevent myself from vomiting. My skin tingled painfully and my vision swam.

"We must finish quickly," I heard Lileen say. The ringing in my ears made it difficult to make out her words. "I don't think Andrew can endure more than a brief exchange."

Rynn said something in response, but I couldn't hear her words. My skull pounded with the cadence of my heart, drowning out all other sound.

Three more pulses of energy passed through me. As the last occurred, I fell to my knees. I held my head in my hands, hoping the ringing in my ears would subside and the roiling of my stomach would abate. My skin burned where Lileen's magic had passed through my hands.

Rynn knelt at my side, concern etching her features. As soon as Lileen stepped away, I stumbled to my feet and bolted for the trees behind my father's frozen form. I only just made it to the trees when I could no longer control my nausea. I retched repeatedly, though little came up.

I gripped the trunk of a petrified tree in each hand, relying on their rigid strength to stay upright. The drumbeat in my skull began to fade after several minutes, but my stomach took far longer to settle. I was weak, my body slicked with cold sweat.

"Andrew?" It was Rynn. She stood behind me, perhaps an arm's length away. I didn't turn, fearing I'd collapse if I tried.

"Never…again," I said between ragged breaths. My voice was roughened from the ordeal and the bile I could still taste in the back of my throat.

"I'm sorry. None of us knew it would affect you this way," Lileen whispered. "When you're feeling better, your father hopes to speak with you again."

I nodded but remained where I was. I'd never felt so weak, not even after my fight with the Venom-weavers. Clearly, my body didn't react favorably to magic of this nature.

I heard Lileen's footsteps as she walked away, and a moment later, Rynn said, "Do you want to sit down? I'll help you if I can." The concern in her tone was evident. "You've gone white as snow."

I turned slightly to peer at her over my shoulder. "I'm afraid if I let go of the trees, I'll fall. Holy hell, I wish Lydia were here."

"I'm not certain she'd be able to help you," Rynn replied, her brilliant blue eyes scanning my face. "The magic caused this… You have no physical injury."

"Fine. Help me sit down…near my father."

She slid an arm around my waist, and I found the chill of her touch helped clear my head. I stumbled as I released my grip on the trees. She staggered under my sudden weight, but managed to keep her footing. We retraced my previous steps, and I sat down heavily, leaning against Zayneldarion's foreleg for support. Rynn knelt at my side and placed her hand on the back of my shoulder, as though she feared I'd topple if she let go for even an instant. I didn't think she was wrong.

Lileen stood a short distance away, speaking to Emmarie in a hushed tone. A moment later, Emmarie bounded toward me and knelt down opposite Rynn. "I can ask one of the birds to seek Galewing. Lydia will come if you ask—"

I managed a weak smile. "No. We should allow Lydia and Alex to enjoy their wedding day."

I knew if Emmarie sent a bird to locate my brother's eagle, Lydia would travel to the grove without hesitation. And I believed Rynn; there was little Lydia could do to assist me in my present state. I was beginning to recover, though I'd need to eat soon in order to regain my strength.

"There is something you *can* do for me," I said after a moment, noting the girl's disappointment. She looked up, eager to assist. "Return to the Citadel and find me something to eat. I don't think I can walk."

She flashed a grin. "I know! I'll find that baker I met when we were here before. He makes the best meat pies in all of the Southlands, or so he said."

Rynn fished a few coins from her pocket and dropped them in the girl's open palm. "This ought to take care of it. Bring me one as well, if you will?"

I forced a smile as Emmarie raced across the grove, dark hair flying behind her, then looked up as Lileen approached once more.

"What happened?" I asked.

"I don't know, though Zayneldarion suggested I speak with one of the others," she replied, gesturing between Caelmarion and Miranetha.

"We believe it has something to do with who you are. Until your arrival, your father had never encountered another skin-changer—he fears his desire to speak with Rynn has caused you harm. We both know how your kind reacts to some forms of magic."

I leaned my head against my father's leg and closed my eyes briefly, exhausted. I heard Lileen's footsteps retreat across the glade as she made her way toward one of the other dragons. Rynn took one of my hands in hers, and I allowed it; I didn't possess the energy to object or break away.

I must have dozed, for when I next opened my eyes, Emmarie had returned with a half dozen meat pies. The aroma was delicious, and my mouth watered in anticipation. I'd eaten nothing since the fruit the night before.

To my delight, the pies were still warm. The poor girl must have run the entire distance to the baker and back, but she didn't appear winded or upset, merely concerned for my wellbeing. I forced another smile and accepted a pie. One bite told me the pies were as tasty as their aroma implied. I devoured three before my hunger was sated, but I felt significantly better. Stronger. My headache receded, and I believed I could stand without aid.

As I finished eating, Lileen returned from across the grove. She'd been speaking with Caelmarion, and I sensed she'd gleaned some knowledge of what had occurred. She took the last meat pie when Emmarie offered it to her, then sat down nearby.

She took a delicate bite from the pie. "Hmm, Roymond's pies have always been my favorite." She smiled for a moment, then her expression darkened. "It seems what we did was incredibly dangerous. Caelmarion was livid and called me a few choice names before I could even frame my question." She frowned at the pie in her hands. "When he finally granted me permission to ask what happened, he said skin-changers are particularly susceptible to the direct effects of magic. If I had prolonged the conversation even a few moments more, it may have killed you. Andrew, I'm terribly sorry! I would never have suggested this if I'd known, and I'd never hurt you. I simply didn't know…" She blinked rapidly in an attempt to stave off tears.

I glanced toward my father. "He could not have known either. He wouldn't have asked to speak with Rynn if he believed it would put me in danger."

"We can't allow anyone else to learn of this." Rynn's voice was firm, but her eyes were wide with fear. "If the wrong person were to learn of this weakness…" She swallowed hard. "I don't want to consider the outcome."

I frowned, perplexed and uneasy. "I've been tended to by healers in the past, with no ill effects—"

"A healer's magic only enhances your body's ability to mend itself," Lileen interrupted. "It's different in its action. Other magic, if directed at you, or *through* you, as happened in this case, disrupts your body in a fundamental way." She sighed heavily and blinked away more tears. "Rynn's right. We can't allow anyone else to learn what happened here. Not even your brother should know unless there is a great need for it."

I crossed my arms and glowered. "Alex would never harm me."

"Perhaps not, but the fewer people who know, the safer you will be," Lileen pointed out. She turned to Emmarie. "Can we count on your secrecy?"

Emmarie nodded emphatically. "I'll never tell a soul."

Lileen studied me carefully. "You're beginning to look better. Your ability to heal is remarkable."

I shrugged indifferently. She wasn't the first to comment on my body's ability to mend itself rapidly, and I didn't believe she'd be the last. "I'd like to speak with my father."

Once Lileen established the connection between us, Zayneldarion's voice echoed in my mind. "Andrew, are you well? What happened?"

I was reassured by his genuine concern and peered toward his face from my place on the ground. I explained what Lileen had learned from Caelmarion. He was silent for some time, and I wished once more I could see the emotions as they played across his features. When next he spoke, his voice was raw.

"If I'd known the toll this would take on you, I would never have asked. You are my son, my *only* son." I heard his sorrow, his remorse, thick in his tone. "If we are ever freed of this blasted curse, Caelmarion will berate me for days. And rightly so, I suppose."

It took me a moment to fully comprehend his words. "You didn't know. None of us did. I still don't understand half of what I am." I frowned then, realizing the full implication of his statement. "Do you believe the curse can be lifted?"

"Yes. But now isn't the time to be distracted by the possibility. There are greater matters demanding your attention. The magi—and your brother—require your aid. The three of us will remain here, locked as we are within stone. There will be time later to deal with our curse." He paused, and I imagined he was contemplative. "If Lileen had not stopped our conversation, I would never have forgiven myself… I won't lose you, Andrew. Not now that I've finally met you."

"I'll be fine," I assured him. "But if I may ask—why did you want to speak with Rynn?"

He chuckled. "That conversation was between her and I. Perhaps later, if she's willing, she'll tell you what was said."

I frowned, unable to mask my irritation.

"She genuinely cares for you," he continued after a moment. "I know you still mourn the loss of your wife, but at some point, you'll need to move on. An unfortunate aspect of our longevity is that any friends we make who are not dragon-kind will eventually succumb to old age. You must learn to accept this. Make the most of the time you are given with each of them."

There was wisdom in his words, but I was unprepared to take the next step. Hoping to change the subject, I said, "Lileen mentioned you'd never met another skin-changer."

"It's true. There were none left by the time I was old enough to understand there were those like you, once." He sighed. "Skin-changers have always been drawn to battle. I suspect it's due to your unusual strength, even in your non-dragon form. Most lost their lives after a few hundred years—they'd become careless and overconfident in their abilities. Even with rapid healing, some wounds cannot be overcome. I hope you'll remember that."

"You said 'non-dragon' form," I said after a moment's reflection. "Were there non-human skin-changers in the past?"

He chuckled. "It gladdens my heart to see you so inquisitive. It's a sign you are recovering." There was a pause, then he said, "To my knowledge, there was once a Merael skin-changer. It was long ago.

There was also a Sevanni somewhere far back in the Tanzarist clan's history. Most have been human. There are fewer magi born to the Merael, and the logistics of mating with a Sevanni are…complicated."

I was unfamiliar with the Sevanni, though I'd heard the term before. I'd had little involvement with anyone but humans and Corodan for most of my life. Emmarie was the first Merael I'd truly interacted with. When I related this to my father, he laughed.

"I'm not surprised. The Sevanni dwell in the sea. They rarely rise to interact with 'surfacers,' and they can't breathe the air as we do. Communications with them have always been difficult if not facilitated by the right type of mage. I recall the story of the Sevanni skin-changer only because it was such an unusual pairing. Dragons can't spend more than a few minutes beneath the water. We can hold our breath, but not long, and we don't swim well, if at all. The skin-changer was the first Sevanni to experience the world above the waves—though there are tales of another who came later. I don't know the details of that story. It's said the skin-changer preferred to remain in the depths with her mother's kind."

"What happened to her?" I asked, captivated by the idea of such a creature.

"She came to the surface at her father's behest during the Mage Wars," he replied. "She didn't survive the battle at the Frostwake. I don't know any more of her story, but you should ask Caelmarion if you're curious. He was present for that battle, though he was considerably younger then."

I glanced across the glade to where Caelmarion stood frozen, wondering what else he must have seen during his lengthy life. The Mage Wars were nearly a thousand years in the past.

"I believe our conversation must come to an end. Lileen is growing weary, and you need rest. If we don't speak again until the coming war is over, know that you will be in my thoughts. Take care of yourself, my son. And take care of Rynn. I know she plans to travel with you."

I nodded. "I will. I'll return when I can, though I fear it may not be for a long while."

FOUR

A pair of men stood outside the entrance to the Oracle's tower, blocking the door upon our return. As our group approached, one of them stood aside and beckoned to Lileen, his features pensive.

"It's not good," he said as he ushered us inside.

The broad foyer at the base of the tower was crowded with the Oracle's various attendants. Most were magi, bearing the ageless countenance I'd learned to recognize. Alexander and Lydia were present, though both appeared confused, perplexed by whatever occurred on the floors far above. When he spotted me, Alexander jogged across the space to stand at my side.

"Did anyone tell you what happened? We came back to gather our things, then the tower was closed to the public." He paused for a moment to study me carefully. "You look unwell, brother."

"He's better than he was an hour ago," Lileen replied briskly, then turned to address the others. She raised her voice to be heard above the murmur of voices and stepped toward the center of the room. "Will someone please explain what has happened?"

The susurration of voices evaporated. A petite woman with olive-toned skin and nearly black eyes stepped through the throng to face Lileen. I recognized her from our previous stay but could not recall her name.

"Lil, I fear the Oracle has done something terrible."

"You must tell me, Canna!"

Canna narrowed her eyes. "You were outside when you should have been here." Her tone was judgmental, hostile.

"We were in the Stone Grove," I interrupted. I wouldn't see Lileen berated for assisting me. "We were speaking with my father—at your Oracle's behest, I might add."

Canna's hard glare met my own. "I suspect this is your fault, skin-changer," she hissed. "Yours and your half-brother's. If not for you…"

"You cannot blame them for what happened," one of the men cut in. "We all know why they came—for asylum, for advice. The Oracle gave it, just as she would have for anyone in their position."

Canna clenched her jaw. "After they left on *his* pilgrimage, she changed. Something happened between them, and they ought to answer for it," she snarled.

"Canna, please," Lileen said evenly, drawing the other woman's attention. "We don't know what occurred. Placing unfounded blame on travelers is uncharitable—and it goes against our code."

Canna deflated at her words and looked away. "You know as well as I that the Oracle locked herself inside her private quarters this morning. She sent the summons out, as *he* requested." She shot Alexander a heated glare. "An hour later, we heard her crying. She was hysterical. Mav knocked on her door, but she refused to open it."

Lileen's gaze swept across the assembly, then she shook her head with a frown. "And where is Mav now? I don't see him."

"He went to the locksmith to have the key repaired," another man said. "The Oracle broke the key to her chamber before she locked herself inside."

"She was crying and screaming," Canna continued after a moment. "Then she fell silent…"

"Stop dancing around the subject," the second man snapped, exasperated. "She's still locked within her room and refuses to meet with any of us."

Lileen stared at him for several seconds, eyes wide, uncomprehending. "No, Erek… Why would she do this?"

"I think we'll learn once Mav returns with the key," Erek replied. "I don't believe our visitors had anything to do with what occurred today. Yes, the Oracle was changed after they arrived," he growled at Canna, "but it was of her own doing."

Alexander shook his head in disbelief. "I don't understand what she's playing at." He eyed me again, critically. "You definitely don't look well, Andrew."

I shrugged, dismissing his concerns. "I'm feeling better than I was, believe me."

Rynn kicked the back of my left boot sharply as a reminder. I needed to end the conversation before Alexander began to question me further.

"It's a story for another time," I added pointedly.

"At least let Lydia look at you," he insisted. "You need to be in top form before you leave. We don't know what you'll find when you reach the Mage's Gate."

He wouldn't relent, so I grudgingly agreed. I allowed Alexander to lead me toward the nearest bench, where I sat down rather ungracefully. Lydia perched at my side, and a green scent reminiscent of herbal tea enveloped us as she channeled her power. I wasn't certain how much damage I'd incurred during the brief conversation in the Stone Grove, but it had felt significant.

After a moment, she shook her head and rose, perplexed. "You're healing from internal injuries, but there is nothing I can do. The damage is almost completely repaired." She frowned at me in concern. "Whatever caused this, I don't recommend you do it again."

"I'll make certain he behaves himself," Rynn replied with a laugh. When I glowered at her, she laughed again. "Someone must look out for you once you're beyond Alex's watchful eye."

I crossed my arms and leaned back in my seat, then closed my eyes. Perhaps if I feigned sleep, she and Alexander would both leave me be for a time. And I *was* feeling better.

We waited another hour before Mav returned with the repaired key to the Oracle's private chambers. We remained where we were while the multitude of assistants ascended the spiral stair and the foyer grew quiet. I didn't believe it was our business to accompany them as they entered the Oracle's private quarters, and I wasn't certain I could make the long trek besides.

"What did your father say?" Alexander asked after a time, taking a seat next to me.

"We discussed skin-changers, and he promised he'd speak with me again when I return. I can't keep Tom waiting much longer," I added.

"Let's visit Bryson Feige this afternoon—if they ever allow us to leave this cursed tower." He scowled. "We'll send Tom a message. He'll be pleased to know you'll be leaving to join him soon."

"I'd like to leave tomorrow afternoon," I replied. "We'll fly to Gwerin's cabin. Once we're through the Mage's Gate, it will be safer to travel at night. I'll be less conspicuous in the dark."

Alexander chuckled. "There will never be a truer statement from you, brother." He sighed then. "I hope at least one member of the Feige family will join me. I'll send you word as often as I can…"

"I know you will." I clapped him half-heartedly on the shoulder. Goodbyes were always so damned hard.

As difficult as it was for us to part, there was no other way. Alexander was committed to gathering an army in the Southlands, while my path led north to our youngest brother's location in the Corodan highlands. And I didn't relish the thought of the lengthy trip through Novania. When we fled, I'd revealed myself to Colin—and everyone else—in my desperate attempt to spare Alexander's life. I'd be hunted mercilessly once Colin was aware of my return.

Colin was a monster made flesh, though I struggled to understand what motivated him. Our relationship had always been strained, and I'd mistakenly believed it was nothing more than rivalry between siblings. But since he was named heir to the throne, his actions led me to believe something more was driving him. I wished I knew what it was.

"Alex," I said after a few moments, "I learned something about mother last night. I didn't have the chance to tell you with all the excitement of the day. She *was* Marked."

Alexander's eyebrows rose. "But how? Father never knew—"

"*My* father said it was on her scalp, beneath her hair," I replied. "Her Mark was not as powerful as yours, but it was there."

Alexander laughed grimly. "I wonder what Colin would do if he knew our mother was Marked. Did you know he called me an abomination when he locked me in the dungeon?"

"I'm not surprised," I growled. "I suppose you'll have to come up with a fitting term for him when next we're graced with his foul presence. The bastard."

Alexander rolled his eyes. "*Tyrannical* bastard is better, but still isn't sufficient. I'll come up with something."

"Perhaps something more…colorful is in order," Rynn offered with a grin. "Based on the stories you've shared about Colin, I'm certain he deserves any name you devise."

"Please don't encourage him," Lydia said, rolling her eyes in mock exasperation.

"I'm not even married a day, and already she's telling me what I shouldn't do," Alexander teased with a mischievous grin.

Lydia laughed in amusement and shook her head, but said nothing more.

Lileen returned to the foyer then, her face red and tear-stained. Erek trailed behind her, along with two others I didn't recognize. No one spoke for several moments; our laughter faltered and died as abruptly as it had bubbled forth.

"The Oracle learned of our conversation from last night," Lileen said in a strangled tone. "She disapproves of my offer to aid you and has given me an ultimatum. If I choose to help you, I will no longer be welcome here. If I remain, I can do nothing but serve a woman who now borders on madness."

Her voice broke, and she covered her face with her hands as sobs wracked her body. One of the women behind her drew her into her arms, offering what comfort she could.

"Lileen, as is her way, refused to go back on her word," Erek said, leveling a steely gaze at Alexander. "I defended her. She has the right to choose her own path. The Oracle ordered me to join her in exile from the tower." He shook his head wearily. "She also claims she believes her child is male, which is improbable. There has never been a male Oracle in all of history."

Alexander shrugged helplessly, uncertainty and confusion clouding his eyes. Like my brother, I didn't understand the implications. What did the gender of the child matter if it was cursed with the Oracle's unnerving brand of magic?

"I don't understand," Alexander said after a moment. "I know that it's my child, but…" He looked down, at a loss for words. Lydia drew an arm around him and he leaned into her embrace.

"If the child has her talent, he will become the next Oracle, yes?" I asked.

Erek frowned. "The Oracles have always been women. She fears what a male child will become."

"And she's *certain* the child is male?" I pressed.

Erek shrugged. "She claimed to have a vision of a male child with Alexander's features."

"That doesn't mean the child she saw was *hers*," Rynn cut in, then nodded at Lydia. "The Oracle isn't the only woman Alexander has slept with."

Alexander flushed and stared fixedly at the tiled floor but made no further response. The room fell silent for a time before Lileen spoke again.

"She said any who choose to follow you north will share our fate," she said thickly. "She has seen something that leads her to believe your plans will succeed, but I don't understand why she insists on our exile. If what she said about the Barrier is true, then we must lend you what aid we can."

"We have already chosen to follow you," Erek added with a sweeping gesture that included Lileen and the others with them. "There will be more. Not everyone upstairs agrees with the Oracle's actions."

"Few do," another man said.

"Canna will never join you." Lileen's tone was bitter. "She sows discord amongst us with her poisoned words. She'll remain in the tower, and I fear all of you must gather your things and leave soon. Canna will make the rest of your stay rather *unpleasant* if she has her way."

"We'll meet you at the inn," Rynn promised Lydia as she began to ascend the stairs toward her room.

I led Emmarie to her room, where she collected her small bundle of personal effects before we descended to mine. Within was the wooden trunk containing my armor and my sword. I tossed the rest of my belongings inside, haphazardly cramming it atop the rest, before hefting it in both arms. When we reached the base of the stairs, Rynn awaited us, her satchel thrown over one shoulder.

"Alex and Lydia have gone. Lileen and the others went with them. Your brother deserves better than this on his wedding day," Rynn stated bitterly.

"He does. I don't understand why the child's gender matters." I glanced toward the tower's top floor, hundreds of feet above. "Or why she's convinced the vision showed *her* child."

"Excellent questions, but we may never learn the answers." Rynn sighed. "You know, I was almost dreading our departure. I've found a good friend in Lydia, and your brother is a decent sort. Leaving them behind is difficult. And then there's the matter of *flying* north—the very idea still terrifies me. But after today's events, I'm now looking forward to leaving the Citadel. The Oracle isn't the same woman I remember from my past."

"You shouldn't be afraid to fly with Andrew," Emmarie said resolutely. "By the time you locate Thomas, I believe you'll even enjoy it."

Rynn laughed nervously and shook her head. "No, I'm afraid that won't be the case. I'm still trying to recover from our first flight, and that was nearly a fortnight ago."

I longed for a way to alleviate Rynn's fear of heights, but I didn't know what to do. Our first flight had been brief, only a few minutes in the air, and she'd been accompanied by both Emmarie and Lydia. I recalled how badly she'd trembled, and it had only subsided once she was safely back on the ground. Guilt gnawed at me, but we'd discussed her decision time and again. Rynn was determined to join me, and despite my initial misgivings, I welcomed her company.

I calculated the journey to the Gloaming Highlands would take the better part of ten nights while flying the entire distance. Rynn knew my plan and she'd assured me her phobia would not pose a problem. She vowed to overcome her fears, and I admired her resolve—but I couldn't shake my worry.

Emmarie shrugged. "I wish I could join you. I love flying." She looked down, a deep sadness in her dark eyes.

"Alex needs you here," I reminded her, not for the first time. "Besides, it would be more dangerous for you to travel with me than it will be for Rynn. The people of Novania aren't friendly to those who are different—a mage can blend in, whereas you can't. I won't see you hurt."

"I know, but I'm scared. Alex has always been kind, but he isn't *you.* You protected me…" Her voice cracked as she dissolved into tears.

I set the trunk on the floor and knelt down to look her in the eye. "Emma, listen to me. I will come back, though it may take some time. You're strong, resilient. Alex will need as many people with your skills as he can find, and he *will* watch over you." I paused to study her, then offered her a smile. "You'll learn to handle your sword better with my brother as your mentor. Alex has finesse, whereas I tend to rely too much on strength alone."

She nodded and wiped her eyes. "I know. He said the same," she sniffed. "I'll miss you, Andrew."

I drew her into a brief embrace. "And I'll miss you. Saying goodbye is never easy—but I promise I'll write to you when I can. You have my word."

When she nodded again, I rose and hefted my trunk, and we left the Oracle's tower for the final time. Outside, the city carried on as though nothing were amiss amongst the magi. We didn't speak during the journey to the inn; Emmarie battled tears, Rynn appeared pensive, and I became lost in my own thoughts. The journey ahead would be lengthy and potentially dangerous, even if all went according to plan.

I spied Alexander speaking with Lileen and Erek outside the inn as we approached. Their two companions were nowhere in sight, though I doubted they'd gone far. When Alexander noted our arrival, he nodded to me in greeting but didn't speak until we'd reached his location.

"The inn has no more rooms available," he said with a frown. "We secured the only room left, which happens to be across the hall from ours, but there isn't enough space for everyone here."

"Emmarie can have the room," I replied without hesitation. "Our tents are in the trunk. I have no issue with making camp outside the city for one night."

"I'll join you," Rynn replied, to which Alexander smirked at me knowingly.

I shook my head, exasperated, but made no reply. Now was not the time to entertain my brother's unfounded notions that there was more between us than friendship.

"Stop by tomorrow before you depart," Alexander said after a time. "I'll send a message to Tom today. We can discuss any news he sends." He looked down, his expression troubled, then said, "I wish you didn't have to go, but I understand the necessity."

"Alex, you'll make a fine leader. I think I can speak for everyone here when I say that." When the others nearby nodded and murmured their agreement, I added, "You won't be alone in this, brother. Trust in those who have put their faith in you. They've all come to assist."

Alexander managed a strained smile. "It's moments like this that reinforce my beliefs. *You* are the leader, Andrew. Not me. I'm little more than a pretender."

"You don't give yourself enough credit," I replied. "You're a mage-warrior. You'll do well—I *know* you will. And if you need advice, you can write to me."

He shrugged uncomfortably. "I'm not the leader you are. I'll never be."

"It merely comes with experience, brother. I have faith that you'll know what to do when the time comes." I clapped him once on the shoulder and hoped my words were encouragement enough to see him through.

"I hope so."

We made camp within the Stone Grove amongst what remained of my father's kin. Rynn left to purchase what provisions she would need for the journey ahead while I pitched the tents.

I planned to remain in my dragon form while we traveled; it would allow us to cover ground more swiftly, we'd be better protected, and I could seek out wild game to hunt from the air. Rynn didn't have the coin to procure enough food for me, and though she disliked the idea of buying only supplies for herself, I insisted. She'd already spent too much on my behalf.

While Rynn was away, I spoke to my father. I didn't think he could hear me without Lileen's assistance, but I shared our plans anyway. If nothing else, I knew he could see me as I moved throughout the glade.

"We'll be leaving tomorrow," I said. "I wanted to thank you again for all you've done for me." I smiled up at the stone face looming above. "I'll return when I can."

I checked the contents of my trunk and packed it more efficiently to pass the time. Stowed inside was the black dragon scale armor I'd acquired in the Dragonlands, my sword, a coil of sturdy rope, an extra set of clothing, and a pair of boots. There was room enough to stow the tents and blankets, and what little Rynn had for personal belongings. Once she returned with the provisions for our journey, we'd have all we required for the trek north.

I still had many questions, but knew my father didn't have the answers to all of them. After the events of the morning, I realized his knowledge was limited. I needed to know more about what had happened, and without Lileen to facilitate a proper conversation, I could not seek his wisdom any further.

My gaze drifted across the grove to Caelmarion Zorai's frozen form. He was the only dragon-magi I could speak to without Lileen's assistance, and was the eldest of their number as well. My father had mentioned Caelmarion had encountered other skin-changers during the course of his long life. Perhaps he could provide the answers I sought.

I closed the trunk and crossed the glade to Caelmarion's location. As soon as I placed my hand on his leg, his voice echoed in my skull. My palm tingled where it made contact with the stone.

"How do you fare, Andrew?"

I smiled uncertainly. I had not expected to hear so much concern in his voice. "Well enough. Better than earlier."

"Good. That fool girl could have killed you—and none of you would have been the wiser for it!" He made a sound of frustration. "Perhaps my anger is misplaced, but if you decide to be party to magical workings again, I'd appreciate it if you would seek my guidance first. I would hate to see you harmed due to sheer ignorance."

I considered his words. I'd come seeking his advice, and it was clear he knew far more about my abilities and limitations than I did.

"I… There is so much I still don't know, and I believed my father could help. But it seems his knowledge is only marginally better than my own." I released a sigh and looked down, terrified my admission would make me seem less in the elder dragon's eyes.

To my surprise, Caelmarion chuckled. "Zayne will do the best he can for you. But he is young, and you are the first skin-changer he has met. I don't believe he took an interest in learning about your kind prior to meeting you. Given his upbringing, it isn't a surprise."

"You mean our family's disdain for people like me." My tone was bitter.

"Yes. It's for the best that he didn't know of you prior to opening the gateway. The elders from most of the other clans would have insisted your mother depart with them, and the Caeins would have resented both your existence and their involvement. You would have been an outcast amongst your own people. Our politics were not so different from those of the humans you've grown up with. Petty and pointless, the lot of it."

"Can you tell me what *did* happen this morning?" I asked before he continued along his present tangent.

"When Zayne asked to speak with Rynn, her…*unusual* nature meant she could not link directly with Lileen. They needed you to act as a bridge between them, yes?"

"That's right."

"I have no doubt you've already discovered you are more sensitive to magic than those around you. The skin-changers of the past claimed they could smell magic as it was being summoned and feel it in their surroundings if it was imbued within a structure or a place."

"Yes. Though with Lileen's particular gift, I can't smell anything. But others… Rynn's smells of wintergreen, and healers tend to have an herbal scent. When we were in the Dragonlands, I could feel… It was as if the very stones were humming." I shook my head, struggling to describe the sensation. "Alex and Rynn both sensed something there, but not as strongly."

"Have you ever wondered why you are this way?" Caelmarion's tone was patient, a teacher guiding his student to find an answer on his own.

"Of course."

"Without magic, you would not exist," he replied. "Your father has the power—as do I—to appear human. But he is *not* human, nor is he a skin-changer. He is a dragon and nothing more. The magic involved is a deception, a trick used to distort reality into something it is not. You were conceived while he was masquerading as Zayne Blackwell. Your mother—as with the mothers of all skin-changers—bore the Mark. Without her Mark, she would have been incompatible with your father. Your very existence is due to the magic borne by your parents."

I nodded, but I still didn't understand why he was telling me all of this. "What does this have to do with what happened this morning?"

He chuckled. "I'm coming to that, Andrew. It seems, like your father, you don't possess an abundance of patience." His tone was amused. "Because your very existence is due to works of magic, you are particularly sensitive to it. Your sensitivity makes you vulnerable. Any magic outside of a healer's ministrations will wreak havoc on your body. If Lileen had used *anyone* other than you as a conduit, they would likely have felt little, if anything. But because you are a skin-changer, your body is intolerant. It is, without a doubt, your greatest weakness. You must be wary around magi, even those whom you consider friends."

"Why can I speak with you, or with my father through Lileen, if I'm so intolerant?" I asked, bewildered.

"The magic I use to speak doesn't pass *through* you. It simply touches your hand," he explained. "No doubt you sense something, even now?"

"My hand tingles," I admitted. "And itches after a while."

"It's the magic. Don't allow any of the magi you encounter to attempt what Lileen did this morning. Her Mark is small and she wields little power, which is why you emerged from the experience physically ill rather than dead. A mage of Rynn's caliber could destroy you in a matter of moments. So quickly, in fact, neither of you may realize the danger until it's too late."

He paused for a moment, and I had the distinct sense he was scrutinizing me. "Your half-brother's power is another matter altogether. I know the two of you have always been close, and you have both been trained as soldiers. His ability will allow him to become faster, stronger, more resilient during battle—but his magic is wholly internalized. He may be the only mage without a healing ability that does not pose a threat to you."

I heard footsteps approaching and looked up to find Rynn walking toward me. She carried a rucksack slung over one shoulder, stuffed to bursting. She flashed a smile as she passed, but I only mustered a solemn nod in return. Even Rynn, who had become a friend during our travels, was a potential threat to my welfare.

She looked at me curiously but went on her way, leaving me to continue my conversation with Caelmarion.

The elder dragon sighed. "I have shared my insights so you can better understand your limitations. Don't question those who clearly care for you. Rynn already knows how Lileen's magic affected you, and I believe she will be vigilant regarding her powers when you're nearby. You'll be as safe with Rynn as you would be with Alexander."

I nodded. He was right, and I was being a fool.

"I understand. I'll speak to her…" I sighed and shook my head, pausing to run my free hand through my hair.

"Andrew."

I looked up at the stone countenance of Caelmarion Zorai expectantly.

"When she spoke with me yesterday, we spent much of that time discussing you." I could hear amusement in his words, but his tone abruptly turned serious. "She will do everything in her power to protect you, even if it means protecting you from herself. You have nothing to fear from her."

FIVE

We'd broken down our campsite and had nearly everything stowed in the trunk by midafternoon the next day. Rynn insisted on keeping a spare change of clothing and some of the provisions in her rucksack, where it would be more accessible.

After we finished packing, we traveled into the city to speak with the others a final time. Alexander and Emmarie were in the stable yard outside their inn, practicing combat stances when we arrived. I waved to my brother as we approached, and he promptly ended the lesson. Emmarie flashed a grin before bounding toward the inn's entrance, no doubt to find Lydia.

"I wrote Tom," Alexander said once she was gone. "He's eager to facilitate the alliance with the Corodan and seems well enough. And our uncle Crossley isn't the only duke to seek out his location. Jon Horace has come as well."

I smiled when Alexander spoke of Duke Horace; he was an old acquaintance of mine and no friend of Colin's. "I'm glad he's found support amongst the nobility."

"I told him I've married," Alexander said after a moment's pause, his eyes flicking to the inn's entrance. "He sent more than his congratulations, Andrew. He… He *accepted* her."

I grinned. Thomas continued to surprise me; I recalled a time only a few months earlier when we'd been terrified to confide in our younger brother. He'd always been interested in law and read much regarding the governance of Novania, and we'd believed revealing our secrets to him would place us in mortal danger.

Yet it was Thomas who had raced to Vinterry to warn me of Alexander's impending execution. It hadn't mattered that Alexander bore the Mark; Thomas' only concern was for his brother. And when I'd revealed what I was, he'd responded with curiosity rather than hostility.

Now, Thomas accepted Lydia—another mage—without question. To our youngest brother, their Marks were irrelevant. He saw them as people, equal to himself and all others, in blatant defiance of Novania's laws—and of Colin's.

I clapped Alexander roughly on the shoulder. "He's accepted *us*, brother. Why wouldn't he accept Lydia as well?"

Alexander shrugged and peered at me sheepishly. "You have a valid point. Tom has risked as much as we have by taking our side, and my Mark wasn't a factor. He helped me when no one else could." He looked up to beam at his new bride as she and Emmarie approached. "I hope they'll have the opportunity to meet one day."

"As do I."

We fell silent. I was no stranger to the ceremony of farewell, but I found this parting more difficult than most. Alexander and I had been through so much in the past months that it took an effort of will on both our parts to go our separate ways. I'd grown protective of Emmarie, and Lydia's kind brand of selfless generosity would be sorely missed. I prayed I'd see them all again.

"Tom sent a map," Alexander said gruffly after a time. He dug into a pocket to withdraw the crumpled sheet of parchment and thrust it into my hands. "I'm not sure how useful it will be from the air, but it's something."

I nodded my thanks. "Take care of yourself, brother. We'll write as often as we can."

"You'd best keep that promise," Lydia cut in. "I expect to hear from you—both of you," she said with a sharp glance at Rynn. "I still believe you're a fool for placing yourself in danger like this, but if any mage can survive in Novania, it's you."

Rynn's smile was tremulous as she blinked tears from her eyes. "I have faith in our ability to survive," she said with a nod in my direction. "He should not make this journey alone, no matter how much he protests."

I rolled my eyes. "I'm right here."

"And you have a history of refusing to listen to reason," Lydia shot back, causing the others to laugh. "Rynn's right. You shouldn't go alone, and despite my concerns, I'm glad she is traveling with you."

Emmarie launched herself into my arms. I chuckled and wrapped her in my embrace. Damn, I would miss her. I'd miss all of them.

"I'll write," I promised again. "This isn't a permanent goodbye."

She sniffled and backed away. "I know. But it doesn't make it any easier."

I replayed our final conversation in my mind as we left the Citadel and returned to the Stone Grove. Rynn was silent, unspoken melancholy in her eyes.

I scanned the grove a final time to ensure everything was in order. Satisfied, I broke our lengthy silence. "I believe we're ready."

She nodded gloomily but didn't respond, her eyes locked firmly on the ground, her face drawn with worry.

I sighed, uncertain what to say next, and waited. I didn't know if she'd become morose after parting with the others or if this was yet another manifestation of her fear of flying.

Slowly, she lifted her gaze to meet my own. "Of course. I'm sorry, Andrew, I was merely thinking…"

"You'll be safe with me," I assured her, deciding the change in her demeanor was the result of her anxiety. "I won't let you fall."

She barked a laugh. "I know. This may surprise you, but I wasn't thinking of the flight. I'm concerned by what must come afterward." She sighed. "I know your brother is accepting of mages, but will those with him feel the same?"

"They wouldn't have joined Tom if they felt otherwise. Everyone in Novania knows what Colin tried to do to Alexander, and my secret is no longer…well, a secret." I shrugged. "If anyone takes issue with your presence, they'll have to deal with me. I won't let anyone harm you. I promise."

She peered at me sharply, eyes narrowed. "I… Thank you." She shook her head slightly, then said, "Shall I go into the trees to give you privacy while you change?"

I laughed. "If that's your wish. I've no issue either way."

She raised an eyebrow in question before disappearing into the trees. I stripped, removed the coil of rope from the trunk, packed my clothing inside, then secured the lid. I placed the rope atop the trunk and stepped away from the still forms of the petrified dragons standing in silent vigil over the grove, then shifted.

The familiar expansion and elongation of my body occurred in an eye-blink, and with it came a rush of power. I now stood at eye-level with the stone form of my father, though Caelmarion's bulk exceeded mine. I stretched my wings and reveled at the heightened sensations my dragon form provided.

Rynn emerged from the trees a heartbeat later. I suspected she'd been watching the transformation from the cover of the surrounding forest, though she didn't remark on it.

As she approached, I said, "I'll need your help to tie the trunk in place." When she nodded, I added, "Climb up. I'll lift it for you."

She collected the rope, then clambered up my scaly side to perch between two of the stiff black spines that ran the length of my back. I felt her tremble as she grasped them, and a pang of concern shot through me. She was confident in all she did, and to witness her terror while we remained on the ground tore at my heart. How could I convince her she had nothing to fear?

"I'm ready." Her voice didn't betray what the tremors in her hands conveyed; it was steady, even, self-assured.

I lifted the trunk by looping my tail around its base, then placed it between the spines directly behind her perch. I craned my neck to observe as she tied it securely in place. She glanced at me when she'd finished, uncertainty clear in her eyes.

"It's not too tight, is it? I don't know how much feeling you have in these…" she gestured toward the spines.

"I feel little sssensssation." I shook my head in irritation. I loathed that I hissed, but I'd yet to learn how to speak in this form without doing so. "It'sss hard to dessscribe. It'sss akin to what you feel through your fingernailsss."

She nodded thoughtfully, then settled firmly in place between my spines. She grasped the one in front of her so tightly her knuckles turned white. "I know you don't like to talk while you're like this, so don't feel obligated to respond if I start speaking. But I… I think it will help if I talk to you, at least at first. It will take my mind off the fact that we'll be flying hundreds of feet above the ground." She shuddered. "Don't mind me. I'll get through this."

I nodded. "If you're ready—"

"Yes," she replied before I could finish. "Let's go."

I leapt into the air, spreading my wings to their full span as we crested above the treetops. I pumped them a few times to gain elevation before we began to soar above the Citadel. I banked northwest to give a wide berth to the Oracle's tower, uncertain if she'd be visible on the balcony. I didn't believe we'd receive a warm farewell from her or the assistants like Canna and opted to keep my distance.

After a few moments, a solitary gray eagle appeared in the sky to our left and flew at my side for a time.

"Galewing." I smiled, and the bird released a shrill cry in response.

Rynn shifted slightly in her seat, and I was surprised to hear her call a greeting. "Give our regards to Alex and Lydia!" She shouted to be heard over air rushing around us.

Galewing shrieked again, then folded his wings and went into a steep dive. He disappeared into the trees and was gone seconds later. I could not see Alexander or the others through the canopy of leaves, but I knew he was below.

"I hope they'll be alright," I heard Rynn say. "This business with the Oracle comes at an unfortunate time."

I agreed. Leaving Alexander had been difficult; knowing he'd be facing Colin's army while the uncertainty of the Citadel loomed behind him made me wish I could remain at his side. But Thomas also needed my help, and I could not be in both places simultaneously. The dragonkind possessed many abilities, but acting in two places at once was not one of them.

I'd been forced to make a decision, and I believed I'd be of greater use to Thomas. I didn't doubt that Alexander would find the means to contact us periodically, with or without the help of the Feige family. He'd always been resourceful.

We flew northwest from the Citadel through the late afternoon and into the evening. Sometime after night had fallen, Rynn began rummaging in her pack. Moments later, she asked if I needed to break for supper. I declined; I would hunt as we came across game below. It was simpler, though I preferred cooked food to raw—but I'd survived on worse.

"Suit yourself," she replied, and I noted her voice harbored more of its usual confidence. "The salted beef I picked up at the market is tasty. I'll eat every scrap if you aren't careful."

I laughed. "You're feeling better."

"Hmm." Her next words came around a mouthful of what I could only assume was the salted beef she'd mentioned. "I suppose so. The darkness helps. I can't see the ground, which means I can't tell how high we currently are."

The night was darker that most; there was no moon, and our flight was illuminated by faint starlight alone. Far below was a road I knew would lead us to the Thornhallow and to the Mage's Gate beyond. There were no major settlements between the Citadel and the Thornhallow, and the landscape was awash in shadow.

The night sky was peaceful and I reveled in the simple act of remaining airborne, exhilarated by the sensation of the wind as it passed beneath my wings and rippled across my scales. Perhaps one day, I'd have the opportunity to fly again simply for the sheer joy of it, as I'd done with Emmarie at the Oracle's Tree.

We made good distance through the night, and as dawn began to break across the eastern sky, I spied a herd of antelope below. My stomach rumbled in anticipation.

I called to Rynn to hold on tightly as I prepared to strike. Her hands renewed their grip, and I arced into a steep dive, arrowing toward the animals below at top speed. Rynn shouted in alarm, but her words were lost to the wind. Her grip remained firm and I believed she was in no danger of falling.

Moments later, I snatched one of the antelope in my claws while the rest of the herd scattered. I beat my wings a few times to soften the landing, then immediately dispatched the terrified creature.

As soon as we were on the ground, Rynn slid down my side. She fell to her knees, trembling violently. Her face was drained of color and her breaths came in rapid succession.

"Rynn?"

She shook her head, and a moment later began to retch into the grass.

I turned away, guilt gnawing my insides. I'd failed to properly warn her of what I planned as I acted on sheer instinct. Hunger clawed at my belly, but I ignored its pangs. While I must eat to maintain my strength, I waited, my concern for her outweighing the ache in my gut.

She walked a short distance away once she'd recovered and turned to face the rising sun. I took that as my cue and rapidly made a meal of the antelope.

As I finished, I raised my head to find she was watching me intently, her sapphire eyes sparkling in the dawn light. She remained a short distance away, her feet planted firmly apart and her hands on her hips. I frowned at her, puzzled.

"You *do* have quite the appetite," she said after a moment. "I didn't believe you when you said it would be easier to hunt than it would be to buy rations for a dragon."

I tilted my head and shrugged. I recalled Alexander had once told me I could eat enough at one sitting to accommodate a small army.

"Are you alright?" I asked.

She nodded and began to walk toward me. "I am now. I knew what you intended, and I thought I'd be able to cope, but… *Damn it*, Andrew, seeing the ground rush toward us was the most terrifying thing I've ever witnessed." She laughed shakily. "I knew you were in control, and the rational part of my mind insisted I was in no danger, but that stupid, *irrational* part wouldn't listen… It required every ounce of my willpower not to scream."

"I'm sssorry." I hung my head in defeat. I didn't know what else to do.

I blinked, startled when she placed one icy hand along the side of my jaw. "I believe I will overcome this fear in time. Each flight will be easier, and I *will* endure." She offered me a strained smile and dropped her hand, then made a face of disgust. "Ugh, you're a mess." Her hand was smeared with the antelope's blood, which was rapidly freezing to her skin. "I believe I saw a lake east of here before you began your dive. Perhaps we should find it, clean up, then rest for a while? I don't know about you, but I need to sleep."

Once we were in the air again, it was easy to locate the lake she'd spied. The water shimmered silver in the sunlight, a beacon against the backdrop of green and brown. Clusters of trees gathered at the water's edge, though most were leafless and dormant so late in the season. I landed near the lake shore, and after Rynn dismounted, I waded a short distance into the water to clean the blood from my face and claws. I heard a splash as she entered the water a few moments later, but she didn't swim to my location, choosing instead to remain near the shore.

As I stood, water dripping from my spines and running in rivulets along my scales, I glimpsed my reflection in the lake's placid surface. I was covered in black scales, with a ridge of stiff black spines running from the top of my head down the length of my back to the tip of my tail. I noted with some satisfaction the trunk with our belongings was still securely in place; Rynn's knots held up well. My wings were folded at my sides, but if I spread them, the leathery undersides and the dusky purple webbing between each segment would be visible.

Looking at my dragon's face was always unsettling. I saw little resemblance to my human form, though the face that stared back at me from the water's surface was identical to my father's. My eyes were the same shade of green in both forms, but as a dragon, the pupils were slit vertically. I wasn't certain I'd ever grow used to seeing my reflection this way.

I turned toward the shore to find Rynn was bathing, her back toward me. If I'd been in my human form, I surely would have reddened, though I was incapable of blushing as a dragon. She stood only waist-deep in the lake, and her mage's Mark was visible to me for the first time. It was a large blue-gray crescent that spanned the width and length of her back.

When I realized she was nude, I dragged my eyes away from her form with an effort of will. She was beautiful, but I would not fall to the temptation she presented. Now was not the time, nor was I ready to pursue a romance with anyone. And I was not the type to seek a woman's bed on a whim, despite my baser urges.

I trundled past her, my eyes focused on the barren trees ahead as I exited the water. The scent of wintergreen permeated the space around her, and I realized belatedly she used her power to prevent the lake water from freezing solid at her touch. I was dimly aware of her laughter as my passage created waves.

My blood thundered in my ears as my desire became undeniable. It was not the proper course of action, and I'd suffer insurmountable guilt afterwards if I acted upon my lust—for that's what it was. I had not been with a woman since Vera's death, and I'd refused to entertain the notion since that night at Vinterry. It would be a disservice to her memory if I were to cave now. It was too soon, and my grief remained raw.

While I knew if I expressed my desire, Rynn would be willing—she'd been waiting for a reciprocal response after she'd confessed her feelings in the streets of Dragon's Feet—she would have been heartbroken to learn I felt nothing more than a profound and primal need. I valued her friendship too much to risk ruining it simply to sate my appetite. I closed my eyes and concentrated on steadying my breaths, desperately trying to clear my thoughts of the image of her bare back side.

Several minutes passed before I heard her exit the water. I risked a glance over my shoulder and noted she'd seated herself near the water's edge, her back once again toward me. She was wringing the water from her blond curls but had not yet dressed. A low groan escaped my lips, and I forced myself to avert my gaze.

Perhaps this journey would prove more difficult than I'd anticipated—for reasons beyond the dangers that lay ahead. I shook my head, unable to rid my mind of the image of her naked form.

Some minutes later, her footsteps ground across the gravelly shore toward my location. I swallowed before I turned to face her. To my relief, she was dressed.

"Andrew, are you well?" she asked, clearly concerned.

I chuckled but didn't trust myself to speak. My mouth was dry, and while the pulsing of my blood had diminished, I continued to feel the residual heat from my sudden and unexpected arousal. Rather than reply, I simply nodded.

She studied me carefully, an enigmatic smile playing across her lips. "If nothing's wrong, then I'd like to rest for a few hours. You ought to sleep too."

I nodded again and settled to the ground, but sleep proved elusive for some time. I lay awake, watching the water lap against the lakeshore long after Rynn had fallen asleep, curled against my scaly side.

When I finally drifted into the arms of slumber, it was almost midday. Mercifully, I did not dream.

Two nights passed before we reached the Mage's Gate. A single cabin stood a short distance from the gate itself, inhabited by a man named Gwerin and his wife, Arabelle. Their duty was to maintain the gate and allow entrance to those seeking asylum in the Southlands.

The Barrier was a shimmering curtain of light streaked with greenish hues as it rose from the ground toward the sky to an interminable height. It stretched in both directions as far as I could see, and so far above it may have touched the stars. It was translucent enough that one could see through it and into the lands of Novania beyond. The area near the Barrier smelled strongly of ozone, but Rynn could not detect the scent, and I assumed it was the magic causing the odor.

The space known as the Mage's Gate was a large, blank area within the Barrier that didn't shimmer or glow as the rest of the construct did. It was a dark, opaque space that magi like Gwerin could manipulate, but few others possessed the same ability.

It wasn't yet dawn when I landed outside of Gwerin's cabin. I hoped to speak with him before we traveled through the gate, but I didn't want to depart until it was fully dark once more. The rumors we'd received from Thomas indicated Colin had positioned a sizeable force not far from the gate, and the Oracle's cryptic visions seemed to confirm them. I wasn't prepared to engage an army and hoped darkness would provide enough cover to slip through without drawing attention. Gwerin should be able to confirm the truth of the rumors.

Since the day was early, I decided to rest. We could talk to Gwerin in the afternoon.

Rynn fell asleep within minutes, and I curled my wing around her to shelter her from the sun's glare. The day dawned cloudless, though the air was cold.

I studied her slumbering form for some time before I drifted off, noting her worry seemed to melt away. In sleep, she'd found a peaceful respite. I hoped I'd find the same.

SIX

I scowled at Rynn as I blinked the sleep from my eyes. I'd been sleeping deeply, subconsciously enjoying the sensation of the afternoon sunlight as it struck my black scales.

"Gwerin wants to speak with us," she said firmly, planting her hands on her slender hips. "You've slept the entire day, Andrew—don't give me that look."

I sighed dramatically. "Fine."

I dug my claws into the ground and arched my back, stretching my wings wide as I did so. Stretching felt *good*. Rynn smirked in my direction, and I shot her a quizzical look.

"It's funny. Sometimes your movements remind me of a cat. A very large, terrifying, reptilian sort of cat." She laughed, then motioned that I should follow. "Gwerin is near the gate."

Alexander and I had encountered Gwerin when we first came through the Barrier. He'd been kind enough to loan me a change of clothing, then traveled with us as far as the Citadel, where he'd met with the Oracle before returning home to his duties as gatekeeper. He stood facing the Barrier and the gate within, but he turned at our approach. His smile was uneasy.

"It's good to see you again," he said. "Your friend tells me you plan to travel north… It's not a path I'd recommend, but she's been quite adamant." He glanced at Rynn briefly and shook his head. "The northerners have an army stationed not two miles from the gate."

I nodded, my suspicions confirmed. "We have to travel north," I replied.

He sighed, resigned. "So it seems. You plan to travel by night, which is wise. I have no doubt the enemy has eyes nearer the gate than what I can make out from here. Darkness may be your ally, and perhaps your passage will go unnoticed. There have been a few refugees trickling through who have managed to evade the king's men. Perhaps you will as well."

I arched an eyebrow. Did any of the "refugees" happen to include the half dozen assassins who had trailed us during Alexander's trials? There was no doubt the men we'd encountered had passed through the Mage's Gate—it was the only way through the Barrier. Gwerin was friendly and amiable, and it would not take a master of persuasion to convince him to open it.

"I had hoped to dissuade you from this fool's errand," Gwerin continued. "Why not simply wait for Alexander's arrival—"

"Gwerin," I said firmly, cutting him off, "We mussst go. What we plan to do will help my brother with hisss plansss."

Gwerin started to protest again, but Rynn spoke first. "I told you what we do is important and will help further Alexander's cause. I didn't want to share the details of our plan in case the gate becomes compromised. The less you know, the safer you will be." She planted her hands firmly on her hips and stared at the other mage fiercely. "Once it's dark, I expect you to open the gate and allow us passage. We have little time and far to go."

Resigned, Gwerin nodded. "Very well. I'll return here in an hour. The sun will be setting soon." He turned to walk back to his cabin.

Once he was out of earshot, I said, "Thank you."

Rynn smiled. "Of course." She studied me for a moment, her eyes unreadable. "There is something I've noticed that may help your speech, if you're open to suggestions?"

I nodded, eager to learn her thoughts if they'd help me overcome the sibilant nature of my words.

"I've been watching as you speak, and it seems your teeth get in the way a bit. That's what makes you hiss." She tilted her head to one side. "I'm not even certain this will work, but I believe if you pull your lower jaw back slightly, your teeth will be better aligned. It may eliminate the hissing altogether."

I considered her words. It wouldn't do any harm to try, and I detested that many of my words came out so damned mangled. It seemed a simple enough adjustment to make.

"Yes, just like that," she said in an encouraging tone.

"Like this?"

I blinked, startled and elated that it had worked on the first try. She grinned, and after a moment, I began to laugh.

"After all this time, all I needed was a simple adjustment." I shook my head, amused. "I have to focus on how I hold my jaw, but given time, it will feel almost natural."

"You sound better already," she replied. "Less reptilian and more...*yourself*."

"How did you come up with the idea?"

She shrugged. "As I said, I was watching you speak. I knew you were uncomfortable, and I thought if I studied you a bit more, an idea would come. And one did. And it worked!"

I laughed; her enthusiasm was contagious. "Thank you. I mean it."

She smiled, and seemingly on an impulse, reached one hand up to pat the side of my jaw. "You are most welcome, Andrew."

We sat near the Barrier as the sun sank lower into the sky and awaited Gwerin's return. Rynn dug through her rucksack and produced another stick of salted beef and an apple, then began to eat as we passed the time. We discussed what lay ahead; Colin's army, the long trek across Novania, and the Corodan lands beyond.

I'd spoken more in the past hour than I had at any other time while in my dragon form, and despite the knowledge that Colin's army was so near the gate, I was strangely content. I was glad Rynn had chosen to accompany me on this journey.

Gwerin returned at sundown as he'd promised. The golden light spreading across the horizon shimmered across the flickering surface of the Barrier for a few brief moments before the disc of the sun disappeared.

We watched the sunset fade into darkness. I turned away from the sky's colorful display to peer at Gwerin, who had remained silent after his arrival. He appeared weary, defeated, perhaps. Rynn lifted a hand in greeting, and he nodded silently in return.

"Gwerin?" she asked after a moment. "Is something wrong?"

He shook his head. "No, not truly. In all my years as gatekeeper, I've never opened the Mage's Gate for someone going north. And the two of you plan to, knowing well that the enemy is but a stone's throw away! It's utter madness."

"We'll be fine, Gwerin," I assured him. "We'll be past the army before they even realize we've been and gone."

He sighed. "I wish I shared your optimism. I knew there would be trouble the day I met you—not that it was your fault. I don't blame you by any means! The story you and Alexander shared chilled me to the core. Now that I've seen the army from a distance, I know I was right." He looked down at his feet and kicked at an imaginary stone. "You're certain you must enter Novania?"

I nodded. "It's the best path forward."

Gwerin's gaze traveled to the opaque space within the Barrier. "I received the Oracle's summons the day before you arrived. I know Alexander plans to travel here, where he'll establish a base of operations. I've never been a warrior, but I've decided I'll help him as I can." He shook his head. "Did you know that since the Novanian army arrived, they've marched to the gate several times? Once, they had a device they pushed along the road. They used it to fling small boulders. The rocks shattered but… How long will it hold? The Oracle's message made it clear the Barrier is failing."

I nodded, finally understanding the man's trepidation. The Barrier could give way at any moment, but I'd been unaware the Oracle included her vision in the summons. That she'd foreseen it didn't mean it was certain to occur, and she'd indicated she refrained from sharing her visions unless she was convinced of the future glimpsed within. I hoped for his sake, and Alexander's, that the Barrier would stand until he could properly defend against Colin's forces.

"The Oracle told us as much," Rynn replied, "but she *also* said she could not foresee *when* it would occur. It could be tomorrow or a century from now. Stop fretting about it. It's out of your control."

Gwerin blinked and looked as though he were about to say something more, but Rynn pressed on.

"I advise you to continue as you've always done. Open the gate when it is needed, and refuse if you believe there is a threat outside. When Alexander arrives, help him as you've promised. Focus on what you can control. You'll be better for it." She crossed her arms as she finished and frowned at the other mage in disapproval.

"I... Yes, I suppose you're right," he stammered.

I suppressed a chuckle. Rynn's forthright nature, coupled with her disdain for those who would wallow in self-pity, had unsettled Gwerin. She'd once told me she'd "lost some of the social graces" that most people expected during her long appointment at the Frostwake. I found her nature refreshing.

We waited until the remaining daylight faded before making the passage through the Mage's Gate. Rynn climbed to her perch on my scaly back and checked the knots holding the trunk in place. Satisfied, she called down to Gwerin that we were ready.

He moved in front of the opaque space as his hands wove an intricate pattern in the air. The sharp tang of vinegar permeated the area as he channeled his magic, and though I tried to hold in the sneeze that threatened, the scent was overpowering. I sneezed twice before Gwerin had opened the gate while Rynn laughed at my reaction.

I was consoled that she found mirth in the situation and was not trembling uncontrollably any longer. Perhaps she was beginning to overcome her fear of flying.

We thanked Gwerin as we passed through the gate. "Close it immediately once we're through," I added.

If Colin's army had eyes in the area as he suspected, I didn't want word reaching my wayward half-brother that there was a potential opening—or that I'd returned to his lands.

On the northern side of the Mage's Gate, the ground sloped away from the low mountain range that lay just south of the Barrier's protection before flattening into a vast plain. We'd travel through the plains for at least two days, and I anticipated we wouldn't be sighted unless we drew too near Colin's army or the road. This area of Novania was sparsely populated.

I surveyed our surroundings but did not immediately see any evidence of Colin's forces. With a glance at Rynn, who nodded once to indicate she was ready, I leapt into the air and rapidly gained altitude. I angled northeast, but kept the road just within my sight. It led due north from the Mage's Gate and would eventually reach the Capitol. I didn't intend to travel in that direction; it would be too heavily fortified, and my presence would undoubtedly be discovered. Instead, I would veer farther east once I spied familiar landmarks.

Though I had not yet told Rynn of my plan, I hoped to stop at Vinterry. I needed to say my final goodbyes to Vera and lay her bones to rest if a burial had not yet been provided. That I'd been forced to leave her lifeless form exposed in the vineyard without properly tending to it had plagued me with guilt for months. She'd deserved better from life than what she'd ultimately received, and I owed it to her memory to ensure her remains were cared for.

I was drawn from my thoughts as hundreds of flickering lights came into view near the road. Campfires and torches marked the extent of Colin's forces, and I gaped at the sheer size of the army he'd deployed on the pretense of pursing me.

I adjusted my course to provide further distance between the road and my position in the sky, hoping to avoid notice. There were a number of trebuchets near the center of the camp, a battering ram, and another device I was unable to identify from afar. Soldiers milled about the campfires while others patrolled the camp's perimeter.

"I had no idea there were so many of them," Rynn said, her voice somber. "Does your brother truly hate you so much? This seems…"

"Excessive?" I asked.

"Yes, I believe that was the word I was looking for."

"I thought Colin was simply seeking revenge, but a force this size indicates he has more planned than the apprehension of a single man." I studied the camp as we flew through the night. "This confirms the Oracle's visions. Colin is not merely seeking me, nor is he seeking Alexander. He is seeking *war*, and by the looks of it, he's going to start one."

I was tempted to fly closer to learn more, but the danger was too great. I'd seen enough to intuit my half-brother's schemes.

After a few moments, the camp faded into the distance, leaving only the twinkling campfires visible as a testament to the army's presence. After a while, those faded from our sight as well, and I pressed on.

Sometime later, I peered over my shoulder, ensuring Rynn was stable. She eyed me curiously.

"I'd like to visit Vinterry."

She nodded. "That's a good idea. Perhaps it will bring closure, or at the very least, peace of mind."

I faced forward with a strained smile. I didn't know what the trip to Vinterry would bring beyond a rush of bittersweet memories, but perhaps Rynn was right. Perhaps I'd find closure at long last.

Two and a half nights passed before we reached the forested area surrounding Vinterry. Our passage through Novania had gone undetected as far as I could determine, and Rynn had grown more confident with each flight.

It was just after midnight. A quarter moon hung low in the eastern sky, providing faint silvery illumination, and the forest was eerily silent. Most of the trees were bare for the winter, their intertwining branches reaching skyward like an army of skeletal hands. I spied the clearing where the manor house had once stood long before we arrived, dismayed by the sight. The grape vines that had once been so well-tended now formed weed-choked rows behind the charred rubble that remained of the house and its adjoining buildings. Clusters of grapes hung from the vines, unharvested and withered by frost.

I landed among the rows of vines, dark memories of what I'd uncovered on my last journey here flashing through my mind. I'd been in my dragon form then as well, but it had been Alexander who slid down my side as we landed that night rather than Rynn. The buildings had been smoldering and smoking, and it had been evident within moments there were no survivors.

Now, the ruins of the manor house poked through a tangle of weeds, its charred stone the only reminder of the tragedy that had occurred. I went to the place within the grapevines where I'd left Vera months before. Nothing remained to mark the violence that had occurred; her body had been moved, though by Colin's lackeys or wildlife, I couldn't be certain. I sighed heavily and lifted my gaze to the sky as grief shredded my heart anew.

Rynn placed one hand on my foreleg. When I looked down, sympathy shone in her eyes. "This can't be easy for you. I'm here for you, my friend."

I nodded my thanks; my throat had become too tight for speech. I didn't feel the sting of tears, but I wasn't certain I was capable of weeping in my current form. My heart ached while my soul contorted itself in a silent scream.

I swept my gaze across the vineyard, seeking some sign of what had happened to Vera's remains. A number of possibilities loomed in my mind, few of them pleasant.

"Andrew, over there."

I turned to follow Rynn's outstretched hand toward the edge of the forest. Several pale stones stood in a row just beneath the overarching branches. The stones had not been there previously, and I knew then that someone had come to Vinterry since my departure. I approached the stones hesitantly, uncertain of what I would find. There were five in total, each planted purposefully. As I neared the stone at the center, the letters engraved on its surface became clear. They were written in a precise and achingly familiar hand.

Vera Sandson, beloved of dragons.

I shook my head, touched by the gesture. "Ah, Tom…"

I would have known his handwriting anywhere. That he'd risked the journey to Vinterry to take care of Vera while I could not was perhaps the greatest gift my youngest brother had ever given me. The inscription said much about both Vera and Thomas; my youngest brother had always held a fervent fascination with dragons long before he'd learned what I was, and Vera had loved me even though she'd known I wasn't fully human.

"Thomas did this?" Rynn asked quietly.

I nodded. "When we first contacted him after reaching the Citadel, I told him what happened here. I didn't expect him to come, to do this… He was running from Colin as well, and this would have been far out of his way." I looked down, overwhelmed. "I owe him so much for this."

"The inscription… Andrew, did she know what you are?" Her voice was filled with wonder.

"When I decided to reveal myself to her, we'd been married only a few weeks. I was terrified she'd flee and send word to the king, but she didn't. She accepted me…" I trailed off as my voice cracked with emotion.

"She was a wonderful person," Rynn replied gently.

"She deserved better than this fate. I loved her. I truly loved her." I shook my head as tears stung my eyes, and I let them fall. Dragons were capable of weeping, after all.

"I know."

"We were married little more than a year," I continued after a moment. "I'd never been so damned *happy*. And to have it ripped away in an instant… For what? What possessed Colin to commit this crime?" I shook with rage, and my next words came out in a snarl. "I will make him pay for this. Damn him."

Rynn's expression was compassionate. "Anyone capable of causing such pain and grief within his own family is an abomination. I'll do everything in my power to help you."

My eyes drifted from Vera's marker to those surrounding it. The pair of stones to her right bore the names of Giles and Gregor. I hung my head, dismayed that Gregor, only ten years old, had fallen victim to this senseless crime. He'd been innocent. He'd dreamed of one day joining the king's army and fighting battles against the Corodan as I had once done, but his young life had been cut short in a senseless act of hatred—an act sanctioned by the king he so revered.

The stones to Vera's left bore the names of Cassandra and Hiram, her cook and vintner. Thomas had met all of them during his brief stay with us the summer before tragedy struck. I recalled Cassandra had often taken lunch to the library when my brother failed to notice the passage of time.

I was beyond grateful to Thomas. I'd fully expected to find the remains of these lost souls laying where they'd fallen, untended and forgotten. Thomas' compassion gave me a measure of solace despite the painful memories that now enveloped Vinterry.

I reached out to touch Vera's marker, recalling the softness of her skin beneath my fingers, how her auburn hair would glint reddish in the afternoon light, the way her blue eyes danced and sparkled when she smiled. I remembered our many nights spent near the hearth in her library as she pored over books about dragons in her quest to learn more of my heritage, and the walks we'd enjoyed during the summers, threading our way through the vineyards.

"Goodbye, my love," I whispered before turning away to face the night-darkened vineyard. More tears spilled from my eyes to run hot against my scales. Vera had been my first love, my *only* love, my greatest friend, and staunchest ally.

After a time, my grief was spent, and I turned to locate Rynn. She'd walked a short distance away, her eyes fixed on the line of stones. Frozen tears glittered on her cheeks in the pale moonlight.

"We should go," I said, my voice roughened by emotion. "We still have far to travel."

She nodded and wiped at her eyes with the heels of her hands. "Yes. I'm glad you could say goodbye, Andrew. Wherever her spirit now resides, I know she'll be comforted by your visit tonight."

"I hope she can forgive me. I wasn't here to stop them… I failed to protect her…" I hung my head, my nose nearly touching the ground.

Rynn strode toward me and placed one hand on either side of my long jaws, forcing me to meet her gaze. "I'm certain she knows you did the best you could given the circumstances. And now, by joining with your brothers to oppose Colin, you will help bring her justice. If I were in her place, I would understand. I would not hold you at fault for the king's actions."

I managed a nod. Her words were a balm to my wounded soul.

I prayed Rynn was right and that Vera—wherever her spirit might now reside—understood.

SEVEN

Three nights later, we reached the northern boundary of Novania Kingdom and a ridge of mountains we called the Gloaming Highlands. I knew little of the lands beyond the border, having ventured only a few miles beyond the kingdom's northern boundary—and only then when I pursued the Corodan during military campaigns. The highlands had always been deemed dangerous until I'd brokered the unlikely truce with the new Hive-queen.

Snow covered the ground, and a chill wind blew relentlessly. I was grateful I was unaffected by cold, though during the third night, the wind gusted so fiercely I scarcely made headway against it. After a few hours in which we made little progress, I decided to land, utterly exhausted from my efforts. I located a wide ledge protruding from a sheer rock face on the leeward side of a mountain and touched down there.

When Rynn dismounted, I noted with weary amusement her blond curls had become windblown and tangled to an extent I would not have believed possible. She cursed as she ran her fingers through her hair in a vain attempt to tame it, then shook her head with an exasperated smirk.

"I'm too tired to climb up and dig through the trunk for my comb," she complained. "Fortunately, your scales remain perfectly in place even in the worst of windstorms."

I chuckled. "At least we've reached the highlands. We'll be safer here. You should rest."

She shook her head. "I'm not ready to sleep yet, not with that ledge so close. Of the two of us, I think it's *you* who ought to rest. I can see the fatigue in your eyes."

Though I wanted to argue, I knew she was right. It had taken more energy than I'd realized simply to remain aloft as we were buffeted through the sky. I was spent. I lay down on the stone with the plan to sleep no more than a few hours, and it wasn't long before I fell into the deep, dreamless slumber of sheer exhaustion.

The sun was high in the sky, and the wind had calmed considerably by the time I woke. Rynn had made a small fire near the base of the rock face, at the point farthest from the ledge. The scent of roasting meat wafted toward me, causing my stomach to rumble loudly.

"Where did you find meat?" I asked, blinking the sleep from my eyes.

She gestured toward the ledge. "A mountain goat found its way up here. It didn't see us at first—I believe it was running from a different predator when it arrived. I froze it since I don't have a proper bow or arrows, and now it'll be lunch. I borrowed your sword. I needed something sharper than a stone to cut with." She arched an eyebrow, eyes gleaming with mischief. "I thought you'd like a *cooked* meal for a change of pace."

After a week of hunting game and eating it raw, the notion of cooked food was certainly appealing. I grinned as my stomach grumbled again, causing her to laugh.

"I'll assume that means you agree," she said. "It'll be a while before it's ready, I'm afraid. I hope you can hold out a bit longer."

I thought over her words for a few moments, savoring the aroma wafting from the campfire. "I didn't notice you climb up to open the trunk. You said you used my sword."

She smirked. "I did, and no, you didn't. You were snoring. All this time, I thought Alexander was merely poking fun at you, but it turns out he was telling the truth." Her expression softened then. "I hope you slept well, Andrew."

"I did, thank you."

I watched in silence as she turned several large steaks over the fire, and I wondered what she was thinking. She'd seemingly mastered her fear of heights since we'd left the Citadel, and while she remained at a safe distance from the edge of the precipice, her hands didn't shake. She was calm and confident. I was pleased that her anxiety was no longer at the forefront of her emotions.

I rose to my feet and stretched languidly. While the air was cold, the sun's rays were warm against my scales. It was a pleasant sensation. If our need to press forward hadn't been so urgent, I would have liked to sit in the sun, basking in the natural warmth it provided. The more time I spent in my dragon form, the more I was surprised by some of my instincts and urges. I would never have known the delight of idling in the sunlight, drinking it in as I did now, if I'd remained in the Capitol and kept my post as commander.

And I wouldn't have experienced the unabashed joy flight afforded me, even when battling a windstorm. As much as I hated Colin for his role in my exile, I also had him to thank for my current state. I reveled in my existence now that I'd begun to truly learn what it meant to be a skin-changer—to be dragon-kind.

I moved toward the ledge and peered at the landscape. The mountains were far steeper than those we'd encountered in the south, and many bore sheer sides with rocky ledges, much like the one we'd landed on. Far below, a silver ribbon marked a river's passage through a rugged and boulder-strewn valley. I followed the course of the river with my eyes until it dropped from a great height to cascade down a rocky cliff face in a misty spray. Rainbows danced in the vapor while raptors circled on unseen thermals above the falls.

I had little to go on in which to locate Thomas. He was somewhere in the Gloaming Highlands near a river and was close enough to one of the Corodan lairs that he'd established trade with them. Locating him would prove difficult, and I was unfamiliar with the terrain. Now that we were safely beyond Novania's borders, I was no longer limited to searching through the night-darkened landscape. Perhaps with the added visibility of daylight, I'd locate Thomas' camp more easily.

As I gazed from my perch, I wondered if the camp was somewhere along *this* river. It was as likely an area to start our search as any, but it was rumored dozens of rivers spilled from the highlands south into Novania. If Thomas had followed this river, it was little wonder he was concerned about discovery. Even from my present height, it was clear the banks were wide and would afford stable passage to those on foot—and Colin had experienced trackers in his employ.

My gazed drifted. I spotted several mountain goats some distance away and marveled as I watched them nimbly scale the sheer cliffs, balancing on invisible footholds. The wind sighed softly around the ledge, and the loudest sound I detected was the crackling of the campfire behind me.

"I think the meat is ready."

I turned away from the spectacular view at Rynn's words, my stomach rumbling again in anticipation. Though the meat was gamey, it was a relief to have it cooked, and I ate heartily. Rynn watched me with amusement in her eyes but didn't speak until I was finished.

"I understand why you insisted I shouldn't bother with provisions for you," she remarked with a smirk. "We would have run out on the first day!"

I chuckled. "With greater size comes a greater appetite, I suppose."

"Hmm." She appeared thoughtful. "At least there seems to be plenty of mountain goats around. It won't be difficult to find game should you need to hunt again." Her gaze left mine and traveled to a point in the distance. "Do you think we'll locate Thomas soon?"

"No." I frowned, troubled. "I don't know the highlands, and we're well beyond where my previous travels have taken me. He could be camped almost anywhere, and we'd never discover the location, given the terrain. But I may have a solution."

She looked up expectantly. "What is it?"

"Tom said he'd been trading with the Corodan. If we locate the entrance to one of their lairs, they may be able to point us to his camp. But… I don't know what sort of reception I'll receive. I killed their former Hive-queen, after all."

She nodded. "Your actions prompted them to broker peace with Novania. They negotiated directly with *you*—and Thomas wrote that they won't ally with him without speaking to you first. I believe they'll be more welcoming than you realize." She studied me for a moment, then said, "Do they know you in this form?"

"I believe so, but I don't know for certain." I shrugged and adjusted my wings. "If I understood the Corodan's method of communication better, perhaps I'd know the answer. They speak amongst themselves over vast distances, and they seem to be aware of one another in a way that defies explanation. It's almost as though when you speak to one, you speak to them all. I don't know if the former Hive-queen was capable of sharing what she *saw* with the rest of them, but in her final moments, she spoke three words the new Hive-queen understood clearly enough."

"What did she say?"

"Danger. Power. Death."

She arched an eyebrow, amused. "I suppose all three words aptly described you, given the circumstances unfolding when they were spoken."

I frowned, working my jaw from side to side. Holding the lower half of it back as Rynn suggested allowed me to speak clearly, but the muscles often became tired and sore. This was one of the longest conversations I'd managed in some time. Given practice, it would become easier, but I needed to rest my jaws at present.

Rynn seemed to intuit my discomfort. "We can speak more later. For now, let's use the daylight for our search. Perhaps we can locate one of the Corodan lairs. Until we speak with one of them, we won't know what their reaction will be."

She was right, but I feared my uninvited arrival at one of their strongholds might provoke them into an unwarranted attack. The only time the Corodan had encountered me in my current form was when I'd been cornered and desperate to survive.

Rynn snuffed out the campfire, then resumed her perch between the spines on my back. I flew toward the rim of the ravine above, hoping to locate the Corodan upon the heights. I wasn't certain I'd find an entrance to their hive there; I knew little of the Corodan's habits beyond battle tactics and what I'd gleaned from them during interrogations. My focus had never been to locate their home.

We spent the afternoon scouting but found no evidence of the Corodan, nor anything to indicate humans were nearby. There were dozens of mountain goats, hawks, and falcons, and above the summits we spied large grazing animals with enormous antlers the like of which we'd never encountered before. Once, we spied a leopard stalking a mountain goat along a sheer cliff face; the big cat was as agile as its prey and maintained its balance where no foothold was visible.

I began to fear we'd traveled too far into the highlands, that we'd passed Thomas' camp during the night and I'd been unaware of it. By the time the sun began to set, I was discouraged. There was no sign of Thomas, no indication of the Corodan, nothing but wildlife, boulders, and wind-whipped trees.

I landed near a small pond. There were no trees at this elevation, though a smattering of prickly bushes thrust their way through the crust of snow capping the peak. The pond was partially frozen, but Rynn had no trouble breaking through the ice near the shore with her magic. The water was cold and clean, and lethargic fish circled in the depths. There were tracks in the snow; I recognized those of the mountain goats, though there were others that appeared to be more predatory in nature. There were no boot prints, nor the jagged footprints left in the wake of passing Corodan.

"This search could take days," I said despairingly. "The highlands stretch along the entire northern border of Novania. Thomas could be anywhere."

"And we'll find him," Rynn replied. "We have little to fear from the weather here, and there is abundant game. We'll survive where others will not. We'll find him, Andrew."

Three days passed before we came across what I believed was an entrance to one of the Corodan lairs. From above, an opening gaped in the side of the mountain, a cascade of rubble framing its rim. We'd covered a great distance during our search, and I was elated to find some indication of those we sought. I landed a short distance from the opening amid the surrounding debris field.

"I don't know how to announce our arrival," I told Rynn over my shoulder. "It feels wrong to enter without permission…"

I moved a few steps closer to better inspect the opening. It was pitch dark within, and I could see no movement. I didn't know if this was typical for a Corodan lair or if this particular entrance had been abandoned.

"Hello?" I called. "I need to speak with someone. Anyone?"

There was no immediate response. I growled impatiently and began to pace.

"Give them a moment," Rynn replied with her usual brand of optimism. "Perhaps it takes a bit of time to—"

She stopped speaking as her breath caught in a startled gasp.

A pair of Corodan emerged from the hole in the mountainside to stop just outside. They assumed a strong stance that indicated they would not allow us to pass any further without a fight.

The Corodan were as large as horses but looked much like praying mantis. They bore thick carapaces that served as natural armor, and their forelimbs were covered in a razor-sharp, serrated edge. I'd witnessed Corodan slice through the best steel armor Novania could produce as though it were constructed of paper. They were fierce fighters, though I'd learned—much by accident—their natural weaponry could not pierce dragon scale.

The Corodan on the right produced a threatening rattle that I recognized as a warning; the sound often precluded an attack.

"I don't wish to fight you," I said evenly. "I only seek information."

I hoped my words would calm the creature, but if it attacked, I wouldn't hesitate to defend myself and Rynn. I dug my claws into the rocky soil, bracing for what was to come.

The second Corodan made an eerie clicking noise, and the first seemed to defer. The two looked at one another for a time, and I sensed they communicated, though they produced no further sounds. After several minutes, the second Corodan approached warily, tilting its head first one way, then the other. It seemed we were being scrutinized.

The first disappeared into the lair once more.

"Kash-kah says wait. I wait. You wait." The Corodan's voice contained a high-pitched, buzzing quality that I could only describe as insectile.

I nodded, recalling Kash-kah was the name of the current Hive-queen. There were few Corodan who could speak our tongue, and the one who faced us now seemed to struggle with our unfamiliar words.

"Kash-kah knows me," I replied. "We negotiated peace."

"Wait."

"I think it wants us to wait for another of its kind, Andrew," Rynn whispered. "This one can't speak adequately."

Several hours passed. Night descended, and the low clouds in the sky above began to drop snow. My breath steamed before me, the only indication I sensed of the temperature's downward slide. The Corodan who waited with us retreated into the entrance of its lair and leaned against the wall, seemingly asleep. Rynn climbed from her perch on my back, a small bit of hard cheese and the remnants of the dried fruit she'd purchased in the Citadel clutched in her hands. I grew restless and hoped whoever was traveling to meet with us would arrive soon.

The Corodan at the entrance alerted me to the arrival of others. It straightened and stood erect, then peered into the dark hole expectantly. After several minutes, a contingent of Corodan began to emerge from the opening. A half dozen marched outside, forming ranks on either side of the lair's entrance, where they stood rigidly at attention. A much larger Corodan emerged from behind them; I knew from experience it was a female—they were always the largest of the species. She moved toward me, unafraid, easily twice the size of the others.

"I am Kash-kah," she said. Her voice was pitched lower than the Corodan who had spoken to us earlier, but it retained the same buzzing quality. At her words, the other Corodan performed a salute, extending their left forelegs toward the sky.

My only encounter with the previous Hive-queen had been in battle, and I was uncertain of the proper etiquette required while speaking with this one. I didn't want to insult her, nor did I want to intimidate her, but I was unfamiliar with the Corodans' customs outside of warfare. I decided the best course of action was to appear deferential and attempt to be as unthreatening as I was able, given my current size and outward appearance.

I bowed my head low. "I am Andrew Caein. I was once the commander of the Novanian army."

The Corodan gathered behind the Hive-queen erupted into a frenzy of excited hissing. Kash-kah lifted her forelimbs in a gesture reminiscent of a speaker attempting to quiet an audience, and the others fell silent.

"I know you," she replied. "We spoke once through my emissary. You relieved our people of the blight that was Krizzt-keh and allowed us to experience peace. I thank you." She paused, tilting her head to one side. "Why have you come here, dragon-man?"

Her words made it clear the Corodan knew exactly what I was, and it seemed Kash-kah wasn't threatened by my presence. That she'd come to speak with me herself was unexpected, but I understood she'd done so out of respect. I hoped she'd be willing to help me locate Thomas.

"I'm seeking my brother. I know he fled to your lands, and he's done some trading for supplies with your people, but I don't know where he is. I must find him."

"He is unlike you," she replied dismissively. "He wishes an alliance but lacks the knowledge to move forward. He doesn't know how to fight. He is like a tiny bird, unable to fly, weak and vulnerable. The red king's men will crush him."

"That's why I'm seeking him. He needs my help."

"You are powerful. You command respect." She tilted her head the other direction, as though peering at me from a different perspective. "I will tell you where he is, and I may even help you fight the red king. But I must receive something from you in return. My people will not offer their services freely—it must be an exchange. If you aid us, then perhaps we will fight alongside you. Or perhaps we will send you on your way to your brother alone."

I didn't know what the Corodan could possibly need from me, but I supposed Kash-kah was justified in asking for something in return for her assistance. It was a negotiation, after all, though one I wasn't certain I was equipped to handle. I glanced at Rynn, who merely shrugged.

"What do you require of me?" I asked.

"There is an upstart in the north. She is called Trelk-keh, and is the child of Krizzt-keh. She plots and schemes, and brings strife to the Corodan once more. She thinks to overthrow me and disrupt the peace of the hive. Defeat Trelk-keh and we will assist you."

I flicked another glance at Rynn. She nodded once in silent agreement. She'd accompany me to face this Trelk-keh, and I was certain her magic would prove useful in the inevitable fight. The Corodan didn't relish cold temperatures, and I doubted they'd fare well against weaponized frost.

"Tell me where to find Trelk-keh and what I should expect to encounter when I reach her."

We would help the Corodan, and in turn, locate Thomas. It was the best I could hope for.

EIGHT

Kash-kah and her entourage led us into the Corodan warrens beneath the mountain, where we were sheltered from the night's chill. The walls and chambers were exceptionally dry and smelled of dust, the warrens were dim, and a maze of networked tunnels branched from the main corridor. Each passage was spacious enough to not only accommodate the largest of the Corodan, but I was unhindered as well. The exposed root tips of plants threaded through the earthen walls, emitting a pale blue-green light strong enough to illuminate our path.

"I will send hive soldiers to accompany you on your errand," Kash-kah said as we traveled. "They will meet you once they are prepared for the journey and will lead you through our hive to the northern exit, where you will travel across the land. There, you will find Trelk-keh. Eliminate Trelk-keh. She seeks to resume her forbear's warmongering without due cause."

We walked through a series of seemingly empty tunnels that wound around and through countless more, and passed more groups of Corodan on occasion. Some were the size of house cats, while others were as large as the Hive-queen's escorts. It seemed the smaller members of the species were responsible for maintaining the warrens; most were at work reinforcing the walls or digging to new areas, while others collected mounds of dry earth for transport back to the surface of the lair. None of the Corodan seemed surprised by our presence; I assumed Kash-kah had informed her people of our arrival and our intentions.

"This section of the hive is under construction," Kash-kah said after a time. "When the hive soldiers lead you to the surface again, you will take a different route. You will see other areas of our home. It is something few of your kind have experienced." She paused for a moment and made a strange rattling sound that I believed was her version of laughter. "Few *humans* have ever come here. You are the first of the dragon-kind to walk within our walls in our collective memory—and our memory is vast."

"You speak as though you know the memories of all Corodan," Rynn said, her voice filled with wonder. "I sense that you speak to them, even now."

Kash-kah turned to study Rynn with her multi-faceted eyes. "It is difficult to explain to outsiders. Our mind is singular, though we each think for ourselves. As Hive-queen, I can influence our thoughts, but we are as *one*. This is why none of the others have approached to inquire about your presence. All were aware of you as soon as the guards responded to your call. We recognized the form of the dragon-man. His presence stirs fear despite his peaceful arrival. We know the destruction he is capable of."

She turned to peer at me sharply. "It is for this reason we must have proof of your good intentions. If you help us, we will help you—but we cannot simply take your word. Your past actions have wounded the Corodan greatly, dragon-man, even if they eventually brought us the peace we long sought."

"I must earn your trust," I replied. "I understand."

"Good."

She turned to resume our tour of the intertwined warrens of the hive. After a time, we came to a spacious ovoid chamber furnished with several large mats of what appeared to be woven grass. There were no Corodan within, and the chamber was accessible only through the passage we'd entered from.

"You may rest here. One of us will bring you refreshments and clear water." Kash-kah tilted her head in contemplation before turning away. "I don't know if we will speak again directly. We will pray for your success tomorrow."

"Well, this has certainly been…interesting," Rynn remarked once we were alone. "I never imagined I'd be trading favors with the Corodan, nor did I believe we'd be spending the night inside their hive. They're not what I expected."

"And what did you expect?" I asked.

"I don't know. After hearing your tales, I thought they'd be a bit more…human-like." She shrugged.

I chuckled. "I fought the Corodan for many years before that final battle you've heard so much about. Perhaps that's why I've come to think of them as I do. They're intelligent, though their mind is clearly different than ours. I've always struggled to comprehend how it works."

"Do you believe we're safe here?" Rynn asked. "I don't think Kash-kah means us any harm, but I can't grasp her emotions—if Corodan are capable of them. There is nothing in her face to convey what she thinks, and her eyes are entirely unreadable."

"I don't believe we're in any danger," I replied. "When we leave to face Trelk-keh, we must be wary. I don't know if the soldiers accompanying us will offer their assistance when forced to fight their own. We may be alone. Be prepared for anything."

She frowned, her expression troubled. "I don't know how insects are affected by cold. They live underground, and the air here is warmer than it was above. I hope I'll be of some use to you in the fight."

"The Corodan dislike the cold perhaps more than most humans do." I paused to settle on my haunches. "It was unusual for them to attack Novania during the winter months. Thomas once theorized they hibernate, but it seems that isn't the case. They simply remain below ground, where they won't freeze." I glanced around the chamber. "I didn't know they were capable of such intricate construction."

Not long after Kash-kah's departure, a smaller Corodan entered the chamber bearing what I could only assume were the refreshments we'd been promised. There was an earthen ewer filled with clean water and a woven tray with an assortment of strange edibles the like of which I'd never seen. The Corodan left the tray in front of Rynn before exiting, leaving us to speculate on its contents.

Rynn picked up a pale, egg-shaped, gelatinous item and inspected it closely. "What do you suppose this is?" she asked, then popped it in her mouth. "Hmm, it's sweet. The flavor is a bit like melon."

Most of the items were palatable, and by the time the Corodan returned to take the tray away, it was decidedly empty. Though I had not found the food filling, Rynn seemed content with her share. I would make time the next day to hunt game once outside, provided our Corodan escorts were amenable.

Rynn fell asleep on one of the woven grass mats not long afterwards. I lay awake for some time, curled against the opposite wall, unable to relax my guard. I'd spent far too much of my life battling Corodan to be completely at ease within their hive. When I fell asleep hours later, it was fitful and restless.

I was roused by the arrival of a number of Kash-kah's promised soldiers. I assumed it was daylight outside, but the dim glow emitted by the roots in the hive walls remained unchanging. The leader of the soldiers was another female, larger and more powerful in appearance than her male counterparts. She introduced herself as Rizzt-tok, and spoke only when necessary; her speech was more broken than Kash-kah's had been.

We followed several winding tunnels and traversed various chambers. Most were filled with Corodan performing various duties, but few turned to observe our passage. As we entered a chamber that appeared to be a sort of nursery, Rizzt-tok waved a foreleg in the direction of the nearest wall, indicating the tiny Corodan nestled within a series of alcoves.

"Those will become workers." She gestured to the opposite wall, which housed a smaller number. "Those will become soldiers." Pointing to a final tiny insect, alone some distance from the rest but tended to by four adults, she said, "That one will become mate of Kash-kah when he grows."

Her explanation made sense but left me with a dozen new questions. Rather than pry, I nodded and followed Rizzt-tok through the chamber. I feared if I began to pepper her with questions, it would be considered an insult, and I didn't want to risk causing an offense while we were hopelessly lost inside the depths of the hive. Our situation was tenuous enough without further complications.

Eventually, the tunnel we followed began to angle upwards, and a short time later, I noticed a brighter light ahead. The tunnel was nearing its end, and sunlight streamed through the exit. Relief washed through me; I'd begun to feel stifled, oppressed from all sides while inside the hive.

And I was hungry. The notion of a hunt, however brief, was appealing.

Rizzt-tok stopped a short distance away from the exit and turned to face me. "It will be another day before we come to Trelk-keh's false hive. Trelk-keh has scouts nearby. We will fight. Will you help?"

I nodded and pushed aside my hunger. I would hunt once I knew the danger to Rynn and the others was past.

"You'll be safer on my back," I said to Rynn as Rizzt-tok began to march forward.

She frowned, her expression unreadable. "I can take care of myself. I don't plan to sit idly by while you do all the fighting. I'm not some helpless damsel who cries at the sight of a broken fingernail."

"I'm sorry," I replied, taken aback by the ferocity of her response. "I know how vicious the Corodan can be, and I—"

"I know you meant well," she said with a sigh, "but it's safer for *you* if I have space to channel my magic. I would never forgive myself if I brought you harm—even if it was by accident." She looked up, concern and fear reflected in her vibrant, blue eyes. "Andrew, I'll be fine. You'll see."

I nodded, resigned. "Very well. Be safe."

"You aren't going to stop worrying about me, are you?" she asked, hands planted on her hips.

I chuckled. "No. It's a habit of mine."

She arched an eyebrow, but said nothing more as we exited the mouth of the hive. We were on a gentle slope blanketed in freshly fallen snow. The sky was heavy and gray with clouds, while a few stray snowflakes floated toward us on an icy breeze. Our Corodan guides huddled together, their discomfort at the marked change in temperature apparent.

"We must move quickly," Rizzt-tok stated. "Shelter is a few miles away. We will rest, then move on in morning."

The Corodan set a brisk pace. The land descended gently for a time as we moved away from the hive's exit, then began to rise again. A few large boulders were visible in the distance, and it appeared they marked our intended destination. As we neared the boulders, the scent of woodsmoke permeated the air. Someone else was already sheltered behind the stones.

"Someone is ahead," I said as softly as I was able. It was nearly impossible for a dragon's voice to become a whisper.

The Corodan halted in unison, and Rizzt-tok spun to face me. She seemed to assessed me, though it was impossible to fathom her emotions. "You sense something, dragon-man?"

"Smoke, perhaps from a campfire. I can smell it."

Rizzt-tok tilted her head. "We cannot 'smell,' as you say. But fire, I know. Fire means people…but whose?"

One of the smaller males parted from the group and began to approach the stones as though he'd been directed to do so. I watched as he cautiously peered around the edge of the rock. Something flashed toward him rapidly, too fast for my eyes to follow, and he fell heavily, his head nearly severed from his body. Blue-gray ichor leaked from his body to discolor the snow.

"Trelk-keh attacks!" Rizzt-tok cried before charging ahead with the other Corodan.

I followed closely, circling to the opposite side of the rocks. A large campfire blazed between the boulders, and a group of five Corodan clustered within, preparing to strike at Rizzt-tok and her people.

I roared a challenge. Two turned just as I swiped a claw through each of them, tearing them asunder. Rizzt-tok was engaged with the largest of the group, who appeared to be their leader, while her remaining soldiers encircled another.

The last of the enemy Corodan charged past and sprinted toward Rynn. She was too far away for me to assist her.

I lashed my tail in anger, striking the Corodan Rizzt-tok faced with enough force that she collapsed to the ground. Rizzt-tok seized the opportunity and leapt on her opponent, skewering her with razor-sharp forelegs.

I glanced up to find Rynn stood her ground calmly, even as the Corodan continued to charge toward her. At the last moment, snow erupted in front of her and shot skyward with such force her enemy was sent flying. Its limbs flailed as it sailed through the air to land just behind Rizzt-tok. Rizz-tok turned and methodically thrust her foreleg through its head.

Rynn strode forward purposefully and shot a pointed glance in my direction. It seemed I'd had no reason for concern, but it was difficult for me to relinquish my role as protector. It was what I'd always done. Who I *was.*

After the last of the enemy Corodan was dispatched by Rizzt-tok's soldiers, they began to collect the bodies of the fallen, heaping them into a pile on the far side of the boulders.

"A warning to Trelk-keh," Rizzt-tok explained. "She will send no others this day."

"Then we're safe for now," I said, then glanced at Rynn. "I need to hunt."

Rizzt-tok tilted her head to the side, contemplating my words. "Kash-kah provided food to you. Royal jelly, meant to fill and give stamina."

Rynn stifled a laugh behind her hand. "I'm afraid she doesn't know the extent of Andrew's appetite. He's been hungry for some time."

Rizzt-tok faced Rynn, the multi-faceted orbs of her eyes spinning slowly. "You must remain with us. Then we know he will return."

Rynn shrugged. "That's fine by me. I'm not fond of flying." She offered me a weary smile, but her expression was troubled. "Be quick, Andrew."

I couldn't fault her for being nervous. While Rizzt-tok believed there would be no further attacks before morning, I wasn't convinced. Having battled Trelk-keh's ruthless and brutal predecessor, I knew what she was likely capable of. An attack during the night was one such tactic, and repeated attempts during the same day was another.

But the Corodan could sense one another in a way that was alien to me. Perhaps Rizzt-tok understood through other means that Trelk-keh would not risk another attack again so soon. Regardless, I needed to hunt if I planned to keep up my strength.

"I won't be long," I promised before taking to the sky in search of game.

It took little time to locate a mountain goat, and I didn't stray far. I was away for less than an hour, but by the time I spied our make-shift camp once more, it was besieged by more hostile Corodan. Frustration welled within me as I surveyed the scene, and I cursed myself for a damned fool. I shouldn't have left simply to sate my hunger.

Rizzt-tok's people were outnumbered and had formed a defensive circle within the stones, but I could not immediately spot Rynn. My heart raced as I propelled my wings forward, beating them more powerfully as I approached from overhead. I would never forgive myself if she came to harm after she'd risked so much to accompany me.

And I'd already lost so damned much in the past year. No more.

I dove toward the ground, bellowing in rage at the attackers as my claws tore into those nearest my landing point. Rizzt-tok took advantage of the sudden chaos my arrival brought with it and charged forward with her people in a wedge formation. Trelk-keh's group continued to press the attack, rushing me thoughtlessly.

I didn't hold back. I unleashed the full magnitude of my strength upon Trelk-keh's minions while I desperately scanned the area for Rynn.

I dispatched a group of enemy Corodan, only to realize another wave charged toward us from further down the slope. I spun to face them, growling low in my throat, challenging them to fight.

Moments later, they were upon us. I took the brunt of the assault while Rizzt-tok's people moved to flank the newest wave of attackers. I tore through several and bashed others with my tail.

I still could not locate Rynn. My concern for her transformed into a white-hot rage that I directed at the enemy Corodan.

I roared and slashed my way through their ranks, tearing, shredding, lashing, and buffeting them with my wings. The snow-covered ground became a mess of slush, mud, and ichor in the wake of my fury. Bits of carapace and severed insectile limbs littered the scene.

I would destroy every last one of Trelk-keh's people if Rynn was hurt. They would rue the day they'd dared to incur my wrath, and I would avenge her until nothing remained of Trelk-keh and her hoard.

As the remainder of the second wave fell, I managed to make brief eye contact with Rizzt-tok. "Where's Rynn?" I growled.

"She is—" Rizzt-tok stopped before forming an answer and turned to face downslope once more.

A third wave of Trelk-keh's people sprinted toward us, an angry buzzing sound accompanying their advance. An enormous female marched behind them; I assumed it was Trelk-keh herself, come to witness the battle.

There was no time to seek Rynn, though I sorely wanted to. I braced myself, roaring another challenge. Let them come. I would tear them asunder as I had those who had foolishly attacked before.

They never reached my location. A jagged wall of ice rose from the ground directly beneath the first line of the assailants. Several were instantly impaled, shards of ice piercing their bodies as it jutted skyward. Those immediately behind the ice crashed headlong into it, unable to stop their momentum in time to avoid a collision.

I released a relieved sigh, then began to laugh mirthlessly. Rynn was alive and making her presence known in deadly fashion.

Corodan began to funnel around one side of the ice. I positioned myself near the edge, tearing into the attackers as they charged around the corner. Rizzt-tok and her people moved to guard the opposite end, slashing and slicing with their serrated forelegs. Soon, there were no enemy Corodan left to continue the assault.

Moments later, the ice wall collapsed and shattered, forming brittle shards that littered the ground. A dozen paces away, the large female who had led the assault stood encircled by dozens of icicles, their jagged ends pointed toward her from every direction. None of the ice pierced her, though she could not so much as twitch if she hoped to avoid injury.

Rynn materialized at my side, her blue eyes ablaze. I grinned, overjoyed to find her well, but her gaze was fixed on the trapped Corodan.

"Trelk-keh," Rizzt-tok spat the word. "Traitor."

She approached Trelk-keh, inspecting the ice crystals carefully before turning her gaze on the other female. They didn't exchange words, though I sensed a form of communication occurred between them. Finally, Rizzt-tok turned away and strode purposefully toward us.

"Trelk-keh asks to speak with you both, ice-mage and dragon-man. I would grant her this final demand."

"She attempted to kidnap me while Andrew was away," Rynn snarled. "I'm not a damned prize to be stolen! I will not speak with her. She is beneath me."

My eyes widened in surprise. "Rynn, I—"

She looked at me sharply. "It's not your fault. She merely took advantage of your departure, though she paid dearly for it, I'd say." She scanned the scene of the battle, frowning at the destruction. "Talk to her if you wish, but she'll receive nothing from me. And make it quick. I've a mind to send every last one of those icicles straight through her."

I glanced at Rizzt-tok, who merely gestured toward the captive. I didn't know what Trelk-keh could possibly want to say. I'd just slaughtered countless of her people, and I was also responsible for the death of her mother and former Hive-queen. With a frown, I lumbered toward Trelk-keh, propelled by morbid curiosity.

I stopped some distance away from the ring of ice. "You wanted to speak?"

Trelk-keh tilted her head slightly. "You defeated Krizzt-keh and sowed peace with Kash-kah. Because of your actions, I became an outcast. Kash-kah knew I would not pass up an opportunity to avenge Krizzt-keh. It is why she sent you here. I have been a fool. I played into her scheme just as she hoped, and now I have nothing. My hive is destroyed by you, dragon-man, and my life is forfeit." She emitted a frustrated series of clicks.

My frown deepened. "Is this what you truly wanted to say?"

Trelk-keh stared at me for several seconds before making a reply. "Kash-kah makes a mistake in her alliance with you, dragon-man. You have always been an enemy."

"I merely fought to protect my people," I replied. "I never wanted the war to last as long as it did. How many times did we capture one of your kind to make an appeal for reason? We didn't want to fight. Krizzt-keh insisted on war. We did not."

Trelk-keh made a rattling sound that I believed was laughter. "You have no 'people,' dragon-man," she replied. "You protect the humans. Why? They are weak, stupid. Look at the red king on his throne in the south. He plays at rule but brings horror to his own people. You would protect him?"

I narrowed my eyes. Could I trust her words? The red king was no doubt Colin, but what horrors did she refer to? Did she know something of Colin that I did not? What had he done while Alexander and I had been away? I decided to ignore her barbed remarks concerning my heritage in order to learn more of my half-brother's recent activities.

"I have been away from Novania for some time. What has the red king done?"

She rattled again. "If you do not know, then it is not my place to say. You will learn soon enough without my words to guide you."

"Tell me, damn you!"

"I owe you nothing, dragon-man. You have taken all I have."

I growled and turned away, frustrated and unsettled by her declaration. She hissed something more, but I didn't hear her words.

Rizzt-tok took my departure as her cue to complete the task her queen had imparted upon us. Trelk-keh made a strangled, gurgling sound a moment after I began to walk away. I peered over my shoulder to find Rizzt-tok a few steps from Trelk-keh, cleaning her forelimbs in the dirty snow.

Trelk-keh sported a pair of gaping wounds in her thorax that oozed blue-gray ichor. She'd fallen forward to collapse into the sharp shards of ice, her carapace instantly impaled. An icicle was embedded in her abdomen, and another severed one of her forelimbs. If she wasn't dead yet, she had only moments remaining.

I turned from the scene to find Rynn staring at me, her expression weary and troubled. We walked silently toward the dying campfire that had somehow survived the battle, while what remained of Rizzt-tok's soldiers began to clear the space of debris.

There were a dozen questions I wanted to ask her, but something prevented me from voicing them. I was thankful she was alive and unhurt, but I was guilt-ridden at leaving her alone and vulnerable.

"Andrew," she said softly after a time, "I'm glad you returned when you did. We were outnumbered, and I…" She shook her head, frustrated. "I didn't think we'd survive. Rizzt-tok is a valiant fighter, but there were so many of them. Even with my magic, we would have been overrun."

"I won't leave you again," I promised. "If something had happened… If I had lost you too…" I looked away, unable to meet her gaze.

I'd lost Vera because I hadn't been there to stop Colin's men. I would not lose another friend in the same manner.

Her icy hand touched my foreleg, feather-light. When I turned toward her again, she gazed at me, her eyes sparkling in the firelight, her expression compassionate. When she spoke, her tone was understanding.

"It wasn't your fault. You could not have known Colin's plans, nor could you have known Trelk-keh's. I know that, and I'm certain Vera did too."

I nodded, though her words didn't assuage my guilt. "I won't leave you again," I repeated stubbornly.

She forced a tired smile, then dropped her hand to her side. "I'm glad to have you at my side. Though I have to admit, your brother was right. You're terrifying in your dragon form, particularly when you're angry."

I chuckled feebly, and some of my tension began to melt away. "When I couldn't locate you, I'd feared the worst. I stopped holding back, and I simply…*raged*."

She studied me silently for a moment. "You've always held yourself back, haven't you?"

"Yes. It was the only way I knew to fit in. I couldn't risk anyone learning the truth of what I am. Over time, it became my norm."

"Don't hold back any longer," she said. There was a ferocity in her tone that I was unprepared for, a heat in her gaze that compelled me to listen. "Alex and Tom both need you at your best, at your most fierce. Be yourself. Be the *dragon-man*. You have nothing left to fear."

NINE

A contingent of Corodan waited for us when we returned to the hive's entrance, Kash-kah amongst them. Rizzt-tok and her people stood in deference before their Hive-queen as she scrutinized them individually. Moments later, they were sent wordlessly inside.

Rynn and I stood a short distance away, but were allowed to observe the Corodan ritual. Finally, Kash-kah beckoned us with a foreleg, seemingly satisfied with what she'd learned.

"You have done my people a great service. Rizzt-tok states you both fought bravely and tells me Trelk-keh's false reign has ended." When I nodded, she continued. "I will fulfill my end of the bargain. After she has rested, Rizzt-tok will lead you to the place where the humans reside. She will bear a gift to the leader of the humans, a symbol indicating I have accepted his proposal for alliance. The Corodan of my hive will fight alongside him when he calls."

"Thank you." I bowed low, genuinely grateful for her promise of aid. We'd need every warrior we could muster to thwart Colin's plans, and the Corodan were fearsome fighters.

"One of the drones will show you to the guest chamber," she said before turning toward the entrance.

The drone she'd mentioned came forward to lead us into the underground warrens some distance behind his queen. It was a male, as all the others we'd encountered were. He didn't speak during the long journey, and I began to wonder if male Corodan were even capable of vocalization. It was possible they could only communicate through other means, those that were utterly foreign to us but that fellow Corodan would comprehend.

"I'll be glad when we reach your brother's camp," Rynn said once we were alone in the guest chamber. "The Corodan have been hospitable, but I don't believe I can withstand much more of this wandering underground. I'd rather have the sky overhead."

I flexed my wings slightly at the thought of the outdoors, then settled into a sitting position. "I know how you feel. I'm not designed for small spaces."

She laughed. "I know what you're thinking. You want to fly."

I shrugged. "I've found I rather enjoy flying, thank you."

"I've noticed." She laughed again, arching one eyebrow. "I believe I've come to *tolerate* it."

I joined in her laughter. "It's a start, isn't it? I was worried during the first days out from the Citadel."

She rolled her eyes. "You worry *far* too much, Andrew Caein. I told you I'd be fine, and I am."

"So you are."

I studied her face in the dimly lit room. She smiled in that maddening, enigmatic way only she possessed, and I had no inkling of what her thoughts might be. She was a complete mystery when she wanted to be, and it seemed she'd chosen this moment as one such occasion.

Rynn sat down on one of the grass mats that furnished the chamber and gazed at me expectantly. "Tell me about Thomas. Since we're to meet him soon, I'd like to know more about him."

"What would you like to know?"

"Anything. We're stuck here until the Corodan see fit to show us the way out, so we may as well talk about something."

I spent the afternoon regaling Rynn with stories of my youngest half-brother. I hadn't spent as much time with him growing up as I had with Alexander or Colin, and by the time Thomas had been old enough to walk, I'd been an adolescent. Alexander had more stories from his childhood featuring Thomas, as they were only three years apart in age. There were thirteen between Thomas and myself.

As we'd grown older, both Alexander and I had become protective of our youngest brother. Thomas had no inclination towards battle and never learned how to properly wield a sword or a bow. He was a scholar, an avid historian, and had a keen interest in the laws of

Novania. He'd been trained as a scribe, a vocation his father believed suited his interests while simultaneously preparing him to assist Colin once he inherited the throne.

Carlton Marsden had done his best to prepare the kingdom and his sons for his inevitable departure. The training my half-brothers received had been dictated by their roles as subordinates to Colin. I believed Carlton had suspected Colin would eventually reject me as the army's commander—our rivalry had begun almost as soon as Colin had learned to speak, and we'd never harbored much love for one another. He'd hoped Alexander would succeed me in that role, while Thomas would assist in a clerical capacity. The late king's best-laid plans had not borne fruit, and Colin had driven all of his siblings away since he'd assumed the throne.

"But the king didn't know the truth about you or Alex," Rynn said after a time. "You've said *no one* knew what you were other than Alex and Vera, and Alex's Mark was only known to you."

I nodded, working my jaw. It was growing tired from our long conversation. "If the king had known about us, I'm not certain how our lives would have played out. Most likely, Alex would have been killed. I don't know how Carlton would have reacted to me. He was a good man, and reasonable most of the time, but he harbored the same irrational fears that have plagued Novanian rulers for centuries."

"But your mother protected you," she pressed.

I smiled fondly as memories of my mother resurfaced. "She did, at much risk to herself, I might add. If we'd been discovered, she would have been executed for treason or crimes against the crown." I shook my head sadly. "It's a wonder she kept us both a secret. She was the queen! And we were not the most well-behaved children. Alex nearly revealed himself on a few occasions before he was old enough to understand the consequences. Fortunately, our mother intervened before anything came of it. It was far easier for me to hide. I simply had to remember to rein in my strength and remain human."

She studied me for a long moment. "This is the longest span of time you've been in your dragon form, isn't it?"

I nodded. "It wasn't until the day at the tourney field that I began to explore what I'm capable of. And I only shifted then because I had no other choice. I was outnumbered, and I wasn't going to allow Colin to kill Alex." I glowered at the floor; the memory still riled my temper. "It was the first time I'd ever attempted to fly. I wasn't even certain I could."

"And only a few months later, flying has become one of your favorite activities." Rynn grinned, her eyes glittering in the dim light. "You've come so far, despite your upbringing and your wicked brother."

I managed a smile in return. "I suppose I have, but I've had help at every turn. I didn't make it this far alone. Alex and Vera helped me learn some things about myself, and I discovered even more when I finally met my father. And you've played a part as well."

"Hmm." She stood up and stretched her arms behind her. "I've only given you a simple suggestion regarding your speech, nothing more."

"That's where you're wrong," I replied. "You've become a true friend, someone I respect. It's nice to have someone I can talk to, and I believe I can talk to you about nearly anything."

Her smile was dazzling, a ray of sunlight piercing the gloom. "Then I made the right decision when I embarked on this journey with you."

"Kash-kah cannot see you off, but she sends her thanks," Rizzt-tok said the next morning. "She has given me directions. I will guide you to the camp you seek. It will take several days to reach on foot. Come."

We followed her out of the guest chamber and into the warren of tunnels beyond.

"And if we were to fly?" Rynn asked, rubbing sleep from her eyes. The Corodan soldier had arrived only minutes after she'd awakened.

"We do not know. It would be faster." Rizzt-tok swiveled her head to glance briefly in my direction. "We did not want to presume the dragon-man would allow me to fly with him."

"Your Hive-queen has agreed to help us fight the red king," I replied. "You're welcome to fly with me."

"We accept your offer." She paused as we turned to wend our way through another chamber. "We are nearly to the surface."

We exited the hive from a different location than we'd entered previously. The sky was gray and threatened snow, though none was falling at present. Rynn clambered up my side and secured the rope holding the trunk in place against my spines, though I doubted it had moved. Her knots were incredibly strong; they'd remained steadfast during the windstorm and the battle, after all.

Rizzt-tok hesitated as she considered her options, tilting her triangular head first one way, then the other. After a moment, she dashed nimbly up to a place a short distance in front of Rynn. She'd moved more rapidly than I'd expected, and her steps had been feather-light. I felt her hook one of her forelimbs around the nearest spine. Though the limb could not pierce my hide, I could feel the myriad serrations that lined its cutting edge.

I craned my neck to ensure they were seated and prepared for the flight, then leapt into the air. Rynn's grip intensified as we gained elevation, but she did not tremble. Perhaps she truly *had* come to tolerate flying as she'd indicated the previous afternoon.

Rizzt-tok's strange buzzing voice carried easily over the rush of wind, much to my surprise. She directed me toward the last known location of Thomas' camp without hesitation. I hoped he had not been forced to move, and we'd locate him without incident. By nightfall, we had yet to reach him, though Rizzt-tok was confident we'd arrive at the campsite before the end of the next day.

We stopped for the night at the lip of a wide canyon. I landed a short distance from the edge for Rynn's benefit, and once she and Rizzt-tok had dismounted, I walked to the cliff to peer below. A river rushed through the canyon, its water churning so swiftly it was white with froth. Huge boulders were strewn throughout its expanse, and the riverbed was littered with sharp rocks. Even from our present altitude, it was clear the riverbank would prove treacherous. Ice coated the banks where snowdrifts didn't obscure them.

We built a small campfire for Rizzt-tok's benefit, taking turns to keep it stoked throughout the night. When I awoke the next morning, snow dusted our camp, and I was coated in a fine layer of it. I shook myself off, thankful once more for my unusual physiology.

Rynn had kept the fire blazing while it was her turn on watch, though its heat had been insufficient to prevent Rizzt-tok from suffering the effects of the cold. She moved slowly and seemed lethargic, though she claimed she would recover in time.

Once we were airborne, Rizzt-tok directed me to follow the river as it knifed through the canyon. "Humans camp in caves near a waterfall. They should remain. The weather is bad for travel."

"Tom spoke of the red king's soldiers in his last letter to me," I replied over my shoulder. "If they've discovered his location, he may have moved on."

Rizzt-tok emitted an amused rattle. "It is unlikely. Our scouts patrol this area. We have seen nothing of the red-king's people for many weeks."

I nodded, but I remained unconvinced and said nothing more. I flew on through the falling snow.

Daylight was fading when I spied an area that matched Rizzt-tok's description. The canyon had narrowed, and the river flowed sluggishly between the rocky cliffs looming on either side. A deep pool had formed on one side where the water eddied in a slow whirl, and a thin layer of ice had crusted over the water. A hole had been cut into the ice near the shore, a clear indication someone had recently been there.

Somewhere beyond the pool was a waterfall. The distant roar of the water as it crashed down from the heights echoed along the canyon, though I could not make out its location through the driving snow. I didn't immediately see an opening that would lead into a cave, but decided to land near the pool to investigate further.

Rizzt-tok had become more sluggish in her movements as the day wore on. She stumbled as she slid to the ground but didn't complain, and I hoped for her sake we'd locate Thomas' campsite soon. She needed the warmth of a campfire and shelter from the elements.

The snow at the edge of the pool was packed down and trampled by numerous footprints, many of which appeared relatively fresh. I followed the prints with my eyes to a rocky outcropping that was free of snow. There, the trail disappeared. I scanned the rocks, though I saw no sign of the cave Rizzt-tok had mentioned.

"Someone has been here," I said after a few moments, "but I can't—"

A whizzing sound cut through the air, and a second later, an arrow struck my hide and bounced harmlessly off to fall in the snow. I glowered at the rocks as Rynn and Rizzt-tok darted for cover behind me. I couldn't locate the archer.

I snarled a warning. A second arrow shot toward me from across the river in response, but was as ineffectual as the first.

I growled low in my throat. "We did not come here for a fight. Show yourself!"

There was a slight movement between the rocks across the water, and I noticed a small crevice between two boulders. A third arrow whistled past my shoulder, missing its mark entirely.

I narrowed my eyes, frustrated. The archer was either one of Colin's men who undoubtedly knew who I was, or one of Thomas' who had mistaken me for an enemy.

I roared, bellowing at the top of my voice. The sound echoed through the canyon and rattled a few small stones loose from its walls, while the abrupt scuttling within the crevice told me I'd startled my assailant. If Thomas was nearby, I had no doubt he would come to investigate. And if Colin was…

I'd do what was necessary to protect Rynn and Rizzt-tok.

Rynn chuckled from behind my flank. "If this man is an enemy, you've just alerted all of his comrades to our location. I hope this is where Thomas is camped, for if it's not, we'd best prepare to defend ourselves."

"I had to do something," I replied with a frown. "I don't appreciate being shot at."

Surprised shouts erupted from somewhere beyond the water, and after a few moments, I heard scraps of conversation near the archer's location.

"No, sir, there's a *demon* outside. *A demon*!"

I couldn't hear the response. There was a pause, and then, "Have a look for yourself. But it seems he's right pissed off."

There was another pause, then a peal of merry laughter I immediately recognized. "Oliver, you damned fool, that's no demon. It's a dragon—and not just any dragon. It's Andrew!"

I heaved a sigh, relieved beyond words. We'd located Thomas at last. It was wonderful to hear his voice as it carried across the water, to learn he'd escaped Colin's clutches and was seemingly secure in his hideout.

I grinned and peered over my shoulder at the others. "It's Tom." Both appeared unhurt by the archer's stray arrow, though Rizzt-tok was clearly miserable from the cold.

I turned back in time to watch several men climb down from the rocks on the opposite bank. Even in the deepening twilight, I recognized Thomas. Duke Jonathan Horace, Duke Everett Crossley, and another man I wasn't familiar with accompanied him.

I motioned to Rynn and Rizzt-tok. It would be easier to cross the river if they climbed on my back and we flew the distance. Once they were secure, I traversed the span in a single leap and skidded to a halt before the assembled men. Thomas rushed toward me, an excited grin lighting up his face.

"When Alex sent word you were on your way, I was thrilled! But I feared you risked too much by crossing Novania. Were you followed?" Thomas peered around me to assess the darkening canyon.

I shook my head. "We didn't see any of Colin's men."

Rynn and Rizzt-tok dismounted once more, and I introduced them. Thomas' face brightened further when he learned I'd secured an alliance with the Hive-queen.

Jonathan Horace moved forward hesitantly, his eyes never leaving my face as he shook his head in wonder. "By all the hair on the damned tyrant's ass, I would never have imagined you were half dragon." He shook his head, bewildered, while I laughed. "Damn it. Now I owe Ev another two silvers."

Duke Crossley crossed his arms with a smirk. "I was at the tourney field that day, as I've mentioned more than once, Jon. You should be wiser when placing your bets."

Jonathan's expression was sheepish as he peered at me once more. "I'll admit, I thought the story of your transformation was just another bit of false propaganda Colin was using to garner support against you. You won't…eat us, will you?"

I laughed at the sheer absurdity of the question. "What makes you think I'd eat anyone? I'm no different now than I was before. The only difference is I no longer have any secrets to hide."

"We have much to discuss," Thomas cut in, "and it's damned cold tonight. Let's go inside where we can talk near a fire. We've got fish stew."

Jonathan grunted. "Fish stew nigh on every night, truth be told. But it's better than nothing."

While Rizzt-tok followed the two dukes and the other man into the cavern, Rynn scrambled up my side to untie the trunk. Thomas lingered not far away, watching silently as I lifted the trunk to the ground with my tail. Rynn opened it and began to rummage inside as I shifted forms.

I felt diminished, *lesser*, after spending weeks in my dragon form, but to be human again was something of a relief. It would be easier to speak with the others, and I wouldn't have any difficulty entering the crevice hidden in the rocks behind Thomas. Rynn tossed me a set of clothing, and I dressed hurriedly. I hoisted the trunk in my arms, then we followed Thomas into the caves.

Once inside, Thomas spun on his heel and drew me into a rough embrace, despite my burdened arms. "It's good to see you. Alex has kept me apprised of events in the Southlands, and… Well, it's good to see you." He paused to glance at the floor, then said, "I apologize for the guard earlier. When I told them to watch for a dragon, perhaps they didn't know what to look for."

"It's alright, no one was hurt. And I'm glad you're safe. The last I'd heard, you were concerned Colin had found your hiding place. If he'd harmed you, I'd have his head, consequences be damned."

Thomas laughed and looked down at his hands. He clasped them tightly to prevent himself from fidgeting. I noted the change in his behavior and assumed it was the work of Duke Crossley.

"Things have grown worse in Novania," he began. "Colin is searching for me, he dismissed all of Father's governors and advisors, he's sent soldiers toward the Mage's Gate, nobody has seen the queen in weeks, and all the while, he continues to round up those bearing the Mark—and anyone caught aiding them. I don't know where he takes them or what is done to them, but the rumors are dark. Most are assumed dead." He spoke rapidly, his words a rush as he finished.

"Let's find that fire you mentioned. We can speak there," I said evenly. "No doubt your uncle and Jon are waiting."

He nodded absently, distracted. "You're right."

He led us deeper into the cave, and I was stunned by its scale. The path from the river outside broke off into numerous small chambers.

Some were utilized as storage areas, others as sleeping rooms. After a few turns in the path, we came to a vast cavern where many fires were lit. I spotted the dukes and Rizzt-tok near the center of the cavern.

Seeing Thomas again brought a rush of memories to the forefront of my thoughts. I set the trunk down and grasped Thomas' elbow before he could move inside the room. Startled, he spun to face me, questions in his blue eyes.

"Tom, there's something I need to say before we're entangled in the business of ousting Colin and it slips my mind."

He nodded. "Go on."

"We stopped at Vinterry on our way here. I needed to…" I shook my head as my voice cracked with emotion, then cleared my throat before going on. "I had to ensure they were laid to rest. That Vera…"

He clasped my upper arm in reassurance. "I know, Andrew. When you wrote that you were forced to flee, I knew you'd been given no time for burials. I went there before I fled to Bridgewaters. Colin didn't believe I'd travel east from the Capitol, and it was the safer route."

"Thank you," I managed. "I didn't know what to expect when I arrived, but I'm grateful you did what I could not."

"It was the right thing to do."

We stood in awkward silence for several moments. I didn't know what more to say, and my paltry words were insufficient to express the true gratitude I felt for my youngest brother's actions.

"I'll speak with the cook. She'll bring us some stew," Thomas said after a time. "It will be good to hear your news. I feared the worst when you didn't arrive a few days ago."

I forced a laugh. "You weren't easy to find. I had to seek the Corodan for word on your location. But we can speak of that later. Let's have supper first."

TEN

After we'd eaten, Rizzt-tok was shown to an area where she could rest. The Corodan drew curious stares, though it was impossible to discern what she felt regarding the attention, if anything. She didn't appear as lethargic as she'd been outside, though she trudged away at a markedly slower pace than her norm.

Rynn sat at my side, but was uncharacteristically silent throughout the meal. The two dukes, Jonathan Horace and Everett Crossley, lingered at our fire. Not long after we finished supper, the man I recognized from earlier joined us as well. He was familiar, though I couldn't place where I knew him from. I studied him intensely, and he offered a wary smile in return. He was perhaps thirty years of age, thin and wiry, with dark hair and soft brown eyes. A scar marred the left side of his face, running from hairline to jaw, just outside the corner of his eye.

"Daniel Clarence," Thomas said by way of introduction, which jarred my memory. Daniel had been one of the lieutenants among the castle garrison before I'd relinquished my position as commander.

"You didn't bear that scar when last we met," I remarked.

He shrugged uncomfortably. "The result of defying the king's orders. I left the garrison soon after I earned it."

"Colin did that?"

He chuckled dryly. "It's the least of his crimes. The past few months have been little short of hell for those who stayed in the Capitol. I arrived here only a few weeks ago. There are many people seeking Thomas' camp, but not all of them are friendly."

"So I've heard." I turned to face Thomas. "You asked outside if I'd been followed. Do you know where Colin's people are located?"

Thomas sighed and stared into the campfire. "No. We've been forced to move our camp twice so far to avoid detection. Our scouts have seen no sign of them since we came here, but I fear it's only a matter of time."

"The Corodan knew your location," I reminded him.

"Yes. We trade with them, and I was hoping to gain the Hive-queen as an ally. I didn't keep my whereabouts secret from them. Thanks to you, that bit of business is complete." He flicked a glance in my direction, his blue eyes troubled. "How did you manage that, Andrew? She wanted to speak with you—and *only* you— regarding an alliance, but I assume there was more to it than mere words."

Rynn snorted, but didn't reply.

"There was more." I detailed our journey through the Corodan hive and the confrontation that ensued with Trelk-keh. When I came to the part regarding Rynn's abilities, I paused and eyed her uncertainly. When she nodded, I proceeded to tell Thomas of her role in the battle.

His eyes grew wide. "A true mage!" He exclaimed, his voice rising with excitement. "Fantastic! You must tell me what it's like."

She flushed and looked at each of the men sitting around the fire in turn. "My ability is limited to ice, snow, frost, and the like. I can freeze or thaw things as I see fit. But, as happens with some mages, my power didn't come without a price." She sighed and leaned back, her gaze drifting toward the cave's shadowed ceiling. "I can no longer safely interact with most people. My skin is too cold. I've given people frostbite without meaning to."

Thomas' gaze flitted between Rynn and myself. "Andrew is unaffected because he's dragon-kind, which means some of those tales I read at Vinterry are true. You *are* immune to the cold, aren't you?"

I stared at him for a long moment, uncertain if I wanted to pursue the conversation any further. Thomas was just as likely to drag us into a historical discussion of my father's people as he was to return to the original topic—our story, and what was necessary to combat Colin.

"Yes, Tom."

"What about the healing power? I read that—"

When I sighed, Everett reached out and placed a hand on Thomas' shoulder. "You can ask Andrew more about what he is later when it's relevant. We have other matters that need to be dealt with before it grows too late."

Thomas' face fell, but he nodded. "Yes, of course." He chewed his lower lip for a moment, then blurted, "Alex said you plan to support my claim to the throne."

I glanced at Everett, who merely shrugged. "I'm not of royal blood," I said, "and Alex is… He feels he'd be a poor choice, given his Mark. Which leaves only you."

He shook his head miserably. "I don't want it either. I've told Alex that, but he ignores my protests."

"Your brothers are right," Everett said evenly. "Colin can't remain on the throne, not with what he's done to Novania's people. And while Alex is technically the next in line, the people will never fully trust him. How many generations have passed since the Mark laws went into effect? It will take time to build acceptance."

"And with some training in etiquette, you'd make a fine ruler," Jonathan added. He'd pulled out a wooden pipe and began to smoke. "You know the laws of the kingdom already, boy."

Thomas frowned into the fire, his expression dark. "It wasn't supposed to turn out this way. Father's plans have all gone awry."

"Had he known of Alexander's Mark, or of what I am, we would be worse off," I replied. "I give thanks every day that mother shielded us from Novania's laws."

"Colin has made them worse," Thomas spat the words. "As I mentioned earlier, he's been rounding up anyone bearing the Mark. There are special details of the garrison sent to each city and town, their sole purpose to seek Marks. Anyone found with one is arrested and taken back to the Capitol for 'trial.' Anyone found hiding a Marked person is likewise arrested. The trials are a farce. Every person arrested is ultimately found guilty."

"The rumors we've heard are grim," Everett agreed. "We couldn't risk traveling too near the Capitol, for fear of recognition, but we've heard plenty of tales describing the king's twisted version of justice. It's no longer mere execution these people face, Andrew. There are rumors of torture, starvation, forced conscription… To prolong one's suffering for the crime of their birth is purely evil. The people arrested are no threat to the kingdom. None have been trained as your friend has been."

All eyes shifted to Rynn, who frowned.

"Do you perceive me as a threat, then?" She crossed her arms defiantly.

Jonathan chuckled. "No, girl. If you're a friend of Andrew's, you're a friend of ours."

Rynn arched an eyebrow, her expression unreadable as she stared at the portly duke. After a moment, he looked away, muttering under his breath.

"Rynn, I'm thrilled to have you here," Thomas said hastily. "What Jon said is true. I suppose in order to help Alex with his role, we need to know as much about the magi as possible. What are your capabilities? How many will join him? Is there anything we need to consider—?"

"Tom," I said, cutting him off with a laugh, "We can answer your questions, but you'll need to ask them one at a time."

I spent most of the next day in conversation with Thomas. I recounted everything that had transpired since I'd fled with Alexander from the tourney field and the scene of his botched execution, while Thomas listened raptly.

"I've never seen Colin so furious," he said after a time. "He knew I'd helped you that day, though he couldn't prove it. I wasted no time in fleeing the Capitol."

I nodded. "I was surprised to learn you'd moved on from Bridgewaters."

He shifted uncomfortably and clasped his hands. "Colin demanded that our uncle return me to the Capitol to face judgment. When he refused, Colin revoked his title and deeded Bridgewaters to his present commander." His expression soured. "Robert Claybourne is underserving of the title *and* the lands."

I stared at him for several seconds. "Colin took the duke's ancestral home?"

"Former duke, and yes." Thomas shook his head and shifted his gaze to the campfire. "Jon has fared no better, you know. His crime was merely friendship with you."

I scowled at the flames. "Damn Colin. And the dukes support you, which will only complicate matters should we fail."

"Then we must make certain we don't."

I nodded, then looked up as Rynn approached, a troubled frown twisting her lips.

"Rynn?" I asked.

She sat down heavily, but didn't speak for several moments. When she did, she eyed Thomas anxiously. "Some of your people are making a point to avoid me."

His eyes widened. "What? I'm—"

She held up a hand. "I was expecting this to happen. I'm a *mage*, Thomas. The first they've encountered. People naturally avoid contact with those they deem…dangerous."

I growled low in my throat. "If anyone gives you trouble, they'll deal with me."

She lifted her eyebrows, her expression unreadable. "I'm capable of taking care of myself, but thank you for the sentiment."

Thomas' gaze darted between us uncertainly for a moment. "I have no doubt you're both fearsome when riled, but I'd hoped to maintain peace within my camp. If anyone stirs trouble, please speak with me or Uncle Everett. We'll see that it's taken care of."

I was stunned by my youngest brother's display of maturity, and simply nodded.

Rynn laughed softly. "I'll be sure to tell you if anything occurs, as will Andrew."

I crossed my arms. "So long as no one else asks me to transform for their mere entertainment, you'll have no trouble from me."

"I've spoken to the sentries," Thomas assured me, not for the first time that morning. "Most are curious—they mean no harm, brother."

I groaned. I should have expected Thomas to take their side. "I'm not in the habit of shifting before an audience, and I'd like to keep it that way, their curiosity be damned."

Thomas heaved a sigh, while Rynn snickered. "Perhaps Jon was right to fear you'd eat people. You're certainly surly enough," she said.

I gaped at her, unable to form a response, while Thomas laughed at my expense. "Speaking of Jon, he wanted to discuss our defenses with you this afternoon. No doubt he's been waiting, and I've kept you too long." He rose to his feet. "He'll be in the training cavern. I'll take you there."

Over the next several days, I learned both of the former dukes had arrived at the caverns with most of their garrisons, along with their families and household staff. Between them, there was a force of nearly two hundred able-bodied soldiers. It wasn't enough to oppose Colin directly, but it was sufficient to keep Thomas secure in our present location.

Jonathan had taken control of the scouts and the cavern defenders, while Everett worked more closely with Thomas on matters ranging from etiquette to securing supplies to interrogating those they considered spies.

I learned several of Colin's loyal soldiers had been captured since their arrival in the caverns. When Everett discovered they'd been seeking Thomas on Colin's orders, he'd been forced to make a decision regarding their fates. Everett Crossley took no pleasure in executions, but he'd believed these were warranted. Thomas' safety was paramount as we planned to oust Colin from the throne.

After I began to understand the workings of my brother's camp and learned its rhythms, I started to spend more time in the training cavern, drilling with the younger and more inexperienced soldiers. It was a role I was familiar with, and most were eager to learn from Carlton's former commander. I was engaged in overseeing defensive maneuvers one afternoon when Thomas burst into the cavern.

"Andrew, I need a bit of your time." He was breathless, as though he'd been running.

"Tom, what—?"

"It's Alex. I have a letter from him." He waved a sheet of parchment in the air.

"We'll continue tomorrow," I told the others before following Thomas to the central fire in the main cavern that had become his primary area of operations. I was eager to learn how Alexander fared.

"Alex asked if you had arrived before anything else," Thomas said as we sat down. "I suspect he'd begun to worry. When he wrote last, you weren't here."

"We all know I would have made it here eventually. It's going to take more than Colin's lackeys to keep me away from this fight. What more does Alex have to say?"

Thomas scanned the note for a moment, then said, "He arrived at the canyon north of the Thornhallow. Some magi were there ahead of him, and he's begun to shape them into proper combat units. He says there are several healers who have come, and they'll be working closely with his new wife…"

"Does the Barrier still hold?" I asked.

Thomas read for another moment, then shook his head. "Alex doesn't mention the Barrier, so I suspect nothing has changed. Several Merael have joined him as well, and have taken up training with your friend Emma. Emma…is that Emmarie? You spoke of an Emmarie."

"Yes, that's Emmarie." I frowned thoughtfully. "From what little I know of the Merael, I'm surprised they've chosen to join Alex. Emmarie was convinced she'd be an outsider amongst her own people for choosing to take up arms."

Thomas shrugged. "The Merael seem to be a fascinating people. I would like to learn more of them."

I chuckled, amused. "Of course you would, Tom."

He blinked in surprise, then said, "The note ends as most do. That we should take care, and if we want to make a reply, to write on the back of this parchment." He paused to study me shrewdly. "Andrew, this is a bit of magic, isn't it? This message-sending can't be anything else."

"Alex doesn't do the sending, only the writing," I replied. "There are a few magi we met—a family—with the ability to send messages like this. Alex writes the message, and one of them sends it here, to you. You received messages from me as well."

"Well, yes, I did. I suppose *you* could not have sent anything using magic." He sighed. "What should I tell Alex?"

"Tell him Rynn and I have arrived, to start," I replied with a grin. "Give him a report of our status. He'll need to know how many soldiers we have and any specific capabilities we possess, which are very few at present. Tell him we've reached an accord with the Corodan, and will have their aid. I'll make it a point to speak with Rizzt-tok tonight. We need to know how many Corodan will join us, if that number has been determined by the hive."

Thomas wrote furiously, though his script was neat and orderly. "I'll tell Alex I plan to have you and Jon take command of our forces here, and against my better judgment, I'll defer to the plan you've hatched for succession. I dislike the notion of ruling—it leaves a sour taste in my mouth every time I think of it. But I suppose anyone would be a better option than Colin."

As Thomas finished writing, the parchment vanished from beneath his fingertips.

Thomas laughed uneasily. "I'll never grow used to that."

"I've often wondered how it worked," I admitted. "Will Alex send a reply?"

Thomas nodded. "It's rare when he doesn't. Stay here for a while. If he sends one, it will arrive near me."

Alexander's response came minutes later. Thomas burst out laughing as he began to read. He handed the sheet to me after he'd finished, still chuckling.

Tom –

I'm glad to hear from you. Tell Andrew to stop dallying in his travels. This was no time for a vacation.

On a serious note, it's good to know the Corodan are on your side. I'll provide further details on our numbers in the south once I have a better idea of what they'll be. Stay safe, brother.

I glowered, feigning annoyance. "I didn't 'dally.' You didn't make it easy to locate your camp."

Thomas laughed again. "I know. I'm glad Alex hasn't lost his sense of humor after all that's happened. When Rynn said he'd been changed, I'll admit I didn't know what to expect. Would it have affected his personality?"

I shrugged. "I don't believe so. Alex knew most of the risks before he started his pilgrimage. What exactly did Rynn tell you?"

"She said that like her, Alex was changed physically when he became a mage. And not in the usual way that magi change, where their age becomes indeterminate."

"Alex is physically stronger than he used to be. So much so that he foolishly challenged me to an arm-wrestling match." I grinned. "He still lost."

"But he believed he could match your strength all the same?" Thomas asked, eyes wide. "That means he must be far stronger than a normal man, even if he's no match for the dragon-kind."

"His change wasn't as severe as Rynn's," I replied. "She's been unable to interact normally with people since she finished her trials. I… I'm the first person she encountered who is unaffected by her change."

Thomas nodded slowly as he considered my words. "Do you know anything of Alex's other abilities when he uses his power? Rynn said she knew little of what he's capable of."

"I know only what Alex was inclined to tell me. He can make himself stronger, faster, and more resilient in battle, but to what extent, I'm not certain even he knows. Yet." I shrugged. "Did either of them—Alex or Rynn, I mean—tell you of Galewing?"

"Is that the eagle?" When I nodded, Thomas' face brightened. "Yes, Rynn spoke of him. Alex has some connection to the bird, and can see as it does. Is that right?"

"According to what Alex told me, yes."

"You've had quite the adventure," Thomas replied wistfully. "I wish I could have accompanied him as well. There is so much we could have learned!" He sighed, a sound filled with regret. "Perhaps one day, when this mess with Colin is over and done, I can travel south myself."

"Tom," I said evenly, "I'm not certain that will be in the cards."

My youngest brother's desire for learning far surpassed my own, and I knew what Alexander and I had experienced could have held even greater meaning if Thomas had been present to give his insights. But the decision had been made.

To restore order to Novania, Thomas must take the throne. The responsibility might become all-encompassing, and his desire to travel and see what we had may never bear fruit.

He deflated and a sad frown crept across his features. "I know, but I'm allowed to daydream on occasion. Perhaps when this is done, I'll write an account of your adventures. It won't be as good as seeing them in person, but it will be better than nothing." He studied me carefully, then asked, "When this is over, what do you plan to do? Will you stay in Novania, or will you return south?"

I shrugged. "I haven't given it any thought."

"I suppose out of all of us, you have the greater luxury of time." He chuckled dryly. "If you make a decision, let me know, will you? I'll need help restoring order, and you're better suited to the task than anyone I know. Alex doesn't take matters seriously enough, and with his new bride, I assume he'll go south with her once this is over. I could use your expertise."

I was loath to tell him no, but I also wanted to return to the Stone Grove to visit my father and learn more about the curse that afflicted him. He'd been certain it could be reversed, and I was in the best position to do so. But Thomas was right—I had the luxury of time. I didn't know what I'd do.

"I don't need an answer today," Thomas said as he rose to his feet. "Think on it. We'll be camped here until the spring thaw. There's no reason to move when the weather is turning foul. You have time."

I nodded absently as he departed and stared into campfire, lost in my own thoughts. There was much to consider, but first, we needed to bring Colin to justice. It would be no easy undertaking, and at present, we were sorely outnumbered.

ELEVEN

"Andrew, I need your opinion on a…delicate matter." Everett kept his voice low so the others could not overhear.

I was in the training cavern, overseeing drills with some of Jonathan's garrison to pass the time, a routine I'd fallen into since my arrival three weeks ago. I motioned for the others to continue without me and followed him outside. The passage between our location and the main cavern was empty.

"What do you need?" I asked once we were alone.

"I think it best if you accompany me to the interrogation cavern. The scouts located two women braving the storm earlier. And one of them… It's Claire." He frowned and shook his head in frustration. "You know her better than anyone. At first, I feared she was here on Colin's behalf, but after seeing her… I don't believe that's true."

"Why would she come here?" I wondered aloud.

Everett moved quickly through the winding corridor toward the entrance, and I lengthened my stride to keep pace.

"That's a question I would very much like to learn the answer to," he replied. "She said she would speak to no one but Thomas, though I believe she may have a change of heart upon seeing you."

I snorted. "Claire bears no love for me and I doubt she ever did. My presence might make matters worse."

"When you see her, I think you'll understand." He frowned, a troubled expression creasing his rugged features.

"And the other woman?" I asked as we made our way into the blustery gray day.

A smattering of snowflakes fell from the sky while the bitter wind whipped around us. Everett was bundled against the weather, but drew his cloak more tightly around his shoulders as we exited the cavern's relative warmth.

"Her name is Leta. A maidservant, it seems."

I nodded. Leta had been a constant fixture in our household and one of Claire's closest confidantes. It was no surprise she'd followed her mistress when Claire left me for Colin, and again when she traveled here.

"I know Leta. Has she been any more forthcoming than Claire?"

Everett grunted. "No. She refuses to speak out of loyalty to her mistress. All we've learned are their names and that they seek Thomas."

We arrived at the smaller cave after a quarter-hour trudging through the snow. A pair of guards were stationed just inside the mouth of the cave, while a fire blazed in a recess behind them. The cave wound around a corner of rock, where a smaller chamber was being utilized as the guards' outpost. Four guards stood on one side, warming their hands over a blazing brazier, while another pair stood near an opening in the rock wall opposite us.

Everett strode to the opening, where he spoke briefly to the pair. A short passage led from the outpost to another chamber furnished with several wooden crates that served as makeshift chairs. Another three guards were within, standing in an arc around the two women, who were seated facing away from us as we entered. A small fire had been lit in one corner of the chamber, but the air remained cold.

At the sound of our approach, one of the women turned. I recognized Leta instantly; she'd changed little in the past two years, though her attire was threadbare and travel-stained. She whispered to Claire as recognition bloomed in her eyes.

Claire didn't immediately turn around. Her hair was loose, and as I neared her position, I was stunned to see bands of silver running through her dark tresses. Claire was of an age with Alexander, far too young to bear such blatant signs of aging. I stopped a few steps away while Leta looked between us expectantly.

Finally, Claire turned, but kept her face down and would not meet my eyes. "I suppose I should not be surprised to find you here, Andrew."

"Claire…" I knelt down in an attempt to peer into her eyes, but she turned away. I frowned, perplexed, and returned to my feet. "Why have you come?"

"We heard rumors that Thomas had established a camp," Leta answered for her. "We are seeking *him*."

I glanced at Everett, who indicated I should continue to ask questions. "Are you here on Colin's behalf?"

"No," Leta replied with a scowl. "Your people have already asked this, and I gave them the same answer I now give you. We came of our own volition."

"Forgive me for my skepticism," I replied bitterly. "Given the last conversation I had with your damned mistress, I'm not inclined to believe she came here for our benefit."

Claire seemed to steel herself, and when Leta began to form a reply, she motioned for silence. She stood slowly, as though the act required significant effort, then lifted her face to meet my gaze. Her dark eyes were the same as I remembered, but the rest of her countenance was markedly changed.

Her nose, which had once been straight and perfectly formed, was now crooked and flat; it had been broken at least once since I'd last seen her. The left side of her face was slightly misshapen, and I recalled a rumor that Colin had broken her jaw. When she opened her mouth to speak, I was appalled to find many of her teeth were chipped, and some were missing altogether.

Lines had formed around her eyes. She appeared to have aged a decade in the span of only two years. When she spoke, it was slowly, as though she had difficulty—or experienced pain—when forming her words.

"I came with the hope I might escape Colin. What I have endured at his hands is unspeakable." She held my gaze unwaveringly. "When I found the means to escape, I seized the opportunity and didn't question my fortune. Your half-brother, if that is what he truly is, has become a monster."

"What has he done?" The words came unbidden to my lips. I was unable to hide my shock at her altered appearance.

"The better question is, what *hasn't* he done?" She laughed bitterly. "I'd hoped to find Thomas here, to bring him word of what has occurred in the Capitol since he left. Much has transpired, and little of it good."

"Before we escort you to the main camp, we need to verify your story as best we can," Everett said from behind me. "Forgive me, my lady, but we must take every precaution."

Claire sighed and resumed her perch on the overturned crate. "I'll speak with you and Andrew, but send the others away. I can't bear a larger audience for the tale I must tell."

I nodded, and Everett motioned for the others to leave.

Claire examined her hands and picked at her nails as we waited. Even her fingers, once delicate and straight, bore signs of injury and past abuse. She'd bruised my heart irrevocably when she'd petitioned for an annulment of our marriage, but despite my bitterness, it pained me to see her reduced to this battered and broken state. No one deserved to suffer as she had.

Once we were alone, she said, "I must appear hideous, given your initial reaction."

"No," I tried to reassure her, but she waved one hand dismissively.

"I know what he has done to me. I've no love for my own reflection in a mirror. My youth has fled in its entirety during the past months." She sighed heavily. "You were always kind to me, even when I was cold to you. I didn't realize how fortunate I was when my father and the king arranged our union. I was a stupid child and threw it all away to grasp at power. It was you who found me in the castle's commons after he beat me the first time. I knew I'd made a grievous error, and I did what I could to escape, but my father had other plans." Her face twisted into a bitter scowl. "My father wanted me to be queen to further his own influence. He signed the marriage contract when I would not, giving his only child away to suffer at the hands of a madman." She looked up to meet my eyes then. "He's dead, you know."

"Duke Ellington is dead?" Everett exclaimed. "He was one of the king's favorites—"

"It seems even a favorite must be dealt with swiftly when he's caught in the bed of the king's mistress," Claire replied acerbically. "Oh, yes, Colin had at least two mistresses that I'm aware of, and there are likely others. He only came to me when he was at his worst. He blamed me when our child was born a girl." Her face crumpled, and she began to weep.

"Shall I tell them?" Leta asked gently as Claire tried to collect herself.

Claire shook her head adamantly, compelled to tell the story on her own. After a moment, she wiped her eyes and drew a shaky breath. "I must begin with the day that Colin threw Alexander in the dungeon. He was abusive before, but I was able to cope then." She paused to stare at her hands before she continued.

"As you know, Colin had begun to enforce the inspections by that time. He was hunting those with the Mark and sent countless to the gallows. Alexander would not abide by it. I attempted to council him against contradicting Colin, but he would not be swayed. Alexander believed it was unjust to condemn people over a matter of their birth, something they had no control over. He confronted Colin, demanding he stop the inspections. I believe Colin suspected something about Alexander prior to that date, for his first course of action was to have the guards seize his brother and strip him of his clothing. Alexander's Mark was revealed for all those present to see. Thomas was there, as were a number of palace guards."

"Tom fled the Capitol and brought word to Vinterry," I said. "I know Alex was placed in the dungeons under guard, and Colin wanted to make a grand example of him. Tom and Alex knew I wouldn't sit by and allow Colin to execute one of his own brothers."

"Did they know what you were?" Claire asked pointedly.

"Alex did. Tom did not."

"I suppose I should not have taken offense that you never bothered to tell me either." She compressed her lips into a thin line, a clear sign of disapproval. "When you transformed on the tourney field, Colin went into what I can only describe as hysterics. Not only had his plot been foiled and Alexander escaped alive, but his life-long rival had come to the rescue and revealed he was much more than meets the eye."

I shrugged uncomfortably but didn't interrupt, recalling Colin's reaction when I'd shifted to defend Alexander. He'd been out of his mind with rage.

Claire paused and looked away, fresh tears in her eyes. "When we arrived back at the castle, Colin had me taken to the top floor of the western tower, where I was kept under guard until he determined 'what should be done' with me. He was convinced I was privy to your secret, that I should have warned him what you were capable of. The next day, guards brought some of my personal effects to the tower, and it was then I realized I'd become little more than a prisoner in my own home."

"The king allowed me to attend her as I've always done," Leta added. "I convinced him she would need my aid to care for their child."

I narrowed my eyes as I realized there had been no news of a child when the pair arrived. "Where *is* the child, Claire?"

She closed her eyes. "I will come to that. Verena is not with us, as you can see."

"Is she safe?" Everett pressed.

The tears Claire had been attempting to hold at bay spilled forth. "No." Her voice was a strained whisper as she wiped briskly at her eyes.

I glanced at Everett as a flash of understanding shot through me. "You left her in the Capitol?"

Claire shook her head, but it was Leta who answered. "No, my lord. Verena is dead."

I stepped back inadvertently, stunned by the revelation, while Everett swore under his breath.

"Holy hell. What happened?" I demanded.

Claire gathered her composure, though when she spoke, her voice was thick with grief. "After Colin locked me in the tower, he visited me perhaps once a week, at most. Each time, he reeked of drink and sought me to sate his…baser desires. He was violent. I learned it was simpler to let him do what he'd come to do. If I struggled, he'd strike me. No doubt you've noticed the state of my teeth by now." She gestured feebly toward her mouth. "A result of my initial struggles."

Even though I was long past bearing love for Claire, her tale filled me with unbridled rage. No man should treat his wife that way. I'd always known Colin possessed a short and rather violent temper, but I'd never believed him capable of the brutality Claire had suffered at his hands.

"Colin had best hope he faces Alexander or Thomas at the end because I will tear him limb from limb," I growled as I began to pace the length of the small cavern.

Ire made me restless. It was fortunate Colin wasn't present, or he'd have been dead in an instant.

"Did no one come to your aid?" Everett asked. "Surely there must have been someone left in the castle who could protect you from him."

Claire laughed mirthlessly. "The nobility who remained departed for their own estates after Alexander's botched execution. My father wouldn't dare cross Colin, and by that time, my life was no longer any of his concern. How well that turned out for him." Her lips twisted into a bitter scowl. "The servants were terrified of him. To cross the king meant a trip to the gallows or to one of his work farms. I'm not certain which fate was worse."

"This is the first I've heard of these farms," Everett replied with a troubled frown.

"It's one of the items I plan to discuss with Thomas—if he's truly here," she replied. "Colin has been sending people caught harboring those with Marks to the farms. I don't know what goes on inside, but I've heard most perish within weeks."

"What prompted Colin to start enforcing the old laws?" I demanded. "It's been at least two generations since the inspections were last enacted, and his father certainly didn't enforce them."

"It started after his new advisor arrived. A man named Claybourne. I didn't know him well, only that he was an old acquaintance of my father's." Claire shrugged. "My father convinced Colin to give Claybourne the post. After only a few weeks, Colin began to meet with the man daily. I believe Claybourne is behind the enforcement of the old laws, among other atrocities."

"Do you mean Robert Claybourne?" Everett asked. When Claire nodded, he muttered darkly under his breath. "Robert Claybourne's first wife was Marked, or so they say. It's rumored he murdered her in a blind rage when he learned of it—though no one has ever managed to substantiate the rumor."

"Isn't he the man Colin named commander after Jerrick Vine?" I asked.

Everett nodded. "The same."

"It's not only the laws regarding Marks that Colin has reinstated," Claire cut in. "There were laws permitting game hunters to seek and kill dragons for sport. He has publicly announced that anyone returning to the Capitol bearing the head of a dragon will be richly rewarded. You're in danger."

I frowned, though I was unsurprised. "Anyone choosing to hunt me will find they've made a grave mistake."

She sighed wearily and rolled her eyes. "Be that as it may, there are assassins and bounty hunters seeking your head. I hope you'll remain vigilant."

We fell silent, and I considered Claire's words. There had been three separate attempts on my life while I'd been in the Southlands. Two had been made by desperate men coerced and blackmailed by Colin. The last had been different; perhaps the men I'd encountered in the marsh had been a pair of bounty hunters seeking glory.

For the first time since meeting my father, I was grateful he was encased in stone. The dragon-magi could not be harmed if Colin's hunters discovered their location—and Colin's edict had been indiscriminate. Every dragon was in danger.

"I should finish my tale," Claire said somberly after a time. "Two months ago, Colin came to the tower. He was rougher than usual, and though I tried to remain silent, I cried out. He caused me such pain..." Her eyes brimmed with tears once more. "When I did, it awakened Verena. She began to cry, and Colin went to her. He shouted, which only caused her to wail all the more. I begged him to let me tend her, but he was in such a rage there was no reasoning with him. When he picked her up, I knew she was in danger. I ran to him, tried to take her from him... He backhanded me so hard that black spots filled my vision and one of my teeth was knocked loose. I fell to the floor."

"Claire..." I knelt before her and took her bent fingers in my hands. I wanted to comfort her further but was uncertain if I should—or if she'd even welcome it.

When she raised her eyes to meet mine, I was struck by the misery I saw within their dark depths. "Verena didn't stop wailing. He screamed at her, called her a failure… Andrew, she wasn't even a year old! She was his daughter, and he…he…" Her words faltered as sobs wracked her frame. She withdrew her hands from mine to cover her face.

I looked helplessly between Leta and Everett. I didn't know what to do, what to say.

"He threw her from the tower window," Leta stated woodenly. "The servants found her in the courtyard the next morning."

"Holy hell," I whispered, rising to my feet. "I didn't believe Colin was so damned heartless."

"I learned a few weeks ago that I'm with child again," Claire said through her tears. "I knew then that I must escape. If the child is another girl, Colin will have me killed. He's desperate for an heir."

"We fled the castle through the servants' quarters," Leta added. "We traveled to Dresdin's Forge. It took many days, and by that time, winter was setting in. We were not dressed for the weather."

"I asked Leta to purchase better clothing while we were there." Claire stared at her hands while she spoke, her eyes distant. "While she was at the market, she heard rumors of Thomas' location. While I didn't know if it was true, it was our best hope. Someone must know what Colin has done, and my unborn child must be protected. I won't allow Colin to murder another."

It was late in the afternoon when we returned to the main camp. Everett led Claire and Leta to a place where they could stow their scant belongings, then took them to speak with Thomas. I returned to the training cavern. After hearing Claire's story, I was furious and frustrated; sparring would alleviate some of my pent-up energy.

As I rounded the corner, I was surprised to find one of the lieutenants working with Rynn. She'd never expressed the desire to learn how to wield a sword when we'd spoken of it. Her back was toward me as I approached, and the man working with her glanced up briefly to acknowledge my presence.

"No, no," he said patiently, "not like that. You'll be unbalanced when you try to parry. Let me show you again."

He moved into the stance he was attempting to teach her. She shifted slightly, but did not copy his form precisely.

I smiled and decided to intervene. The man could not touch her to help correct her footing, whereas I could. I moved forward and gently took her by the arms to shift her balance subtly.

"Like that," I said. "Do you feel how you're more centered? You'll be harder to knock over."

"Andrew," she breathed, startled, "I didn't hear you approach."

I chuckled and backed away to allow the pair space to continue. Her eyes lingered on mine for a few seconds before she turned to face the lieutenant once more. I crossed my arms, watching as Rynn parried several strikes successfully. The wooden practice blades clacked loudly with each impact.

Perhaps I would spar another day. The desire to vent my rage on an unsuspecting soldier had inexplicably fled when I'd noticed Rynn.

A short while later, Everett appeared in the cavern, Claire and Leta with him. I nodded toward them in acknowledgment, then turned back to watch Rynn. She was struggling with another defensive form, and I moved in again to help her plant her feet correctly. She offered a brief smile as I backed away.

I glanced toward the entrance once more. Everett and the others were departing, but Claire lingered a moment, and her dark eyes sought mine. An expression of longing crossed her once beautiful face. After a moment, she followed the former duke from the cavern with a sad shake of her head. I frowned; her reaction was puzzling.

"Who was that?" Rynn asked. She handed the practice blade to the lieutenant, hilt-first, then turned to face me. "Damn, I think I'll be sore tomorrow."

I chuckled. "I'm surprised you were training with a blade at all."

She shrugged. "I can't always rely solely on magic for protection, can I? Who was that?" she asked again.

I sighed. "That was Claire."

Her eyes widened. "*The* Claire? The one who left you for that shit who now calls himself king?"

I winced. "Yes."

"Hmm." She paused, contemplating her next words. "I suppose that explains the look she gave you just now. Is that where you were all day? Tom said you'd been summoned to the interrogation cave."

"Yes," I said again. "We allowed her to come to the main camp because she has suffered greatly at Colin's hands. She seeks refuge, protection. I'm not certain she'll be safe here, but it's better than she had in the Capitol." I released a breath and raked a hand through my hair. "I hope she wasn't followed."

"If she's here, it means you don't believe she's a spy." Rynn peered at me, her expression unreadable. "Based on your description, I expected she'd be an exotic beauty. And she looked rather older than I believed her to be."

"She's been through hell, Rynn," I replied. "Colin treated her poorly. I was shocked by her present appearance as much as you were. I…pity her."

Rynn raised her eyebrows. "Pity? You were furious, Andrew. You loathed her for what she did to you… What occurred today that changed your mind?"

I motioned for her to follow me. "I'll tell you everything. Let's find a place where we can speak without interruption, and perhaps we can find supper as well."

TWELVE

More refugees from Novania braved the highlands, combating the winter storms as another month went by. Amongst them were a few minor nobles and their households; most had fallen into disfavor with Colin for one reason or another. The number of soldiers at our disposal grew, and I spent my days in the training cavern—when I wasn't called away to Thomas' fire to discuss strategy.

We received word from Alexander every few days. He was having success recruiting in the Southlands, and the number of people following his command had rapidly outpaced our own. The Corodan promised to supply as many soldiers as they were able, but I had not yet gleaned an exact number from Rizzt-tok. Once the land began to thaw and spring neared, we planned to march.

Thomas usually wrote our replies, but on occasion, I was granted the opportunity. I wrote not only to Alexander, but to Emmarie as well. She seemed to be thriving, though I still feared what the coming war would do to her.

As I oversaw training drills one morning, I was surprised to see Claire enter the cavern. She was markedly out of place in her long dress and knit shawl; she hadn't made the journey to take lessons in combat. Rynn was working with some of the guardsmen, and though she was often frustrated by her self-proclaimed "slow" progress, she'd improved substantially. I watched her train as Claire moved to stand at my side.

"Did you need something?" I flicked a glance in her direction, but she faced forward, her eyes on the sparring match.

"I spoke with Thomas last night," she replied. "He told me what happened at Vinterry. I wanted to give you my sincerest condolences."

I sighed and dropped my gaze to the cavern floor. "I should have been with her. I could have protected her."

"Even if you'd known Colin's men would resort to murder, you still would have risked everything to save Alexander." Her tone was matter-of-fact and non-judgmental, but the statement rankled all the same. "Perhaps if there had been some indication of Colin's plan, things would have turned out differently."

I grunted in irritation, though I knew she was right. It didn't mean I had to like it.

"Regardless, it seems you've moved on."

I looked at her sharply. "What do you mean? I loved Vera—"

Claire arched an eyebrow, her dark eyes piercing. "I know you did. But you look at *her* in the same manner you once did Vera." She gestured toward Rynn. "I must admit, I'm a bit jealous. Even when we were married, you never once looked at me that way."

I shook my head, uncomprehending. "What do you mean?"

She rolled her eyes but didn't elaborate. I turned away to continue watching the drills, and my eyes found Rynn of their own accord. She had taken a break and was resting near the far wall. When she caught my eye, she flashed a grin. I couldn't help but smile in return.

"*That*," Claire said pointedly, "is what I mean. The look in your eyes—you care for her a great deal."

"She's a good friend," I replied defensively.

"Oh, a *friend*," she sneered. "Your expression says volumes, Andrew. She may only be your *friend* at present, but mark my words, she'll become more—whether you admit it now or not."

Her tone sparked my anger. Claire's judgmental nature had long been a source of contention between us, and it was one aspect of my previous life I didn't care to relive.

I scowled. "Is this why you've come? To goad and to mock?"

Her expression was stony. "It seems I've struck a nerve. I'll leave before this escalates into yet another senseless argument." She sighed as she turned away, muttering furiously under her breath. "Some things will never change."

I rolled my eyes, exasperated, and glowered at her back as she walked away. Some things never changed, indeed.

We'd been married for a little more than four years, and during that time, Claire had never ceased her criticisms of me. Ours had been a tumultuous relationship marred by many heated exchanges, and I'd often avoided her for hours afterward. I had deluded myself into believing I loved her, but I knew now that wasn't true. I'd tried to do right by her, hoped to give her the life she deserved, but it had never been good enough.

I shook my head as she disappeared from the cavern, fuming. It was a wonder she'd deigned to speak with me at all, given that I'd never managed to meet her lofty expectations.

"Trouble?" Rynn asked as she stopped to stand at my side.

"With that woman, always," I growled.

"I'm finished with drills for the day," she said, mercifully changing the subject. "Would you care to walk with me? Perhaps a friendly ear will lighten your mood."

I nearly declined, but something in her tone caused me to reconsider. "Very well."

Rynn flashed a smile. "We'll go outside. I promised Everett I'd clear the ice from the pool today. I also need to check the ice bridge. It's been cold enough that it should remain steadfast, but I don't want to risk someone's life if it was weakened by yesterday's sun."

I nodded and followed in brooding silence until we exited the cave. Fresh snow was falling from the leaden sky, but the wind was calm. The guards stationed at the cave's mouth were huddled near a fire, their cloaks drawn up around their shoulders. They nodded a greeting as we passed but said nothing.

"Tell me what the exiled queen wanted with you," Rynn said as we approached the near side of the ice bridge.

The tang of wintergreen struck my nostrils as she summoned her power. I scrunched my face as I attempted to stave off sneezing, which gave me a moment to form a response. It was one of the few times I was thankful for my sensitivity to magic.

I wasn't certain if I should divulge the full conversation since much of it had revolved around Rynn. I didn't know what her reaction would be, and I wasn't even sure what my own thoughts were on the matter.

I valued Rynn's friendship, and I would do anything in my power to protect her, but my emotions were conflicted when I considered the possibility of anything more.

When she glanced at me expectantly, I knew then that I'd tell her everything, despite my better judgment. It was becoming increasingly difficult to keep secrets from her.

She reinforced the bridge, methodically making her way to the other side, while I relayed the brief and exasperating conversation I'd had with Claire. Rynn was silent for a time after I fell silent, and I wondered what thoughts ran through her mind. She finished working on the bridge, then turned around, hands on her hips.

"Was she right, Andrew?"

The question hung in the frosty air between us for several long seconds. I chewed on my lower lip, then shrugged. "I…don't know."

"Well," she said slowly, "you've known for some time what I feel for you. I'll take your uncertainty over the blatant refusal I received in Dragon's Feet." Her smile was mischievous. "We'll call it progress."

She spun away, headed toward the pool where our scouts often strung nets to catch fish, leaving me to stare after her, speechless. The water had frozen over the holes they'd carved, but Rynn cleared the ice away from the surface in moments. I watched as she worked her magic, self-assured and seemingly content.

I heard footsteps crunching in the snow behind me and noted several scouts had ventured across the newly fortified bridge. They carried additional nets and fishing gear, baskets, and extra cloaks. Rynn waved as she finished clearing the surface of the pool.

"Good luck," she called as she passed them to rejoin me at the bridge. She paused to peer up at me, an enigmatic smile on her lips. "Let's walk. We can gather firewood as we do so. I'm not ready to go back inside."

I nodded and gestured for her to lead the way. She seemed to have an agenda, though what it was, I couldn't fathom.

We followed the river north toward the waterfall. This late in the season, the water was frozen, and enormous icicles hung from the cliff face to glitter dully in the stormy afternoon's light. A grove of trees grew along the riverbank near the waterfall, and Rynn's path led us there.

"I spoke with Thomas last evening," she said after a time. "He said Alex has gathered a sizeable army. He also gave me this." She pulled a folded bit of parchment from her pocket. "It's from Lydia. I…haven't read it yet."

"Why not?" I asked. "The two of you are close."

Rynn shrugged uneasily. "It has been seven weeks since we left the Citadel, by my calculation. She didn't send any messages until yesterday. What if something happened?"

"Or perhaps she's been busy and only now found the time to write you," I suggested. "You won't know until you read the letter."

"Very well."

She stopped to unfold the parchment. I watched as she read, oblivious to the swirling snow around us, while a cascade of emotions crossed her face. Abruptly, she flashed a grin.

"Andrew, Lydia says she's with child!"

I laughed. "That means we were both correct. Something *did* happen, and she *has* been busy." I smirked. "Alex wasted no time in becoming a father, did he?"

"I should write her back when we return to the cavern. She's no doubt been waiting for my response." She shook her head. "Ugh, I'm a terrible friend."

"I'm certain she'll understand."

She flashed a smile. "I hope so. I'm glad I waited to share the news with you. It seems…better, somehow."

We collected suitable branches for firewood in companionable silence. The snow was falling heavily by the time we were finished, and we were both covered in a dusting of flakes when we returned to the cavern. I sought Thomas once I'd stowed my bundle of kindling amongst our stores. I knew he'd be thrilled by Lydia's news.

Thomas was speaking with Claire at his fire, but at our approach, she rose abruptly to level an icy stare at Rynn. She turned on her heel and marched away, leaving a frigid chill in her wake.

"I thought *I* was cold," Rynn muttered. "Holy hell."

I chuckled and took the seat Claire had vacated. "Don't mind her." I turned my attention to my brother. "Tom, I have news. Or rather, Rynn does."

Thomas looked at her expectantly, but she merely handed him the letter, careful to avoid direct contact. He laughed with delight as he skimmed it.

"I'll have to remember to congratulate our brother when next I see him," he said with a grin. "You know, I always wondered why Alex seemed wholly uninterested in the court ladies. Now that I know of his Mark, it makes sense." He paused thoughtfully. "Lydia is Marked as well, isn't she?"

"Yes," Rynn replied. "She's a healer."

"Will their child bear the Mark?"

I chuckled as Thomas' mind embarked on its latest scholarly tangent. He ignored my amusement and focused on Rynn.

"It's never a certainty," she replied. "My father had two siblings with the Mark, but neither finished their trials successfully. Before them, I don't believe our family had a history of magi. Lydia also came from a family who didn't bear Marks. She's the first."

"Much like Alex," Thomas replied thoughtfully.

"Actually, Tom, I learned something about our mother." I ran a hand through my hair, uncertain how he'd respond to the news. "She was also Marked. According to my father, my existence would have been impossible without it."

Thomas stared at me for several long seconds, blue eyes wide as he digested my words. "Mother was Marked?"

I nodded. "My father said her Mark was hidden beneath her hair."

He stared at the fire, contemplative. "That makes sense. I recall one memory that lends credence to your father's claim. It was summer, and I was very young. You were no doubt off on campaign, though I can't be certain. Mother was in the solarium, sewing, while one of the tutors was busy with Alex. I wasn't old enough for lessons, but I remember playing with a wooden horse. One of the ladies in waiting was combing Mother's hair, then exclaimed loudly. She was clearly frightened, and Mother was furious. I'd never witnessed her wrath so acutely—before or since. I don't recall seeing that lady around the castle again."

I arched an eyebrow. "She was angrier than when she found out I'd lost track of Alex during his first campaign, when he'd been surrounded by Corodan?"

Thomas nodded emphatically. "That was a rage borne of concern. What I witnessed as a child was borne of self-preservation. Mother must have sent the woman away."

Rynn tilted her head to one side thoughtfully. "Andrew mentioned you've studied your kingdom's history extensively, as well as it's laws. Do you know how the laws regarding magi or dragon-kind came to be? It has always puzzled me. We're people, just as you are."

"The dragon-kind, I have a true answer for," Thomas replied. "My great-grandfather, Philip, was a boastful man and a renowned hunter. The stories say he was always striving for bigger game and greater challenges during the hunt. He was prolific. Moose, elk, bears—legend states he even sought a great, tentacled sea monster. It was during his reign that a law was enacted that stated any dragon-kind caught within the borders of Novania would be hunted for sport. He was—"

"What sort of horrible *shit* puts a law like that into place?" Rynn demanded, outraged.

"Just the sort I've been describing," Thomas replied with a dry chuckle. "Philip wasn't liked by the people of his time. I believe he made a grievous mistake by declaring the dragon-kind inferior, little better than beasts. The stories say it wasn't long after the sport-hunting law was signed that the dragons began to search for the means to leave this world. We are all poorer for their departure." He met my eyes, and I detected a well of sympathy within. "Some of us more so than others."

Rynn nodded, her expression troubled. "Was Philip ever…successful?"

"With hunting dragons? No," Thomas replied with a smirk. "Nor was anyone who came after. The dragons departed from the skies of Novania and weren't seen again. At least as far as most historians were aware of." He frowned. "From the histories I've read regarding King Philip Marsden, I imagine he wasn't so different from Colin. Perhaps his tenure has given Colin inspiration for his own reign."

"Is Colin truly so barbaric? Hunting his own brother for sport?" Rynn demanded, flicking a fearful glance in my direction.

"If what Claire said was true, he is," I growled. "Colin and I never had much love for one another. After he learned he was the true heir to the throne, he went out of his way to antagonize me. I wouldn't be surprised if he called a kingdom-wide hunt with a dragon as its greatest prize. You both know what Claire said. He's offered a reward for my head."

Rynn's expression soured, and Thomas released a heavy sigh.

"You know of the assassins," Thomas said to her. "If he learns Andrew is here, I fear that a hunt—or something akin to one—is inevitable. Colin is mad with power and unafraid of those who oppose him. If anyone possesses the audacity to hunt a dragon for sport, it is him."

"Ugh, it's disgusting." Rynn scowled at the campfire. "The more I learn about this brother of yours, the more I'd like to see *his* head on a pike." She paused to shake her head. "What do you know of the laws regarding magi and the Mark?"

"The histories are much less clear on those," Thomas replied. "There are many conflicting stories in the archives and several theories about why they were enacted, but none can be verified."

"May I borrow your quill, Tom?" Rynn asked suddenly.

Thomas blinked, confused. "What? Of course…"

Rynn managed a smile. "While you tell me your stories, I'd like to write a response to Lydia. You always have a quill and ink nearby."

"Oh, yes, I do."

He flushed slightly and fumbled amongst the items on the overturned crate at his side. He produced a quill and ink, then handed the items to Rynn. She promptly turned over Lydia's message and began to write. When Thomas didn't begin his tale, Rynn paused to peer at him sharply.

"Tom?"

"Oh, yes, my apologies," Thomas replied. "One story claims the law was put in place as a result of something called the Mage Wars. I could locate nothing in our archives that described such an event, but it's not unusual. Most documents that mentioned magic or magi were destroyed centuries ago."

"I can tell you of the Mage Wars," Rynn replied as she continued to write. "But not yet. Finish your tale first."

"There's also a story about a Novanian king whose daughter was very ill. It was said the king sent for a healer to look after her, but when the king refused to pay for the treatment, the healer cursed the girl instead. She was transformed into a tree in one version and a statue in another. The king the story refers to wasn't named, so I can't verify if he even existed."

Rynn snorted. "That story is preposterous. A healer is a healer. Their gift can't be used for anything but promoting a person's natural healing response. If the story were true, the king mentioned must have hired a mage with a completely different talent. It could not have been a healer." She shook her head. "I've never heard of a mage capable of transforming a human being into a tree or a statue either."

"That story ends with the king signing the first Mark laws, and bearing the Mark became a crime punishable by death. It's the same law in place today."

"Tell me," Rynn said as she finished writing and the parchment disappeared, "if you succeed in ousting your brother, what will you do?"

"I will repeal both laws immediately," he replied without hesitation. "As you've said, you are people, just as we are. We ought to learn how to live together peacefully."

"You make it sound as though magi are a different species," Rynn said with a laugh. "We aren't, you know." She glanced at me, a mischievous smile on her lips. "I can't say the same for Andrew, however. He is, without question, *different*."

"That's a bit unfair," I replied, feigning hurt.

Thomas laughed. "If Alex were here, I'm certain he'd back your statement." Thomas studied me carefully, then said, "Since that evening when we reached the tourney field and you revealed what you are, I've been wondering..."

"Go on." I crossed my arms and leaned back, curious to learn what he'd been stewing over.

"Mother must have known what you were from the start. How did she hide it from my father? Or from the court, for that matter?"

"I don't have any clear memories of my youngest years," I replied. "But by the time I was five years old, I knew I must not change forms, even when I was upset. I knew that doing so was a risk to my life. I asked Mother about that once I was older. The winter after my sixteenth name day—that would have made you perhaps three years old—mother convinced the king to allow her to travel to the royal manor in Summerdale. She asked me to lead the escort guard."

"I'd forgotten about Summerdale," Thomas replied. "Father didn't seem fond of the place."

I chuckled. "No, he wasn't. Perhaps it's why Mother asked to go there. It's remote, and surrounded by forest." I shrugged. "We spent a few weeks in Summerdale. During one of our final days there, mother asked me to walk with her into the forest. She wanted to see me in my other form, as she hadn't watched me transform since I was small. In fact, I wasn't even certain I would recall *how* to shift when she made the request. I'd been human for so long…"

"Did you?" Thomas asked.

I nodded. "It's not something one can forget, Tom. Once I shifted, she said, 'You look so much like your father.' We spent the afternoon talking. I asked her how she'd managed to hide my secret, and she said, 'There's a reason why there are six years between you and Colin.' She wanted to ensure that I understood the dangers of shifting before she was willing to bear another child. I didn't have a nursemaid, much to the king's chagrin. Mother insisted she tend me herself until I was of a proper age. Your father didn't question her and believed she was simply enamored by her firstborn. I'm not certain how he would have reacted if he'd known the truth."

Thomas frowned thoughtfully. "Father was a reasonable man, but knowing that Mother had lain with a dragon-mage before meeting him might have spoiled much of their relationship. He always held her in high esteem. He believed she was the greatest woman to have ever graced the royal castle. The truth would have ruined his perception."

I shrugged. "He loved her, but I understand why she never told him about me, or Alex, for that matter. Even if he'd deigned to change the laws, we would have both been made outcasts. People fear what they don't understand."

Rynn made a sound of disgust. "Is that why half the people here give me a wide berth and whisper when I pass? Is it why Claire stares daggers at me whenever she's given the opportunity?"

"I've made it very clear to everyone that you're a welcome guest and an asset to our cause," Thomas replied evenly. "But perhaps they *are* afraid of you. You're a mage, and most here have never encountered one before. Beyond that, most are unused to a woman who relies on no one but herself—or one who happens to be as capable as you are."

Rynn frowned. "I suppose I should take that last as a compliment."

"As for Claire," I cut in, "there are other factors behind her animosity. I don't believe she gives one whit about you being a mage."

Rynn stared at me for several seconds, but her eyes were unreadable. "I believe I understand based on our earlier conversation. Is she always so petty?"

Both Thomas and I laughed. "It's the way of noble ladies," Thomas replied with a shrug. "They have too much time on their hands and not enough to keep themselves occupied with. They resort to gossip and provoke court scandals. Claire has known no other life."

"And you don't believe she'll cause a scandal here?" Rynn asked. "How could one grow up in such an atmosphere? I'd be dead of boredom by the time lunch came around."

I chuckled. "It's expected of noble ladies. They consider it demeaning to take up a profession."

"That's an utterly useless part of your kingdom's society," Rynn declared with another frown. "Where I'm from, it's expected that *everyone* takes up some sort of profession. Those who are Marked have more specialized work. If I hadn't undergone the trials, I'd likely be on the lake with my brothers, setting fishing nets and bringing in the catch." She glanced at me, smiling faintly. "If I hadn't undergone the trials, I wouldn't be sitting here now. I'd like to believe I've made the right choice."

Thomas raised his eyebrows and shot me a pointed look. I wasn't about to take the bait.

"Well," I said awkwardly, "I'm certainly glad we have your assistance."

She smiled knowingly and I felt my face redden beneath their combined scrutiny. Both Alexander and Thomas seemed to believe there was more between us than mere friendship, though Thomas was tactful enough not to state it outright. In fact, I rather enjoyed her attention, but I was unwilling to admit it to my brothers. Now was not the time.

Thomas cleared his throat. "If I've answered all of your questions, I must meet with Jon and Uncle Everett before long. I'll leave the two of you to your evening."

As Thomas took his leave, I groaned while Rynn laughed merrily.

"Holy hell, Tom's going to think there's something between us. And if *he* thinks that, he'll tell Alex." I ran one hand through my hair. "What am I to do with you?"

She laughed again. "Let them wonder, Andrew. It's just a game."

"Is it?" I asked.

She smiled enigmatically. "Yes, unless you want something more. I'll leave that decision to you." She rose and stretched her arms behind her. "I'd best return to my training. Lieutenant Corin is expecting me."

I watched her as she strode away, unable to make sense of the exchange. She left me feeling both awkward and wanting more, and I was uncertain how to proceed. In the short time we'd been away from the Citadel, Rynn had managed to weaken my resolve, and I'd failed to realize it until now.

I groaned and stared at the cavern floor. Friendship was acceptable, but something more? I shouldn't even consider it—now was *not* the time.

THIRTEEN

The next few weeks went by in a whirlwind of activity. Thomas devised a plan to scout the landscape surrounding the caves in a systematic manner, but it was Jonathan Horace who came up with the idea of sending me to surveil the landscape from the air.

Thomas protested the idea initially—he hoped I'd take up command of the soldiers—but the approach made sense, and I agreed. The scouts could only cover so much ground during the day, but I could easily fly three times their distance during a single night. I also held the advantage of keener night vision, and it helped that my dragon form was covered in black scales; I'd be difficult to spot against the night sky. Jonathan would assume command of the soldiers while I was otherwise engaged.

Each night, a new soldier was assigned to ride with me, bundled against the bitter cold and biting winds. Some enjoyed the task, while others openly feared the assignment. As my two half-brothers liked to remind me, I was intimidating in my dragon form, even when I didn't mean to be.

Jonathan outlined the destinations each night before we departed. Often, it was simply to fly in a set direction and see what lay below. I'd fly until midnight or until my rider became uncomfortable with the chill, then return to the caverns, often as the sun was breaking over the horizon. I'd report any findings we'd made, take a meal, then sleep for several hours. The schedule provided me with little opportunity to speak with Rynn—or with anyone else, for that matter.

With the help of the two former dukes, lengthy exchanges with Rizzt-tok, and his long-distance collaboration with Alexander, Thomas was beginning to formulate a plan for Novania. As the days passed, my nightly outings began to take on greater meaning. I remained in the highlands during each excursion, as Thomas would not risk a flight through Novanian territory without further preparation.

As I landed in the gray pre-dawn light one morning, there was immediate movement at the cavern's entrance. My scouting missions had become commonplace by that time, and the guards no longer exited to investigate my arrival. The movement and accompanying voices drew my attention, and I glanced back at the scout who had traveled with me during the night, a woman named Hulda, whom Everett had recruited for her cartography skills. She'd been sketching as we flew, noting the landmarks and terrain on a sheet of parchment cleverly held to a board with a set of strong clips at either end. She often accompanied me when the moon was bright and the skies were clear.

"It sounds as though they've been expecting us," I said over my shoulder.

She laughed as she slid to the ground. "No, my lord, they've been expecting *you*. I'm merely a scout. I'm not important."

I frowned as I noted the thin film of frost coating her garments and gloves. "Were you warm enough?"

She cut me off with another laugh. "Oh, yes. I have two more layers beneath what you see. This frost is no bother. I'll tell them you'll just be a moment. I'll bring your clothes."

Moments after Hulda disappeared into the cavern's entrance, Thomas emerged carrying the bundle of clothing I'd left behind the night before. I shifted as he tossed them toward me.

"I don't think I'll ever get used to watching that. It's fascinating, yet so *unnatural* at the same time." I heard him chuckle as I pulled the shirt over my head. "Your skin-changing ability isn't why I've come, however."

"Why did you come?" I asked as I pulled on my boots. "You know I always report to you or Jon as soon as I return."

He grimaced. "There's been a bit of an incident. I don't know how I should handle it, and I hoped you'd help."

I lifted my eyebrows in question as I rose to my feet, silently prompting him to continue.

"Some of the men were drinking last night, and one of them began to harass Rynn. He—"

"Is she hurt?" I asked, then inwardly winced. I'd spoken too quickly, but Thomas didn't seem to notice.

"No, she's not hurt. It wasn't *that* sort of harassment, Andrew. He attempted to incite a riot against her because she's a mage. He was loud and unruly, and several others thought it'd be fun to join him. She's upset by their behavior, and rightly so." He released a sigh and seemed to deflate. "I believed we'd made it clear such behavior wouldn't be tolerated. Jon had the lot locked in the brig, under guard. I wanted to speak with Rynn before we decided on their punishment, but she is refusing to speak to anyone—even me."

I raked my fingers through my hair. "Where is she?"

Thomas gazed at me for a moment before forming his reply, his expression guarded. "She barricaded herself in the cavern we use for drills. She walled off a portion of the cavern with a solid block of ice. It's just clear enough that I can see her silhouette pacing within, but she won't speak to me—or to anyone else who has tried. I was hoping, given your...*friendship*, that she'd talk to you."

"I'll see what I can do," I promised, though I wasn't certain she'd be willing to speak with me if she'd refused Thomas.

"Please tell her what I've told you. We'd like to speak with her, and the men have been detained. I need her to understand she's safe here and that I won't tolerate their crude behavior."

I studied Thomas thoughtfully. "Despite your protests, I think you're going to make a worthy king."

He laughed humorlessly. "We've a long way to go before it comes to that. I'm only trying to do what's right."

"My point exactly." I walked with him into the cavern. "I'll speak with her now—*if* she's willing, that is."

"I have every confidence that she will be." Thomas clapped my shoulder and turned to leave. He smiled knowingly as he walked away, and I was left to wonder yet again what my brother believed he knew of my relationship with Rynn.

Rynn's barricade had taken over one corner of the training cavern. Through the translucent ice, I could make out her silhouette, pacing the length of her self-imposed prison. I rapped on the ice in an attempt to garner her attention.

"I've already told you lot to leave me be!" Her voice was hoarse, as though she'd been crying.

My heart wrenched at her tone. "Rynn, it's me."

"Andrew?"

There was a heavy sigh, followed by the overwhelming scent of wintergreen. Moments later, a hole opened in the ice large enough to accommodate me. Without waiting for further invitation, I stepped inside. Rynn closed the ice behind me, then sat heavily on the cavern floor. The air on this side of her barrier was frigid and my breath steamed in the air.

"Tom told me what happened," I said.

She turned to meet my gaze. Her blue eyes were tortured and the frozen remnants of tears clung to her face. "I'll never fit in here. I've known since I first proposed coming with you. But that isn't what has me so upset." She looked at the ground and began tracing her fingers over the uneven stone.

I studied her for a moment before taking a seat beside her. She'd never displayed such fragility before. I wanted to comfort her, to act as the friend and protector she so obviously required, but uncertainty staid my hand. Instead, I drew my knees up and rested my arms across them.

"Tell me."

"I wasn't prepared for the pure hatred in their faces." Her eyes became shiny with unshed tears. "I've as much a right to exist as any of them. *Why?*"

"I wish I had an answer. I truly do. You're not alone in this."

She snorted. "You make it sound so simple, but you and I are not the same to these people. They know you. They remember you from *before*, their brave commander who won ever so many battles. You're Thomas' brother. They have a measure of respect for you that seems to overshadow their fear of what you are."

I swallowed any further response I might have made. She was right—we weren't the same, would never *be* the same.

I settled for another tactic. "How can I help you? I'm here for you."

She laughed nervously but didn't look up. "When you say things like that, I…" She sighed and shook her head. "Ah, never mind."

"The men who were bothering you have been detained," I said in an attempt to change the subject. "Tom wanted to speak with you before meting out punishment."

"I don't want them punished. I want them to *understand*."

Her voice was tremulous. I didn't think of what I did next; I simply reacted. I slipped one arm around her shoulders and drew her close. She needed comfort, physical contact, and it was something only I could provide.

She inhaled sharply and looked at me, startled. "Andrew?"

"Hush."

I knew my action would further complicate my feelings toward her, but in that moment, I didn't care. She needed me, and I would do all I could to help her through this situation. Despite my previous hesitation, I found my resolve was rapidly eroding. I'd been lonely since Vera's death, and I enjoyed her company. Perhaps, I chided myself, I enjoyed it too much. And I was only acting as a *friend*.

After a moment, she relaxed and leaned into the embrace. She rested her head on my shoulder and closed her eyes. "I suppose I've only made matters worse by walling myself off like this." Her voice was subdued, riddled with exhaustion.

"No one blames you, Rynn," I said softly. "Those men were out of line."

"Hmm."

I held her in the cold confines of her barricade for several minutes before I realized she'd fallen asleep. I smiled and studied her face as her breathing steadied and her expression became serene. As gently as I could manage, I shifted into a more comfortable position against the cave wall, and soon found myself drowsing as well.

When I awoke a few hours later, Rynn was still sitting at my side, though she no longer leaned against my shoulder. She smiled apologetically.

"I didn't mean to fall asleep," she mumbled. "It was nice to feel secure, and I drifted off."

I smiled and blinked the sleep from my eyes. "I didn't mean to fall asleep either, but I *was* awake all night."

"We ought to speak with Tom," she said after a moment. "He was no doubt expecting you hours ago."

I shrugged. "Hulda gave her report to Jon when we returned. I have nothing more to tell them, and…" I studied her for a moment before I made the decision to continue my train of thought. "Some things are more important than scouting reports. I had to make certain you were alright."

It was in that moment I realized how much I truly cared for her. If it had been anyone else in the camp, I didn't believe I would have reacted the same way. I didn't know if what I felt was love, exactly, but it was far more profound than simple friendship, and I struggled to characterize the emotion. When it had come to Vera, my feelings had been crystalline; I'd known what I felt, what I wanted. With Rynn, I was uncertain, though I could no longer deny I wanted her in my life.

She smiled warmly. "I'm much better than I was, thanks to you."

It took her only moments to dissolve the frozen barrier. Some of the soldiers in the training cavern gave us strange looks, and a few whispered as we passed. Rynn kept her eyes down as we walked, and I hoped she was unaware of the pointed glances we received. She'd endured enough misguided judgment during the night—and I feared I'd only added to it.

But damn, it had been worth every moment just to see her smile again.

Thomas was in the main cavern, speaking with Jonathan and Everett as we approached. When I stopped just out of earshot, Thomas motioned for us to join them at his fire.

"We've been expecting you," he said, a faint smirk on his lips.

"No doubt," I replied guardedly.

"I've determined a likely route south from our present location based on Hulda's sketches," Jonathan broke in. "We were just discussing how best to proceed."

"That matter can wait," Thomas replied briskly. "We must deal with the incident from last night now that Rynn appears ready to speak with us."

Rynn drew a deep breath. "I told Andrew I don't want them to be punished. I simply want them to understand I'm here to help. I'm no threat to any of you, so long as you keep your distance."

"Besides," I cut in before Thomas could reply, "your men will need to adjust to the idea of mages. Alexander is one as well, and we both know *he* won't be lenient with certain individuals. We'll be meeting up with his forces eventually—and he is not the only mage amongst them."

Thomas nodded thoughtfully. "Yes, we discussed that earlier today as well. Our people must learn we are allied with the magi of the Southlands." He shook his head, perplexed. "I'd believed the alliance with the Corodan would be more difficult for them to accept."

"You're certain they should receive no punishment?" Jonathan asked, mystified. "Their behavior was unacceptable."

Rynn nodded firmly. "I'm certain."

"Very well…" Jonathan wasn't satisfied with the outcome, but I knew he'd do as she asked.

"Jon," I said after a moment, "warn them that if they attempt a repeat performance, they'll have to deal with me."

I was aware my statement would only give them cause to further question my relationship with Rynn, but I wasn't going to sit idly by when I could do something about her present situation. And as she'd pointed out, the men knew me. If they didn't respect my previous post as commander, they'd at least fear the threat of my wrath as dragonkind.

Jonathan chuckled. "That's more like it. I'd best get to it, then." He rose, and Everett joined him with the promise he'd return later in the evening.

"I have things I must see to as well," Thomas said after a moment. "I'll return in an hour. We can speak more of our plans then."

"I'll be here," I replied as he departed.

"You're mighty protective today," Rynn said once we were alone. "Not once, but twice. Andrew…"

I shrugged awkwardly but didn't know what to say. I couldn't explain the tangled mass of my emotions to myself, let alone to the woman who managed to evoke them in the first place. I felt my face redden under her continued scrutiny, and after a moment, I turned away to stare into the fire.

"Something changed, didn't it?" she asked softly.

I nodded. Yes, something had changed; had, in fact, been changing for some time.

I considered the events of the past few months, the times we'd shared together, and a slow realization came over me. I'd begun to heal—*truly heal*—after we'd visited Vinterry. Knowing Vera had been properly laid to rest had been a profound relief, and since then, I'd been dwelling on her loss less often. The nightmare scene Alexander and I had uncovered the day Colin's men had murdered her hadn't plagued my dreams in weeks. Rynn had encouraged me to travel to Vinterry, and that action had led to my present conflicted state.

"Take your time," she said. "You don't have to say anything now, or even tomorrow, or next week."

I smiled, grateful for her patience and understanding. She would never know how much her words meant to me, and I was unsure if I'd ever summon the courage to tell her. When it came to hostile enemies out for blood, legions of Corodan on the battlefield, or facing incomprehensible foes like the Venom-weavers, I was unafraid and unflinching. Yet when it came to matters of the heart, I was inexplicably terrified.

I was spared from further discussion regarding my confused feelings when Jonathan returned. He sat heavily across from us and offered a smile.

"I'm glad that business is over and done. Your brother's right, you know. These people need to learn to accept the magi. Like it or not, we'll need their help to defeat Colin." He crossed his arms and turned to face Rynn. "I think they'll leave you be from now on. There's a certain measure of respect—and fear—they have for Andrew's declaration, and I made certain they were aware of it."

Rynn scowled into the fire. "I'd rather not rely on the reputation of others to resolve this mess. I'm unused to it."

"And they are unused to you," Jonathan replied evenly. "Give them time. I know it's been almost two months, and most have accepted you, but there is still much we don't understand about magic. It certainly doesn't help that you distance yourself from everyone. I know your reason for it, as do Thomas and Ev, but most of the others don't. They fear what they don't understand, and given the stories we grew up with, there is much prejudice to overcome."

Rynn looked down at her hands and sighed despairingly. "I knew before coming here that I'd be considered an outsider. I don't know what else I can do to make these people see I'm no threat to them."

Jonathan tilted his head thoughtfully to one side as he studied Rynn, then he turned his gaze to meet mine. "There may be something, after all."

"What are you thinking?" I asked, immediately suspicious.

A crooked grin spread across his face. "I may be presuming a bit here, but I have an idea that may help with this situation. Most of the soldiers know you, and they all respect you. Your reputation as the former commander has preceded you."

"Jon…" I said in a warning tone. I suspected I knew where his train of thought was leading, and even after the events of the morning, I was unprepared to take the next step.

"Hear me out, Andrew," he said with a laugh. "What I'm proposing is this: Rynn will join you on the scouting missions. It will give the soldiers an opportunity to learn more about her, and they'll behave themselves in your presence." He paused to smirk at Rynn. "Particularly those who are already wary of your dragon."

"That just might work—" I began, as Rynn said, "I'll agree to those terms."

We looked at one another, startled, while Horace laughed genially.

"The two of you seem to have an understanding," he said, still laughing. "I think this will work out well. As for tonight, you should rest. You haven't had a night off in over a fortnight, and I need more time to determine your next destination. You can resume tomorrow under this new arrangement."

I shifted my gaze to Rynn. "You're certain?"

She nodded. "Though I'm not fond of flying, it's better than the alternative."

"It's settled then." Jonathan rose to his feet with a grin. "Enjoy your evening."

She flicked a gaze at Jonathan's retreating form, then smirked at me. "I'm surprised you didn't object when he called you 'my' dragon."

FOURTEEN

"Hulda won't be joining us tonight," I said with a frown. "Jon's determined another path for us to follow based on her sketches, but someone else has been assigned the duty."

I hesitated, uncertain how Rynn would react to the news. We stood at the cavern entrance, watching the sky darken from sunset to true dusk while we waited for Jonathan's scout to arrive. A chill breeze wafted toward us from outside, but it was no colder than it had been on previous evenings.

"Who is it?" she asked without turning to meet my gaze.

"His name is Evan. I've flown with him several times, but I'm not certain how he feels about magi."

She crossed her arms. "He was one of the men Jon detained. Why would he assign him to this duty straightaway? What's your friend playing at, Andrew?"

Knowing Jonathan as I did, he was likely attempting to ascertain how the most contentious of his people would react to the new arrangement. If Evan reacted favorably, the others would be less problematic, but if he reacted poorly, Jonathan would seek an alternative before the matter escalated further. His tactic made sense, though I was concerned for Rynn.

"He's paired us with the worst of the offenders first," I replied. "It will get better from here on, I promise."

She shook her head and stared outside, her jaw set and her expression aggrieved. "I want to believe you, but after what he and the others said, I have my doubts."

"Let's see how this evening plays out," I said in an attempt to encourage her. "It may end better than we anticipate."

She managed a smile. "I'll have you with me this time. I hope you'll keep your word."

I chuckled darkly. "I will. He'll watch his tongue, or he'll regret ever opening his mouth."

"Hmm."

She fell silent as she contemplated my words. Her blue eyes were focused on the sliver of sky visible above the rim of the canyon far above, where the pastel shades of twilight rapidly transitioned to the inkwell of the night, spattered by countless stars.

I knew I must leave her for a few moments and go outside to shift forms, but I was loath to do so. She'd never appeared so vulnerable. Instinct drove me to protect her, to shield her from any harm the ignorant amongst the Novanians might inflict. Alexander had often teased me for being protective of those I cared for—perhaps it was but another sign of my burgeoning feelings for Rynn. I lingered at her side for several minutes, hoping my presence would somehow ease her mind.

The sound of footsteps in the cavern drew my attention, and I turned to find Evan striding toward us. He was bundled in multiple layers against the winter's chill and appeared ready for the night's work. I nodded a greeting and murmured to Rynn that I must go outside.

I heard her voice in conversation with Evan a few moments later, though by that time, I'd walked far enough that their words were lost to the icy breeze. I knew if he caused her any trouble, she would not hesitate to tell me, though I couldn't help but fret over her in my brief absence. Since our time within her barricade the previous morning, she'd been ever-present in my thoughts.

I didn't want to delay our departure any longer than necessary, and stripped hurriedly. I heard laughter seconds later as Rynn emerged from the cavern with Evan in tow.

I lifted my eyebrows in surprise when she smiled up at me. I'd feared the worst, but it seemed my concern was misplaced.

"I think we'll be fine," she said softly as she collected my clothing to return it to the guards' post inside.

Evan took up his position between the spines on my back. "The dukes said we'd be following a new path tonight," he said. "They also said your girl will be joining us. She seems nice—"

"Rynn is my *friend*," I growled.

He snorted. "I'm not certain you can say that any longer. Everyone in the training cavern knew you were in that ice-wall of hers for hours."

I groaned. "I fell asleep—"

He laughed. "Sure, you did. Anyhow, I've apologized to her… I was out of line for what I said. And I certainly wouldn't want to cross you. I've heard stories, you know."

"You can't believe everything you've heard, especially if you've heard it from any of my brothers."

Though I was encouraged by his words and pleased he'd apologized for his misdeeds, I was becoming irritated as well. It seemed everyone believed something was going on between us, even though I'd failed to sort out my own thoughts on the matter. I hoped he'd drop the subject; I disliked being the target of idle gossip. It was too reminiscent of my years at court.

Evan laughed nervously as Rynn approached once more. "Well, as I said, I've heard stories, and not from your brothers, I assure you. The whole kingdom was talking about you after the failed execution. Alexander's Mark was news, but your transformation into a dragon to save him? *That* was the real story. I didn't believe half the rumors until you arrived here. And now, well… You *are* a dragon."

"I'm certainly glad to see my scout is so damned observant," I growled as Rynn climbed up my side to take her place. "This isn't the first time you've flown with me."

My patience was rapidly dissolving and my temper was primed to flare.

"Oh, Andrew, the poor man is terrified of you," Rynn said with a laugh. "There's no need to intimidate him further."

I craned my neck to frown at both of them. "I'm not trying to intimidate anyone."

Rynn smirked at me while Evan stared at me wide-eyed, his face ashen.

"To be honest, sir," Evan stammered, "you are intimidating whether you're trying to be or not. I dread this assignment each time it's given, and after what happened the other night… I believe Duke Horace gave me this task as punishment. He knows that I'm… I'm…"

I stared stonily at the man, willing him to finish his sentence.

"Andrew," Rynn said gently from behind him, "when you wear that expression, it doesn't help matters, particularly when you're in this form."

I sighed wearily and faced forward. Perhaps I was being too hard on Evan, but after he'd caused so much turmoil and distress, I wasn't feeling lenient. He could remain terrified for all I cared, so long as he left Rynn alone.

"What I'm trying to say is… I'm afraid of you, sir. And I'll not do anything to the lady again, I swear it!" Evan's words toppled over one another in a rush.

I smiled grimly. At least something had come of our pointless conversation.

"See that you keep your promise," I snapped as I leapt into the air to begin our night's work.

Rynn and I fell into a routine with our nightly scouting missions. While some of the scouts who accompanied us were at first uncertain of the change, most seemed to accept it well enough after one or two outings.

Even Evan began to relax somewhat; I learned he wasn't truly afraid of Rynn and his previous actions had been borne of ignorance and his upbringing. Most of his skittishness was due to his fear of *me* and what I might do should he cross me a second time. After a few conversations, Rynn convinced him I wasn't to be feared so long as he didn't make me an enemy.

I was irked by my failure to make him see it myself, but was grateful for Rynn's involvement. She'd managed to smooth things over where I'd floundered. Perhaps she and my brothers were right, and I was intimidating due to who and what I was, but I didn't know how to remedy the situation. I couldn't change the fact that I was half dragon.

As the nights went by, the weather became progressively colder and the winds more unpredictable. After ten outings, I was forced to end the scouting missions for the season. Hulda was with us on that final night, and the wind became so fierce I could scarcely make any headway against it. After only a short while, I returned to the cavern entrance, exhausted and utterly defeated. Hulda shivered uncontrollably beneath her many layers.

Though it was late, Thomas remained at his fire with Everett. I was grateful he wasn't abed. I collapsed into a seated position between the pair and apprised them of the situation.

He nodded, resigned. "I've been afraid of this for some time. The weather is worse with each passing day. Our people are still catching fish from the river well enough, but for how long? Our other provisions should last another month at least, perhaps two, but we'll need to seek additional supplies soon." He shook his head and scratched at his beard. "I hope my decision to over-winter here has not been a mistake."

I studied him for a moment in the flickering firelight. Thomas' blue eyes were weary, ringed by dark circles. His brow was lined with worry and fatigue. He appeared both older and younger than his twenty-five years.

"Is there anything more I can do? Scouting must be put on hold for a time, but surely—"

He waved one hand in the air dismissively. "No, you've done more than enough so far. This is my burden."

"Be that as it may, you don't have to bear it alone," I replied.

He chuckled. "I have help from many people. Perhaps you don't see it, since you've been sleeping for most of the daylight hours. I know I'm not alone, but…the strain wears on me." He shrugged. "I worry about everyone and everything. I want to do right by our people, but I continually wonder if this is the correct path. The winter has proven to be harsher than I'd anticipated."

"Lord Marsden, we've been over this," Everett said patiently. "Our stores will be sufficient for some time yet. You needn't fret."

Thomas sighed and stared into the fire. "And yet, I do." He forced a tired smile. "Food is but one of my concerns. We require more wood each day to provide warmth and light, and the grove near the waterfall dwindles. I can't allow my people to grow cold and hungry. They're depending on me. Colin forced them to flee their homes, and despite the weather, more continue to find their way here. As the weather worsens, trade with the Corodan becomes more difficult. Rizzt-tok has relayed my concerns to the hive, but there is little they can do until there's a break in the storms. I can't—"

"Tom," I said evenly, "our people know you're doing your best. Most have done what they can—and more—to help. You're doing better than most others would have, given the situation."

"It isn't enough, Andrew. It isn't enough." He groaned in despair. "When I fled here to avoid Colin, I never imagined so many would follow."

"You're the only son of Carlton Marsden worthy to rule in his place," I reminded him gently. "I know you never wanted this, but you've done a damned good job of keeping order, and the people here respect you. I suspect many of them know you're the only person who *can* succeed Colin."

"But Alex—"

I shook my head. "We've discussed this. Alex bears the Mark. The people would not readily accept him. The incident with Rynn two weeks ago is proof of the fear they bear for magi. It will take time for that to change."

He averted his gaze. "I'm beginning to understand why Alex respects you as he does. I wish we'd had more time together while we were growing up or that I'd followed you into soldiering. I wish I would have known you better before all of this happened."

"What's important is that we're together now."

Thomas had been a toddler when I began to leave each summer on campaign, and during the winter months, I'd spent much of my time in the practice yard honing my skills with a sword. In truth, I hadn't known Alexander well until I was nearly twenty-five, when he began to accompany me north to battle the Corodan. Alexander and I had grown close quickly, but since Thomas' interests had always differed from ours, I'd been afforded little opportunity to truly know him. Perhaps this business with Colin would have some good come of it, after all—it placed me in a position to learn more of my youngest half-brother.

"Your brother is right," Everett said after a moment. "If there is nothing further you need of me, sire, I'll take my leave for the evening." When Thomas nodded absently, he rose and made good on his word.

Once we were alone, Thomas shook his head miserably. "I don't know what the right course is. There are several before me, and if I choose the wrong path, it will doom us all." He groaned and stared up at the cavern roof. "I'd like to speak with Jon about your scouting… I'd rather have you here, where you can offer your advice when it's needed. And I don't believe there is much more we can learn of the landscape, in any case."

"I'll do whatever you need of me," I promised. "If that means I remain here, then I will."

He forced a weary smile. "Thank you. I'm glad I gathered the courage to ask for your aid, and I'm fortunate you had enough faith in me to risk the journey here."

I studied him for a moment, puzzled by his statement. I believed I'd always made it clear to my brothers that I'd help them if they asked. That offer had once extended to Colin as well, but he'd proven unworthy after his attempt on Alexander's life.

"Tom, you should have known I would come."

He chuckled. "As I said, I never had the opportunity to know you as well as Alex did. And Colin never had anything positive to say… I was uncertain that you'd keep your word." He looked down as a shadow seemed to pass over his face. "Between Colin and Alex, I didn't know who to believe. After Alex began to go off on campaigns, he idolized you. And Colin—well, he was himself, I suppose you could say. Bitter, jealous, itching for your rivalry to escalate into something more. It was only after he killed our father that I realized he was a monster. There *were* signs before then, though I was blind to them at the time."

"Were you able to prove he did it?" I asked.

Thomas shook his head glumly. "No, much to my continued sorrow. And as you know, things with Colin only escalated after our father's death. If even half of what Lady Claire has told us is true, our brother is without conscience, a monster unmatched by any in our known history." He sighed heavily, but his next words were filled with conviction. "He *did* kill Father. I'm certain of it."

"If we can find proof, we may be able to avoid a war—" I began, but Thomas cut off my words with a bitter laugh.

"We searched for weeks, Andrew, and then for months. We found nothing to tie him to the crime." He shook his head. "Perhaps if we'd been in the Capitol when he committed the act, things would have turned out differently. I'm certain Colin made the decision to act when he did because we were away. He'd planned for months, perhaps years. It's likely he destroyed what evidence there might have been long before we returned to the Capitol."

I looked down, morose. They'd been visiting me at Vinterry when their father died. Guilt writhed in my gut, even though I knew none of us could have foreseen what Colin had planned. Until that day, I'd considered Colin an annoyance, something I could ignore if I put my mind to it, but nothing more. When he'd forbidden me to return to the Capitol with my half-brothers to pay respects to the man who had raised me, every shred of respect I'd once held for him was destroyed. Even after so long, the memory rankled and stoked my rage.

"There is something else I need to say," Thomas said after a time. "Alex thought me foolish when I suggested it to him, but I truly believe Colin forbade you from returning to the Capitol with us for a reason deeper than his mere hatred of you. I believe he fears you, and I think he ordered you to stay away because *you* would have uncovered the truth of his crimes. Did you know the first thing he asked when we returned was if you'd obeyed his command? There was no greeting, no expression of sorrow for our father, no condolences… Only that question, straight away."

"I didn't know," I replied with a troubled frown. "Alex doesn't like to speak of that time, and I never pressed him for details. I should have spoken to you sooner, but we've all had more immediate matters to attend to."

"Alex helped me look into Father's death in the beginning, but once Colin began the Mark inspections, he became relatively scarce. I didn't realize why until later—and you know what happened afterwards." Thomas shook his head sadly as he gazed into the fire.

"Why do you believe I would have uncovered evidence of Colin's crimes when you and Alex failed?" I asked.

"You were on good terms with so many people around the castle. You knew them better than either of us could have ever hoped to." He shrugged. "I believe if you had been there, we would have learned something. Perhaps Alex was right, and I *was* being foolish." He rose, stretching as he did so. "It's growing late. We'll talk again tomorrow."

I nodded as he turned away. There was much to consider; if we could find evidence of Colin's involvement in the late king's death, we might spare Novania undue bloodshed. Locating the evidence now, however, would prove incredibly difficult, if not impossible. I didn't doubt Thomas' assumption that Colin would have destroyed anything tying him to the crime. Colin was nothing if not clever.

I sighed in frustration before an idea occurred to me. Perhaps Claire could provide the information my brothers had been searching for.

FIFTEEN

The next morning, I located Claire sitting alone in an alcove off the main cavern, sipping what appeared to be rapidly cooling tea while she frowned at anyone who walked past. I wondered where Leta was; it was unlike Claire to be seen unattended.

She scowled at my approach. Clearly, she was unhappy to see me—her reaction threatened to sour my mood, but I quashed my rising anger. I'd come for information, not another senseless argument.

As I sat down on the rough floor across from her, she sniffed and tossed her head imperiously. "Why are you here?"

I lifted my eyebrows. It was rare that Claire would forgo formalities and move straight to the point.

"It seems I've come at a bad time." I rose to my feet, prepared to leave. "I'll return later—"

She huffed and shook her head. "No, you may stay. I'm feeling rather unwell today, and the cause puts me in a foul mood." She frowned and surveyed the main cavern behind where I stood. "I hope Leta returns soon. One of the apothecaries has a remedy of sorts. It makes the sickness more tolerable." Her eyes flicked back to meet mine briefly. "Sit down. We'll talk."

I paused to study her before resuming my seat. As I marked each of the changes in her appearance—a line here, a scar there, the poorly-healed break in her nose—regret lanced my gut. While she'd never borne much love for me when we'd been married, she hadn't deserved the treatment she'd suffered at Colin's hands. I understood her sickness stemmed from her pregnancy, which was just beginning to show. I hoped for her sake we'd move the camp nearer to a proper city before she came to term; I wasn't certain if anyone present possessed the skills required to assist in childbirth.

"Don't look at me like that, Andrew," she snapped. "I've endured enough from everyone here. I don't need your pity as well."

"Claire, I—" I began, then stopped myself with a heavy sigh. As was typical of our conversations, it had already become tense and combative. "I don't want to argue. I simply came to ask a few questions."

She crossed her arms, her dark eyes unreadable and her jaw set. "Then ask. I've nothing else to occupy my time."

I nodded, frustrated she'd already forced me to go on the defensive. Perhaps my coming had been a mistake.

"I spoke with Tom last night regarding Carlton's death. He's convinced Colin was involved, and I wondered if you knew something—"

Claire rolled her eyes, exasperated. "Are you accusing me of this too?"

I shook my head hastily. "No! Please, hear me out."

Her continued glare indicated she awaited my next words.

I groaned and raked a hand through my hair. "I thought perhaps you may have seen something, heard something, a rumor … You were closer to Colin than any of us were at the time."

She sat back, and her expression softened from stony hatred to bitter resignation. "I have no doubt Colin has committed murder. He wasn't above throwing his own child from the tower window, after all. But I'm afraid I can't help you. Even then, I lived in fear of him. I kept my distance as much as I was able, and Carlton's death came as a shock to me, just as it must have to you. I didn't see or hear anything that implicated Colin as the killer, though I have no doubt he was capable of the crime."

I looked down, deflated. I'd known the likelihood of Claire having usable information was low, but I'd clung to the stubborn hope she knew something.

"I anticipated you'd return with your brothers after Colin sent his message to Vinterry," Claire said after a time. "It puzzled me why you didn't. Carlton always held you in high esteem, even though you weren't his son."

"Colin didn't tell you?" I asked, and she shook her head. "He forbade my return. I assumed it was a final jab, one meant to gut me and cast me in a poor light. He always knew how best to throw salt in my wounds."

She nodded and pursed her lips. "It makes sense. He felt your presence was an affront to the royal family, an insult as it were. I was forced to endure enough of his tirades on the topic to understand his mindset, whether I agreed with his position or not."

"And did you?" I asked sharply, unable to stop myself.

She laughed bitterly. "In the beginning, yes. I was *livid.* When my father arranged our marriage, I was elated—I was to be your queen. To learn four years later that it was all a sham was devastating. My dreams were shattered, and I was married to the queen's bastard son, with no hope of ruling if I remained at your side. I wondered what else you'd withheld from me, what more I'd find out…" She trailed off, and as she did, a faint, amused smile crossed her lips. "I suppose I learned more than I'd bargained for that day at the tourney field. If Colin hadn't been so furious, perhaps I would have had time to realize what a wonder it was that I'd been married to a dragon."

I shrugged uncomfortably. "I'm only *half*—"

She laughed, much to my surprise. "I was a fool to have left you, and I know that now. But that chapter of our lives is well behind us, and we have both moved on—one of us to a much better future than the other." She sighed, her gaze dropping to the slight swell of her belly. "Colin can't learn of this child. If I have to spend the rest of my life in hiding, then so be it. I will not lose another by his hand."

"If there is anything I can do—"

She shook her head, a look of confused wonder on her face. "Even after all I have done to you, all I have said, it amazes me that you continue to offer your aid. No, we're finished. Though I appreciate the offer, there are others who would benefit more from your attention." She crossed her arms, the steel returning to her gaze. "You can't look after everyone, even given your unusual abilities. I won't ask for your help, and I don't expect it from you. I… It's past time I learned how to cope on my own."

I sighed, disappointed by her words, though I believed I understood. "Very well."

Her expression softened once more. "Please know I will always regret the days in which I sided with Colin against you. It was unfair to you, and I was a foolish girl who didn't understand what I'd relinquished until it was far too late. But I also can't accept your offer. This is my penance, perhaps, for past wrongs." She glanced beyond me for a moment, then sighed softly. "Regardless, there is another woman who requires your attention, it seems."

I turned to peer over my shoulder. Rynn stood near the center of the cavern, speaking with Thomas at his fire. Her back was to us, and she didn't see my lingering gaze. Claire was right; I needed to be there for Rynn. More so, I found that I *wanted* to.

When I turned around, Claire was smiling wistfully. "If you had looked at me even once during our marriage as you looked at her just now, I may not have been so hasty to end it. We were a poor match, you and I." She rose slowly and arched her back. "I must find Leta. I bid you a good day, Andrew."

I remained seated while Claire departed to seek her maid and considered her parting words. She'd matured since our time together, though it was clear our relationship would always remain somewhat contentious. She wasn't the same Claire from my memories. She was an older, broken, and bitter version of that woman, though stronger and more determined.

"That looked a bit heated," Rynn said from behind me. "I didn't want to interrupt, so I spoke with Thomas for a time. May I join you?"

I smiled over my shoulder. "You don't need to ask."

She lifted an eyebrow as she sat at my side. "She seemed unhappy when she left. Or perhaps she was simply disappointed to see me. What did you speak of?"

I chuckled and recounted the conversation.

"Hmm, so it *was* me," Rynn said after a moment. "It's a shame she didn't know anything about Thomas' father."

"That's something we agreed on, at least," I replied. "Even though she expressed her regrets, she's still angry with me. I don't understand."

She tilted her head thoughtfully, then said, "Walk with me, Andrew. I need to clear the ice for the fishermen again, and I think you could use some fresh air." She flashed a mischievous grin as her gaze flicked deeper into the cavern. "Claire is there, watching us."

I rose and offered Rynn my hand. She glanced furtively toward Claire before reaching to take hold, then pulled herself upright.

"She may growl, but she won't do anything to harm you," I said.

Rynn nodded and released my hand reluctantly. "Nevertheless, she was once a very powerful woman. She still *is*. I've never spoken more than a passing greeting to her, and I have the distinct impression she despises me."

I chuckled, following her toward the cavern entrance. "Don't take her moods personally. She reacts as she does to you because of your proximity to me."

Rynn frowned. "Because we're friends?"

I felt my face flush despite the biting wind that struck us from the mouth of the cave. I knew I'd have to gather the courage to tell her my feelings were evolving into something more profound than mere friendship, but I feared how she'd react to my confession. Though I knew she sought more, I hesitated to take the next step. Instead, I managed a stiff nod.

As we approached the ice bridge that spanned the river, Rynn began her customary checks along the structure, ensuring no cracks or weak spots were present. The weather had been sufficiently cold, and there was little evidence of melting. We reached the opposite bank within a few minutes.

She turned to face me, a puzzled look in her blue eyes. "May I ask you something?"

I shrugged. "Of course."

"Thomas explained how names are often passed down in Novania. He said he was named for some hero of legend, and Alexander was named after one of his father's cousins. Colin was named for one of the Novanian kings from several generations ago." When I nodded, she said, "When I asked about your name, Thomas said you were named for your mother's father, which given the circumstances of your birth, was unusual. He also said you bear no second name."

"That's true," I replied slowly. "All of my half-brothers bear a second name because they're of noble birth. I don't because my father's name doesn't appear on my official birth record. I'm sure Tom filled you in on the intricacies of the laws regarding naming and inheritance?"

She nodded. "He did, but my mind wandered. I find law a rather dry subject."

I chuckled. "As do I." After a moment, I continued. "Since the official record doesn't list my father, I'm not considered nobility, even though my mother was from the Winston line. I couldn't be given a second name under the kingdom's laws. I should have been named for my father, but since my mother withheld his name, I wasn't. She chose to name me for her own father instead."

Rynn nodded thoughtfully and began to make her way toward the pool where the fishermen had cast their nets. "She was protecting you."

I smiled. "Yes. If she'd named my father in the records, my secret would have been revealed before I was old enough to defend myself. Zayneldarion isn't a human name." I studied her for a moment. "And what of you, Rynn? Where does your name come from?"

She sighed. "I suppose it's only fair that I share it with you. I was named for my grandmother, Rynnalda. I don't like the full version of my name, so it's a rare occurrence when I share it with anyone." She shot a pointed look in my direction. "I expect you will keep that information to yourself. To everyone else, I am simply Rynn."

"What's wrong with Rynnalda?" I asked, genuinely interested to learn more.

She rolled her eyes with an exaggerated sigh. "It sounds too…prim. And I like to think I'm not. I used to become furious with my mother when she'd call me by my full name. Usually, it was because I'd done something I shouldn't have, but it still infuriated me. And my brothers found it an endless source of amusement." She shook her head. Her next words were spoken in a tone I could only assume was a mimicry of her mother's. "Rynnalda Gwyneth, if I don't see your face in this house by the count of ten…"

I laughed, having heard similar statements from the maids who had watched over me as a child. "You have a second name, as well?"

She blinked, startled, then nodded, her face flushing slightly. "Yes. It's commonplace in the Southlands, you know. I was surprised when Tom informed me they're only reserved for nobility in Novania."

"In terms of being called upon when I was causing mischief as a child, I suppose I was more fortunate than my brothers were." I flashed a grin. "When I used to return to the Capitol in the summers, particularly when Alex and Tom were young, the nursemaids were *always* shouting their second names. If I had a copper for every time I heard Alexander Carlton or Thomas Winston shouted, I'd have been a very rich man. I've always been just Andrew."

She laughed. "Oh, I can't *wait* to tell Lydia I know Alexander's second name. According to her last message, he's been trying to make her guess what it is and refuses to give her any hints."

"That sounds like Alex." I grinned and shook my head, amused. "If you tell her, he's likely to blame me as the source of her information, you know."

She arched an eyebrow. "Then he won't be wrong. You *are* my source, 'just' Andrew."

We'd reached the edge of the deep pool, where a pair of men worked on one of the fishing nets as they sat near a small fire. They nodded in greeting as Rynn began to clear the ice away from the nets that remained in the frigid waters. Afterward, the fishermen thanked her and we departed.

"You know," Rynn said as we began to cross the ice bridge, "I'm almost looking forward to the spring. Marching south and leaving this place and its monotony behind will do us all good. I know we're but half way through the winter, but—oh!"

Her feet slid from beneath her, and her arms pinwheeled for balance. I reacted on instinct and reached toward her, catching her in my arms before she fell from the icy span.

"Are you alright?" I asked as she slowly regained her footing.

She gripped my arm fiercely, her eyes wide. She nodded and looked down to study the bridge between her boots. "Yes, I think so. I didn't realize the span was so slick here." She raised her face, a shy smile playing upon her lips. "At least you were here to arrest my fall."

I felt my pulse accelerate. I wanted to draw her closer, to learn what it would feel like to kiss her frozen lips. I held her, neither acting on my sudden desire nor releasing her. I wanted to do right by her, but what was the correct path?

She held my gaze for some time before she slowly moved one of her hands from my forearm and raised it to touch the side of my face. Though her fingers were colder than the winter air, I felt my skin grow hot beneath them.

"Andrew…" Her voice was breathless, a mere whisper. There was a longing in her gaze that mirrored my own feelings.

I closed my eyes, knowing I was unable to resist any longer. I wanted her, *needed* her as more than a friend. I drew her further into my embrace and my lips found hers almost of their own accord. She didn't pull away, and when I began to draw back a few moments later, she pulled me back in. I laughed through our kiss, surprised and thrilled by her reaction.

Finally, breathless, we both stepped back. She was beaming, her eyes alight.

"I've dreamed of this moment," she said, her eyes locked on mine. "For months, I've dreamed of this…"

"I feared your reaction," I admitted, my voice low with desire. "Even though I recall every word you said in Dragon's Feet, I was afraid you'd changed your mind."

Her laughter was bright. "I watched you stand against assassins in the marshlands and slay Trelk-keh's people by the dozen, courageous and unflinching, even in the face of death. How is it you're afraid of *me?*" She shook her head, smiling coyly. "You have *nothing* to fear from me, Andrew Caein. Nothing."

I grinned. I had no words to describe the tangle of my emotions, though I was elated and content in a way that I hadn't experienced in some time. Perhaps, I thought wryly, it was fortunate Thomas had placed Jonathan in charge of the soldiers. I'd been distracted by Rynn's mere presence of late, and now the effect she had on me would become even more profound.

"We should head back," she said after a few moments. "I told Thomas—"

I nodded and dropped my arms to my sides reluctantly. "You're right."

I glanced toward the cavern entrance to find several of the guards stationed there peered toward us with undisguised interest.

"It seems we have an audience." I frowned in their direction.

She laughed again. "They're no bother," she replied, taking my arm as we crossed the rest of the bridge toward the onlookers. They scrambled toward the entrance in a belated bid to appear busy. "Nothing and no one can ruin my mood, not even your surly expression."

"My…what?" I certainly didn't feel surly; quite the contrary, in fact.

She smirked knowingly. "I know you don't like the attention you often receive, and you always get the same look on your face. Surly is the only way I know to describe it." She shrugged. "It doesn't matter. I'm happy, and I'm with you. After all this time, I can finally say it. I'm with you."

Sometime between midnight and dawn, I was awakened within the little alcove I'd claimed as my sleeping quarters by a fit of powerful sneezes. It took me a moment to realize the scent of wintergreen filled the air, nearly overpowering in its intensity. It was dark enough that even with my superior night vision, it still took several seconds to locate Rynn. She was near the small crevice that served as an entrance to the alcove.

As I sat up, my blankets fell away. I glimpsed her eyes in the darkness as she glanced toward me briefly. She was building a wall of ice, blocking the entrance of the alcove from within. I watched as she worked; her hands moved subtly across the frozen surface, and it thickened and grew opaque in response. I sneezed again.

"I'm sorry. I'll be just another moment," she said softly. "I wanted more privacy."

I didn't have to ask her intent. There was but one reason why she'd come to my quarters in the dead of night.

"I apologize for waking you like this." After a moment, she dropped her hands to her sides. "That ought to do."

"Are you certain?" I asked as she turned to face me.

I had to be sure before this went any further. I wanted her and had for some time, but I needed to hear her say it was her desire as well.

She grinned. "Yes, Andrew. I am."

"There will be talk, you know," I said as she kicked off her boots.

She laughed softly. "I have no doubt there will be. Let them talk. Yours is the only opinion that matters."

She pulled off her tunic and discarded it on the floor as she sauntered toward me. I drew a breath, surprised at the strength of my desire.

"Rynn…"

She tumbled into my arms, her lips seeking mine in the darkness.

"Don't speak, Andrew. Let me have this night with you."

"Gladly."

Late the next morning, I awoke to the sound of voices in the corridor, but they were muffled behind the wall of ice that blocked my alcove from the cavern beyond. There was a small hole in the roof almost directly above the ice wall, and through it, I spied a swatch of blue sky.

Rynn lay beside me, her head resting on my shoulder. I remained still, afraid to move for fear of waking her prematurely. She seemed at peace. I smiled as I gazed at her features, memorizing every detail in the morning light.

I no longer had any reservations. I would follow the advice my father had given me and relish every moment I was granted with her. After all, her time on the earth was far more limited than mine. To deny her would be selfish.

The voices in the corridor grew louder. I listened for several moments but could not identify the speakers. There were at least two men, perhaps a third. Likely, they'd come to this remote portion of the cavern to speak privately; few others strayed toward my alcove due to the hole in the roof and the chill it represented. Most knew I rarely bothered to light a fire.

"Don't the lot of you have work to do?" Another voice demanded sharply.

It was louder than the others, harsh, and distinctly Claire's. A shadow passed across the frozen barricade from the other side as she walked past our location.

There were muttered protests from the men, followed by an exasperated sigh from Claire.

"Begone, all of you! Andrew and I may not be amicable, but even I respect his privacy. Now, go!"

I raised my eyebrows, stunned by the vehemence in her tone, and even more so that she'd chosen to defend me. Perhaps it was an attempt on her part to make amends. I would thank her later for clearing out the curious onlookers the ice wall had attracted.

Rynn stirred languidly in my arms. When I turned to look at her, she blinked sleepily, then offered me a smile.

"Good morning," I whispered.

"Hmm. I could grow used to this." She glanced toward the ice wall. "I thought I heard…*something* when I woke."

"Voices in the corridor. Nothing to worry about," I assured her as I cupped the side of her face.

"When I completed my trials and realized what my power had done to me, I never believed I'd know a man's touch again. I'm happy to learn I was wrong." She grinned. "I fell in love with the man who was appointed my guardian, you know. We spent many nights together, but after I changed… He left me after a time. I couldn't blame him—we could no longer touch. But you… What I feel for you is so much stronger than those long-ago memories I have of him." She shook her head and looked down. "I don't know why I'm telling you this."

I studied her for a moment, taking in every detail of her ageless countenance, the way her curls fell haphazardly around her face, the striking vibrancy of her blue eyes. Why had it taken me so long to realize how much she truly meant to me? It was more than mere attraction, more than friendship, though it wasn't the same as what I'd felt for Vera. Was it possible love could take on more than one form?

"What's going through your mind, Andrew?" she asked softly. "Sometimes you have this look of such…*intensity*. I wonder what you're thinking, and when your gaze is fixed on me, I feel as if I will melt—despite my condition."

I laughed, taking immense pleasure from her words, then pulled her closer. Our lips met, and I lost myself in her embrace for a time.

"I was thinking of you," I replied when we parted for air. "And I was kicking myself for having waited so damned long… I keep thinking back to that day at the lake when you were sitting on the shore with your back to me. The sight of you…" I sighed, frustrated at my inability to articulate my feelings. "I wanted you then. But the timing wasn't right, and I wasn't ready. I didn't want to hurt you. You deserved better than I could hope to offer you."

Her smile was brilliant. "And now?"

"Now, I'm ready." I touched the side of her face. "I want this, Rynn. I can't think of anyone else when you're near."

"I didn't realize the effect I had on you. And that day at the lake? I'd gone into the water to bathe. After I touched your face, my hands were sticky with gore." She laughed. "I'll have to remember dragons make for poor dinner guests. Not only will they eat every morsel you have to offer, but they'll make a terrible mess too!"

"You've had an effect on me for some time," I admitted with a smile. "I tried to ignore it, to push it aside. I told myself time and again it wasn't right, that there were other matters, more important matters…"

She arched an eyebrow. "What changed?"

I thought over all that had occurred since we'd left the Citadel, and nothing stood out in my mind. I shrugged. "I don't know. But I'm glad it did."

"As am I."

She rose slowly, and as the blankets fell in a puddle around her feet, I was afforded a moment to appreciate her beauty in the daylight. She began to locate her scattered clothing, but I remained where I was, enthralled by her mere presence.

"I wish we had more time together, but I promised Corin I'd meet him at noon," she said. "I need to become proficient with a blade. And I'd like to scrounge something for breakfast before I meet him."

"If you'll give me a moment, I'll join you."

My clothing was stashed in the trunk with my armor and the other supplies we'd traveled from the Southlands with. I'd placed it at the rear of the alcove, where it was out of the way. I rose and dressed, then turned around to find Rynn appraising me with a small smile.

"Let's go face the day, whatever it may bring," she said, her smile widening. "I plan to return here later—as long as you'll allow it?"

I knew she teased, but I could no longer resist her charms. "You'll always be welcome here, Rynn."

SIXTEEN

Each day blurred into the next as the winter marched on, and soon, another month had gone by. While I kept busy during the day running drills or plotting our next moves with Thomas, I looked forward to the nights spent with Rynn in my arms. It had taken less time than even I had anticipated for word of our union to circulate, and though there were many whispers and glib remarks for a few days, they soon faded.

The attention of the bored rumor-mongers shifted abruptly when one of Jonathan's daughters was found sleeping with Claire's handmaiden, Leta. For a noblewoman to be caught with a common servant was scandal enough, but when the servant happened to be in the employ of the queen, it created a veritable firestorm.

At the end of the month, we enjoyed a string of four days in a row without snow and began to seriously plan where and how we'd move the encampment. Rizzt-tok joined in the discussions, adding the hive's knowledge of the landscape when relevant. The Corodan would rendezvous with us at a place she referred to as the river-junction, a broad valley where the river outside our camp met up with another.

The hive cautioned patience, and we agreed to wait another two weeks before marching. The weather, though clear at the time, was primed to take another stormy turn, according to their sources. Two days later, several inches of new snow fell.

During the storm, I received a message from Alexander. I was surprised; he'd been sending all of his correspondence directly to Thomas since my arrival at the camp. It was unnerving how the message simply appeared in the air before me as I strode through the caverns, hovering expectantly.

Plucking it from the air, I unfolded the note just enough to glimpse Alexander's handwriting and Rynn's name alongside mine. I slipped the message in a pocket—I'd read it with Rynn later. She was in the training cavern working with Corin once more, and I had agreed to spend the afternoon with Jonathan as he assigned our collective soldiers to individual fighting units. Alexander's message could wait.

I spoke with her that evening. She met me in the main cavern for the evening meal, where I sat alone near one of the cavern walls. When I told her of the letter, she placed her hands on her hips.

"What does it say?"

"I haven't read it yet," I admitted. "He addressed it to both of us."

She groaned. "I suppose it means Lydia has finally told him about *us*. Now I'm not so certain I want to know its contents. I know how Alex likes to tease."

"He doesn't mean any harm by it," I replied.

"I know, but things were simpler before both of your brothers were aware of our new circumstances." She sat down, a small smile playing across her lips. "At least Thomas has been kind. I feared what he might say when he learned. At times, he's so...*proper*, and our being together has gone against the Novanians' standards of etiquette. Truly, my own brothers would likely disapprove as well."

I studied her carefully, alarmed by her admission. "Is it because we're unmarried?"

I liked her brothers, and I certainly didn't want to be the source of tension between Rynn and her family. Though we hadn't spoken of marriage yet, I would ask her to become my bride one day, but it was too soon.

She tilted her head. "They wouldn't care if we married. No, it's because of what you are. I'm not certain how my brothers will react to the news of you being a skin-changer. I didn't tell them when we visited Dwymm."

"I believed you had," I said, surprised. "How did you explain why I'm unaffected by your condition?"

She chuckled. "I didn't. They never asked, and I never told them. It seemed easier at the time. We'd only known one another for a week, and though I would have been lying if I'd said I didn't find you attractive, it was too soon to know how I truly felt. I told them you were a friend—though at the time, I felt even that was a stretch."

"You thought I was attractive?" I pressed, intrigued and unable to stop myself.

She laughed. "Of course I did. Do you not see it yourself? Most women practically fall over themselves in vain attempts to secure your attention, even those who know what you are." She paused to study me for a moment, amusement dancing in her eyes. "You don't see it. Your expression tells me as much. Oh, Alex truly wasn't jesting when he said you were oblivious. And I thought it was only with me you seemed so unaware."

I shook my head helplessly and shrugged. I didn't know what to say, though I sensed she spoke the truth. Alexander found my lack of awareness regarding women a continuous source of humor. During my time with Claire, I'd been made aware on multiple occasions that she was furious with many of the court ladies based on how they reacted to my presence. I'd never noticed, which caused Alexander endless mirth and Claire's bitter jealousy.

Rynn laughed softly and took one of my hands in her own. "Don't let it bother you. I don't want you to change, and truly, the fact that you don't see this about yourself is rather endearing."

I rolled my eyes. "Endearing" was not a term I used to describe myself, though I supposed it could have been worse.

"Shall we see what Alex has to say?" I asked, hoping to change the subject.

"Yes, let's." She released my hand with a smirk.

Andrew and Rynn –

I must admit, I rather like writing that. It's taken you long enough, brother! But enough on that. Lydia says she'll have my head if I poke too much fun at you, and I'd rather not be the target of her wrath.

I have some news that may be of interest to you, and I didn't want to pass it through Tom. He means well, but he simply doesn't understand the workings of the Oracle, though I've tried to explain it to him. Perhaps he'll better understand if it comes from one of you.

I received a message from the Oracle not long ago. It was insufferably vague, as most of her words are, though Lydia insisted I mention the one item that seemed clear. She has seen something of Tom's future and wrote this: "Andrew must remain vigilant at his brother's side, for unseen danger lurks nearby."

Lydia believes she refers to an assassin, though Tom has been extraordinarily careful in his dealings with the refugees. I don't know if the person is in his camp, but if they are, my advice is to keep your eye on Claire. I've never trusted her—even when she was married to you, brother. Keep Tom safe.

And Rynn, I wish you the best of luck. Andrew can be difficult at the best of times. Lydia sends her love to you both.

–Alex

"We need to warn Tom," I said as I finished reading the message, while Rynn smirked at me. I shrugged, though I knew why she looked at me as she did. "What?"

"Difficult, he says. I rather like the challenge you represent." She grinned mischievously for a moment before her expression became serious. "But you're right. We need to warn Tom."

Thomas was seated near the fire at the center of the main cavern, speaking with Everett and Daniel Clarence when we arrived. He looked up briefly at our approach but didn't wave us over to join him until the former duke had taken his leave. I wanted to get straight to business, but I didn't feel it wise to broach the subject until Daniel left as well. Though I knew Daniel from my time as the late king's commander, I was uncertain if he could be trusted, given Alexander's warning. We made small talk for a time before Thomas dismissed Daniel.

"I've learned enough of your habits to know you didn't come here for trivialities, Andrew," Thomas said once we were alone. "I noticed your patience was beginning to wear thin."

I grunted in acknowledgment, then proceeded to tell him of Alexander's message and the warning it contained.

Thomas shook his head with a slight frown. "This business with the Oracle makes little sense. I've gathered enough from Alex to understand she's something of a leader in the Southlands, but he bears little love for her."

Rynn leaned forward, her gaze intense. "The Oracle isn't merely 'something' of a leader. She is *the* leader. Much like your kings in the north, though she acts as a guide rather than a ruler. Her word is taken as law, and her visions are heeded when she believes them true. You must take the warning seriously."

Thomas glanced at me uncertainly, his skepticism clear.

"I can't explain it well," I said. "But I know one of her visions regarding Alex has already come true. Before we began his pilgrimage, she claimed he'd encounter something called a cursed blade. I didn't know what her words meant at the time. While he was in Dragon's Feet, he obtained a sword—it's bound to him in some manner, but it's the cursed blade she'd seen. I'd forgotten the Oracle's vision until I saw him with it… The Oracle is a mage, but her gift is incredibly rare. While I don't agree with how she's treated Alex, I believe Rynn is right. You should heed this warning."

Thomas sighed, and for a moment, he appeared far older than his twenty-five years. "I suppose I could ask for no one better to act as my personal guard than you, Andrew. I fear Jon and Uncle Crossley will both find this news difficult to comprehend, and if there is someone plotting to harm me, I don't know who it is. And the dukes will be unlikely to accept the word of this Oracle."

"Alex believes we should watch Claire," I said, "but I don't think she's involved. She has suffered too much at Colin's hands and is no longer loyal to him. And she fears for her child too much to risk its safety."

"If we begin to list everyone who might have a reason to betray me, we could easily name most of the people sheltering here," Thomas replied bitterly. "There are many who have come for reasons of their own, but have they been truthful to us when questioned? I can't say."

"Whether the dukes agree or not, I will remain at your side whenever possible," I promised. "You must be protected. Without you, the kingdom will be leaderless—and Colin can't remain on the throne."

Thomas sighed heavily and dropped his gaze to the sputtering campfire. "Such matters never end peacefully. There would be in-fighting, perhaps even a prolonged civil war. No—I can't allow that to occur." He looked up, his blue eyes troubled. "If you're to become my personal guard, then so be it. But remember—this campaign also needs *you*. Some of the plans we've drawn up hinge upon your unique abilities."

"I heal rapidly." I flashed a feral grin.

"That wasn't my point—" he began, but was interrupted by Rynn.

"Andrew has armor. He can wear it while on duty if it makes you more comfortable with the situation."

Thomas nodded thoughtfully. "Yes, the dragon scale. I'd forgotten. I would very much like to see this armor put to use and learn its true capabilities. Alex mentioned his armor is remarkable. It protected him from several direct arrow shots."

Recalling our brief battle in the marshes, I couldn't help but remain frustrated with Alexander for his recklessness that day. He'd acted as he did to protect me—one of the few instances when our roles had been reversed—but we'd both known the archer who pursued us had tipped his arrows with a deadly poison. Its lethality was proven hours later when Chela succumbed to its effects, despite Lydia's tireless ministrations.

The dragon scale armor had kept him safe through his brazen charge toward our assailant, even when one of the arrows was fired from close range. It had bounced harmlessly away, unable to penetrate his armor.

"Alex was a damned fool to test the armor as he did," I growled. "But your point has been made. I'll wear it if it will ease your mind. From here on, you'll have me as your shadow."

He managed a weary laugh. "I suppose I must learn to become accustomed to this. If we topple Colin from his throne, I'll have guards following me everywhere for the rest of my days, just as Father once did." His expression darkened. "How did Colin bypass father's guards? I've wondered that for some time. None saw him in the corridor that night—or at least, none would admit to it."

I shrugged, helpless to provide him with answers. "Perhaps one day we'll learn the answer, but we're in no position to do so at present."

He chuckled. "I was merely thinking aloud. If justice can be achieved for Father, I hope I'll have the opportunity to question Colin myself. For now, I must wait."

I nodded. "Now that this matter is settled, I'd like to write to Alex. I'm sure you have a quill somewhere?"

Thomas produced it after a moment's search. "What else did our brother have to say?"

Rynn laughed and proceeded to tell him of Alexander's jesting. I allowed her to tell the story as I wrote a brief response on the back of the parchment. It had been hours since the message arrived, and I knew Alexander would be impatient for my reply. I told him of my plan to remain at Thomas' side, and as I was about to sign the message, Rynn deftly took the quill from between my fingers, leaving a smudge of black ink across my thumb. I glanced at her, perplexed.

She flashed a grin. "I'd like to write something to Lydia before this disappears."

Thomas chuckled at the exchange. "I'm glad you've found one another. It's good to see you happy again, Andrew."

When I gave him a questioning look, he said, "Alex wrote to me during your journey in the south. He was concerned for your wellbeing. He said you were in a very dark place, and he didn't know how to help you overcome your grief. I had no advice to give since I didn't know you as well as he did, and I had other matters to preoccupy my thoughts. Perhaps all you needed was time—and the right person to walk into your life."

I smiled at Rynn as she finished her brief message to Lydia. It seemed time had helped mend my wounds, but having someone to share both joy and sorrow with was a gift unlike any other. I'd been adrift and alone for months after Vera's loss.

But Rynn had broken through my sorrow to show me I still had much to look forward to in life, a feat even my brothers could not have managed. I'd found not only comfort in her embrace, but peace as well.

I hoped we'd share many more memories, well beyond the conclusion of the coming war.

SEVENTEEN

I awakened as the dawn began to color the patch of sky visible through the hole in the roof of the alcove, disentangling myself reluctantly from both Rynn and our scattered blankets. She remained abed as I rose, her eyes tracking my every movement.

I began to remove the various pieces of my black dragon scale armor from the trunk and set them aside while I rummaged for my sword. Rynn continued to watch as I dressed and buckled on my armor, though she didn't rise to join me. It was the first time I'd donned it since retrieving it from the Caein family vault, and I was pleased with how well it fit my frame.

"You look so official," Rynn said after a few moments. Admiration shone in her sapphire eyes.

I chuckled as I buckled on the sword belt and slid my weapon into its sheath. "I suppose I must, but as Tom said, there's no one better suited to the role of protector. It has always been mine."

"Your brothers are fortunate to have you."

I picked up my helm but didn't put it on, then knelt beside Rynn as I prepared to leave. "I'll return tonight."

She smiled and sat up, resting one hand along the side of my jaw. "I'll be here."

With her free hand, she gestured toward the entrance of the alcove. The sound of ice shattering echoed through the cavern as the wall she'd erected the previous evening was destroyed. I returned her smile and kissed her briefly before departing. Though I wanted to linger, I had a duty to Thomas.

I passed through several corridors to another remote alcove that Thomas had selected for his sleeping quarters. A pair of Jonathan's men stood sentinel outside, and as I approached, they nodded in silent greeting.

"The duke said you'd be coming this morning," one said. "It seems Lord Marsden has begun to recruit his personal guard."

"About time he did, I say," the other replied with a firm nod.

"I can take over from here."

They grinned and took their leave with a brief salute. In the alcove, I heard Thomas begin to stir in the darkness.

"Andrew?" he asked quietly after a few moments.

"Yes, Tom. I'm here."

"Ah, good. I heard voices, but I wasn't fully awake. I can't see anything but your silhouette in the doorway. I wasn't certain it was you. Give me a moment. I'll dress, then we can make our way to the main cavern." He ended his statement with a loud yawn.

"Take all the time you need, brother," I replied with a laugh.

Though the corridor was dark, I could see well enough to know we were alone. When Thomas emerged from the alcove, he was shivering despite the thick cloak he'd drawn around his shoulders. It was cold in this remote part of the caverns, though the air was warmer here than in my own sleeping quarters.

"Let's get you to a fire."

He shook his head stubbornly. "I'll be fine. It's the same every morning, you know." He glanced at me, his expression drawn into a thoughtful frown. "Or perhaps you don't know. From what I've read of the dragon-kind, you're unaffected by the cold. Do you sense it at all?"

"Of course, I can sense it. I don't shiver, and I can't get frostbite, but I'm aware of changes in temperature."

"So, when you're with Rynn—?"

"Oh, hell, Tom!" I laughed, unable to stop myself. "Yes, I'm aware of *her* temperature. I'd expected this question from Alex, but not from you." I shook my head and laughed again.

Even in the darkness, I could see the color rising in Thomas' cheeks. "I was merely curious. Before I fled, I made it my objective to learn as much as I could about dragons and, well, *you*. Nothing I read explained the immunity to the cold…" He shrugged helplessly.

"I can only tell you what I know myself." I smirked, though I doubted he could see my expression. "I'm certain you'll have plenty of time to ply me with questions and sate your curiosity over the next few weeks." I paused to study him thoughtfully for a moment. "We'll need to enlist one or two others we can trust with your safety as well. While I'm perfectly capable of shadowing you throughout the day, I do require sleep."

"Yes, that's a good idea. Jon posted the men at my door last evening, though I don't know either of them well." He sighed. "It will take me some time to grow accustomed to this. I've never required a personal guard. I was Father's youngest—there was no need for it. All my life, I believed it would be you on the throne one day. Then Father revealed the truth. And now Colin has ruined all that our father built!"

It was rare to witness an outburst from Thomas, no matter the circumstance. His eyes glimmered fiercely and his jaw was set in anger. I didn't believe he would have spoken if we hadn't been alone; my reserved younger brother would have bottled the emotions tightly if faced with an audience.

"We'll make this right."

"I certainly hope so," he replied, his tone weary. "I never wanted this. I'll do my best, but I don't know if it will be enough."

"Your best is all you can do." I turned to step in front of him and placed a hand on each of his shoulders. "You are not alone. Never forget that."

He nodded once. "I'll try."

As we entered the main cavern, the air grew noticeably warmer. Several campfires had already been lit, including the one at the center where Thomas spent most of his time. Everett sat near it alone, apparently awaiting my half-brother's arrival. At our approach, he stood to bow once to Thomas, then nodded a silent greeting in my direction.

I placed my helm on the overturned crate Thomas often used as a writing table, then took up a position a few paces behind him, where I could observe the cavern but wouldn't be directly involved with his more private conversations. It had been many years since I'd acted as a personal guard, and though I knew the task could become tedious, I didn't mind filling the role for Thomas.

"I'm glad you've finally taken our advice on the matter of guards, my lord," Everett said after Thomas had seated himself near the fire. "Our numbers continue to grow, and as I've stated many times, I don't know how many people we can truly trust. What changed your mind?"

"Andrew convinced me it was in my best interests," Thomas replied, clasping his hands to still them, "though I doubt you were waiting to ask me this. Why have you come?"

Everett sighed. "Our scouts found a group of refugees late last evening. They'd become lost in the storms while searching for your camp. The survivors spent the night in the interrogation caves. Several of their number perished, and most of the survivors will likely lose fingers and toes due to frostbite. I thought you should know before I departed to question them further."

Thomas' morning was filled with many such conversations. Jonathan stopped by for a time, as did Daniel; both had updates on training drills and the dwindling inventory of supplies. Even if the weather didn't break soon, we'd be forced to move on in order to replenish our stores.

Rizzt-tok brought news from the hive, stating their "sensors" felt it would be safe to travel in approximately eight days. Thomas didn't ask what the "sensors" referred to, and I assumed he was familiar with the term.

There were others as well, each seeking Thomas for their own purposes. He handled it well, taking each new development in stride. At times, he made notes in his personal journal, and at others, referred to previous entries. I was impressed with his organizational skills.

It wasn't until late in the morning that Thomas received a break from his visitors. I wondered if all of his days were spent in this manner, or if this was simply a busier day than usual. He stood and heaved a sigh while stretching his arms behind him.

"Andrew, sit with me for a while," he said. "I've some questions for you… And I'd like to examine your armor a bit more closely, if you don't mind."

"Of course." I gestured to the helm resting on the crate alongside his writing implements. "Look for yourself."

As he picked it up, he blinked in surprise. "I expected it to be heavier," he said, marveling. "And it's as strong as Alex says? It can stop arrows?"

"Among other things."

He lifted an eyebrow, making it clear my answer was insufficient.

"Did Alex tell you of my last campaign against the Corodan? I refer to the true story, not the one I gave your father."

Thomas shook his head. "No, I only know the official account. It states you killed the former Hive-queen single-handedly, along with a number of her warriors. It makes for a good story, but how *did* you do it?"

I gave him the true version of events—my unfortunate fall into the Corodans' trap and the certainty that if I'd remained human, I would not have survived. I'd shifted, and during the course of the fight, learned even the Corodans' sharp and serrated forelegs could not penetrate my hide.

"I learned more while we traveled through the Southlands," I continued. "There, I could truly be *myself* for the first time without fear of what would happen if anyone learned what I am. I was allowed to explore my capabilities, though there are still some things I've yet to fully understand."

Thomas' eyes were alight with excitement. The thrill he received from gaining new knowledge must have been akin to what I experienced when flying. He continued to examine my helm for a time, turning it over in his hands as he did so.

"Alex said it took a long time to heal after you gave up your scales. I know dragons are supposed to heal rapidly. If it took weeks for you to heal, I assume the wound was severe."

"I… Yes, I suppose it was. I couldn't see it myself. The scales were taken from between my wings. When I was finally able to return to this form, the wound was between my shoulder blades. And the extraction…" I shook my head, recalling the excruciating pain I'd suffered as the smith had wrenched each scale free. "I don't believe I could go through it a second time. I've never experienced pain of that magnitude, and I don't wish to again. A dragon's scales aren't meant to be removed."

Thomas chewed his lower lip and nodded thoughtfully. "Does Alex realize how fortunate he is? I've read through all of the official records we had of your battles, and I know you've been through some terrible ordeals. If the pain was so great…" He trailed off, his eyes locked on the flames of his campfire, his expression troubled.

"Alex tried to talk me out of it," I said quietly. "He spoke with my father and understood the sacrifice I planned to make. He didn't want me to go through with it, but I'd already made up my mind."

Thomas smiled knowingly. "Your stubbornness is almost legendary. Father once told me when you set your mind on something that it would take nothing short of a miracle to sway you from your course. When I was a child, I used to ask him to tell me stories of the great heroes of our kingdom. Sometimes, he'd tell tales of your exploits. It was during one such tale that he spoke of your…tenacity, shall we say."

"I never knew that."

I studied Thomas carefully, wondering what else I'd learn from my youngest brother in the days to come. It was a source of pride to know the late king had thought of me as a worthy enough subject to inspire his tales. I'd always harbored great respect for him, and it seemed he'd reciprocated the sentiment.

Thomas placed my helm carefully on the crate. "I've been wondering: Have you decided what you plan to do once this business with Colin is over and done?"

I looked down, uncertain. When he'd asked me previously, I'd pushed the notion firmly out of my mind—there were more important matters requiring my attention. While I knew he'd accept my help if I offered it, I didn't want to linger in Novania. My time in the south had shown me what life could offer when I wasn't forced to masquerade as fully human. Thomas sought to change the kingdom's laws, but it would take years for true acceptance to take root.

There was also the matter of my father and the other dragons. I hoped to return, where I might assist in breaking the curse of the Stone Grove.

And no matter what I decided to do after we were finished with Colin, I would remain with Rynn. We hadn't yet spoken of that seemingly distant future, but my heart was set. There would be no changing that course so long as we both survived the coming conflict.

I looked up, startled to find Thomas was studying me intently. "I don't know yet, Tom. There are many factors to consider."

"I understand. I hope when you make a decision, you'll let me know. If you choose to leave the kingdom, I won't attempt to change your mind." A deep sadness marked his features and he would not meet my eye.

"What's wrong?" I asked, concerned.

He forced a tired smile. "I was merely thinking of how wonderful it would be to follow my own path, as Alex has done and as you will do. But for the good of Novania, I can't… Someone must take the burden of leadership. It seems that mantle has fallen on my shoulders." He released a sigh. "Don't mind me. I'm simply daunted by what we must do—what *I* must do. I'm wholly unprepared for this."

"There's a reason your father looked to the governor's council for advice," I reminded him. "He also had quartermasters, provisioners, a chamberlain… You don't have to do everything yourself, and you're certainly not alone."

"Thank you," he replied after a moment. "I know it's not the first time you've said this, but it seems I'm prone to forgetting I have help. Ah, I hope this becomes easier with time." He paused and stroked his beard thoughtfully, then peered at me sharply. "One position you failed to mention in your list was the commander of the king's army."

I suppressed a groan. I'd expected Thomas to bring up the topic eventually, but I couldn't accept the position. I was certain my time as commander was over and done.

"I don't believe I can return to that post. Not after everything that has happened."

"You mean now that everyone knows your secret."

I nodded grudgingly.

"That shouldn't matter! You're a good man, and the soldiers under your command had great respect for you." His tone rose in pitch, betraying his frustration. "That you're not fully human shouldn't be a mark against you."

I shrugged, skeptical. "My arrival at your camp comes to mind. The guard shot at me several times, claiming I was a demon. And don't forget several generations of Novanians have grown up under a law that states I ought to be hunted down and killed for *sport*. I think it best if you find another commander when the time comes."

I averted my gaze, but my eyes landed on Rynn. She walked toward us, her eyes questioning.

I offered her a strained smile in greeting, then refocused my attention on Thomas. "I think my path lies with hers. Wherever she goes, I'll follow."

Thomas nodded and waved to her, an invitation to join us. "I was afraid to say this before, but I think she's a better match for you than anyone else has been. I know you cared deeply for Vera, but seeing you with Rynn is markedly different. With Vera, you were overly careful, as though you feared you'd harm her with your mere presence. With Rynn, you act like yourself. And you're certainly prone to smiling much more often than I'd ever believed you capable of."

As he finished, Rynn sat alongside me. "What were we talking about?" she asked, flashing me a smile.

I laughed, even as I continued to mull over Thomas' words. It was true—I felt differently about Rynn, but I'd been unaware it was plain to those around me.

"We were discussing future possibilities," I replied.

"Oh?" she asked.

"Andrew claims he doesn't know what he plans to do once Colin has been ousted," Thomas cut in with a smirk. "But it seems to me that his mind is made up."

I frowned at Thomas. I had not yet discussed the future with Rynn, and he was forcing my hand.

"Andrew?" Rynn asked, a touch of concern in her tone.

"Thanks, Tom," I muttered darkly before turning to face her once more. "I… We haven't talked about this yet. You and I. And, I… Well…" I sighed in frustration, running one hand through my hair. I continued to struggle when it came to conveying my emotions to her. "I told Tom my path lies with yours. Wherever that might lead."

She beamed at me, then reached over and drew me into a fierce and sudden embrace. As she released her arms, Thomas laughed heartily.

"I believe you've made the right choice, Andrew," he said with a smile.

"Yes, well, it looks as though Jon has need of you," I said as I noticed the former duke standing a few paces away.

I was relieved someone had come to divert his attention away from me. I stood and made my way back to the spot I'd occupied for most of the morning, where I could better monitor the other people within the cavern. Rynn followed my lead.

"Do you always talk about such things with your brothers before you talk about them with anyone else?" she teased.

I sighed. "I hadn't meant the conversation to go that way. Tom asked what my plans were, and… You heard what I said." I shrugged uncomfortably. "He was trying to see if I had any interest in remaining in Novania."

"And do you?" she pressed.

"No."

"Then it's settled." She fixed me with a knowing smile. "We'll finish this business with your brothers, then we'll go south. We can determine where we go from there later."

"I believe Alex and Lydia will return to the Southlands as well," I replied. "I can't imagine him staying, given that they're both Marked—and starting a family. Even if Tom changes the kingdom's laws, Alex will still be considered an outcast by most, no matter that he's a Marsden."

I paused to scan our surroundings. More people were entering the cavern as midday approached, and the men and women working the fires on the northern side were busy preparing another batch of stew. To my eye, nothing appeared out of place, and no one seemed to be acting suspiciously. Thomas was safe, for now.

"May I stay here for a while?" Rynn asked. "I don't wish to impose—I know you have a job to perform."

I grinned at her. "You may stay as long as you like. It breaks the tedium, and I can easily watch over my brother while you're here."

The afternoon was a mirror of the morning. Thomas met with various people, made notes, and scarcely had any time to himself. I left him to his tasks, surveying those around him as he worked. As the day wore on, I began to notice patterns, but there was nothing that seemed out of the ordinary. I hoped the Oracle's vision was merely a warning that we should be more cautious, but I knew from experience her words should not be dismissed lightly.

Rynn lingered for much of the afternoon, leaving only to bring Thomas and I some stew once he had a break between visitors. Though she'd done her best to keep her hands on the edges of the tray, the chill emanating from them was strong enough to cool the food before she returned. She apologized several times, her words directed at Thomas, who merely laughed and told her he didn't mind.

The following days were much the same, and we fell into a routine that was only broken four days before our planned departure. At that time, Thomas began to directly oversee the packing of supplies, though I tried to persuade him Everett and Jonathan were more than capable of the task. He insisted, however, and I accompanied him as he made his rounds.

The day before we planned to leave, everything was in hand, organized and planned meticulously, as was Thomas' way. Thomas summoned Rizzt-tok to ensure the hive remained amenable to a rendezvous in the valley as we'd agreed previously. The hive was eager to lend its aid to its new allies, and Rizzt-tok assured him the Corodan would make good on their word.

Kash-kah would not accompany the hive's warriors. The journey had been deemed too dangerous by the majority of the hive's voices, and they collectively refused to lose another queen so soon after Krizzt-keh's demise. Rizzt-tok would lead the hive's forces in the queen's stead, as she had when we'd faced Trelk-keh and her minions.

The world beyond the cavern was beginning to thaw from the long winter's freeze. With the spring, we would march south into Novania and make the bold statement we sought to oppose Colin's reign.

I had no doubt Colin had forces awaiting us, though we still believed he'd be stunned by the numbers we'd gathered. He'd sent a large portion of his army toward the Mage's Gate, where Alexander was planning to make his stand.

Alexander wrote that he was ready for anything the blasted tyrant might throw at him, and I believed his words were more than mere bravado. The magi of the Southlands had joined him in droves, as had the Merael.

We were on the precipice of war, brothers pitted against brother in a fight that would likely change the course of Novania's history forever.

EIGHTEEN

I'd been through the Northern Marches of Novania in the past, but I'd never set foot within the city of Dresdin's Forge, my mother's hometown. The path we'd taken out of the highlands after our rendezvous with the Corodan led us directly to the city. Our journey had taken the better part of two weeks, but for most of it, the weather had held and we'd suffered few delays.

We made camp a mile beyond the city gates. Thomas and I prepared to march into the city with a small contingent of his personal guards selected by Jonathan Horace. At my half-brother's insistence, I'd act as part of the guardsmen and wear my armor and helm. He feared the reaction I'd evoke amongst the people should I be recognized—as did I.

Jonathan sent a scout ahead to inform Duke Winston of our arrival. The scout returned with word that the duke was expecting Thomas and seemed amenable to his proposed meeting.

Elias Winston was our mother's cousin, though he'd rarely made the long journey to the Capitol from Dresdin's Forge. I'd met him once when I was a child; he'd visited the Capitol during the summer after Alexander's birth and had remained in the castle for several months. I remembered he bore much of the family resemblance from my mother's side—wavy blond hair and green eyes—though I recalled little else of the man. Thomas had visited Dresdin's Forge on two occasions and seemed to know the duke far better than I did.

Dresdin's Forge was surrounded by a thick stone wall, a relic of the long years when the threat of being overrun by Corodan was ever-present. Today, the gates to the city were thrown wide in welcome, but

I noted a large number of soldiers atop the ramparts. They paid close attention to our approach and eyed us warily, but said nothing as we passed and continued toward the duke's manor house at the city's heart.

The manor house was a sprawling, three-story structure with matching outbuildings and gardens surrounded by a second, lower stone wall. We were met at the gate by a pair of soldiers and a man whom I could only assume was the duke himself. He looked like an older version of Alexander, the first hints of gray streaking his temples.

Both Thomas and Jonathan stepped forward to greet the duke, who appeared sincere in his welcome. His eyes scanned the guardsmen Thomas had brought along, his gaze lingering on mine for several long moments.

"Let's go inside where we can talk without an audience," he said after the initial greetings were finished. His gaze flicked to mine once more. "And bring your guard-captain. He ought to hear what is said."

Thomas' confusion at the last statement was evident, but Jonathan understood immediately and beckoned to me. It seemed I'd been recognized after all.

I nodded and followed the others into the manor house while I attempted to ignore my sudden unease. We were shown to a parlor by a pair of servants who collected the others' cloaks and bade them to be seated. A platter of tea cakes was set on the low table in the center of the room, though it was left largely untouched by the duke's guests. Thomas and the two dukes sat on a pair of cushioned benches, facing one another across the table. I stood to one side, maintaining my guise as Thomas' guard.

Duke Winston scanned the room before he began to speak, ensuring none of the servants lingered. "When I received your message, I was pleased to hear you were well. Word came from the Capitol that it was likely you'd perished, cousin."

Thomas forced an uneasy smile. "The winter was difficult, but I haven't allowed the weather to best me. There are other, more important matters that require my attention before I depart this world."

"Yes, your brother." He frowned and dropped his gaze to the polished floorboards. "I understand what you plan to do, and it's not without merit. The king is a menace, but I cannot openly support your cause without risking undue harm to my family. The king has made several threats already."

"We have a plan," Jonathan cut in. "We don't want to place your family in danger, but we ask that you take in some of the women and children who travel with us. They won't be safe with the army—and we both know battle is inevitable."

"Before I agree to anything, I must learn the details of this plan." His eyes moved to Thomas, then flicked toward me. "No doubt you *both* have had a hand in it."

I nodded but allowed Thomas to speak, as was his place. We'd devised our scheme, such as it was, along the trek from the highlands. If it worked, it would divert a portion of Colin's forces away from the Mage's Gate and provide Alexander an opportunity to strike at the army in the south.

"Yes. It was largely Andrew's idea." He shrugged uncomfortably, unused to his new role as our leader. "I ask that you send word to Colin. Tell him of our army here… And that Andrew is with me. He won't pass up the opportunity to seek his misguided revenge. I'll tell you where we plan to march from here, and you'll include the location in your message. You'll remain in his good graces, your family will be protected, and it will further our own goals."

Duke Winston crossed his arms and leaned back in his chair, an amused expression on his face. "You're asking me to send word to the king that your army is here? You're *looking* for trouble, cousin, and I'm tempted to oblige… But there is something I must know first." He looked up at me, green eyes glinting with mischief. "Do I tell him I've seen Andrew, or that I've seen a ferocious, winged beast clad in black scale? I'd like to know if the rumors from the Capitol are true."

Both Thomas and Jonathan turned their attention to me. I scowled, but nodded in confirmation. "The description is a bit lacking, but yes, what you heard was likely true."

"So dear Carra wasn't infatuated with a mere merchant, was she?" he mused. "Her father—your grandfather—suspected she was with child before Carlton ever set foot within this city. But Carlton was captivated by her, and it seems, was willing to allow her previous transgressions to fall by the wayside. Tell me, Andrew, did your mother know the sort of being she carried within her womb? Or did she learn the truth after the fact?"

I narrowed my eyes. "She knew."

"When your father left, she was devastated. She wanted nothing more than to leave with him, but her father would never have allowed it. Love has no place in the marriages of nobility, and she was to succeed him as ruler of the duchy. Your father wore the guise of a merchant, but his apparent status was insufficient to appease your grandfather. But he was happy enough when she managed to enchant Carlton and became queen."

He paused to study us, his expression unreadable. "To learn Carra bore not only a child with the Mark, but a skin-changer as well came as a shock to the family. There was significant unrest in the city for several weeks, and the king sent men to 'deal with the situation.' The townsfolk suspected the Winston line was cursed. Colin was not kind nor gentle to my people, and those he found with the Mark were…dispatched. Those who had been sheltering them were marched away, though I don't know where they were taken." His eyes grew hard and he clenched his jaw in momentary anger. "I bear no love for the man who defiles Carlton's throne. I will send your message. I wish you success in your endeavor."

"Thank you, cousin," Thomas said. "This means much to me—to all of us."

"Don't thank me yet," the duke replied with a bitter laugh. "If you're right and the king sends his army to intercept you, the war that ensues could well tear the kingdom apart. Is that what you truly wish to achieve?"

Thomas gazed at the duke levelly for several seconds before making his reply. "I want what's best for Novania. My brother is cruel and heartless, and I believe he's unfit to rule. Someone must oppose his tyranny, and given our unique family history, I'm the only one who can replace him."

"You're reluctant."

"What I want doesn't matter," Thomas replied, clasping his hands. "I must do what is best for this kingdom, regardless of the cost to myself. My brother must be stopped, Elias."

Duke Winston broke into a sudden and unexpected grin. "Ah, there's the determination I recall from your father. This is good. You'll need it in the coming months." He glanced at the table between them, then gestured to the untouched food. "Please, enjoy what hospitality I have to offer before you depart. I'll accompany you to the outskirts of your camp. I'd like to see what you have assembled before I send word to the king."

"Of course," Thomas agreed.

"Ah, we ought to warn you about the Corodan, sir," Jonathan said uneasily.

"Corodan?" The duke narrowed his eyes in suspicion.

Thomas held up his hands, placating the duke. "They are here as allies, not enemies. There are many within the camp, and they were instrumental to our survival throughout the winter. They're not to be feared."

"The news you bring continues to grow more peculiar," the duke remarked. "First, you order me to send your whereabouts to the king, the very man who has been seeking you for months, then your…*half*-brother confirms he's dragon-kind. Now you tell me you're working with the Corodan! Times can't become any stranger."

"That remains to be seen," Thomas replied cryptically.

The duke arched an eyebrow. "There's more?"

"Yes, cousin, and you'll hear of it eventually." Thomas steeled himself before continuing. "I don't want to burden you with more 'strangeness' since it may put your family in further danger. If Colin suspects you're aiding us, he'll show you no mercy."

The duke nodded slowly. "Very well. I thank you for listening to my concerns. There is one other matter that troubles me, however."

"And that is?" Thomas pressed.

"Where is Alexander in all of this? The rumors claimed he fled south with Andrew, yet Andrew stands here in my parlor."

Thomas and I exchanged a meaningful glance. We'd agreed Alexander's whereabouts and the portion of our plans that concerned him would remain unspoken.

"Alex isn't with us," Thomas replied. "He's well, but I can tell you nothing more."

The duke nodded, but a sad smile creased his features. "I'm glad he's well. Carra used to say he reminded her of me when I was younger. I believe it was four years ago when I last saw him—he traveled here with you." He shook his head, smiling wistfully at the memory. "Carra was right. It was like peering into a mirror of my past."

We lingered a short while before departing with the duke to our camp. During the journey, he and Thomas spoke of their last meeting, both reminiscing on better times from their shared past. We didn't reveal anything more of our plans.

As we neared the camp, it became apparent to the duke that the Corodan had a sizeable presence amongst us. While most of our people had accepted them by now, the duke was stunned.

"I don't believe I've ever been so close to these creatures," he breathed. "I'd heard they were veritable giants and built for battle, but this is astounding."

"The largest one, there," Thomas said, gesturing at the distant figure of Rizzt-tok, "is the leader of their warriors. She commands them at the behest of the Hive-queen."

He nodded, surveying the camp with keen eyes. "I have agreed to write a message to the king and to shelter those unable to fight—the old, the young, and the women who choose not to battle. May I request one thing in return? I must sate my curiosity before you depart."

"If there is something we can help you with, name it," Thomas replied without hesitation.

He turned toward me, a wicked grin spreading across his features. "I want to see the dragon."

I sighed but realized belatedly that I should have known this request was coming. The more we spoke, the more he reminded me of Alexander; had their positions been reversed, Alexander would have asked the same.

"I'll need to go to the outskirts of the camp," I replied with a frown. "There isn't enough room here—"

"Andrew, don't be daft!" Thomas cried out, though he was laughing. "I don't think it's wise to reveal yourself yet—"

"Thomas, he's going to send the letter to your brother regardless," Jonathan interjected. "I don't see the harm in it. Besides, if others also send word to the king, his story will be corroborated, which plays right into our plans."

Thomas was clearly exasperated, but he held his tongue.

"Then you'll do it?" the duke asked, his voice betraying his excitement. "Had I known the merchant my cousin was dallying with was truly a dragon, I don't think I would have left the poor man alone to do his work. I've always wanted to meet a dragon, and it turns out I have… I simply didn't know it at the time."

I chuckled. "Yes, I'll do it. Yours is not the first request I've received, and I'm certain it won't be the last."

Elias Winston's reaction to my rapid transformation was akin to that of many others, though beyond his initial shock, he kept his thoughts to himself. He walked in a wide arc before me, first one way, then the other, as he scrutinized my dragon form.

"I think I know exactly what I'll write to your brother in the Capitol," he told Thomas after a few moments. "I can provide a detailed enough description that he'll have no cause to doubt my words… Are you certain you want me to do this?"

"Yes," Thomas and I said at the same time.

The duke looked up at me, startled. "I wasn't certain you'd be capable of speech with those teeth of yours. But if you're both certain, then I'll do as you ask. You'll have your battle soon enough."

"Thank you, cousin," Thomas said.

"I'd best return to the city before long," the duke mused. "Send those who can't fight to my manor, and I'll ensure they're kept safe as we've agreed." He glanced up at me once more. "Protect your brothers, Andrew. They'll need it."

I nodded as he and Thomas began to make their way back toward the opposite end of the camp. Movement to one side caught my eye, and I turned to find Rynn walking toward me. I flashed a grin.

"You can't help but show yourself off in front of family, can you?" she teased.

"He asked." I closed my eyes and shifted, then began to dress.

"And you didn't object to the request, either." She crossed her arms with a smirk. "Admit it, Andrew—you've come to enjoy the attention more than you let on."

I grunted. "I'm not certain it's the attention. I've become more used to my dragon form. And I rather like it."

The admission felt strange, but during the winter, I'd spent almost as much time as a dragon as I had as a man. I no longer felt awkward or unseemly when I shifted. Instead, I was comfortable no matter which skin I wore.

"Well," she said as a mischievous smile spread across her face, "I rather like you in *this* form. But I suppose your dragon form has its merits too."

I chuckled and drew her into my arms, matching her smile with one of my own. "I'll show you merits—"

"Andrew! There you are!"

I released an irritated sigh and dropped my arms to my sides. I turned to see Claire striding briskly toward us. She was breathing heavily as though she'd been running, and her eyes were wide with fear.

"Where is Thomas?" she demanded.

I gestured vaguely in the direction he'd gone. "He's with Jon and Duke Winston."

She nodded once, then turned briskly on her heel. "I must find him."

I knew something was amiss, and based on Claire's unusually forthright manner, it was nothing good. I jogged a few steps to catch up with her as Rynn followed in our wake.

"Claire, what's this about?"

"It's Leta." She scowled, and her dark eyes flashed with unmitigated fury. "She has been acting strangely of late, and I've kept a close watch on her activities. She disappeared two hours ago. While she was away, I took the opportunity to go through her things. That little bitch has betrayed me, and she's still working for Colin!"

She increased her pace, forcing me to lengthen my stride. "Is Tom in danger?"

She flicked her gaze to meet mine. "Yes. We must stop her."

We crossed through the center of the camp where Thomas' tent had been erected, but he wasn't there. I suspected he was walking to the perimeter with our cousin and told Claire as much.

She broke into a run. "Then we don't have much time. I believe she'll take the opportunity to strike now that you're not at your brother's side."

"There!" Rynn called from behind us as we rounded another set of tents.

Thomas was speaking with Elias, though I didn't immediately see Jonathan with them. I scanned the area for any sign of Leta; this close to the camp's perimeter, it was a hive of activity as our people engaged in trade with local merchants, and the curious drew near to investigate our presence. After several seconds, Claire pointed savagely to my left. Following the direction she indicated, I spied Leta crouching between a pair of oak barrels, a bow in her hands. An arrow was nocked as she prepared to fire the missile.

"I can stop her arrows," Rynn stated confidently. "Go. Now!"

I broke into a sprint, charging toward her from the side as she let her first arrow fly. I trusted Rynn's ability and resisted the urge to follow the arrow's path with my eyes. I knew I must keep Leta in my sight.

Leta frowned and swiftly drew another arrow. She carefully took aim; it was obvious she was not only familiar, but well-practiced with the weapon. I was almost upon her when she fired the second shot. Her focus was absolute. She was unaware of my presence until I knocked the bow from her hands and shoved her roughly to the ground.

Her eyes widened in surprise even as she scrambled to her feet. "Andrew?"

I lunged and took hold of one of her wrists in an iron grip. She struggled futilely even as I pulled her in front of me and secured her other wrist behind her back.

"What's the meaning of this?" she demanded, feigning outrage.

"I ought to ask you the same," I growled. "Who were you aiming for, Leta? This is no practice yard in which to hone your skills."

Now that she was disarmed, I risked a glance toward Thomas. He and the duke were speaking with Rynn while they made their way toward us. Elias held a crystalline object in his hands, marveling at it. It was one of Leta's arrows, encased in ice.

"I was—" Leta began, but was cut off as Claire appeared at our side.

"You were attempting murder," Claire hissed in a venomous tone. She stepped in front of Leta, an expression of unadulterated hatred twisting her features. "You have betrayed my trust, and I will not allow it to stand."

Leta twisted suddenly in my grip, a desperate bid to regain her freedom, but I held firm. When I increased the pressure of my hands, she snarled in frustration.

"Why?" Claire demanded.

"He told me he would make me his queen." Leta's words came through clenched teeth. "All I must do is remove Thomas as a threat. My shots would have been true if not for that ice-wench."

I growled a warning, tempted to squeeze her wrists until they snapped. It would not take much of my unusual strength to break them, thin as they were, but I resisted the urge.

Claire darted forward. Her movement was so swift that it took me several seconds to realize what transpired. She drew a knife from somewhere within the folds of her skirt and plunged it into Leta's heart, twisting the blade savagely in the wound as she glared a challenge at her former handmaiden. Claire gripped the hilt and held it steady for a few seconds, then forced the blade deeper. Blood spurted onto Claire's hands and stained Leta's dress.

Leta's mouth dropped open in shock as the color drained from her face. "Lady Claire…"

"You will not address me," Claire replied contemptuously. "You have failed, assassin, and you will never see your lover's face again."

She wrenched the blade free with some effort, stumbling backward as she did so. She nearly crashed into Thomas as he ran toward the scene with Duke Winston on his heels.

Leta slumped forward, no longer struggling in my grip. Stunned, I released her and backed away. She fell to her side, one hand feebly reaching toward the wound Claire had inflicted as her life's blood spilled across the muddy snow. I gaped at Claire, stunned that she'd taken it upon herself to kill Leta, shocked she was even capable of the act. Claire dropped the knife into the snow, her eyes fixed on the fallen form of the woman who had once been her closest confidante and friend.

"Tom, are you alright?" I asked after a moment in which we had all stared in stunned silence.

Thomas nodded slowly, though he was clearly shaken. "Yes, thanks to you and Rynn." He turned to Claire. "What happened, my lady?"

Claire's face crumpled in anguish, but she did not weep. "I will give you the letters I found amongst Leta's things. They'll explain her plans far better than I can." She paused to draw a breath, then shook her head.. "I was a fool to have trusted her. I should have left her in the Capitol when I fled."

"Do you believe Thomas was her only target?" Elias asked. He still held the arrow in his hands, though the ice enveloping it had begun to melt.

"I don't know," Claire replied unsteadily. "I must…retrieve her letters. I'll find you once I have regained my composure." She turned to leave, and to my surprise, Rynn followed her, shooting me a knowing glance over her shoulder.

I stared at Leta's lifeless form, surrounded by a bloody patch of snow. She'd grown still, her eyes unfocused as they stared at the brilliant spring sky.

"As the duke, I ought to take a statement from Claire," Elias said solemnly, "but given the circumstances, it won't be necessary."

"You bore witness to the attempt on my life." There was a tremor in Thomas' voice. "The law dictates that would suffice as evidence."

"Yes. I'll have one of my men write up a report, though I think I'll give Lady Claire the benefit of a false name when I do so." Elias turned his gaze to meet mine, tearing it away from Leta's fallen form. "We are both fortunate you were here. Please extend my thanks to Rynn as well."

"I'll have someone help me take care of this." I gestured at Leta's body.

I was stunned by what had transpired and didn't fully comprehend the duke's final words. I'd known Claire could be vengeful and vicious, but I'd never believed her capable of taking a life.

"I expect to see you at my tent within the hour, Andrew," Thomas said, breaking through my reverie. "I want you present when Claire brings the letters she spoke of. And I believe we have another matter to discuss, as well. Elias, you should go. Your absence from the city will draw notice."

"I hope the next time we meet, it will be under better circumstances," Elias replied somberly as he turned to depart. "Holy hell, this is madness."

NINETEEN

It was dark by the time Claire arrived at Thomas' command tent. I stood opposite my brother at the table set up within, while Jonathan paced along one side of the canvas wall, agitated and on edge. Everett lingered near the tent's entrance, his expression dour.

The table had been cleared, though a stack of correspondence and various maps were piled haphazardly on one side. Several candles had been lit to illuminate the space, and a trio of braziers arranged throughout the tent glowed faintly, emitting enough heat to keep the interior comfortable. Despite the welcoming atmosphere, tension vibrated in the air.

Thomas and I had related the afternoon's events to both former dukes, then had been forced to explain the Oracle's message during the course of the conversation. Jonathan was hesitant to believe the threat to Thomas was over, and I was inclined to agree. Without knowing exactly what the Oracle had seen, I couldn't be certain if Leta's attack had been the focus of her message, or if she'd seen something else entirely.

While Jonathan seemed to accept the Oracle's words now that something had come of them, Everett remained skeptical. He was loath to trust the word of anyone he'd never met in person—particularly when it came from someone as contentious as the Oracle.

When Claire arrived, I noted she'd changed into a clean set of clothing and had regained her carefully-crafted composure. Rynn accompanied her at arm's length. I was stunned the two had remained together throughout the afternoon and that they'd appeared to have come to an understanding. Claire's typically venomous glances were markedly absent, and though Rynn's eyes revealed her uncertainty, she seemed less unnerved by Claire's presence than I'd come to expect. Once they entered, Rynn made her way to my side.

Claire placed several sheets of parchment on the table between us. "I discovered these amongst Leta's things while you were in the city. I believe this will illuminate the situation, and I hope it will bring clarity regarding my own actions."

Claire held her head high, her expression imperious. It was a look I'd grown to know well during our years together.

I frowned and averted my gaze. She'd often looked at me in the same manner—when we'd been arguing, when she'd found fault with my actions, when she grew suspicious of me for one reason or another... The expression drew on a wellspring of unpleasant memories that I'd long hoped were forgotten. Claire hadn't been focused on me this time, but it was difficult to look at her with Rynn standing at my side.

"Is something wrong, Andrew?" Claire's voice was steely.

I clenched my jaw. "No. I was simply thinking...of our shared past."

She studied me for a long moment, then her dark eyes softened. "I believe I understand."

Thomas pored over the messages Claire had provided, holding each as close to the candles as was possible without catching the sheets ablaze. He shook his head as he set down the last document, a troubled frown etching his features.

"All this time, Leta was working for Colin?" When Claire nodded, he grimaced. "He *ordered* her to accompany you when he learned you planned to flee. She was to report on your whereabouts, and mine if they were discovered... How did she know you'd seek my camp?"

"I was under the false assumption she could be trusted," Claire replied bitterly. "As I was preparing to leave the Capitol, we spoke of my plans. She insisted on accompanying me. After all, I had no experience with life beyond the royal court—or the tower-prison Colin had created for me. It's likely I would never have found you without her assistance. Leta had been in my employ since before the time of my initial engagement to Andrew. She came from a family of servants, but we were close in age. She was perhaps the closest thing I ever had to a true friend... Until the snide bitch betrayed me. I didn't know she was one of Colin's mistresses, nor was I aware of his promise to her. Not until today."

"Given what happened and her damned attachment to my daughter, I can't help but wonder if she used Carinna as a means to gather information," Jonathan spat the words and resumed pacing. "I hope this serves as a lesson to my wayward daughter that not all maidservants can be trusted, no matter how pretty they are."

"I believe it has been a lesson for many of us, my dear duke," Claire replied somberly. "I should have seen through her deception, but I didn't believe she'd side with Colin. She was in the next room when he threw my child from the tower window! How could any woman yearn for a life with such a monster?" While she spoke, her voice rose in pitch as she struggled to contain her anger and grief, but she shed no tears.

"Did she know you were with child when you left the Capitol?" I asked gently.

Claire managed a tremulous smile. "I suppose that's the one bright point in this mess. I didn't reveal it to her until we were well into the highlands. I was feeling ill one morning, and she became concerned. Or rather, she *appeared* to be concerned. I can't be certain now. I was forced to tell her then. She never had the means to send the news to Colin." She scowled at the floor. "If she had succeeded today, I have no doubt she would have informed Colin within hours. What the idiot girl didn't realize was he'd never make good on his promises. She was a commoner. She could never become queen."

"You forgot to mention Colin's word has never been any good to begin with," I said dryly. "Even as a child, he'd promise whatever was necessary to get what he wanted, consequences be damned. He never followed through."

Claire looked down at her hands, her expression carefully composed. "I wish I'd listened to you. There were countless times you cautioned me against working with him. I simply believed it was sibling rivalry and misplaced anger behind your words. I knew you never saw eye-to-eye, but the last two years have shown me the truth."

Claire would never outright apologize for her past animosity, nor would she apologize for destroying our marriage, such as it had been.

Her words now were as close to an apology as I was likely to receive. I nodded once in acknowledgment.

"You'll be safe enough here, Lady Claire," Jonathan stated after a moment.

She turned to face him, her dark eyes narrowed in suspicion. "By 'here' do you refer to this camp, or do you refer to Dresdin's Forge? I've no intention of remaining behind in the city, Duke. I'll be safer within the camp."

"My Lady, please see reason," Everett interjected. "A military camp is no place for a woman expecting a child!"

"I've learned a good deal about bandaging wounds and splinting broken bones since Colin began speaking with his fists," Claire snapped. "Once I was locked in the tower, I was left to tend my own injuries as best I could. I can assist the surgeons, and such work might give me a sense of purpose. I *will not* remain behind."

Thomas looked first to Jonathan, then to Everett, his expression thoughtful. He stroked his beard for a moment, then shifted his gaze to Claire. "You may make your own decision, Lady Claire. The dukes make a fair point, however. Your child's safety can't be guaranteed if you choose to remain with the army."

Claire nodded stiffly. "Thank you for giving me a choice in the matter. I fear if I stay within *any* city, Colin will learn of my location. He'll come for me, and if I survive his punishment for leaving the Capitol, I'll wish it were otherwise. I can't return, not so long as he remains king." Her next words were a somber whisper. "Perhaps, not even after he's gone."

"Then you may stay," Thomas replied, "but I can't spare fighting men to act as guards. You'll be somewhat on your own."

Claire narrowed her eyes, and I knew from her sudden change of expression she was about to lash out at Thomas. I held up one hand, placating her.

"I believe you'll be safer here than in the city, where one of Colin's sympathizers might recognize you," I said, hoping to diffuse the situation before it became heated. "I'll do what I can to make certain you're protected."

She studied me for a long moment, her expression unreadable. "It's a continuing source of wonder that you still offer your help,

Andrew. I am unworthy of such charity, given our past, but I thank you." Her eyes shifted to Rynn. "You're more fortunate than you know."

Rynn made no reply, though her hand sought mine and gave it a squeeze.

Claire closed her eyes for a moment, seeming to gather her strength. "I'll leave you now. You may keep Leta's letters from Colin if you wish. I hope never to see them again."

"You seem to have come to an understanding with Claire," I said to Rynn as we walked to the tent we shared. "I'm not certain what to make of that."

It was fully dark as we threaded our way through the campsite, though several cookfires provided a dim illumination to our path.

"She needed to talk with someone, though she would never have admitted it," Rynn replied with a shrug. "I believed I could help, but I wasn't certain it would do any good at first. She's a difficult woman."

I snorted derisively. "That's a very kind description of my former wife."

"Oh, Andrew, after all she's been through, I think you ought to give her some leniency." She paused to study me, a smirk playing on her lips. "She told me some things about you."

I groaned as my face flushed and was grateful for the darkness. I hoped Rynn could not see my reaction.

"What did she tell you?" I asked guardedly, and immediately regretted voicing the question.

She laughed softly. "There was little I haven't already learned myself, and nothing you need to worry over." She took my hand in hers. "But…there was something she mentioned that I'd like to learn more of."

I was silent for a time, uncertain what Rynn had learned from Claire. Finally, I said, "What is it?"

"Claire said you often wouldn't sleep well for weeks after returning from campaigns. That you'd relive the battles in your dreams." She paused for a moment, contemplative. "I know you've been a soldier for most of your life. Do you regret that decision?"

No one had ever asked me that before, and I had never taken the time to truly assess my thoughts regarding my life's path. It was what had been expected of me, and I hadn't questioned it. I'd been eight years old when Carlton Marsden informed me that I was to begin training as a soldier and would one day become part of the castle's garrison.

I recalled I'd been excited by the prospect, but I'd been a child and didn't understand what would be asked of me later. I didn't realize the toll my path would exact; the loss of friends and loved ones, the brutality of battle, the violence, the sheer struggle to survive. I learned how to adapt and overcome, but I'd never been given a choice in the matter.

"Andrew?" Rynn asked uncertainly.

I chuckled. "I'm fine, Rynn, I'm just…thinking. To answer your question, that path was decided for me. But even so, I don't regret that it was made. It led me to where I am now. If things had been different, I wouldn't have been able to save Alexander from Colin. I wouldn't be an asset to Tom, and I would never have met you."

"Perhaps," she replied slowly. "No matter what path your life may have taken, you'd still be a skin-changer. You would have protected Alexander regardless of your military training. You would have always been an asset to Tom, no matter your profession. He's fascinated by the dragon-kind, and we both know he'd never have passed up an opportunity to learn more about you. I believe you'd still be right here, in this moment."

"I'm not so certain," I replied. "If the former king had pushed me toward another occupation, perhaps it would not have sparked my rivalry with Colin. He's no warrior, and because of that, he's always viewed me as a threat. He can't match me in strength or size, and he never showed any inclination toward swordplay."

I sighed, recalling a conversation I'd had with Vera long ago. Though I still mourned her passing, the pain I once felt was now less poignant, more subdued. Rynn had been instrumental in my healing, even after I'd tried time and again to push her away. Her persistence was admirable—and wonderful.

"Vera once told me Colin acted as he did because he knew he was outmatched physically," I said. "What Colin failed to understand is that

I wasn't trying to compete with him, nor would I have ever harmed him intentionally. He's my brother, just as Alex and Tom are."

"You mean *before* he tried to have Alex executed?" she asked pointedly.

I nodded. "He went too far. Alex is his brother, and his Mark was harmless at the time. He wasn't a threat. Nor was Vera, or even Tom. I wonder if he can be redeemed, even after the tales we've heard. He can't possibly be responsible for so many horrors… And yet, I know in my heart he is."

Rynn stepped in front of me and turned, blocking my path. "I understand. I have two brothers myself, though neither can be compared to Colin. If you ever need to talk, all you need do is ask."

I smiled, thankful she'd walked into my life. "I know. There are many times I realize I should open up to someone, but I've always had difficulty expressing my feelings. It doesn't come naturally, and I don't like to burden others with my troubles, perceived or otherwise."

She laughed softly. "You'll never be a burden. Speak what's on your mind any time you wish."

"Thank you." I looked down for a moment, then said, "I suppose what I've been trying to sort out is what I'll do when we finally face Colin. He's done so much damned harm. I know he must be brought to justice, but I don't know what *I* will do when that time comes. A part of me wants to tear him limb from limb, but another part reminds me he's my brother, he's family… I'm not certain I'd act as Claire did toward Leta. The two may not have been family in the truest sense, but I believe Leta was the closest thing Claire had to a sister."

"Blood ties are the hardest to ignore," she replied, reaching up to touch the side of my face. "No matter what happens when you meet, I know you'll make the right decision. You strive to follow the right path, and this situation will be no different."

"I hope you're right." I raked a hand through my hair. "I learned much about myself during Alexander's trials, and one important item was my unexpected longevity. I don't want to commit an act that I'll regret for centuries, no matter how justified it may seem at the time."

"I stand by my previous statement," she said softly, withdrawing her hand. "I know you'll do the right thing. Your words only serve to reinforce my belief." She looked around briefly, seemingly startled. "It has grown very dark, hasn't it?"

I chuckled. "It has, and we've strayed from the nearest campfires. Don't worry. I can see well enough to lead us to our tent."

Rynn was silent for a time as we walked. Though it wasn't late, there were few others outside and the camp was quiet.

"She was right, Andrew."

I glanced toward her, puzzled by her statement. When she didn't immediately explain, I was forced to voice my question. "Who was right about what, Rynn?"

She smiled faintly. "Claire was right when she said I was fortunate. I've been in high spirits, despite everything that's happened around us." She paused to glance at me, mischief glinting in her eyes. "It's your fault, you know."

I laughed. "I'll gladly take the blame. I've been happy too. It's not something I believed I'd ever feel again."

"I know you miss her, Andrew. I simply hope I can be but a shadow of what she was to you. That would be enough, so long as you're content."

"I am, Rynn."

And I was. Though she was far different than Vera, I cared for her just as deeply.

TWENTY

It was not quite dawn when I awoke the next morning. There were a dozen items demanding my attention that I'd postponed due to Leta's attempt on Thomas' life, and I couldn't linger at Rynn's side any longer. We'd be departing Dresdin's Forge the next day, and Thomas expected that I'd be available to assist him with preparations for the move.

I had dressed and seated myself near the tent's entrance to pull on my boots when Rynn stirred within our blankets. She sat up slowly, blinking the sleep from her eyes, then sighed as she noticed I was preparing to leave.

"Ah, I suppose we both have many things to accomplish today," she said, her tone filled with both longing and disappointment. "Why didn't you wake me?"

I smiled. "You needed the sleep, and it's still early. I know you would have found me after you awakened."

She rolled her eyes as she stood and kicked the blankets away. "I would have, but that wasn't my point."

I studied her as she moved about the tent locating her clothing in the pre-dawn light, unable to tear my gaze from her nude form. Seeing her like this made my leaving all the more difficult.

Noting my heated looks, she peered at me sharply. "What is it?"

"You're beautiful," I blurted, feeling my face flush with the admission. I had long thought it but had never said the words aloud.

She laughed, her blue eyes dancing with mirth. "And it seems I have distracted you yet again."

She pulled on her clothing, smiling all the while. I remained seated at the entrance to our tent, captivated by her every move, enthralled by the vibrant soul who had inexplicably captured my heart. This unabashed attraction was a new experience, one that I could not fully explain even to myself. Neither Claire nor Vera had mustered such power over me that I'd become loath to depart, if only for a few hours.

Though she seemed unaware of the effect she had on me, Rynn now commanded my attention, my desire, my future—and I didn't want to leave her side. Not today, nor any other.

"Knowing Tom, he's been expecting you for some time," she stated as she pulled on her boots. "You shouldn't keep him waiting, not after what happened yesterday."

I nodded, steering my thoughts back to the more important matters at hand. But *damn it,* I was helpless in her presence sometimes.

"You're right, and I shouldn't." I rose reluctantly and went to retrieve my sword belt where it rested against the canvas nearby. "Do you believe Leta was the assassin the Oracle referred to?"

Rynn shrugged. "Perhaps, but I don't think we should relax our guard. There may be others." She studied me, hands on hips, while I donned the belt. "You aren't wearing your armor today?"

I shook my head. "I can go one day without. We'll be packing and preparing to leave, and it's easier to maneuver when I'm not encased in dragon scale."

She smirked as we ducked outside. "That's only true while you're in *this* form."

I snorted. "Yes."

We walked in silence for a time, threading our way through the still-sleeping camp. A few sentries strolled along the perimeter, though there was little movement elsewhere until we neared the center. Closer to the command tent, a number of guardsmen drilled in the open space nearby. I spied the portly figure of Jonathan Horace gesticulating as he spoke with a pair of soldiers outside Thomas' tent, while my brother stood to one side. A roaring campfire blazed not far from the tent, and a number of people busied themselves around it, preparing breakfast.

Rynn breathed in deeply, then broke into a broad grin. "Bacon! I didn't realize how much I'd missed that until now. Do you think they'd let me have some? I know they're cooking for Thomas and his guard, but *you* are part of the guard, and *I'm* with *you*…"

I was unable to contain my laughter. "I'm sure they'll spare some for you."

"My family has fished Lake Dwymm for generations," she said after a moment. "I never once believed I'd grow tired of eating fish. It was our livelihood. But after nothing *but* fish all winter, I've changed my mind."

As we drew nearer, Thomas motioned for me to join him. I left Rynn at the cookfire and strode to where Thomas stood near his tent.

"I received word from Elias," Thomas stated. He fidgeted, a sign of his anxiety. "He has made arrangements to take in those who can't follow us to war. I—"

"Tom," I said evenly, cutting him off, "slow down. Take a deep breath."

He heaved a sigh and gazed skyward, scowling in frustration. "How can I, Andrew? There are so many lives depending on my actions, and I don't know what to do!"

"We have a plan," I reminded him. "And we know our enemy. I've always believed the most important part of any strategy is understanding your opponent, and in this case, we know him far too well."

"You've also said time and again that even the best-laid plans tend to disintegrate during the heat of battle," he shot back, his tone laden with despair. "What if we're wrong in pursuing this path?"

I studied him carefully for a moment, noting the fear in his eyes, the lines of worry that creased his forehead. "With all that we've learned, would you rather Colin remained on the throne?"

"No! He must be stopped." Thomas looked down, deflated. "I never realized this would be so damned *hard*. Did you truly understand what you asked of me when you and Alex hatched this plan?"

I looked away, guilt writhing like a fetid worm in my core. Alexander and I had assumed much when we'd nominated Thomas as Colin's logical successor. We'd never given our youngest brother an opportunity to choose his own path—we'd acted according to what we believed to be right. I owed Thomas an apology, though I wasn't certain he'd accept it. It was too late, and I'd failed to foresee the repercussions of our decision until now.

"Tom, I'm sorry." He deserved more from me, but I found it difficult to articulate what I needed to say.

"You did what had to be done." Thomas' tone was somber. "I understand that, and I wasn't laying the blame on you. But I'm at a loss when it comes to leadership. They're depending on me to see them through to victory, but I feel like a fraud. The plans we've made come not from me, but from Jon, my uncle, you…"

I cracked a smile. "Tom, think of your father. He was no warrior, but…" I trailed off and studied him for a moment, then said, "We never gave you the opportunity to turn us down, did we, brother? For that, I am truly sorry."

"Someone must take the throne once this is over," Thomas replied, quiet determination in his words. He clasped his hands to still them and drew a breath, his spine straightening. "The Marsdens have ruled Novania for over six hundred years. If Colin is unfit for the throne, then it must fall to me. As you've often reminded me, Alex can't do so, and you… You are a Caein." He shook his head. "If only Father's conscience hadn't intervened, he could have named you as his heir."

"Alex expressed that same sentiment to me once," I replied. "Even if he had named me, I wouldn't have lasted long. It would have become apparent after a few years that I'm different. As you know, I don't age."

Thomas nodded thoughtfully. "There were some rumors, even before father spoke to the council regarding his successor. A number of courtiers remarked that you appeared younger than Colin, or even Alex at times. I remember Alex once told a woman you kept yourself clean-shaven so you didn't appear as old as you truly were."

I grunted. "Leave it to Alex to come up with a story when he doesn't know even a sliver of the truth. It was Lydia who told him that I don't shave, by the way. I'm not certain he would have figured it out on his own."

At that, Thomas broke into a laugh. "I hope we'll see Alex again soon. I never thought I'd say this, but I sorely miss him."

I nodded in agreement. "As do I."

A messenger strode toward us, her breath steaming in the cool morning air. She paused a respectable distance away and knelt in deference to Thomas.

He clasped his hands and drew a breath. "What news do you bring?"

"A message from Duke Winston, my lord." She withdrew a folded sheet of parchment bearing the duke's seal from within a pocket and offered it to Thomas.

He took it from her but did not immediately open it. "Thank you. You are dismissed."

He waited until she'd moved toward the cookfire before he broke the wax seal and began to read. I watched as a slow smile spread across his face.

"Elias has sent our message to Colin. He says he provided a rough estimate of our numbers and mentioned a black dragon specifically." Thomas looked up with a chuckle. "He did not mention the Corodan. He claims he rather likes the notion of that unwelcome surprise when Colin's forces arrive."

I laughed. "Holy hell, our mother wasn't lying when she said Alex reminded her of the duke."

"No, she wasn't. Elias goes on to wish us luck and promises again that he'll provide for the refugees as well as he can." He paused as a troubled frown creased his features. "I hope the keep Jon has chosen as our staging point will hold up as well as he claims. Colin will undoubtedly send a significant portion of his army to our location once he receives the news."

"He will, and we're counting on that response—as is Alexander." I crossed my arms. "Jon's more familiar with his lands than most noblemen are, and I trust his judgment. The keep is ideal. It's located at the end of a wide valley and is accessible only from one side. It's defensible. And while he mentioned some of the walls may require repairs, we'll have some time before Colin's arrival to bolster them. Don't worry, brother. I believe in our plan."

"Then I will too." He crumpled the message in his fist and strode toward the cookfire, where he tossed it promptly into the flames.

When I glanced at him questioningly, he shrugged. "I promised Elias I'd leave nothing behind to implicate him in our schemes. Like you, I strive to keep my word."

The next day, we began our march toward the keep. It was slow-going given the size of our army, and I anticipated we'd manage only a few miles each day. It would take at least five days to reach the keep, provided we encountered no resistance along the way, and the route Jonathan had outlined was indirect. It would lead us through farmland, but would not take us near any cities or sizeable towns. We hoped to avoid any skirmishes until we were in place and had prepared our defenses.

With so much of the king's army staged near the Mage's Gate, I believed Colin would be forced to divert a portion of that force in order to muster soldiers enough to face Thomas' army. Unless he'd recruited more soldiers since I'd fled the Capitol, he wouldn't have the manpower at his disposal to oppose us in any other manner. It was a gamble, but given Colin's behavior since he'd ascended the throne, I was confident he'd take the bait without question. He'd been itching to take my head, after all.

During our fourth afternoon of travel, Hulda returned in a rush, her expression frantic. Rynn and I were walking near Thomas and the two dukes at the center of our long column when she arrived. Jonathan called a halt to the march while we spoke with the harried scout.

She knelt before Thomas swiftly. "My lord, I have news. Callen sent me back while he continues the watch. We don't know if who we saw is friend or foe."

Thomas nodded, his expression pensive. "Go on."

"There's a band of men, soldiers by the look of them, about a half mile ahead," she continued. "There were ten, by our count. They bear the colors and coat of Duke Everly."

Jonathan swore in frustration, and I sighed. Duke Everly was a contentious man, though military-minded and a veteran of many campaigns. If he had come to intercept us on Colin's behalf, it was likely the ten soldiers Hulda spied from afar were but a fraction of his force.

Everett frowned but maintained an air of calm. When he spoke, his tone was one of wary curiosity. "What is Jonas doing so far east? His lands lay west of Duke Winston's."

"Indeed," Jonathan groused. "Why *is* Jonas Everly on *my family's* ancestral land?"

"Duke Crossley—Uncle," Thomas cut in, "I require a delegation of men. We need to send word of our presence to Duke Everly and assess his intent. I will speak with him directly."

I watched my youngest brother with interest. His mind was working furiously, and his blue eyes were sharp and calculating. I had no doubt Thomas was forming a plan.

"My lord, I advise against this," Jonathan stated gruffly. "Jonas Everly is no friend to me, nor to your brother."

"Nevertheless," Thomas replied evenly, "I must speak with him. He has traveled far from his home, and I want to know why." Thomas turned to peer at those around him, steel in his gaze. "Dukes Horace and Crossley, you will remain here. If my plan doesn't work, you'll know how to best lead our people." Ignoring their spluttered protests, he turned to me. "Andrew, I want you at my side. We'll take a dozen soldiers with us, and we *will* learn why he has strayed so far from his lands."

When I nodded, Rynn made a noise of frustration. "I'm coming with you," she stated fiercely. "I'll not let the two of you get yourselves captured if this proves a mistake."

"Rynn—" I began, but was stopped with a gesture from Thomas.

"You may come as a part of the guard," he said. "Your abilities may prove useful."

Several minutes later, Thomas strode past the ranks of our army, his chosen guard surrounding him. I didn't know what his plan was beyond speaking with Everly, but I hoped he'd share it with us before we drew too near the man's location.

"Why does this Duke Everly dislike you and Jon?" Rynn asked after we'd passed the head of the column.

"Jonas is a difficult man," I replied with a scowl. "He's experienced in battle. Like me, he spent most of his life fighting the Corodan, but he and I were never on friendly terms. Initially, he believed I was an upstart who knew nothing, even after the king named me commander.

He believed I was given the post since I was the king's son. Even after I'd been commander for several years—and largely successful, I might add—he was…prickly, for lack of a better word."

"And what of Jon?" she asked.

"They have some history between them that even I don't know the details of," I replied. "They have never liked one another, but they are capable of working together when necessity dictates. Even in the best of times, things between them are tense."

"What is Tom planning?"

I shrugged. "I wish I knew. I hope he knows what he's doing."

Ahead of us, Thomas chuckled. "While Duke Everly has had his disagreements with you, I've always found him to be a reasonable man. He would not be so far from home without good cause, and if there are only ten men in total, they are too few to oppose us. I don't believe they'll be a threat, particularly once they learn our true numbers."

"Hmm." I hoped Thomas wasn't placing himself at risk simply because he was too trusting. Everly may have been an ally once, but nothing was certain any longer.

"My lord," one of the soldiers ahead called, "I can see them."

We crested a hill. A short distance ahead, Everly's soldiers gathered near a copse of trees, resting in the shade. They were clad in the colors of the duke's house; blue and white livery adorned with the stag motif that had long been the Everly family's insignia. I spied the tall, stern figure of the duke amongst them, but he made no move toward aggression. He stood with his arms crossed, watching our progress with steely eyes, silent and impassive as stone.

I motioned for the soldiers accompanying Thomas to fan out and stand ready as we approached the duke's location. Though Jonas had not rallied his soldiers for an attack, I didn't trust his apparent amicability to last.

"Duke Everly," Thomas said by way of greeting. "We didn't expect to meet you during our journey."

The duke knelt swiftly before Thomas and bowed his head. I was stunned at his display of deference toward my brother, but it wasn't enough to shake my skepticism.

"My lord Marsden," he said, "I'm not seeking a fight. I'd heard rumors you were heading this way, and I'd hoped to find you. I've come to offer my services."

I lifted my eyebrows, stunned. I'd rarely witnessed the duke act so deferential toward anyone. What had transpired between Jonas Everly and Colin to cause such a drastic shift in his allegiance? He'd always been loyal to the crown.

Rynn gripped my elbow and leaned toward me to whisper, "Andrew, he bears the Mark."

I spun to face her, eyes wide. Her expression was grave, and I understood in an instant why Jonas sought Thomas over Colin. I glanced at Thomas, who nodded once. He'd heard Rynn's hushed statement.

Had the duke's past animosity toward me been borne of fear? He'd never been privy to my own secret—no one but Alexander and Vera had been prior to that fateful day at the tourney field. If he'd known the truth about my heritage during our years of soldiering, would he have been less hostile?

"I believe we know why you're here," Thomas said after a moment's pause. "We would welcome your aid, and you offered it freely without knowing my purpose. I hope you understand my hesitation. Please stand."

Jonas nodded and rose to his feet, casting an uncertain glance in my direction. "May we speak privately for a moment, my lord?" he asked, flicking another glance toward me. "If I'm not mistaken, that's your brother as well. I'd like to speak with him too."

I smirked and removed my helm, following the duke and Thomas to an area just beyond earshot of the others.

"I was present at the tourney field last year," Jonas said without preamble. "I saw what the king planned to do to your brother. I knew he'd eventually send his men north to conduct further inspections, and it would only be a matter of time." He sighed, then turned to look at me, his eyes keen. "I also saw what you did to save Alexander. I know we've never been on good terms, but know that it was not because I disliked you. It was because I feared you—you were in the employ of the king, and I perceived you as a threat."

I nodded. "Rynn—the woman with us—told us you bear the Mark. You have nothing to fear from us, Jonas."

He scowled. "How could she possibly know?"

"She's a trained mage," Thomas replied. "She can sense the power in others—and she sensed yours."

He crossed his arms, clearly uncomfortable with the situation, and glanced around to ensure no one had strayed too close. He shifted his feet, drew a breath, then began to speak.

"The king's men came to the Northern Marches in autumn. They traveled to each city, each town, to conduct the Mark inspections. When his men arrived in Summerdale and came to my estate, I refused them entry. My men are loyal to me, and they followed my command without question. We sealed the estate, then escaped through the ancient tunnels that run beneath the walls. We fled with what little we could carry, and I've been running ever since. But my men… They don't know my secret, though I've no doubt some suspect it."

"How many fled with you?" Thomas asked. "Are there more than those here?"

Jonas nodded. "There are another two dozen at the valley keep. We discovered the place by accident, but it was fortunate we did. It provided shelter during the winter and is defensible enough. One of my men was scouting two days ago and heard rumors that you were traveling with a large contingent of soldiers. I wanted to be certain it was you and not one of the others who still blindly follow the damned, bloody tyrant who dares call himself king." His last words were spoken with such vehemence that I lifted my eyebrows in surprise.

To his credit, Thomas betrayed nothing of his thoughts, his expression carefully neutral. Everett Crossley would have been proud to see his work with Thomas during the past months was coming to fruition. Thomas was no longer the fidgety, uncertain youth he'd once been—so long as he remembered to maintain his composure.

"We are planning to move to the valley keep, as you call it," Thomas replied evenly. "I must warn you that I've made arrangements for Colin to learn of our location. We will provoke him into a fight."

Jonas studied Thomas for a moment, then flicked another wary glance in my direction. "Does he know your brother accompanies you?"

I chuckled in response, while Thomas said, "Yes."

"Good. Then we know he'll come." Jonas smiled grimly. "I've been waiting for an opportunity to bloody my damned blade and take the fight to him."

Thomas cast a glance toward me, and I shrugged. "I told you Colin would come."

"In the weeks following your…spectacle, the king was incensed. He hired assassins to follow you and offered a hefty sum to anyone who returned to the Capitol bearing your head." Jonas' scowl deepened. "I don't know how many took up the quest, Andrew. I was preparing my own escape and paid little attention to the missives. If the king was willing to execute his brother for bearing the Mark, he would not hesitate with a duke, no matter how loyal I may have once been."

"Colin is a menace who must be stopped," Thomas replied heatedly. "He has revoked the titles and lands of others whose only crime was helping me, or who were allies of my brothers. No doubt he's done the same to you."

Jonas' laugh was bitter. "I'm certain of it. I defied his orders and fled. Based on the reports I've heard from the Capitol, one does not do that and keep his head for long." He studied me carefully for a moment, then said, "I should like to speak with the woman who accompanies you, if time allows. I… I have questions."

I nodded. This was the most I'd spoken with Jonas Everly about any one topic without our words becoming heated and hostile.

"I'm certain she'll oblige," I replied. "I can speak to her if you'd like."

"I'd be grateful." He extended one hand toward me, and I shook it. "I've always been wary of those in power, and you worked for the king. If I'd known you were a skin-changer, perhaps our relationship would have been grounded in friendship rather than animosity. But you must understand, I was simply protecting myself."

"I know. Perhaps we can leave the past where it is and start anew."

Relief washed across his weathered features. "That's more than I could have hoped for. I'm not certain I deserve this chance, but since we'll be working and fighting alongside one another again, I'll take it."

TWENTY-ONE

Jonathan Horace remained wary of Duke Everly's intentions throughout our march to the keep, though Thomas had assured him the duke truly was an ally. We agreed to keep Jonas' Mark a secret; he could tell the others if he saw fit, but it was not our place to do so.

The keep was nestled at the far end of a wide, grassy valley, surrounded on three sides by sheer cliffs. A stream cut through the valley some distance from the keep's walls, but near enough that we could draw water as needed. Its outer walls were crumbled in places, but would still provide a measure of defense—and we believed they could be repaired and fortified further before Colin's army arrived. The keep itself was mostly intact, though some of the smaller outbuildings had fallen into disrepair. The building that had once been a granary lacked a roof, and the forge had but two walls that remained standing. Many of the windows were broken, though Jonas' garrison had boarded many of them up to conserve what little warmth could be generated within.

We'd begin work reinforcing the walls the next day, while Rizzt-tok's people agreed to enhance our defenses by digging trenches across the valley beyond. The Corodan were better suited to digging the earth and had often used pitfalls in their many battles against Novania. They would employ the same tactics in the battle to come—and I doubted Colin would be prepared for them. The Northern Marches had been the locus of Novania's previous battles, and with two of its three dukes amongst our ranks, it was unlikely Colin's latest commander would be familiar with the Corodans' methods.

I fervently hoped that was the case—much of our strategy hinged on the commander's inexperience with our insectile allies. And if Elias Winston was as good as his word, Colin's forces wouldn't be expecting them. The trenches would prove a nasty surprise.

Jonathan assigned soldiers to watch duty as we began to settle in, then dispatched three pairs of scouts to act as lookouts at various points surrounding the valley. If Colin's army approached, we'd be warned well before they were within sight of the keep.

I remained with Thomas, Rynn, and the three former dukes as our forces began their assigned tasks. Thomas insisted that I stay near; he wasn't convinced Leta's attack would be the last attempt on his life.

While Thomas discussed strategy with the others, Rynn and I stood off to one side. We were near enough to answer questions and give advice when asked, but far enough to converse quietly without interrupting the others.

It was growing late by the time Thomas decided to turn in for the night. He'd been given a room that had once belonged to the lord of the keep. The room was unfurnished, but it would be warmer and more comfortable than the lodgings he'd taken in the caves. Both Jonathan and Everett departed when Thomas did, but Jonas lingered. He'd been waiting for an opportunity to speak with Rynn, and I was curious to hear what he planned to ask her.

I formally introduced the two, and when Jonas moved to shake her hand, Rynn drew away instinctively.

"I'm sorry," she said. "It's not safe for me to touch you. The magic I possess physically altered my body when I became a mage."

I studied him carefully, gauging his reaction. To his credit, he nodded thoughtfully and dropped his hand.

"Andrew said you wanted to speak with me," Rynn said after a moment of awkward silence. "You may ask me anything, though I don't claim to know everything there is of magic."

"Thomas said you're a mage. Not just Marked, but a true mage."

Rynn smiled. "Yes. I've been through the trials and am in control of my abilities, as much as I can be."

"You're from the Southlands, then?" When she nodded, he said, "There were many times during my life that I considered undertaking the journey to the Mage's Gate, but Novania is all I've known. And now I'm old enough to believe the journey is beyond my reach."

"I will not lie to you," she replied evenly. "The trials are dangerous. It's not unheard of for someone your age to undertake them, but it tends to be more difficult... Younger magi are often more resilient."

Jonas turned toward me, his eyes piercing. "I've been wondering where Alexander is in all of this. It's obvious he's not with you. Is he in these trials you speak of? I've long assumed you took him away from the kingdom."

"Alex survived the journey and the trials. He's gathering his own army in the south," I replied. "We're hoping to draw some of the men Colin sent to the Mage's Gate here, to give Alex the opening he needs to take the offensive from his position."

Jonas' gaze shifted between mine and Rynn's for a few moments as he contemplated the news. "Is your brother's ability akin to what she's capable of?" He asked, gesturing toward Rynn.

Rynn laughed with a shake of her head. "Alexander's power is far different than my own. He is difficult to read since it's largely internalized. He's what we refer to as a mage-warrior. His magic enhances his physical strength and his battle prowess, if you will."

"And he has been itching to find out exactly what he's capable of," I added dryly. "I just hope he doesn't do something reckless and get himself killed in the process. I've always been there to protect him in the past, but this time, he's on his own."

We had not received word from Alexander in over a week, and I was becoming concerned. I'd managed to keep my misgivings to myself, though I'd spoken to Rynn about them. When last we'd heard from him, Alexander was readying his people to pass through the Mage's Gate and into Novania, but he didn't plan to strike without informing us of his plans. With the bulk of Colin's army stationed just a stone's throw from the gate, any number of possibilities could account for his delay. The longer we went without hearing from him, the more worry gnawed through my gut.

"Yes, I recall several times when you went out of your way to save your brother," Jonas mused. "I admit that I've always been impressed by your selflessness and bravery. I'd chalked it up to a desire to protect your kin, but it seems there has always been more to your actions than what is immediately apparent."

"You mean that I'm a skin-changer." I braced myself for further questions, certain he had many, just as everyone I met seemed to.

He nodded, but didn't press me for further details. "My grandfather used to trade in secret with the dragons of the highlands," he said. "It wasn't a fact that our family shared with anyone outside the duchy, for obvious reasons. If the king had learned of my grandfather's actions, he would have been executed for treason, and my family would have fallen into disgrace." He shrugged. "It seems he only delayed the inevitable. My defiance of the king's inspections may not prove that I'm Marked, but it will certainly lead the kingdom to believe that I'm at the very least a sympathizer. My fate would be the same if I'm caught."

"How is it you avoided Colin's men for so long?" I asked. "You overwintered here without carrying supplies, though it seems you've managed to acquire all that you needed and more."

Jonas' men were well supplied. Crates of food, casks of wine and ale, barrels of oil, blankets, and clothing were in abundance within the keep. They had arms and armor that did not bear the duke's colors or insignia—we'd learned during our journey to the keep that he'd insisted they don their Summerdale gear specifically for the meeting with Thomas. He'd risked much by doing so, gambling his very life on the rumor that Thomas was sympathetic to those who opposed the king.

Jonas looked down, a troubled frown creasing his weathered features. "If you've heard there was an increase in bandit activity, that was largely the work of my people. I'm not proud of what we did—we were forced to stoop to the level of common criminals in order to survive the winter, but it became necessary. When we fled Summerdale, there was no going back. My people don't know my reasons for leaving, nor why I've chosen to defy the king, and I would like to keep it that way." He paused to study us in turn. "I made it a point to leave the common people be. They don't deserve to be caught in the crossfire of my grievance with your brother. We only attacked merchants bearing the king's banners and took what we required from their wagons. Common merchants had nothing to fear from us."

"You speak as though it was only you and your soldiers who fled," Rynn said slowly. "Do you not have a family?"

I smiled at her question. She didn't know Jonas Everly as the rest of us did, though learning he was Marked explained many of his life's choices. He'd never married and had named his sister's son his successor. He was the last of the Everly line.

The duke shook his head. "No, I have no family. I've lived alone many years, fearing my secret would be uncovered should I become involved with anyone." He looked up at me then, his gray eyes probing. "Your brother was the same. I've heard he balked each time your father—*his* father—brought up the prospect of marriage."

I nodded. "Alex planned to remain a bachelor as long as he stayed in the kingdom. He's married now, you know."

He chuckled. "A woman from the south, I presume? Good for him."

"She's another mage," I replied. "A healer. Perhaps if our plans go as we hope, you'll meet her one day."

"She travels with him, then?"

"Her skills will be invaluable when things become bloody," Rynn said. "And I doubt Alex could say anything to prevent her from marching at his side."

Jonas studied her for a moment, then said, "Much like you, with Andrew." When I lifted my eyebrows, he chuckled. "It's plain to anyone watching that the two of you are together. If you're half as capable as you seem, Lady Rynn, you'll be an asset to the army."

Rynn flashed a grin. "I'll consider that a compliment. Thank you."

I paced the ramparts the next morning, a short distance away from Thomas, who was speaking privately with the three former dukes and Rizzt-tok. The quartet were acting as his primary advisors, and each held a different opinion on how best to prepare the keep's defenses.

I was restless, itching for the battle we knew was on the horizon. Rynn was somewhere below, amongst the ranks of soldiers setting palisades and repairing the keep's stonework. Alone, I was left ample time with my thoughts. Thomas had insisted I remain nearby, and I'd be there for him in whatever capacity he required.

Even from a distance, it was clear Jonathan and Jonas were unable to shake the decades-long animosity they held for one another. I was glad I'd taken the time to speak with Jonas the previous night. Now that we had a better understanding of one another, I felt our past tensions would not resurface. Jonas Everly had always been a valuable tactician in our campaigns against the Corodan, and his expertise in this matter was welcome. I'd shared my thoughts with Thomas before we arrived on the ramparts, and he agreed to include Jonas in any discussion regarding the looming conflict.

My gaze wandered to the activities unfolding below. Several groups of soldiers worked to clear rubble from the areas deemed essential for our defenders, a few hammered the larger blocks into more manageable pieces, while others sharpened stakes or repaired crumbling stairs. The Corodan were digging a trench that spanned the width of the valley, just within archery range of the outer walls. Rizzt-tok planned to place sharpened stakes into its depths, then cover the trench to appear invisible to our attackers—it would prove lethal for those who stumbled into it.

If time permitted, a second trench would be constructed closer to the walls. The Corodan were efficient, and I was grateful to have secured the alliance with them.

Thomas called to me after a time, and I turned away from the view. The others were still with him, but it seemed he required my input as well. I'd expected it, but was surprised it had taken him this long to ask.

As I strode toward the group, Thomas thrust a sheet of parchment into my hands.

"It's from Alex," he said, relief evident in his grin.

"It's past time we heard from him," I replied, thrilled that we'd finally received word. It had been too long since we'd last heard from our brother, and I'd begun to fear the worst.

I took the sheet and began to read.

Tom,

I've some good news for you. It seems our plan is working!

There has been movement within Colin's troops, though I don't yet know how many of them are planning to depart. We'll continue to monitor their activities and inform you when we have a true idea of the numbers marching toward your location. Once their departure is complete, I will wait two days before launching my strike against those who remain at the Mage's Gate.

My people are ready and eager to begin this fight. I've no doubt Andrew has been worrying over the delay since my last message to you, but tell him all is well. Bryson was ill and could not accommodate sending messages for a time. Lydia has seen to him, and he is recovered now.

Take care, Tom. And tell Andrew not to do anything reckless. We'll need him more than ever now that things are finally coming to a head.

–Alex

I snorted as I read the last lines of Alexander's message. It was usually *me* who cautioned Alexander against recklessness; I was unused to warnings coming from him regarding my own tendencies. I shook my head and handed the message back to Thomas, who immediately began to pen his reply.

"He's not wrong," Jonathan said as he studied my reaction with an amused smirk. "We'll need you more than ever. The presence of a single dragon could change the outcome of a battle."

"Like it or not, you're without a doubt one of our greatest weapons," Jonas remarked, his tone grave. "Alexander is right to urge caution."

I crossed my arms and frowned as my temper rapidly shifted toward surliness.

"Andrew, we *do* need you," Thomas said, pausing in his writing to peer at me with an earnestness that shot a bolt of guilt through my core. My irritation had been misplaced.

I sighed and raked a hand through my hair. "Fine, you've made your point. I'll stay at Tom's side until the battle."

Everett shook his head sternly. "You will not deploy with the other soldiers. We've devised a plan—and you are key to its success."

I stared evenly at the duke, silently willing him to elaborate. This was not the news I'd expected, and I hoped it was clear to everyone present that I was disappointed—and furious—they'd made the decision without seeking my opinion or agreement first.

"We'll start the battle traditionally," Jonathan cut in. "When the time is right, the Corodan will enter the fray. It's my hope they'll be a rather unpleasant surprise for the king's soldiers."

"We are capable," Rizzt-tok stated, tilting her head to one side. "The Hive-queen will be proud."

"Once the battle is well underway, we'll have you shift and wreak whatever havoc you can manage," Jonathan continued, a gleam of mischief in his eyes. "Our secret weapon is a dragon."

I clenched my jaw and suppressed a sigh. "You know I can wield a sword just as well—if not better—than most of the soldiers down there. I'd like to be there—with them—as I've been trained to do."

"We need this victory, brother," Thomas said evenly. "We can't fail. And we need you, as a *dragon*… I don't know if we can defeat Colin's army without you."

My frown deepened. "Colin knows I'm here. My presence is no secret."

"Ah, but how many of Colin's men have seen a dragon, Andrew?" Jonathan asked, his face alight with devious glee. "I'd wager only a handful, and they don't know what you're truly capable of. You may have revealed yourself last summer, but you did nothing save fly away from the scene once Alexander was freed. Colin doesn't know your strength. We need you to do this."

I turned to face Thomas directly. "Do you believe there's any chance Colin may have learned more of what I am? My strengths and…weaknesses?"

Thomas raised his eyebrows, skeptical. "When did Colin ever bother to read, let alone research anything? It's not his style."

I wasn't convinced Colin would arrive unprepared. While he may have little interest in research himself, he was now king, and could order others to do the work for him. I continued to learn more about myself with each week and didn't fully understand some of my own shortcomings. I wasn't invincible, despite what the others seemed to believe.

I was overcome with the sudden desire to speak with my father or Caelmarion, though I knew it was impossible. There wasn't enough time, and I wouldn't risk leaving Thomas alone for even a single day. I'd do the best I could, given our present circumstances.

"I hope you're right," I replied wearily. "I don't want to consider what might happen if you're wrong."

"We can't prepare for everything, Andrew," Everett interjected. "I know this goes against your philosophy, but it's the truth. The plan we've laid out is our best chance for success, and for it to work, we'll need you to agree to our terms. You're one of the greatest assets this army has in its possession."

I nodded but made no reply. It was frustrating to realize I'd been reduced to nothing more than a weapon, a tool to be used in our effort to stop Colin's tyranny. If Alexander had been present, he would have insisted I have a voice in the discussion. That realization made me miss him even more.

"Andrew, please—" Thomas began, but I held up a hand, and he broke off.

"I understand your line of thinking well enough." I was unable to keep aggravation from seeping into my tone. "I'm not happy about this, but I'll do it if you believe there is no other way."

"We don't believe there is." Everett looked down at his boots as he spoke, uncomfortable with the turn the conversation had taken.

I scowled. "Fine."

"Then you'll do it?" Thomas asked hopefully.

I nodded once and held his gaze steadily. "Yes. I'll do it for you, brother, though I hope that next time you'll ask me first. I don't enjoy being reduced to the same status as a mere possession." I shook my head and turned away, fuming. "I need time to think. I'll be…elsewhere."

As I strode away, Thomas began to protest, but Everett advised it was best they allow me to go. Thomas would be safe enough in the presence of the dukes, and I needed to do something to vent my anger. I recalled the soldiers who'd been tasked with breaking down blocks of rubble and decided the opportunity to demolish stones was exactly what I needed.

Thomas and I would speak later, once my temper had cooled.

It was well past sundown when I returned to the keep. I'd spent the afternoon breaking stones, and the physical activity had served its purpose. My frustration had evaporated, but was replaced by a brooding resignation.

I located Thomas in the great hall near one of the fireplaces, speaking with Everett. I nodded to them as I passed, but I didn't stop to speak. I wasn't ready to talk with Thomas about his decision or continue our previous conversation.

Instead, I made my way to the eastern tower and up the narrow, winding stair to the top floor. Rynn and I had claimed the room as our own the previous night. Four of the six windows ringing the circular room were broken, and the door leading onto the wide balcony hung haphazardly from rusted hinges. The room was exposed to the elements, and the nights were still cold; no one else had desired the space, which suited my current mood splendidly. I needed more time alone.

Rynn wasn't there when I arrived, but I knew she'd find her way to me eventually. I crossed the room to throw the balcony door wide, then stepped outside to study the darkened valley below.

The night was clear. Myriad stars were visible in the sky above, and a crescent moon shone near its zenith. Below, dozens of torches blazed, twinkling in the night. The occasional call of the guardsmen on the ramparts could be heard, acting counterpoint to the hooting of an owl. The night was tranquil, serene, and harbored the false impression of peace. Soon, it would be riddled with screams, the crackle of fire, the clash of steel.

Once Colin's army began to move north from its post at the Mage's Gate, it would be less than two weeks before they arrived at our location. It was time enough to shore up the remainder of the keep's defenses and finalize our strategy. But two weeks was fleeting—the days would flow by swifter than the spring wind that tousled my hair.

I stood at the balcony's cracked railing for some time, leaning my forearms against it as I surveyed my surroundings. When I heard footsteps on the stairs, I assumed it was Rynn, but I didn't turn to greet her. I continued to grapple with my thoughts and how best to speak with Thomas.

When the footsteps stopped in the doorway, I resisted the urge to glance over my shoulder. There was a sigh, followed by more footfalls, and I recognized the sound as belonging to Thomas. He came to stand alongside me, but said nothing.

After several seconds, I turned to fix him with a steely gaze. Thomas' arms were crossed as he looked down at the ramparts, his expression troubled. I looked back into the night, waiting for him to break the silence first.

"You were right to be angry." His tone was weary.

I risked a glance in his direction. I didn't trust myself to speak, fearing my temper would flare and make matters worse.

"We assumed you'd take no issue with our plan," he continued after another long pause. "Andrew, I never meant for you to feel…*used*, for lack of a better term. You're my brother, and you've done so much for all of us. I…I'm sorry our discussion followed the course that it did."

"I assumed I'd be part of the main attack," I replied, my eyes locked on the landscape below. "It's where I've always been, even when I was your father's commander. But that was before anyone knew my damned secret."

"Jon was merely trying to utilize your strength," Thomas explained, his tone wavering toward despair. "We never meant for this to upset you…"

I swallowed my frustration; Thomas hadn't meant any harm. "I misunderstood your intentions. I can't go back to the way things used to be, no matter how much I want to." I sighed, morose.

"I *am* sorry, Andrew. I'll make certain we consult you before we make our next set of plans. You deserve that much after all you've done and all you've been through." He shook his head and pinched the bridge of his nose, remorse etching lines in his brow. "During the past few months, I began to believe I truly knew you, but it seems I still have much to learn."

"I meant what I said earlier," I replied with a shrug. "I'll follow your plan, but there is something I'll need from you first."

He nodded, awaiting my next words with a wary frown.

"I'll need a signal, Tom. When you're ready for me to join the battle, use it, whatever it happens to be. I'll be watching for it. This balcony is an ideal place to take to the skies. Can you do that?"

A small smile quirked the corners of his mouth. "Yes, of course. I hadn't considered how we would inform you, but a signal makes great sense."

"Rynn plans to take part in the battle as well." I studied him, gauging his reaction.

I was about to divulge a secondary source of my previous anger, and I was unused to sharing such details with him. If Alexander had been there, my concerns would have been relayed much sooner, but I was less certain of what I could share with Thomas in confidence.

"If I'm to attack from the air, it will be difficult for me to keep her safe. She's never been through something like this. I'd hoped to be near her." I sighed heavily. "Please promise me you'll have her remain on the ramparts with the archers, or near you as one of your personal guards. Anywhere that isn't the front lines… I can't bear the thought of losing her too."

Thomas nodded in understanding. "I'll do all I can to make certain she remains safe. You have my word."

While Rynn would never truly be safe so long as the battle raged, she'd be better off if she remained at a distance from the front lines. I'd do everything in my power to ensure she survived, and it was a relief to know I could count on my brother for help.

"I'll leave you for the night," Thomas said after a pause. He turned to walk slowly across the balcony.

"Tom," I said as he reached the door, "thank you. I can't lose her. I can't go through that again."

What I didn't tell him was that I feared what I would do, what I would potentially become, should Rynn fail to survive the battle. The very notion of her death left me teetering on the brink of a hollow, dark void from which I was certain I'd never return should I fall into its deadly embrace. I'd lose myself in a black, destructive rage, one which could prove fatal to anyone who stood in my path, whether they were friend or foe. The prospect of losing Rynn—and subsequently myself—was terrifying.

He nodded once, pausing at the threshold. "I understand. We'll keep her safe, Andrew."

TWENTY-TWO

I resumed my duties as Thomas' personal guard the following morning and went about the day as though nothing had transpired between us. Thomas was clearly relieved when I arrived outside his room that morning, and it was only then that I realized I'd been too hard on him. He was still learning the role of prospective king, and he'd never meant to draw my ire. With a night to sort through my grievances and misgivings, I was in a better temper and had come to accept my place in his army.

It was nearing midday when one of the forward scouts returned from the field, bearing urgent news. He made his way directly to the great hall and Jonathan, where he began to speak, gesturing animatedly.

I watched the exchange from near the fireplace where I'd taken up my post. Thomas was in a discussion with the quartermaster regarding bread and ale stores and didn't pay any mind to the scout's return. The scout spoke between gasps, panting as though he'd run a great distance. He handed the former duke a sealed roll of parchment, and immediately the pair turned to stride purposefully toward us.

As they neared, I could make out the insignia impressed into the red wax seal—the royal Marsden boar. Colin had made his first move.

When Thomas took note of the parchment in Jonathan's hands, he dismissed the quartermaster. "Jon, find the others. I want everyone present when I read this."

The duke nodded and handed the parchment to Thomas before departing. The scout lingered, his eyes darting between Jonathan's retreating form, myself, and Thomas.

"Tell me your name and how you came by this message," Thomas stated.

"Lance Markley, my lord. I was on duty at the mouth of the valley, patrolling the perimeter." He spoke matter-of-factly, unperturbed by the prospect of speaking with his future monarch. "I didn't see the shooter, but this scroll was attached to an arrow. A fine arrow it was too, with tawny goose feathers used as fletching. The arrow struck the trunk of a tree a few paces ahead of where I stood. When I saw the seal, I knew I must bring it to you directly."

"Thank you, Lance." Thomas studied the scroll and turned it over in his hands. "Do you recognize the design?"

Lance shook his head. "No, my lord, but it looked important."

"It is. Thank you for bringing it to me." Thomas sighed and leaned back in his chair. "You may return to your duties."

Lance saluted before backing away. I glanced around the hall, noting Jonas was striding toward us, and not far behind was Everett. Rizzt-tok had been overseeing the construction of the trenches and the traps being laid within; it was no surprise she had not yet arrived.

"What is Colin playing at?" Thomas mused, casting a curious glance in my direction.

"I suppose we'll know more once you read his message," I replied with a shrug. "Though I'd bet he sends this as a warning. Or perhaps it's meant as an affront. We'll see."

Thomas shrugged. "I'm surprised he bothered to send a message at all."

I chuckled humorlessly. "I'm not. Colin has always had a flair for the dramatic, and he has never passed up an opportunity to goad me."

While I didn't believe he'd send threats or taunts meant for Thomas, I had no doubt he'd saved at least one pointed barb for me. We fell silent as we awaited the others. The dukes recognized the king's seal immediately, but refrained from asking questions until Jonathan returned with Rizzt-tok.

Thomas gave me a meaningful glance before breaking the wax seal. I didn't have to ask if he was concerned or afraid; both emotions were evident in his blue eyes. He read the contents, frowned, read them again, and closed his eyes with a pained expression. He thrust the scroll toward me without looking, his free hand covering his face.

"Tom?" I asked, concerned.

"Colin is a unique brand of bastard." His words came through clenched teeth. "Read it, Andrew."

I studied my youngest brother for a few moments before dropping my gaze to the sheet of parchment clutched in my hand. Whatever was coming, we'd face it together—and I hoped Thomas understood that.

I unrolled the scroll, noting with mild surprise that Colin had written the note himself. His handwriting was an untidy scrawl, yet unmistakable in its familiarity.

My dear brother Thomas,

I received the most distressing message from our cousin in Dresdin's Forge. I have dispatched this note with the hope my messenger finds the information I was given is false. Should he find an army where Duke Winston suggests it is and this letter finds its way into your hands, I will be sorely disappointed.

How can my only true brother turn against me? We are the only viable Marsdens left in this kingdom, and as such, we should strive to work together. We should stand in solidarity as we seek to eradicate the threat the Marks pose.

If the rumor of your army is true, then the other part of our cousin's letter must be as well. How did it come to pass that the vile beast who masquerades as a man managed to slip his way into Novania without my knowledge? Why have you turned your back on your family and allied yourself with a monstrosity? He was never our brother, Thomas, and it pains me that you've chosen that creature over me. It is the greatest of insults.

Know this: As king of this great land, I will ensure you are rightfully punished for your insubordination. This ridiculous notion of rebellion must be stopped. I cannot be lenient with you any longer.

As the tone of the message became angrier, the handwriting became sloppier and was marred by several ink blots. Colin had signed the letter with an angry flourish which ran to the edge of the page. A scratch marred the parchment where the quill had dug savagely into the paper. He'd been furious as he'd inked the message.

The words themselves were typical of Colin's rhetoric, and I didn't immediately understand why Thomas was so visibly upset. I found it both amusing and irksome that Colin avoided calling me by my name throughout the message, resorting to base insults instead. I'd expected nothing less from him.

"Tom, are you alright?" I asked as I passed the letter to Everett.

Thomas stared bleakly at the floor, his head in his hands.

When he looked up at me, his eyes were hard. "I anticipated threats and a poor attempt at reasoning, but I never believed he'd completely disown you and Alex! And he wouldn't even write your name!" He crossed his arms, outraged. "How are you so damned calm?"

"I expected it," I replied with a shrug. "I've been called worse than a beast in my time, though 'monstrosity' is new. Colin is merely posturing. Don't let it bother you."

"I believe we should be more concerned with the threats he has leveled against *you*, my lord," Jonathan cut in, his tone grave. "If this rebellion goes poorly, you'll need an escape plan. I'd hate to see what the tyrant has in store for you, should you be captured."

"We agree," Rizzt-tok added. "The Hive-queen offers shelter if you must flee the red king, but we do not believe it will come to that yet. Our defenses in the valley are strong. Our warriors are ready. We stand with you."

"Thank you," Thomas replied numbly, looking down at the floor once more.

"Colin didn't mention the Corodan." Jonas glanced between Rizzt-tok and Thomas. "I don't understand how Duke Winston could betray your location—and Andrew's presence—without the realization that they accompany you. He was the arrangement you contrived, wasn't he?"

"Yes, and Elias elected not to mention the Corodan," Thomas replied. "We both thought it would be a nice surprise for the king."

"Wise." Jonas nodded thoughtfully.

"We are happy to help with your surprise." Rizzt-tok's words elicited a laugh from the group, breaking the tension.

"Our scout was ranging some distance away from the valley when the message was delivered," Jonathan said after a moment. "I wonder if the messenger drew close enough to report on our activities and numbers. Lance never saw the archer, so it's difficult to be certain."

"He's fortunate the archer was only here to deliver the message," Everett replied with a frown. "He could have been the target of that arrow. I hope your scouts will be more vigilant from here on. We'll need every soldier we have to make this work."

We received another message from Alexander two days later. Thomas and I were in the great hall, enjoying one of the increasingly rare moments when no one was seeking his approval or his opinion. We were alone when the message appeared in the air between us, hanging like a beacon. The note was brief but held significant meaning.

Alexander wrote that Colin had pulled just over half of his troops from the Mage's Gate, leaving a much smaller force behind. He stated he'd make his first strike the next day. The tone of his message was confident, and I hoped for his sake the battle would go in our favor. He promised to write often, though I suspected he'd be far too busy for regular updates once the battle ensued.

"I wish I possessed a fraction of Alexander's mettle." Thomas shook his head in disbelief. "He's gone so far as to plan on a rendezvous point in which to meet us. I don't know how he'll travel north without Colin noticing—and after engaging the king's army at the Mage's Gate!"

"Tom," I said evenly, "remember this is Alex we're speaking of. He's always been optimistic, and in this case, it can't hurt to think ahead. Our plans can be changed if needed. We must be flexible, but knowing our potential next step is a good idea."

Thomas sighed wearily. "I suppose you'd know better than I do. The location he mentions… I'm not familiar with it, though I've heard the name. The ferry crossing at Willever."

"The second year Alexander joined me on campaign, his company met up with our main force at Willever," I replied. "A good friend told Alex the area was defensible, so long as the enemy didn't come from the river. It's a reasonable location for a rendezvous. We often used it as the first staging point when moving toward the highlands."

That friend had been Jerrick Vine; a good man, a loyal soldier, and someone who I sorely missed. If I were able to speak with his widow after this was over, I'd tell her what transpired between us in the forest north of Crystal Crags. Jerrick had deserved a better fate. His loyalty to Novania had been shattered, his faith in his king destroyed, and he'd forfeited his life in a desperate attempt to shield his family from further harm. Though it was my blade that had ended his life, Jerrick's death was ultimately the result of Colin's merciless schemes.

"Does Colin know of Willever?" Thomas asked pointedly.

I shrugged. "He may not know himself, though I'd expect his commander to. Should we agree to Alex's plan, we must prepare for resistance along the way. Willever is only a three-day march from the Capitol. It's a logical half-way mark between our location and Alex's, though the proximity to Colin may prove problematic. We'll have to adapt as we learn more."

Thomas frowned in frustration. "Is it always like this? The uncertainties, and 'ifs' and 'shoulds?' All of our plans—are they nothing but a waste of time?"

"No," I said, mildly amused. "Having a plan in place is important, but battles rarely go as anticipated. As I've said, we must remain flexible. We may have to change our plans or scrap them entirely, depending on the outcome. I'm telling you this so you understand the reality of the situation. It's not going to be easy, no matter how the fight goes."

Thomas looked down and covered his face with one hand. In that moment, he looked older than his twenty-five years, and the toll that bearing the mantle of leadership cost him was clear. When he looked up again, an array of troubled emotions flitted across his features, and he suddenly appeared every bit my younger brother as I recalled him from a decade past.

"Andrew," he said, his voice strained, "I need to know—do you truly believe we can win this war?"

I studied him carefully for a moment while formulating my response. "I know things seem uncertain right now, but I believe we can do this. We have to."

He nodded and closed his eyes briefly, seemingly relieved. "If you believe it, then I will too."

"We're in this together." I offered him a strained smile. "You, me, and Alex. Between the three of us, we'll find a way to succeed. We'll make things right for Novania."

Footfalls echoed behind me. I turned to find Claire, a carefully tied bundle cradled in her arms. Elanor Horace was beside her. Like Claire, she could not be persuaded to remain behind in Dresdin's Forge, even though her children had. She'd always been loyal to the duke and refused to leave his side.

Claire placed the bundle on the table between us. "Is Rynn here?" she asked, casting a glance around the room.

I shook my head. "No, she went to spar with Jon's scouts an hour ago."

Claire nodded once, her expression neutral. "She should be here for this since it was partially her idea."

"I'll send someone to fetch her," Thomas replied, "though I'd like to know what this is about, Lady Claire."

Claire shrugged noncommittally, as if to say we would learn soon enough. With an amused shake of his head, Thomas motioned for one of the nearby soldiers and asked her to locate Rynn and request her presence in the great hall.

"I hope this is a good time, my lord," Elanor said after the soldier was gone. "You didn't seem busy, though your discussion appeared serious."

Thomas waved his hand dismissively. "It's no trouble, Lady Elanor. Andrew and I were speaking of our brothers. Please sit down while we wait."

Claire raised her eyebrows as she perched on the edge of a nearby stool. "Then we may well have interrupted something of importance, given who your brothers are."

I glanced at Thomas and offered him a knowing smirk. "You're no bother. Sometimes Tom needs a break from his duties, and interruptions can be welcome. I doubt he'd admit it himself, but it's the truth."

Thomas chuckled. "I'm right here, Andrew." To Claire, he said, "I could use a diversion, and now you've piqued my curiosity."

Elanor rose to wave animatedly. I glanced over my shoulder to see Rynn had arrived. At the sight of the other women, she broke into a wide grin. She took the empty seat next to mine, quivering with excitement. Whatever the three had hidden inside the bundle must have been something of importance.

"My Lord Thomas," Elanor began, smiling graciously. "We've made this for you, and we hope you're pleased with the results." She pushed the bundle toward him, indicating he should unwrap it.

Thomas looked at each of the women in turn, unspoken questions in his eyes.

"For the love of all that is holy, just open it, Tom!" Rynn cried, her tone a mixture of exasperation and unabashed excitement. She turned briefly to look at me, a mischievous grin on her face. "I hope you like it as well."

"Rynn," Elanor said in a warning tone, "please don't spoil the surprise."

Thomas began to unwrap the parcel, uncovering a bundle of cloth. As he unrolled it, a standard was revealed; the background was comprised of two blocks on a diagonal, one crimson, the other ivory, the ancestral colors of the Marsden family. Embroidered in the center of the banner was the silhouette of a black dragon with its wings spread.

"Colin bears the boar sigil of house Marsden on his standards," Claire said, breaking our stunned silence. "Though you're a Marsden too, you require your own standard. Something to differentiate your people from those of the tyrant's, something that will inspire them to greatness. It seemed fitting, given your unusual alliances, that yours bears a dragon."

I turned to give Rynn a meaningful glance. I had no doubt she was responsible for the sigil, but I was rendered speechless. I'd become the symbol of hope for Thomas' army. She honored me beyond words.

Rynn beamed. "The dragon was my idea. I hope you don't mind."

I shook my head and managed a crooked grin. "Not at all. It's—"

"It's perfect," Thomas said, awe-struck, as he admired their handiwork. "Where did you find the cloth? We've been scraping for supplies…"

"I cut up some of my gowns." A bemused smile crossed Claire's lips. "I insisted on coming with you, and this was the least I could do to help your cause. I feel as though I've done something worthwhile, that I've contributed in my own small way."

Thomas looked up to study each of the women in turn. "Thank you, all of you. This means more than you will ever know."

When his eyes met mine, hope shone in their depths, something I'd missed seeing in Thomas for some time. "This is proof of your words. We *are* in this together, no matter the outcome. We'll hang this from the ramparts, where it will be seen by all who approach. It will travel with us when we move on, borne at the forefront of the army. It is a symbol—*our* symbol—of defiance against Colin's tyranny. It's a promise of hope, a promise that I can make this kingdom a better place. For everyone."

I grinned at my youngest brother. That such a seemingly small act by the three women could inspire Thomas to such determination was a wonder. He'd been frustrated and overwhelmed for months, uncertain of himself and our plans. Though I'd sought to ease his mind and help him as much as I was able, it had been this unforeseen act of charity on the part of Elanor, Rynn, and Claire that sparked the renewed sense of purpose within him.

Rynn stared at Thomas for several seconds after he'd finished speaking, her eyebrows lifted appraisingly. "Keep talking like that, Tom, and the whole of the kingdom will follow your lead. I didn't realize you had it in you."

Thomas reddened but continued, undeterred by her praise. "Our people need hope, and I must be the one to inspire them. I see that now. The knowledge that you believe in me enough to create this… It means *everything*." He looked down and chewed his lower lip. "Does everyone have such faith in this cause?"

I laughed. "They wouldn't follow you if they didn't."

"Andrew is right," Claire added. I blinked in momentary surprise; it was a rare occurrence to hear those three words spill from her lips. "Everyone here wants to contribute in whatever way they can. We want you to succeed. It's why we're here."

"I didn't realize how much support I truly had," Thomas said, mystified. "I assumed they came because I am the only logical successor to Colin, not because they believe in *me*."

"We *do* believe in you, my lord," Elanor replied. "Though the path may be grueling, I have no doubt you will persevere. You have the support of every duke in the Northern Marches, Alexander's army in the south, the Corodan, and the last of the dragon-kind as well. If anyone has the means to overthrow the tyrant-king, it is you."

TWENTY-THREE

Eleven days passed before Alexander's next message arrived. We'd received brief notes from Lydia, though she could tell us little about the battle other than the magi had taken few casualties. Over time, I grew anxious; I needed to hear from Alexander himself.

Thomas and I had been walking the ramparts as he oversaw the last of the fortification efforts for the keep when the message arrived. He snatched it from the air, unfolding it eagerly. I watched an array of emotions play across his features as he read and knew without asking that it bore good news—or at the very least, hope.

"Alex is victorious," he murmured, staring at the message in his hand as though it were a thing of wonder. "He says Colin's forces have been routed, and the few who refused to surrender have fled." He looked up, unable to conceal his smile. "I can't believe… I *wanted* to believe this would be the outcome, but it seemed impossible. And yet, Alex has done it!"

He thrust the message into my hands, and I scanned its contents quickly.

Tom –

I wish I could have written sooner, but things were a bit more chaotic than I'd planned. I've been busy dealing with Colin's men. What is left of the army has either surrendered to us or fled toward the Capitol.

It's clear Colin was wholly unprepared for an army of magi. The poor bastards facing us had no inkling of how to defend themselves. I almost pity them. Though we fought for many days, we sustained very few casualties and will be moving toward Willever's ferry tomorrow. We'll defend that location until you arrive, however long that may take. If my calculations are correct, the men Colin sent to your location should arrive within the next few days. We will likely reach the ferry ahead of you.

I gave the soldiers who surrendered the option of joining us or abandoning their arms and returning home. Much to my surprise, most chose to join forces. It seems they fear what Colin will do to their families if they return home in disgrace and he learns of it.

I don't know what our brother has done, but the rumors are ominous. We must stop him, one way or another. Take care, Tom. We'll meet again at Willever.

–Alex

"I hope Alex keeps a close eye on the men who decided to join him," I replied, handing the letter back to Thomas. "I wouldn't be so trusting, given the assassins Colin sent after me and what Leta attempted with you."

Thomas shrugged. "Perhaps you're right, but Alex seems confident enough."

"And that's why I worry. Alexander's optimism sometimes blinds him. He fails to see enemies until they've already struck. And I'm not there to protect him…" I sighed and ran one hand through my hair. "I suppose with as many magi as he's gathered, he'll be safe enough."

Thomas nodded. "Of course. I've seen some of what Rynn can do, and she's spoken of the abilities of others. Alex will be fine. Besides, I need you focused on the battle *here*. We both know Colin's men will arrive any time, even without Alexander's warning."

I nodded. Thomas needed my help and I'd promised he'd have it, yet I was worrying over Alexander, who was far beyond my reach.

"You're right. I'm sorry."

He chuckled. "You don't need to apologize. I've known for many years that you and Alex are far closer than you and I will ever be. I don't fault you, but there is nothing you can do at present to help him. And *I* need you." He paused to look out over the valley. "Every preparation has been made. Is the waiting always so difficult?"

I shrugged. "It can be, though I've seldom been on the defensive, as we are now. My battles with the Corodan were markedly different."

"At least this time, they're on our side." Thomas gestured toward the completed trenches, furnished with sharpened stakes and false coverings designed to collapse beneath the weight of a man or a horse.

"They certainly know how to engineer traps. Did you encounter many during your campaigns?"

"On occasion," I replied. "They didn't furnish them with stakes then. I'm fairly certain Jon put that idea in the hive's mind."

Thomas shuddered inadvertently. "I'm certainly glad they're allies now. Rizzt-tok and her people seem fierce enough, but after learning what they're truly capable of, I wouldn't choose to cross them."

I opened my mouth to respond when I detected hurried footfalls approaching us. Turning from our view of the valley, I saw Everett sprinting toward us. I shot the duke a questioning glance as unease writhed in my gut. Had Colin's forces finally been sighted?

Thomas spun at my reaction, then his eyes narrowed in concern. "Uncle? What is it?"

"One of Jon's scouts returned a few minutes ago," he replied. Though he'd been running, he wasn't short of breath. "The tyrant's army has been sighted just beyond the mouth of the valley. They'll be visible from the walls before dusk." He shot me a pointed look. "The man who gave us his report recognized their leader. It's Robert Claybourne."

I grimaced. "Claybourne is the man responsible for Colin's desire to enforce the old laws. Colin knows I'm here, but why has he sent Claybourne? I'd half expected Colin to lead the army himself."

Everett shrugged. "I don't know the reason, but I find it worrisome. Knowing Colin as we do, I expect he has something else planned, something we may not have prepared for. Claybourne is—*was*—a minor lord, and had never been invited to court until after Carlton's death. To become so influential so quickly is unusual."

Everett's implications were clear. Claybourne had convinced Colin to trust him and promote him to a higher status. He'd become the ruler of the late Duke Ellington's lands and had been granted Bridgewaters as well. It seemed the man's ambition had no bounds. He was now leading Colin's army, but I doubted he had much experience in battle, if any. I would have remembered him if he'd been on campaign against the Corodan during my time as commander.

I glanced at Thomas. "We should speak with Claire. She knows more about this man than we do."

Thomas nodded, but his demeanor had become subdued. "Yes."

"Tom?" I asked, concerned.

He laughed nervously. "I suppose I should not have been complaining about the wait. Now that Colin's men have been sighted…I'm…" He shook his head as though to clear it, and when he met my eyes, his terror was written plainly across his features.

"We'll get through this," I assured him. "Let's speak with Claire while we have the opportunity to do so."

I knew we'd only have a brief window in which to finalize our plans, and we must make the most of it.

We made our way back to the main keep, but news of Claybourne's arrival had preceded us. Most stood at attention as Thomas passed or made brief statements regarding their commitment to his cause. It was heartening to see our forces remained steadfast even with the enemy on our doorstep. The experience seemed to strengthen Thomas' resolve, allaying some of his fears. By the time we entered the great hall, he'd regained his composure.

I was more certain than ever that Thomas was the right choice for Novania's next king.

Thomas led us to the table nearest the fireplace, asking one of the soldiers we passed to locate Claire. Jonathan entered the room not long after we'd taken our seats and strode toward us with a glower.

"It's Claybourne, is it?" he asked, sitting down heavily. "I've heard rumors of the man, none of them good."

"The scouts report he wears the cloak of the commander," Everett replied with a frown. "We know little about him, and it worries me."

Thomas rose, his gaze focused beyond the dukes. "Lady Claire," he said, motioning for her to take the empty seat next to Everett. "Thank you for coming."

She nodded as she adjusted her skirts and sat down gracefully. "I'm aware Claybourne leads the king's army," she replied coolly. "I expect you wish to know what information I might provide?" Her dark eyes were focused solely upon Thomas, her face betraying no hint of emotion.

"Yes," Thomas confirmed. "We hoped you may know something of his methods, his temperament… Anything that can help with our strategy."

She drew a breath as though steeling herself, then closed her eyes briefly. "Robert Claybourne came to the Capitol during the weeks following Colin's coronation. I didn't see him again until Colin began to execute people for bearing the Mark, and then he became a fixture in the Capitol. Colin named him advisor, and when the previous commander chose to step down from his post, Claybourne was given that as well."

Her dark eyes flitted toward me for a heartbeat. "It was Claybourne's idea that a spectacle be made if anyone of importance was discovered with the Mark. The festivities, the musicians, the storytellers and fire-breathers… All of it was at the behest of Robert Claybourne. When Alexander was arrested, Colin sent word to him immediately. He bears a hatred for those with the Mark unlike anything I've ever encountered, and his influence over Colin is undeniable. Together, the two are a menace to the very foundations of this kingdom."

As she'd spoken, the still-smoldering rage at the injustice of what Colin had attempted to do was rekindled in my heart. If Claire's words were true—and I no longer had any reason to doubt her—Claybourne was just as responsible as Colin was for the events leading up to Alexander's failed execution and the murder of Vera and her staff. If I was granted the opportunity, I would make the bastard pay for every drop of blood he'd spilled.

It was Thomas who voiced the question that whirled through my own mind. "Do you believe Robert Claybourne is ultimately responsible for what Colin attempted to do to Alex?"

Claire looked down at her hands, her expression unreadable. "I can't say for certain. Colin was searching for a reason to imprison your brother before he began the executions. He told me Alexander had become a larger thorn in his side than he'd ever imagined possible." She met Thomas' eyes unflinchingly. "He knew you were investigating your father's death, and he wanted to stop it. He believed if he found a means to silence Alexander, you would no longer oppose him."

Thomas scowled. "He was wrong, but that's irrelevant. We need to know what sort of man Robert Claybourne is."

Claire nodded. "I didn't know him well. By the time he became a permanent fixture in the royal castle, I was imprisoned in the tower.

What I can tell you is this: He is manipulative, vindictive, and from the glimpses I've seen of his work, he is without mercy." She shifted her gaze to meet mine. "You must ensure Rynn stays clear of him. She's a mage, and he won't hesitate to kill her, given the chance."

"Rynn will remain on the ramparts," Jonathan interjected. "We made that determination previously based on other factors."

"Nevertheless, she must be made aware of the danger she's in," Claire persisted. "I don't want to see her harmed. She has already risked so much by traveling here."

I studied Claire carefully for several moments, convinced there was something more behind her words. Her concern for Rynn appeared genuine, but the simple fact that she *was* concerned gave me pause.

Claire frowned imperiously. "Do not look at me so, Andrew. I've come to consider Rynn a friend—much to my own surprise. She is headstrong… I fear what will happen should she find herself too near Robert Claybourne. You have no reason to remain suspicious of me! I've done everything in my power to help Thomas' cause."

I nodded once and muttered an apology. Perhaps I was being unfair, but I could not shake my wariness of her motives so easily after all she'd done. Her decision to annul our marriage and unite with Colin had wounded me more deeply than even I had realized, and it was difficult to trust her implicitly—particularly where it concerned Rynn.

"I'll speak to Rynn once we're finished," I said guardedly. "I want to believe you mean her no harm, but after everything that's happened between *us*…" I shook my head, frustrated. "This matter can wait for another day."

Claire crossed her arms as a bitter sneer twisted her features. "I agree, though I'd like to point out that it is *you* who can't seem to relinquish the past, Andrew."

I rolled my eyes, exasperated. "Claire…" I growled a warning.

"*Enough!*" Thomas rose from his seat, glaring angrily between the two of us. "Now is not the time for your petty arguments. Andrew, I need you focused on the coming battle." Claire smirked at me, only to have Thomas turn on her seconds later. "And Lady Claire, if there is nothing more you can tell us of Robert Claybourne, you may go."

Claire nodded once as she rose carefully. "There is nothing more, my lord."

Once she was gone, Thomas glowered at me. "Go. Speak with Rynn. Your part in the battle has already been determined, and you know what you must do. I'll send word if anything changes."

I blinked and forced myself to nod, unused to the note of authority in Thomas' tone. I shouldn't have allowed Claire's words to provoke my temper, but the woman had always known precisely what to say to spark an argument. She was maddeningly frustrating, and I'd always paid the price.

Reluctantly, I departed as the others began to discuss strategy. I knew our forces were in capable hands; Jonathan Horace and Everett Crossley were both experienced leaders. Despite this knowledge, it was difficult to walk away after years spent as the former king's commander.

As I reached the door leading to the keep's courtyard, I glanced over my shoulder, longing to participate in the final stages of battle preparation. But my time as commander was over and done, and I must accept my role as an "asset" to the army. I ground my teeth and whirled away.

When I had parted ways with Rynn earlier in the day, she'd mentioned she would be with Jonas' forces most of the afternoon. Jonas and his soldiers had been assigned to fortify and defend the keep's inner walls. When Thomas had asked her to join them, she'd accepted without hesitation. It was a relief to know she'd be with them, and I trusted Jonas Everly.

It didn't take long to locate her along the wall. She was alone, gazing toward the ramparts and the land beyond. I could just make out the first ranks of Claybourne's forces as they began their descent into the valley, marching steadily toward the keep. Rynn glanced at me briefly as I came to stand alongside her, then returned her attention to the oncoming army.

"I thought you'd be with Tom and the others, but I'm glad you're here."

I nodded, sharing the sentiment. In the few months that we'd shared together, Rynn had evoked a subtle change in me, one that I'd failed to recognize until that moment. For the first time, I wanted more from life than a mere continuation of what I'd always known and done. And I wanted to share that life and all its possibilities with her.

I drew a breath and focused my thoughts. I'd sought her for a reason.

"The man who commands Colin's army is dangerous. He bears an unparalleled hatred of magi—and those with the Mark. Promise me you'll keep your distance."

She turned toward me, her cerulean eyes unreadable as she studied my features. "I've been assigned to the inner walls. I doubt I'll see much action, if any."

"Things can change rapidly during the course of a battle," I replied stubbornly. "Please, heed my warning. I need you to remain safe. I can't…" I shook my head and turned away, unable to finish the sentence. The notion of losing her was almost too much to bear.

"Andrew, I'll be fine. You'll see."

When I nodded, she said, "Promise you'll return to me when this is over."

I was startled that she seemed just as concerned about me as I was about her. "I will."

"You'd better, Andrew Caein," she replied, forcing a strained smile. "I didn't go to all the trouble of undertaking this long journey only to have you slip away."

"I'm not going anywhere."

"Good."

She reached out, taking one of my hands in hers. We stood on the wall for some time, watching as Claybourne's forces took up their positions at the far end of the valley. We didn't speak, but we didn't need to; there was little else to say before we were forced to part ways.

I was content to stand at her side, prolonging our time together, even if it was spent in relative silence. Her presence was soothing, a balm to my soul. There was no one else I would have rather been with as I watched Claybourne's soldiers spread across the valley like a plague.

I knew in that moment, as we stood atop the wall of the keep, that I loved her.

TWENTY-FOUR

"My lord."

I pulled my attention from the ranks of enemy soldiers below and glanced at Rynn before turning to face the speaker. I didn't know his name, though I recognized him as one of Jonas' people.

"Lord Marsden requests your presence above the lower gate, sir."

I drew a breath and nodded. "Tell my brother I'll be there."

He saluted and strode away, leaving me alone with Rynn once more. I studied her face in the fading light, memorizing its every detail. She smirked, amused by my sudden scrutiny, but said nothing.

"I'll return if I can," I promised.

"I know you will. Go, Andrew. Thomas needs you."

I nodded and pushed away from the wall to begin the trek to my brother's location. The gates to the keep were closed and barred, and the inner courtyard teemed with alert soldiers. I glanced toward the top of the wall as I walked through the throng, but was unable to catch a final glimpse of Rynn.

I passed through the narrow gate leading from the inner courtyard to the outer, then through the bustle of activity as final preparations were made for a siege. I threaded my way through the masses, making for one of the narrow stone staircases leading to the outer wall's ramparts. I took the steps two at a time in my haste to reach Thomas.

The last rays of the setting sun slanted through the valley, painting the worn stone beneath my feet in an orange-yellow hue. He stood directly above the keep's gate, flanked by the three former dukes, the dragon standard unfurled proudly above him. In the shadows of the guard tower behind, Rizzt-tok paced restlessly.

Thomas motioned for me to join them as I approached, then gestured to the valley below. "We've received word that Claybourne wants to speak before the matter 'escalates.' Some of Jon's people have gone out to act as an escort. I don't want him to learn of the fortifications we've constructed in the valley. We need the trenches to remain secret until he begins the attack."

I nodded my agreement while Everett said, "Claybourne's message stated he hopes to end this 'debacle' without bloodshed. I've no intention of backing down. We all know his words can't be trusted."

Jonathan chuckled grimly. "If we surrender, the king will march us to the Capitol for execution. We're all guilty of defiance—akin to treason in his eyes—and he hasn't been lenient with others. We won't survive the encounter if even his most trusted advisors failed to do so."

I knew he spoke of Duke Ellington. There had been others as well, based on the rumors we'd received throughout the winter, but Ellington was the first who came to mind.

I turned to Thomas. "Why have you called me?"

Thomas glanced at Everett uncertainly, but the duke merely shrugged.

"Claybourne's message hinted at a trade of sorts," Thomas said. "If we surrender you, Claybourne will leave without further incident. I don't trust a word he's written, and I will *not* allow you to be taken into his custody. Colin has made multiple attempts on your life, and I'm not going to stand idly by as he attempts to kill you like he tried to do with Alex."

I shifted my gaze to the valley and the army camped on the far side as I considered his words. The first pinpricks of firelight appeared, glimmering gold and red in the distance, a reminder of the army I'd flown past near the Mage's Gate. Colin had sent assassins for my head on more than one occasion, but now Claybourne was tasked with my capture. I didn't dispute Thomas' assessment; if I surrendered, I'd inevitably be killed—but after I reached the Capitol. I narrowed my eyes, frowning in thought while I attempted to understand the reason behind Colin's apparent change of heart.

"We can't give him what he seeks," Jonathan said. "I hope you're not contemplating going along with this madness. This is not a battle with the Corodan."

I cracked a grim smile at the memory. No, this was a much different situation, and I no longer held the element of surprise. Claybourne knew what I was, and if he was even passably competent as commander, he would have learned some of my strengths and weaknesses as well.

I shook my head. "I won't surrender. It goes against my nature, Jon. I was merely trying to puzzle out why Colin would offer to let the rest of you go in exchange for me. He's made it rather clear he wants me dead, and mercy isn't one of his notable virtues."

All four of the men appeared relieved at my response, but it was Jonas who voiced it. "It's good to hear you weren't going to attempt another foolish scheme. You may have survived the former Hive-queen's ambush, but I'm certain this would have ended far differently."

"We didn't know he was the dragon-man," Rizzt-tok said from the shadows. "If Krizzt-keh had known, she would not have sprung the trap."

I turned to study the Corodan warrior. "Claybourne knows what I am, and he still demands my surrender. I don't like it."

Rizzt-tok tilted her head, contemplating her next words. Perhaps she was communicating with the hive, though it was impossible to know simply by watching her movements. When she spoke, her voice was grave.

"We believe he has learned how to...counteract your abilities, dragon-man. Some of the smaller members of the hive have uncovered troubling signs. They scout and report, but have not yet been seen by the enemy. I can influence them to gain more intelligence if you desire."

Her words sent an icy finger down my spine. "What have they seen?"

She tilted her head the other direction. "The apparatus...the stone-flingers... They have been modified. The enemy has created nets, bundled in a specific pattern. We believe these are meant to be hurled through the air."

"When you speak of 'stone-flingers,' do you mean trebuchets?" Everett asked.

"Yes." Rizzt-tok appeared agitated. "The nets are large. Meant for capturing enormous prey." An angry hiss emanated from her thorax.

"I cannot force the scouts to go nearer, or we will be discovered. We cannot risk this."

"We understand," Thomas assured her. "What you have told us is invaluable. Give my thanks to your scouts, then pull them back." He turned to face me, his expression strained. "Andrew, he means to capture you one way or another."

I nodded my agreement. "Thanks to the Corodan, we know of the nets. I won't be caught by surprise."

"Just…be careful," Thomas replied guardedly.

"Thomas," Jonathan interrupted gruffly.

He gestured to the valley, where a pair of torches were making their way steadily toward our location. Three of his scouts accompanied a single man, wearing the crimson cloak of the king's commander over a heavy set of plate mail. Two of our scouts flanked him, and the third followed behind; all three appeared apprehensive.

The cloaked man could be none other than Robert Claybourne. He walked with an air of authority and a haughty confidence borne of his station. He was not a tall man, but was solidly built and would seem formidable to some. His head was shaved, and it gleamed dully in the torchlight as he approached. The scouts halted his progress once they stood within arrow range of the ramparts. He stared at our group, his square jaw set in defiance.

I stared at him, only then realizing we'd met once before. I'd knocked him unconscious and stolen his armor to use as my own the night before Alexander's failed execution.

"Lord Marsden," he called in a gravelly voice, "I expected a warmer welcome from the king's only brother! Was my earlier message insufficient to relay my peaceable intentions?"

Beside me, Thomas bristled, but before he made his reply, he drew a deep breath and steadied himself. "Your message was clear enough, but I will not allow anyone to surrender to you, least of all one of my brothers."

"You have but one brother, my lord," Claybourne retorted. "He awaits you in the Capitol, and asks you to put this foolishness behind you. He will accept you with open arms, if you would only allow me to take that creature beside you into custody."

I clenched my jaw and held my tongue. Thomas had proven himself thus far, and it wasn't my place to interrupt—though I sorely wished to. My rage burned white-hot at being relegated to the station of a mere creature; Colin no longer saw me as a man. I realized after a moment that I was visibly shaking as I struggled to contain my fury.

"*Andrew* will not be going with you this night, nor any other," Thomas replied evenly.

I was impressed by how well he kept his composure in the face of Claybourne's insults. His uncle's lessons were serving him well.

"That's a shame," Claybourne replied with mock sympathy. "The king promises that you and those with you won't be judged, if you would only submit to this simple wish."

"He lies," Jonas growled.

"Then I'm afraid I must disappoint you," Thomas stated. "I won't comply with a malicious request, even if it comes from the king."

Claybourne seemed to have expected his answer. He smirked knowingly at our group, his dark eyes hard. "Very well. My men will prepare the same response that we gave to that traitorous bastard, Alexander. You'll wish you'd accepted my terms, young Thomas, just as I'm certain he wishes for it as well." He looked down for a moment, picking at his fingernails with an expression of bored superiority. "I must say, you hold that creature in far too high regard. You've made him the harbinger on your banner—but a harbinger can be construed as a symbol of doom just as easily as it can be one of hope. You'll rue the decision to engage me." He straightened to his full height, which was still less than any of the scouts surrounding him, and began to march back toward his own camp.

I stared at Thomas for several seconds as Claybourne made his departure, my previous anger dissolving as I registered his parting words. "He doesn't know Alex defeated the other half of his army."

"What?" Thomas asked, startled. "Yes, you're right." A slow smile spread across his face. "We may be able to play that to our advantage. It will take another few days before he learns of his defeat in the south."

Jonathan chuckled. "At first, I wasn't keen on the idea of this instant communication the mages use, but it *has* proven useful, hasn't it?"

"I wish we could send word to Alex as quickly as he can send word to us," Thomas lamented. "There is much he should know regarding today's events."

"Perhaps we can assist," Rizzt-tok offered. "We have scouts who ranged beyond the enemy's camp. One can speak as I do. I can influence her to travel to Alexander's location. She is adept at camouflage."

Thomas nodded thoughtfully. "Yes, that would be a great help. How long would it take your scout to reach the ferry? Ah, how long would it take for Alex to reach that point?" He asked of me.

I shrugged. "I don't know the route he planned to take."

Thomas released a heavy sigh, then shook his head, determination in his eyes. "It can't be helped. We're as ready as we can be."

"I will send the scout to Willever," Rizzt-tok said. "She can wait there for instruction. Once we learn Alexander's location, she will know as well. The hive knows what each of its members learns."

"Good, send her," Thomas replied decisively. "When Alexander writes next, I'll inform him of your scout." Thomas looked at each of us in turn before dismissing us to go about our assigned duties. "Andrew, wait a moment," he said as I began to turn away.

He waited until the others were gone before speaking again. "I saw your anger at Claybourne's words. For what it's worth, I'm sorry for what Colin has done—"

I shook my head. "It's not your fault, and you shouldn't apologize on his behalf. He'll regret what he's done before we're finished."

"Even so, he has forsaken both you and Alex," Thomas persisted. "It's so damned *wrong*. I'll make things right, brother. You have my word."

"I know you will," I replied. "Colin wrote me off long before he took the throne. My rage wasn't from that portion of Claybourne's message, in any case."

Thomas appeared perplexed, then he gaped as he realized what I referred to. "It was his insult, wasn't it? He called you a 'creature.'"

I nodded grimly. "He'll pay for that too. But I ought to thank you for your own response. It means much, knowing you're on my side."

"Whether or not Colin will acknowledge it, you *are* my brother. When we finally face that unworthy, murdering bastard, I'll be the first to remind him of it."

"Hmm." I stared out over the ramparts once more, taking in the sight of the two opposing camps, marked by torchlight and cookfires. "Colin should hope you get to him before I do. I'm not certain I'll have any restraint left, and he'll wish he'd never crossed me."

Thomas snorted. "Alex has shared the same sentiment. If Colin is to come out of the encounter unscathed, he ought to hope it's me who comes for him. Even then…" He shook his head and shrugged, but left the thought unfinished. "I still believe he killed father, and he must answer for that crime."

"It was the first of many transgressions."

"Yes." Suddenly, he brightened. "Claybourne called you the harbinger on my banner. A harbinger is more than a mere symbol—it's a sign of things to come. Perhaps Rynn's idea of placing a dragon on my standard was more meaningful than any of us could have anticipated."

I spent the night atop the keep's wall with Rynn, awaiting Claybourne's first strike. Though she slept for a few hours, her blond curls resting on my shoulder as we sat with our backs to the stone, I was too tense to rest myself. I rarely slept on the eve of battle, my overwrought nerves unable to settle as my mind whirled through countless possibilities.

The keep was largely silent throughout the night, but there was an increase of movement amongst those assigned to guard and watch duties. I peered through the darkness, but could see little beyond our own walls and the distant pinpricks of firelight at the far end of the valley. It seemed Claybourne awaited the dawn.

It was still dark when Jonas began to rouse those under his command. Reluctantly, I rose from Rynn's side, pausing to caress the side of her face a final time. We didn't speak, but I saw all I needed to in the depths of her sapphire eyes.

I strode away with the unspoken wish she'd remain safe, then made my way inside the keep. Thomas was near the fireplace, which was unlit and cold, pacing the length of the hearth. Everett was with him, speaking in low tones. The former duke nodded a greeting as I passed on my way to the tower's winding stair. Thomas called a reminder that I should await the appointed signal before engaging, and I waved in acknowledgment. It was Jonathan's duty to light the signal fire that indicated it was time for me to join the fray.

By the time I reached the balcony at the tower's apex, the sky was beginning to lighten, but dawn would not break for another hour. As I strode across the room, I noted a familiar silhouette on the balcony, her back toward me as I approached. Claire's hair was unbound, the dark tresses cascading to her waist. She didn't turn toward me, even as I took my position at the balcony's railing a few paces away from her. Her dark eyes were fixed on the scene unfolding far below.

"It won't be much longer, will it?" she asked breathlessly.

"No."

Even with my superior eyesight, I could not yet detect any movement within the ranks of Claybourne's forces. I believed he'd strike soon, but our long days of preparation gave me confidence that we'd repel the initial attack.

"Elanor said I should stay inside the keep," Claire said with a toss of her head. "I find it difficult to sit about wondering what occurs outside. I came here to gain a better vantage point." She turned to face me, compassion in her gaze. "I thought you might need someone to speak with while you wait. I know we have often argued… But that isn't why I've come."

I nodded, relieved but wary. I said nothing and awaited her next words.

She sighed and turned away with a frown. "To be honest, I'm terrified. During the few short years we were together, you left every summer to fight the Corodan. I was never worried for your safety then—somehow, I always knew you'd return. This time is different. I fear for Thomas. I fear what might happen should this battle go in Claybourne's favor. I fear for Rynn. I fear for dear Everett, and Jon, and Elanor… I fear for my child."

She looked down as her voice broke and tears began to stream from her eyes. In all the years I'd known Claire, I'd only seen her weep a few times. She was frightened, but not for herself; her fear was so powerful she could no longer maintain her carefully composed emotions.

"Claire..." I said softly, uncertain of what to say.

She shrugged and wiped at her eyes. "There are very few people in this world who have seen me like this. I've made mistakes, and you were forced to pay dearly for many of them. I know I should have said this to you long ago, but I truly am sorry for all I've done. You were a far better husband than I deserved."

I drew a breath and looked down at the courtyard. "I wanted to do right by you. When that wasn't good enough..." I growled and raked a hand through my hair. "It doesn't matter anymore, does it? The past is done and gone."

When I looked up once more, she was smiling through her tears—a genuine smile, despite the broken state of her teeth. "I didn't believe you would ever forgive me, Andrew."

I was tempted to tell her that I'd never believed she would apologize, but I decided against it. She was attempting to mend the rift that had grown between us, and it would serve no purpose to provoke her anger now. Instead, I merely shrugged. I didn't have anything meaningful to say.

"May I ask you something?"

I glanced at her briefly, then nodded.

"I have seen you as a dragon several times now, but I have never watched the transformation itself. May I...?"

She appeared so uncertain, a reaction I'd rarely witnessed from her, that it caused me to laugh aloud. "Of course you may," I replied with a grin. "It's only fair, given that I was once forced to keep it a secret from you."

"If the laws in Novania had been different, would you have shared that part of yourself with me?" Her dark eyes were filled with intensity.

I nodded without hesitation. "If I could have done so without repercussion, and if the king had not forbidden me to speak of my heritage, I would have."

She nodded and looked across the valley as the gray pre-dawn light continued to strengthen. "If he had been your father, things would be so much different. I don't know if they would be better between *us*, but for the kingdom, it would be a much happier time."

"Perhaps."

I leaned my forearms against the balcony's railing, noting Claybourne's army was beginning to stir. Ranks were forming, and several trebuchets crawled slowly through the throng. It wouldn't be long before Claybourne issued the order to storm the keep and the true battle would ensue.

I turned to Claire once more, noting the swell of her belly as it pressed against the railing. She'd been unable to hide her growing pregnancy for some time, but it didn't deter her from following Thomas' lead and lending her assistance to his cause.

"It won't be much longer." When she nodded, I continued. "I'm going to shift forms. Afterward, you should leave the balcony and go somewhere safer. The trebuchets look as though they're capable of quite a range."

She smirked. "I've already told Thomas I plan to help the wounded. As I mentioned to you once before, I was forced to learn bandaging and splinting while you were away in the Southlands. Jon has told his people to bring the injured to the great hall. I'll be safe enough there, and I won't be alone. Elanor will be there as well."

I nodded and began to remove my boots and clothing. It was awkward; though Claire had seen me disrobed numerous times during our marriage, there was much that had happened—for both of us—since that time. We'd changed and grown in the intervening years, and I no longer knew her as I once did. I felt my face flush as I tossed my belongings through the open doorway and into the tower's room.

"It will be safer for you from the doorway," I said. "There's only just enough room on the balcony to…accommodate my other form." My face heated further.

She nodded and moved gracefully to the doorway. Once I was certain she wouldn't be harmed by my rapid transformation, I closed my eyes and shifted. My estimation of the balcony's size relative to my own had been accurate. There was little space remaining.

I swiveled my head to look at her.

She smiled, her eyes sparkling with unshed tears. "Thank you," she said with emphasis. "I'll leave you to your watch. Be safe, Andrew—for *her* sake."

I nodded. "Take care of yourself, Claire."

TWENTY-FIVE

Perched on the tower balcony, I was provided an unobstructed view of the valley below. The movements of Claybourne's men as they began their steady march toward the keep, Thomas' defenders on the walls and ramparts, the trebuchets making their slow progress across the field, even the faint outlines of the covered trenches where the Corodan lay hidden in wait were all visible. The thin clouds scattered across the sky began to tinge in hues of orange and gold as dawn approached, but the valley itself would remain shadowed for at least another hour.

I stretched my wings, eager to leap into action, though I knew it would be some time before the signal fire was lit. Waiting patiently was not one of my strengths, but I understood the necessity of Jonathan's tactics. The balcony wasn't large enough to allow me to pace its length, and I was forced to sit as I awaited my cue. There was little else to do but watch as the battle unfolded below.

As Claybourne's men reached the halfway point in their trek across the valley, the first rank of soldiers suddenly fell as the earth appeared to open up and swallow them whole. From a distance, I was unable to hear the cries of those who fell, though I was certain many exclaimed in surprise while others screamed in pain or fear. As the first line of soldiers stumbled into the trench's maw, the second continued to press forward, unable to stop their momentum fast enough to prevent more from falling into the Corodan trap.

I noted the crimson-cloaked figure of Robert Claybourne, riding a chestnut horse some distance behind the front lines. He shoved his way through the ranks toward the trench to survey the cause of the sudden turmoil and unexpected delay, his mouth working furiously. I frowned as I watched him force his way forward, trampling some of his own people in the process.

The man's lack of empathy for his subordinates was appalling. I now understood why so many of his soldiers had chosen to join Alexander after their defeat at the Mage's Gate. I'd always believed a commander should lead by example, not through terror or displays of brutality. Robert Claybourne was a merciless bastard—much like his chosen king.

Claybourne gestured animatedly, pointing forward toward the keep, his expression thunderous. Minutes later, the lines began to advance once more, despite the trench that obstructed their passage. Some soldiers attempted to leap across the gap while others used their fallen brethren, some of whom were impaled on the sharpened stakes, as human bridges to the other side. I imagined the horror those trapped must have experienced as their commander wrote them off as expendable and urged the remainder of the army relentlessly forward.

It was inexcusable, and I vowed he'd pay for his crimes just as Colin would. Damn them both.

Though Claybourne had taken some losses already, his soldiers still outnumbered those within the keep's walls. They reformed their ranks once across the first trench, leaving the fallen in their wake as the sun began to beat down on the blood-soaked valley. Our people remained steadfast behind the walls, awaiting the next signal.

As Claybourne's forces marched within archery range of the keep's ramparts, several loud horn blasts sounded from the guard tower above the main gate. Seconds later, scores of Corodan emerged from the second set of trenches, racing forward to meet the enemy in a chitinous swarm of serrated limbs and deadly efficiency. Warning shouts erupted from the enemy as the distant sound of blades connecting with insectile shells reached my ears. Screams and curses cut through the air as the Corodan sliced and skewered those on the enemy's front lines. I'd witnessed the finest set of steel plate rent asunder in a single stroke by a Corodan's natural weaponry countless times—and I was grateful that in this fight, they were our allies.

By midmorning, it was evident Claybourne's foot soldiers were no longer making any headway in their march across the valley. The

Corodan had fallen back slightly, but it was a tactical maneuver to draw the enemy nearer to the archers stationed on the keep's outer walls. Arrows rained down on them as Jonas signaled the archers to fire time and again.

Claybourne pressed his forces to continue the fight, undeterred by the mounting casualties. He was as single-minded in his pursuit as he was ruthless.

The trebuchets stalled as they reached the first trench. They'd been dug wide enough that the enormous machines could not risk crossing them without first constructing a solid bridge. Several small clusters of soldiers toiled near the trenches while the trebuchets lined up to await their turn to cross the gap. The trebuchets would need to reach the second trench before they would be within range of the keep.

I observed it all from my vantage point on the balcony, growing increasingly impatient for the signal fire, my cue to join the fight.

As noon drew near, I heard movement in the tower behind me. I turned to find Claire had returned. She bore a tray of food and placed it carefully just outside the doorway.

"Jon sent word that he'll be lighting the beacon soon," she said. "He asks that you target the trebuchets before they come within range of the keep." When I nodded, she continued. "Thomas thought you might like something to eat, and he asked that I remind you of Rizzt-tok's warning."

I nodded again as I recalled our conversation from the previous afternoon. The trebuchets weren't only armed with traditional ammunition, but nets. I had no intention of being captured; I'd remain vigilant as I began my assault to ensure I didn't become entangled. I was certain I could break free given enough time, but it was a risk I was unwilling to take.

"Thank you," I replied, indicating the tray with a dip of my head. I hadn't eaten since the previous evening and knew I should do so before I was summoned to the fight.

I waited for her departure before consuming the contents of the tray. Rynn liked to tease me that dragons made for poor dinner guests, and I didn't want Claire to bear witness to the mess I'd inevitably make. She would have been appalled.

It was another hour before the signal fire bloomed to life atop the guard tower. I roared my approval, my voice echoing from the walls and ramparts, then leapt into the air to circle the keep once before I entered the battle. I flew low over the keep's inner wall, seeking a glimpse of Rynn as I passed. When I located her, she was speaking with Jonas Everly, but paused to look up as my shadow fell across them. She grinned, despite the tension that creased her features. Jonas nodded a greeting, his expression stoic.

As I soared over the keep's outer walls, the gate was winched open and a contingent of soldiers poured through to reinforce the Corodan in the valley. Jonathan Horace was at the forefront of the charge, his sword raised high. Once through, the gate was closed behind them.

I focused on the trebuchets. There was a sudden increase in activity near their bases, and I was certain it was due to my appearance. Several were being primed to fire, and as I studied them more closely, I noted they'd been heavily modified from the version I was used to. These could swivel on their bases, allowing their aim to be rapidly adjusted—they'd been designed to strike at moving targets.

I growled low in my throat. I'd be within targeting range in a matter of seconds. I pumped my wings to gain elevation, hoping to outdistance the war machines with altitude until I was in a position to strike myself.

From my new vantage point in the sky, I bore witness to the terrible scope of casualties Claybourne's army had taken while crossing the first trench. As I watched, several soldiers pulled bodies from the main area of fighting and tossed them amongst the dead and dying already trapped within.

Sharp fury lanced through my core. Some of the soldiers might have survived their injuries given time and treatment, but Claybourne himself was directing his people to move those unable to fight any longer to the confines of the trench. Those still conscious fought feebly against their brethren, though most were too weak to break free. Claybourne shouted threats and curses at those tasked with clearing away the dead and wounded, urging them to work more efficiently and harden their hearts. He'd written off the casualties as irrevocably lost.

I was sickened by his behavior. I wondered if Colin knew how his soldiers were treated under their latest commander, then realized with a heavy heart it was likely Colin didn't care. Colin was driven by ambition alone and cared little for anyone who stood in his way, whether it was intentional or not. Claybourne needed to be stopped, just as Colin did. Their mistreatment of good men and women, soldiers who had once proudly enlisted to protect their kingdom, was an atrocity beyond words.

I banked away from the view of the trench and Claybourne's fallen soldiers, my attention drawn toward the trebuchets as a trio of soldiers fired in my general direction. I was too high for the shot to reach my position, but it provided a brief opportunity to study the nets they'd devised.

Once unfurled, it was large enough to envelop me, and as it flashed by below, I spied a glimmer of metal within its depths. The net was constructed of wide bands of a black material I didn't recognize that flexed strangely in the wind.

The first cold pangs of dread niggled at my gut as I observed the net in flight. Had Colin or one of his cohorts been studying the dragon-kind after all? Had we been wrong to dismiss the notion?

I shook off my unease to focus on the trebuchet that had fired the poorly aimed net. The soldiers surrounding it loaded another net into the sling, while a fourth pulled the throwing arm into its firing position. I was almost directly above them. If I remained there, they could not achieve the proper angle to land a shot anywhere near me. Small groups clustered around the other trebuchets, but on closer inspection, I noted only two others had nets near enough to deploy them at present. I was beyond the range of one, but the other's crew rapidly swiveled the machine to better face my current location. I had little time to act and could delay no longer.

I folded my wings and arrowed toward the first war machine, achieving rapid acceleration in seconds. The air was cool against my scales as I rushed toward the ground, and I released a furious roar. At the last moment, I pulled out of my dive and grabbed the trebuchet by its throwing arm while the soldiers around it scattered and shouted curses. The sling pulled free and sent the net flying over my head and into the ground a short distance away.

I strained to gain altitude with the additional weight of the machine, but managed to fly just high enough that I was certain it would break on impact with the ground when I released it. I dropped it above a cluster of Claybourne's soldiers. The trebuchet twisted erratically in the air as it fell toward the earth, but it shattered as I'd hoped it would.

I glanced to my left and noted the other trebuchet was in position and primed to fire. I beat my wings rapidly, ascending higher into the sky to avoid their strike. I would not allow the easy success of destroying the first machine to cloud my judgment. I could afford no mistakes.

I was unable to gain sufficient elevation before the trebuchet fired, but I dodged the net's trajectory. It sailed past harmlessly to land in a heap not far from the trench. I repeated my previous maneuver and dove toward the trebuchet. I grasped its throwing arm before its crew had reloaded the sling and tugged it skyward, then dropped it over the crew's location. I watched as it fell to splinter much as the first one had.

I flew higher, surveying the remaining war machines. There were eight more by my count, and I was currently well beyond their reach. Soldiers toiled along the trench near each one, working to build additional bridges. Others milled near the base of each as they waited for an opportunity to cross.

As I considered my next move, the cloaked figure of Robert Claybourne pushed his way toward the trebuchets. He bellowed orders while simultaneously cursing at his people, then gestured forcefully in my general direction. I smirked, taking grim pleasure in the fact that I'd disrupted his carefully laid plans.

Several long, low notes echoed across the valley, cutting clearly through the air despite the raging battle. I knew the sound well; Jonathan Horace carried a horn into battle to signal his commands. This series of notes indicated something had gone awry.

I turned toward the sound, flying high over the valley as I sought his position. Seconds passed before I located him; he and two others had been cut off from our forces and were engaged in a fight for their very survival. As I neared, Jonathan sounded another series of notes, leaving his right side momentarily vulnerable. He was struck savagely by one of his attackers and crumpled.

I released a bellow of rage and dove. I tore into the enemy before I'd planted my feet on the ground, my talons slashing mercilessly. I wouldn't allow Jonathan to perish on my watch. He was one of my oldest friends and had remained steadfast and loyal throughout Thomas' exile.

"My lord!"

I recognized Hulda's voice. I spun to find she was one of the two soldiers with the former duke. She supported him, even as she defended herself from several strikes by an enemy soldier. I was impressed by her technique, but didn't have the time to compliment her on it.

I lashed my tail at several of the king's soldiers even as I slashed at others who stood before me. I would clear a space around them, and Claybourne's men would suffer for it.

Something struck my left flank. I spun to find a soldier had attempted to stab my side while my attention was focused elsewhere. The blow had been ineffectual, his sword unable to pierce my scales. I narrowed my eyes and drew myself up to stare down at him menacingly.

The man's eyes widened within his helm, and the sharp tang of urine hit my nostrils as he stumbled backwards. He understood his attempt to flank me—and grant himself misguided glory—had failed. I swatted him away with the back of my hand, irritated with the distraction he'd posed.

When I turned to face Jonathan once more, the duke was visibly pale, and blood streamed down his side. We'd cleared the attackers from the area for a few moments, but I'd have little time to deliver him to safety.

"Can you make it back to the others?" I asked Hulda and the man who stood behind her. She nodded, her eyes fierce within her helm.

"I'll take him back to the keep. Go!"

I took Horace into my arms, careful to avoid nicking him with my talons, then nodded at Hulda. She wasted no time in departing, her sword a blur as she cut down another of Claybourne's men.

I looked down at Jonathan as I leapt skyward. He managed a pained smile that immediately soured into a grimace.

"I was stupid," he managed through clenched teeth.

"Save your strength. We'll be back to the keep soon."

He chuckled briefly. "Things were going so smoothly. I made a rookie mistake. I was…arrogant…" He shook his head weakly, his strength rapidly waning.

We were nearly to the outer walls of the keep, but I didn't know if I'd reach Claire and the physicians in time to save him. My hands were already sticky with his blood, and it continued to spill from his wound. I shoved my emotions aside and pushed my wings to move faster.

"We're almost to the keep," I said, attempting and failing to keep the grief from my tone.

"Tell Elanor…" his breath was labored, even as I sped toward the entrance of the great hall.

"Jon, stay with me," I pleaded. "You can tell Elanor yourself."

He shook his head stubbornly. "Tell Elanor I love her. Tell her… I'm sorry."

I was met by a pair of Everett's men as I landed outside the keep's entrance. They took the duke from me and carried him into the great hall where he could receive treatment for his wound. I was torn between returning to the battle and staying to watch over my friend.

A few moments later, Thomas appeared at my side, out of breath from sprinting. "Andrew, was that Jon…?"

I nodded. "He was wounded. I hope I arrived in time."

Thomas clenched his jaw and steeled himself. "I'll speak to Elanor and the others. Go, Andrew—we need you out there. You've done all you can for him at this time."

I nodded. He was right, but I was reluctant to leave all the same. I hung my head and closed my eyes briefly, hoping what I'd done was enough to save his life. Colin's madness had claimed so many souls already; I didn't want Jonathan's name added to the lengthening tally.

"Andrew," Thomas said gently, "we'll do all we can. I'll see to it myself. Now, go."

I don't recall many of the events of the afternoon, preoccupied as I was with thoughts of Jonathan Horace. My concern transformed into a black rage after a time, and based on the reports I heard later from our soldiers and the Corodan present on the battlefield, I destroyed several more trebuchets, raining the broken pieces of the war machines down on Claybourne's forces relentlessly. The debris killed dozens. As the daylight began to fade, I was on the ground alongside a contingent of Corodan, slashing at enemies even as Claybourne sounded a retreat.

The battle wasn't over. It was clear the fighting would resume with the dawn.

The enemy's retreat gave us time to collect our wounded and dead from the field, and we carried them into the confines of the keep. I assisted with the task for several hours, all the while adding to my mental tally of those I'd lost. Among the dead were Daniel Clarence and the scout named Evan, who had so recently reconciled his differences with Rynn.

It was nearing midnight when I returned to the great hall. I'd flown to the tower first to shift forms and dress, though I was certain my fatigue was apparent to those I passed. Dozens of wounded lay within, tended to by a handful of men and women who had volunteered for the task. I spotted Claire kneeling alongside a boy of no more than fifteen; he sported a deep gash on his forehead but appeared well enough otherwise. On the far side of the hall near the fireplace, Elanor knelt beside her husband. I strode toward her and prayed he still lived.

She looked up at my approach, her eyes moist with unshed tears. She held one of his hands between her own, but he didn't stir. His armor had been removed, the wound in his right side had been bandaged, but blood continued to seep through the cloth. He was breathing, much to my relief, but it was labored and shallow.

"Elanor," I said as I knelt beside her, "I—"

"Don't speak," she managed in a choked whisper. "We have done all we can. He fell unconscious not long after you brought him here. I…I don't believe he'll last the night." She swallowed hard, then fixed me with her grief-stricken gaze. "Thank you for giving me the opportunity to say goodbye."

I shook my head, stubbornly refusing to believe he would not survive. "Elanor, he'll make it through. Jon's always been strong—"

She blinked away tears and took my hand. "I know, but I also understand when the end is near. He considered you one of his greatest friends. He was a good man and a good husband. I will miss him dearly." She closed her eyes for several seconds, then squeezed my hand briefly before releasing it to take her husband's once more.

"I wish I could have done more."

I hung my head, clinging to the dwindling hope that he'd pull through, that I would wake up the next morning to find him sitting up and laughing as though nothing had happened.

"You've done enough," she replied without looking away from her husband.

"He said something to me as we were nearing the keep," I said, my voice hollow to my own ears. "He wanted me to tell you he loved you, and that he was sorry."

She managed a strained smile, the tears that had been threatening finally spilling forth. "I didn't want him to lead the charge. I feared… He isn't as young as he used to be, but he had it in his fool head that there was no other way. He wanted to do his part, to prove his loyalty to Thomas—and to you. After twenty years of marriage, I knew he wouldn't listen to me, but a part of me hoped I'd be wrong." She sighed heavily with a shake of her head. "We had many good years together. He'll be remembered for his part in this war, and I'll see to it he is buried with honor."

I began to reply, but she cut me off with a weary shake of her head. "Thank you. There's a woman waiting to hear from *you*, and no doubt she's anxious to learn how you fare. Go to her. You don't know how long you have together, so make the most of the time you have now."

I nodded, aware that her words were eerily reminiscent of my father's. There was wisdom in them, and she was right—Rynn would be waiting for me.

I found her in the tower with a tin of stew that had begun to grow cold. I was relieved to see her well, and we spent a few hours in quiet company. She seemed to understand that I didn't want to talk, but her mere proximity soothed my aching soul.

We were standing at the balcony railing when word came from Thomas that Jonathan Horace had breathed his last. He would be buried along with the others we'd lost in the keep's inner courtyard.

Wordlessly, Rynn took my hands in hers and drew me close as I silently grieved. With another close friend added to the growing list of casualties, my resolve to see this through was solidified. Colin must not win.

Jonathan Horace had deserved better than to be slain at the hands of the tyrant's men.

TWENTY-SIX

"Sir, Lord Marsden requests your presence on the outer ramparts."

I nodded and rubbed my eyes as I turned away from the door. I'd managed only a few hours of sleep and it was well before dawn, but Thomas would not have sent for me without reason.

As the messenger disappeared into the stairwell, I took Rynn in my arms. "Stay safe. *Please.*"

She laughed softly. "I'll be on the inner wall. Don't fear for my safety—you're the one in real danger."

I nodded but could not set aside my worry. Rather than saying anything more, I pulled her in for a desperate kiss, memorizing the chill of her lips against mine. After a moment, she pushed away.

"Don't keep Tom waiting. We'll speak again later." Her eyes were fixed on the floor, unshed tears gleaming in her eyes.

I paused, reluctant to leave her, yet unable to voice the dozens of things I wanted to say. Finally, I nodded and turned away.

When I reached the ramparts, I was met by Thomas, Everett, Rizzt-tok, and Jonas. They stood beneath the dragon banner as it hung in the still night air, their conversation subdued. Clouds had blanketed the sky while I'd slept, bringing with them an oppressive atmosphere that threatened rain. A single torch placed in a rusting bracket nearby provided flickering illumination.

Thomas waved briefly as I approached, while the two older men merely nodded. Rizzt-tok watched the exchange silently, tilting her head first one way, then the other.

"I'm sorry to have awakened you." Thomas paused to stare into the darkness beyond the wall. "There are matters we must discuss before daybreak."

I studied him as he spoke. He wore the same set of clothing he'd been in the day before, his eyes were ringed by dark circles, and his face was pale. It was unlikely he'd managed a wink of sleep himself. A wave of guilt crashed over me for resting the few scant hours that I had, while I'd left my youngest sibling to manage the keep alone.

Thomas turned to the others. "Jonas, I'd like you to take command of our soldiers in Jon's stead. You have experience leading men in battle. Andrew has told me you were with him during many campaigns."

Jonas bowed his head. "I'll do my best, but Jon was the better commander."

"As I continue to be reminded, we're all in this together," Thomas replied, his voice weary. "I believe you're the best choice, and I believe the soldiers will respect you, just as they respected him."

Jonas nodded. "I won't disappoint you, my lord."

"How do your people fare, Rizzt-tok?" Thomas asked, turning to the tall Corodan.

"We lost fewer than a dozen warriors yesterday," she replied. "The battle flowed in our favor. The hive stands ready for the next assault." She tilted her head to one side, the torchlight reflecting from a thousand points in her compound eyes. "Our scouts say the war machines have breached the second trench. They are near enough to strike our walls."

Thomas flicked a glance toward me. "It's fortunate Andrew dismantled so many of them yesterday. How many remain?"

"We have counted four," she replied. "The remains of the others were used to stoke the fires of the enemy. They could not be salvaged. The damage was too severe."

"Perhaps," I replied grimly. "Or perhaps Claybourne merely couldn't be bothered to take the time to repair them, much like he couldn't be bothered to help his own wounded."

The memory of injured soldiers being dragged into the trench to die would forever haunt me. Claybourne's act was unconscionable.

"Regardless of his reason, Claybourne has less than half the trebuchets as he started with," Thomas said. "This keep may be old, but with the fortifications we've made, I believe we can withstand an assault." He turned to Everett. "I know we took some casualties, but how do our people fare today?"

"There were many who returned with minor injuries, and most are fit enough to fight again. In truth, our losses were minimal, thanks to Rizzt-tok and her people." He offered a weary smile to the Corodan. "I will ever be grateful to the hive for its assistance."

"As will I," Thomas stated earnestly. "Without the hive, we would have been outnumbered."

"The hive welcomes the offer of continued peace with the humans," Rizzt-tok replied. "Peace cannot be maintained under the banner of the red king. Kash-kah knows this."

"We lost a few dozen people yesterday," Everett continued after a moment. "Based on the reports I've received, Claybourne fared worse. After his behavior on the field, it's likely he'll continue pressing the damned attack until he has no one left to fight for him. The man is ruthless."

Thomas nodded and stifled a yawn with the back of his hand. "My apologies," he said with a shake of his head.

"Tom, you need to rest," I said. "We can manage for a few hours without you, brother."

He shook his head stubbornly. "I'll rest once this is over. Our people need to know that I'm here, that I support them in this cause, that I'm *one of them*. I can't be what they need if I'm abed."

Though I wanted to say more, to persuade him to do what was best for his welfare, I knew my protests would go unheard. Thomas and I were more alike than either of us had realized; time and again, I'd acted as he did now, refusing to sleep, to eat, to take care of my own needs if those of my soldiers weren't met.

With each day I spent with my youngest brother, I was more confident in our decision to place him in the role of prospective king. Though he was young, he had a good heart, a sound mind, and an overarching desire to do what was best for his people—*all* of his people. He'd earned the respect of many, and his selflessness would garner even more.

We spent another hour finalizing the day's plans. Jonas remarked at the oddity of issuing orders to his former commander, but I shrugged it off. Thomas had made the decision to leave the battle in the hands of the dukes, and I respected his choice. Regardless, Jonas was better suited to issuing commands from the ramparts than I would be from the air.

It was decided that ranks of Corodan and human soldiers would enter the field well before sunrise to engage the enemy before they were fully prepared for the fight. Rynn and a number of archers would remain on the ramparts, attacking from afar. A sizeable force of ground troops would also remain inside the keep, to act as reserves or as a second wave when Claybourne's people began to tire.

Jonas stopped me as we began to depart. "Do what you do best today. Sow chaos amongst them—but please don't get yourself caught in one of those damned nets."

I laughed grimly. "I won't give Robert Claybourne the satisfaction of obtaining what he came for."

"Good." His steely gray eyes were unreadable in the torchlight. "I'd hate to be forced to tell Rynn that news. She's strong, but I fear what it will do to her."

I nodded, sharing his concern. "Watch over her for me, Jonas."

"I will," he promised. We shook hands before going our separate ways.

I turned to gaze out over the valley, noting the locations of the trebuchets in the darkness. Rizzt-tok's information had been good; there were four left, and they'd moved closer to the second trench. They were near enough to strike the walls if Claybourne ordered them to do so. Stone and other large debris were piled near each. While we'd slept and mourned our fallen, Robert Claybourne had been fortifying his position.

I had no doubt the order would be given to strike the walls, and I suspected each trebuchet had likewise been supplied with a number of his damned nets. Despite the nearer location of the trebuchets, I didn't detect the movement of soldiers near them, which was puzzling. I wasn't sure what it meant, but Jonas needed to know.

I turned away from the view, noting the duke had not traveled far. I broke into a run and caught up with him as he neared the narrow stone stair leading to the keep's courtyard below. As I relayed what I'd seen, he displayed no emotion, though his gray eyes were calculating.

"Do what you can to disable those damned machines," he said after several long moments of thought. "I don't believe Claybourne will strike before dawn, which gives us another hour to prepare. Luck be with you, Andrew. We'll need it."

I nodded once. "You as well, Jonas."

It began to rain as I strode across the courtyard toward the main keep. The drops were fat and cold, and what began with only a smattering of drops rapidly became a steady downpour. If the storm continued for even another hour, the courtyard and the battlefield beyond would be transformed into a muddy mire. I took the steps up to the tower two at a time, hoping I'd see Rynn before the battle resumed.

She was seated on the stone floor, pulling on her boots as I entered. She smiled up at me in the darkness, then rose and pulled me into a rough embrace. "I'm glad you returned before I was forced to leave. I...I needed to see you before..." She looked down with a shake of her blond curls and didn't finish her statement.

I drew her closer, wrapping her frigid form in my arms. I understood her unspoken concerns all too well. We'd both lost friends, and it was impossible to know what the new day would bring. My father's words came to my mind then, and though the context of our conversation had been markedly different than the present circumstances, they still held great meaning. I could not know what the outcome of the battle would be, nor if I would survive, but I knew I must not waste this moment with Rynn.

I lifted my hand to touch the side of her face. She peered up at me, her normally vibrant blue eyes subdued.

"You must come back," she whispered fiercely. "I could not bear... I'm not as strong as Elanor."

"You know I can't make that promise," I replied gently. "But I'll do my best."

She sighed heavily and dropped her gaze. "I know."

"Rynn, I—"

Her eyes met mine, and she reached up swiftly to press one cold finger against my lips, effectively silencing what I'd planned to say.

"Don't say it, Andrew—not unless you truly mean it." Her voice was strangled and a profound longing was clear in her expression.

I stared at her for several seconds, surprised she'd intuited what I'd planned to say. Slowly, she withdrew her hand while I continued to hold her gaze. Her expression revealed the depth of her feelings, her desire, her hopes for our future, her unbridled love.

It was time to speak the words—and I was finally ready.

"I love you."

She looked down as a smile spread across her face. "And I love you still. Even after you rejected me in Dragon's Feet, I refused to let go. I knew that one day… One day, we would come together, and when we did, it would be the most wonderful day of my life." She forced a laugh. "To finally hear those words… No matter what happens today, know that right now, I am content."

I smiled and kissed her forehead. "I'm sorry I've taken so long to say it. I've known for some time."

She shook her head, still smiling. "I've suspected it. You aren't terribly adept at masking what you feel in your expressions. And I've come to understand you struggle to *speak* of your emotions but will share them when you are ready to do so."

A horn sounded in the courtyard below, the low notes muffled somewhat by the rain.

Rynn sighed, a flicker of disappointment crossing her fair features. "I must go. When this is over, I expect you to finish this conversation." She took a step back, and I released her from my arms. "Be safe, Andrew."

"You as well."

I watched her depart, hoping she'd remain unharmed as the battle unfolded around us. It was only after she disappeared into the darkened stairwell that I began to go about my own preparations for the day. I removed my clothing and left it folded atop the chest containing my armor and sword. I shifted as soon as I walked onto the balcony.

The rain had intensified, and the courtyard below had become slick with mud. Though dawn wasn't far, the cloud cover was so thick the valley was cast in perpetual twilight. I watched as Jonas directed various groups toward the gate or onto the walls to bolster our defenses. I spied Rynn briefly as she crossed the muddy courtyard toward the outer wall.

Panic lanced through me. She wasn't supposed to be on the outer wall. Something had changed in our plans, but why?

I shoved my concern aside. That she'd be nearer to the battlefield was worrisome, but she was capable of defending herself, and I trusted Jonas to keep his word. I needed to focus my attention elsewhere, but it was one of the most difficult tasks I'd undertaken. I began to understand why the king had discouraged his soldiers from becoming romantically involved with one another.

The attachment, coupled with the near certainty that each battle was predictably unpredictable, coalesced my worry into blinding distraction. Distraction led to miscalculation, something I certainly could not afford in my unique role.

I groaned and shook my head in an attempt to clear it, while I silently prayed Rynn would be safe, that we'd reunite after the battle had reached its inevitable conclusion. I needed to trust in her skills, in Jonas' tactics, and focus solely on what I was required to do.

Stepping aside was not something I was accustomed to, and this time it was so damned difficult.

A horn sounded below, breaking my reverie. I peered down to see the gate had been winched open and ranks of human soldiers interspersed with their larger Corodan counterparts were beginning to stream through. Shifting my gaze to the valley beyond, I saw little movement amongst Claybourne's army. Our soldiers seemed to march through a twilight gloom to their assigned positions as the storm continued to rage.

Not long after the gates were closed, I detected movement across the valley. Claybourne was preparing to renew his assault; his soldiers reformed their ranks beneath the boar banner of the tyrant king and my half-brother.

A flare of light caught my eye. The signal fire was lit, sputtering in defiance of the storm for a few brief moments before it succumbed to the deluge.

I leapt into the air. I had only a short window of time in which to dismantle some of the trebuchets before their operators returned. The rain continued to fall steadily, and I was forced to narrow my eyes and blink frequently to clear my vision as I flew toward my intended target—the trebuchet located near the center that had been placed in line with the keep's gate.

We couldn't afford to lose the gate, and although some of the outer walls weren't capable of withstanding a sustained assault, the gate itself was priority. And with the downpour, we couldn't rely on the archers to deter Claybourne's soldiers from attempting to storm the gate if it was weakened. There were still no soldiers in the immediate area of the war machines, but I knew they'd arrive soon.

I reached the trebuchet well before the group of soldiers moving toward it did so. Lifting it by its throwing arm as I'd done to the others the previous day, I hefted it skyward, then allowed it to fall. It splintered on impact with the ground, just as the group of soldiers I'd spied reached the debris pile that would have supplied it with ammunition. One of the men was forced to jump backward as an enormous wooden shard bounced erratically off the ground and hurtled toward him. He appeared unscathed, though shaken.

I regained altitude and soared above the valley as the two armies began to fight in earnest. From my vantage point, it appeared our soldiers now outnumbered Claybourne's. His army had taken many losses, more than we had, but the numbers didn't add up. Either he had ordered a sizeable number of his soldiers elsewhere, or he'd been plagued by a vast number of desertions during the night. Regardless, his army had dwindled.

It was a good sign for Thomas.

A crash drew my attention from the battlefield, and I noted with some alarm that two of the remaining trebuchets had targeted the same location along the keep's outer wall. It was an area that we'd taken time to fortify, but it remained one of the weaker locations. The first trebuchet hurtled a small boulder toward the wall, hitting its mark. As I watched, the second launched a stone at the same location, and it also hit its mark. The wall held, but I feared it would not last much longer.

Another crash resounded through the valley as the third trebuchet began its attack as well. That section of the wall appeared sturdier than the other. I chose to ignore the lone trebuchet for a time in favor of dismantling the other two.

In the muddy field below, our forces were holding their own against Claybourne's, who continued to struggle with the combined might of the human soldiers and our Corodan allies. As I watched, the Corodan began to shift toward the perceived threat to the wall, the bulk of their forces moving to defend the point the two trebuchets had targeted. Rizzt-tok believed as I did, though her command left the other section of the wall decidedly vulnerable.

Claybourne galloped behind the lines of his soldiers, shouting commands and angry curses from the back of his chestnut steed. He drove his soldiers relentlessly onward, despite their mounting losses, as though they were expendable and his actions of no consequence.

The man was a damned monster. I yearned to target him directly, but knew that action was folly. Jonas' plans required that my attention be on the war machines.

I wheeled overhead, flying high above the field as I prepared to strike at the nearest trebuchet. The soldiers were focused solely on their attack and didn't look skyward until I grasped the trebuchet and wrenched it from their midst. They scattered as I lifted the machine into the air, uttering cries of surprise. The second trebuchet wasn't far, and with significant effort, I tried to fling the one I carried into it. Even with my brute strength, I was unable to achieve the distance required. The machine splintered into the ground a dozen paces from its counterpart. While it served to startle the nearby soldiers, they resumed their task moments later, unfazed.

As I rose skyward once more, I noted Claybourne had marshaled his forces toward the point in the wall where the other, more distant, trebuchet had begun its attack. It would take them a while to reach the wall, but I wondered at the abrupt change in his commands.

Though I was tempted to strike the remaining trebuchet below my present location, I needed to learn the enemy's true intent—and Claybourne's movements indicated this pair had been little more than a diversion. Claybourne's reaction had been so precise, so calculated, that I believed he'd planned it. I didn't like the notion that he'd anticipated our actions.

I circled the battlefield once before changing course, then flew toward the point where Claybourne's forces were rapidly surging forward.

I was still some distance away when the trebuchet hurtled another stone toward the wall. The stone smashed into it only a few feet below the ramparts, cracking in half as it struck. The wall visibly shuddered, then a section of the ramparts gave way. I watched with dismay as at least three of our defenders fell to their deaths while the stones crumbled and fell away beneath them. There were two distinct figures near the edge of the resulting precipice, and as I drew nearer, a paralyzing fear gripped my heart.

I pushed my wings faster. I needed to reach the broken section of the wall before any further damage was incurred. The figure nearest the edge had fallen and was slowly dragging themself backward toward the nearest guard tower and a point of greater stability. Her blond curls were unmistakable, even from a distance.

My thoughts coalesced into a singular driving force. I must reach the wall before any more of it gave way. If Claybourne had anticipated this action as well, then so be it—I was confident I could break free of his nets if I became trapped. My strength was unparalleled.

I would protect Rynn regardless of the cost to myself. I wouldn't lose her as I'd lost Vera. I couldn't bear it. She was my everything.

I roared her name as I approached, desperately hoping I'd reach her in time.

TWENTY-SEVEN

"*RYNN!*" I shouted again as I neared the wall.

She glanced in my direction, and as she did, I knew she was in tremendous pain. She continued to push herself awkwardly along with the heels of her hands and her right leg, but her left leg was badly injured, perhaps broken. The wall sloped at a precarious angle as she struggled toward safety, the ramparts slick from rain. I needed to act quickly before it collapsed.

"Andrew," she said through gritted teeth, "you should not have come. This was a trap."

I nodded. I'd already come to the same conclusion. "I know."

I sought a handhold along the crumbling lip of stone and shoved the wall upwards with all of my strength, straining against the weight. I beat my wings powerfully to keep aloft, but I was nearing my limit.

I could just make out Rynn's retreating figure over the ledge. My efforts to level the wall were working; she made better progress as she inched along. I ignored the clamor of battle behind us, my focus solely on her.

I refused to lose her too.

My gaze was drawn further along the wall as I heard rapid footfalls approach, and Jonas sprinted toward Rynn. He'd wrapped a cloak around one of his arms to protect himself from her frigid nature in order to escort her to safety.

"Andrew!" Rynn cried in alarm, her gaze fixed on a point beyond the keep's walls. "Andrew, they're loading a net. You must let go!"

I shook my head stubbornly. "I'll let go when you're safe."

She blinked several times, attempting to stave off tears. "Andrew, no. Please…"

Jonas knelt swiftly at her side, offering his cloak-wrapped arm. She looked at him, both fearful and grateful. Hesitating only a moment, she accepted his arm and allowed him to help her to her feet.

"You'd better keep your promise, Andrew Caein." Her voice was tremulous.

As she attempted to put weight upon her injured leg, she cried out in sudden agony and stumbled. Jonas adjusted his arm to provide better support, and he nodded to me once. She would be safe with him.

Holding up the broken wall was taking its toll. My muscles began to shake from exertion, but I could not release my grip yet. I kept my gaze on Rynn as Jonas led her away, ignoring the warning that Claybourne's men were preparing to launch a net in my direction. I wouldn't lose Rynn, even if that meant I'd be captured by the enemy.

Colin would not take her from me. He'd already taken too damned much; he would not have her. And I was confident I could break free.

"Rynn," I said as they reached what appeared to be stable ground, "I meant what I said earlier."

She turned with a shake of her head, her expression filled with despair. She flicked her eyes toward the battlefield. A low moan escaped her lips, the sound filled with anguish. "*Andrew!*"

I turned to see the net hurtling toward me. I didn't have time to evade.

I released my grip on the wall, content that Rynn and Jonas were safe. As I did so, a portion of the wall collapsed, enormous blocks of stone raining down to litter the sodden earth below. I had but a heartbeat in which to brace myself for the impact of the net. I glimpsed metal flashing in the dim light an instant before I was ensnared.

I struggled as the weighted ends twined around one another, securing me firmly within. I plummeted toward the rubble-strewn ground below and instinctively twisted to land on my side. My shoulder could take the impact, but I couldn't risk landing on my wings. They were more fragile, and I didn't relish the notion of breaking one.

I landed heavily on my left side, striking with such force the breath was knocked from my lungs. I gasped for air, but otherwise, I'd sustained little more than bruises and a spattering of mud.

Taking a moment to regain my breath, I lay still, enshrouded in the net as though it were an enormous cocoon. The sounds of battle drew nearer to my location, and I spied Robert Claybourne near the forefront of a group of soldiers pressing toward the shattered section of the wall.

I began to struggle in earnest. I must free myself before he arrived.

Something sharp dug into the unprotected underside of my right wing, and I immediately reconsidered the metallic flash I'd seen as the net had drawn itself around me.

The net was made of an unfamiliar material that stretched well beyond that of conventional rope or cloth. Each time I strained against it, the net snapped firmly back into place around me. Even with my innate strength, I couldn't overcome the material's elasticity and was unable to shred it with my arms and legs pinned at my sides.

Frustrated, my only option was to shift into my human form. When I attempted to do so, a sharp tug in my right wing prevented the transformation. Whatever was lodged in my flesh wouldn't allow me to switch forms.

My mind raced as I grappled with the sudden onset of panic. I was thoroughly trapped, and Claybourne was only moments away. I twisted within the net, hoping to dislodge the object embedded in my wing, but only succeeded in entangling myself further.

I roared in frustration, unable to free myself. I was resigned to watch as our forces fell away before Robert Claybourne's final push toward my location.

He was going to get what he'd come for, after all.

Claybourne removed his helm as he approached. He was stoutly built, though not tall, with a craggy, pock-marked face. His pale blue eyes were steely and cold, though his brows were midnight-dark. I noted his baldness was not due to age, but because he shaved his head; a thin layer of dark stubble was beginning to regrow. He sneered from atop his chestnut steed, then gestured to the soldiers around him.

As they began to encircle me, I struggled furiously from within the confines of the net. The soldiers maintained a wary distance, even as Claybourne laughed mirthlessly and spat to one side.

"His Majesty's brightest engineers designed that contraption," he leered. "It was built for a single purpose, and that was to capture a creature like you. You'll be unable to break free of it, even with your supposed strength."

I growled low in my throat. "You'll regret this."

He laughed again, the cold, hollow sound of a man without empathy. "I wasn't certain you'd be capable of speech, but it matters not. The king will have your tongue when we reach the Capitol."

I clenched my jaw and glared at him through the strands of net. It was no wonder Colin had taken such a liking to the man—they were two of a kind.

His smirk dissolved into a glower. "My little diversion worked much better than I'd anticipated." He gestured to the ruined section of the keep's wall behind me. "I knew the battle would be lost before evening fell yesterday, but I wasn't going to quit the field empty-handed. In a word, I needed you. Without that woman, you wouldn't have come here. But you did. Who is she, monster?"

I continued to glare at him. He wouldn't learn anything of Rynn from me.

"Finished talking, I see," he replied, acid in his tone. "Very well. Men, you've been preparing for this moment for some time. Do what you were sent here to do."

The soldiers encircling me began to take tentative steps forward, their boots squelching in the mud. Many were hesitant, and I decided to play that to my advantage. I struggled and thrashed. Several backpedaled and eyed me warily.

"The king said you wouldn't willingly leave the rebels," Claybourne continued, unperturbed. "He said you wouldn't make it easy if you were captured. But I've devised a solution. A little something that will force you to cease your pointless struggles." He smiled grimly, but his eyes remained as cold as a midwinter's morning. "With the king's resources at my disposal, I've had ample opportunity to ensure your capture, and unlike my sovereign, I'm not opposed to sifting through moldy books to learn all I can of the enemy." He paused to smirk, then spat again. "Or soot-covered tomes, as the case may be."

Rage ignited in my core at his insinuation. He'd been in the Captiol when Vinterry was attacked, but it was clear he'd been there at some point to loot what remained of Vera's library. I thrashed in my bonds again, but to no avail.

He gestured to one of the soldiers, and the man nodded in acknowledgment. He withdrew a glass flask from his belt and walked forward, his eyes locked on mine. I didn't know what he planned or what was in the flask, but if he attempted to force me to drink whatever foul concoction was contained within, I'd make him wish he'd never approached me.

I'd assured Jonathan I didn't eat people, but at present, my teeth *were* the only weapons available.

When the man was a few paces away, he threw the flask, never drawing near enough for me to attempt a strike. The flask landed inches from my face, spraying glass shards as it shattered. I was startled by the action and blinked in surprise as he hurriedly backed away. The rest of Claybourne's men maintained their distance as unseen fumes began to pour from the broken container. The odor was foul; both rancid and cloyingly sweet.

Within moments, I became sluggish. It was increasingly difficult to keep my eyes open as the fumes sapped my strength. The desire to allow sleep to overtake me was strong, but I tried to resist it. I feared what Claybourne would do if I fell unconscious.

I glanced toward the keep's wall. Rynn and Jonas were no longer atop the ramparts, and I hoped he'd taken her to the great hall where her leg could be tended. If Claybourne's words were true, the battle would be over within hours, and I took a measure of comfort in the knowledge that Thomas' forces would emerge victorious from this bloody struggle.

I'd find a means to escape, given time. I'd have to if I was to be of any further use to my brothers.

Thomas, Alexander, and I had come so far that I was unwilling to surrender, even now. I thrashed feebly against my bonds, felt the object in my wing snag and pull painfully at my flesh. The net snapped into place around me, time and again.

I wouldn't escape Claybourne this day.

Darkness encroached on the edges of my vision and an incessant ringing filled my ears.

Dimly, I was aware of several horn blasts echoing from within the keep. Jonas was sending the second wave of soldiers into the battle. Perhaps they were on their way to me, but I had a sinking feeling they'd never reach me in time. I struggled weakly within the confines of the net, determined to remain awake to continue my fight.

"Another dose," Claybourne ordered. "This fucking storm is diluting the first."

Moments later, a second flask shattered near my head. The fumes were overpowering, and my vision swam. I strained against the net, but my body began to feel heavy as a cold numbness settled over my limbs. The willpower that had so often driven me rapidly vanished, drained by Claybourne's foul concoction. I blinked to force my eyes to remain open, but I was losing the battle with consciousness.

I wasn't fully aware of Claybourne's next set of shouted orders. In my last moments of lucidity, I prayed that I'd muster the strength to break free when I awakened. I'd promised Rynn I would return, and I was a man of my word.

But she was safe. My sacrifice wasn't in vain.

I pictured her mischievous grin, the sparkle in her sapphire eyes, the way sunlight would shine across her blond curls. She was worth everything—and I would never fail her.

With a final, despairing sigh, I closed my eyes and succumbed to the darkness, knowing she was alive, that she'd be safe now that Claybourne had fulfilled his orders to the king.

The Caein Legacy will continue in Legend

THANK YOU FOR READING HARBINGER!

If you enjoyed reading this book, please consider leaving a review.

Information about new books and their release dates will be posted on my website (www.ajcalvin.net), as well as shared via my newsletter. If interested, you can subscribe by visiting my website and clicking on the "Newsletter" tab.

ACKNOWLEDGMENTS

First, I'd like to thank my biggest supporter in my writing endeavors, my husband. His endless patience (particularly when I'm grumbling about formatting or revisions) means the world to me. There are certainly times when I'm not fun to be around when I'm working on book projects, but he has always been understanding.

And then there's the team of various people who also helped make this book come to life:

Jamie Noble, whose artwork is on the cover,

Dewi Hargreaves, who drew up the map from my scrawling attempts at it,

Sheena Sampsel, my editor and comma-wrangler,

My brother, Patrick, a major inspiration behind Alexander's personality and his interactions with Andrew throughout the series,

And lastly, but most importantly, my readers. Without you, none of this would be worthwhile. I truly hope you enjoyed reading Harbinger and will continue with the series from here. (There's only one more book—and it's coming soon, I promise! Just turn to the next page for details.)

NOW AVAILABLE:

LEGEND: BOOK FOUR OF THE CAEIN LEGACY

War has come to Novania as brothers fight brother for control of the throne. Colin is an unyielding and ruthless ruler without remorse for the atrocities he has committed. He has disowned his half-brother, for Andrew is dragon-kind. He has exiled Alexander for bearing the Mark of the Magi. He forced Thomas to flee under vague threats of assassination.

Now his brothers have gathered allies in order to oppose him. Oppressed Novanians have rallied to their cause, the Corodan have gathered, and even magi from the Southlands have offered their unique talents in the fight. The kingdom burns and the blood of thousands is spilled.

Under Colin's command is a man as ruthless and cold as his king: Robert Claybourne, whose sole motivation is to annihilate the magi – and any who choose to support them. After seeing the power Andrew is capable of, Claybourne makes it his secondary objective to slay the last of the dragon-kind as well.

ABOUT THE AUTHOR

A.J. Calvin is a science fiction/fantasy novelist hailing from Loveland, Colorado known best for The Caein Legacy and The Relics of War series. A former microbiologist, she lives with her husband, a turtle, a bearded dragon, and a salt water aquarium.

When she is not working or writing, she enjoys scuba diving, hiking, and playing video games.

For more information on the author and news about her writing, please visit her website at www.ajcalvin.net.

www.ingramcontent.com/pod-product-compliance
Lightning Source LLC
Chambersburg PA
CBHW021621030826
48979CB00035B/1396/J

* 9 7 9 8 9 8 8 3 1 9 3 9 9 *